Tales from the Hakawati

Traditional tales, fables, and sagas

from the Arabic tradition ...

Compiled, Adapted & Edited by Clive Gilson

Tales from the World's Firesides

Book 2 in Part 4 of the series: The Middle East

(al sharq al awsat)

Tales from the Hakawati,

edited by Clive Gilson, Solitude, Bath, UK

www.clivegilson.com

1st edition © 2024, Clive Gilson

Printed by IngramSpark

ISBN: 978-1-915081-15-5

I have edited Clive Gilson's books for over a decade now – he's prolific and can turn his hand to many genres. poetry, short fiction, contemporary novels, folklore, and science fiction – and the common theme is that none of them ever fails to take my breath away. There's something in each story that is either memorably poignant, hauntingly unnerving, or sidesplittingly funny.

Lorna Howarth, The Write Factor

Tales From The World's Firesides is a grand project. I've collected '000's of traditional texts as part of other projects, and while many of the original texts are available through channels like Project Gutenberg, some of the narratives can be hard to read by modern readers, & so the Fireside project was born. Put simply, I collect, collate & adapt traditional tales from around the world & publish them as a modern archive. Amongst others, *Part 4* covers a host of nations & regions from the Arabic & Turkish speaking peoples. I'm not laying any claim to insight or specialist knowledge, but these collections are born out of my love of storytelling & I hope that you'll share my affection for traditional tales, myths & legends.

Cover image by Dorothe from Pixabay

Chapter header image by Gordon Johnson from Pixabay

CONTENTS

ORIGINAL FICTION BY CLIVE GILSON

- Songs of Bliss
- Out of the Walled Garden
- The Mechanic's Curse
- The Insomniac Booth
- A Solitude of Stars

AS EDITOR – *FIRESIDE TALES – Part 1, Europe*

- Tales From the Land of Dragons
- Tales From the Land of The Brave
- Tales From the Land of Saints And Scholars
- Tales From the Land of Hope And Glory
- Tales From Lands of Snow and Ice
- Tales From the Viking Isles
- Tales From the Forest Lands
- Tales From the Old Norse
- More Tales About Saints and Scholars
- More Tales About Hope and Glory
- More Tales About Snow and Ice
- Tales From the Land of Rabbits
- Tales Told by Bulls and Wolves
- Tales of Fire and Bronze
- Tales From the Land of the Strigoi
- Tales Told by the Wind Mother
- Tales from Gallia
- Tales from Germania

EDITOR – *FIRESIDE TALES – Part 2, North America*

- Okaraxta Tales from The Great Plains
- Tibik Kìzis – Tales from The Great Lakes & Canada
- Jóhonaa'éí –Tales from America's Southwest
- Qugaaĝix̂ First Nation Tales from Alaska & The Arctic
- Karahkwa First Nation Tales from America's Eastern States
- Pot Likker Folklore, Fairy Tales, and Settler Stories from America

EDITOR – *FIRESIDE TALES – Part 3, Africa*

- Arokin Tales – Folklore & Fairy Tales from West Africa
- Hadithi Tales – Folklore & Fairy Tales from East Africa
- Inkathaso Tales – Folklore & Fairy Tales from Southern Africa
- Tarubadur Tales – Folklore & Fairy Tales from North Africa
- Elephant And Frog – Folklore from Central Africa

Preface

I've been collecting and telling stories for a couple of decades now, having had several of my own fictional works published in recent years. My particular focus is on short story writing in the realms of magical realities and science fiction fantasies.

I've always drawn heavily on traditional folk and fairy tales, and in so doing have amassed a collection of many thousands of these tales from around the world. It has been one of my long-standing ambitions to gather these stories together and to create a library of tales that tell the stories of places and peoples from the four corners of the globe.

One of the main motivations for me in undertaking the project is to collect and tell stories that otherwise might be lost or, at best, be forgotten. Given that a lot of my sources are from early collectors, particularly covering works produced in the late eighteenth century, throughout the nineteenth century, and in the early years of the twentieth century, I do make every effort to adapt stories for a modern reader. Early collectors had a different world view to many of us today, and often expressed views about race and gender, for example, that we find difficult to reconcile in the early years of the twenty first century. I try, although with varying degrees of success, to update these stories with sensitivity while trying to stay as true to the original spirit of each story as I can.

I also want to assure readers that I try hard not to comment on or appropriate originating cultures. It is almost certainly true that the early collectors of these tales, with their then prevalent world views, have made assumptions about the originating cultures that have given us these tales. I hope that you'll accept my mission to preserve these tales, however and wherever I find them, as just that. I have, therefore, made sure that every story has a full attribution, covering both the original collector / writer and the collection title that this version has been adapted from, as well as having notes about publishers and other relevant and, I hope, interesting source data. Wherever possible I have added a cultural or indigenous attribution as well, although for some of the titles, the country-based theme is obvious.

This volume, *Tales from the Hakawati*, is the second in a set of collections covering indigenous tales from what we in Europe know now as The Middle East. *Tales from the Hakawati* concentrates on telling stories from the broader Arabic diaspora, with a particular focus on telling stories from beyond the usual *One Thousand Nights And One* boundary.

In putting this small collection of tales together I've found the process to be particularly rewarding. Arabic folklore and fairy tales reflect the deep cultural roots and diverse traditions of the Arab world. The stories are embedded with cultural symbols, practices, and values, offering a unique window into the rich heritage of the region.

I've also been impressed by the diversity of the narratives. Arabic storytelling encompasses a wide range of tales that vary across different regions and communities. Reading these tales exposes you to a wide range of themes, characters, and settings, so much of it stemming from the strong oral traditions of the wider community.

Many Arabic folktales have been passed down through generations via this oral tradition. This continuity connects contemporary audiences with the storytelling practices of their ancestors, fostering a sense of cultural continuity and identity.

In particular I've found that by exploring Arabic storytelling, I have gained a better understanding of the perspectives, beliefs, and worldviews of the wider Arab peoples, which can only help to foster cultural empathy and help break down stereotypes. I believe wholeheartedly that engaging with the world's storytelling promotes cultural exchange and mutual understanding. It allows us to connect with the cultural expressions of a community and fosters appreciation for the similarities and differences that make our global society so diverse and so engaging.

Arabic folklore and fairy tales also include a wealth of imagination and creativity. That creativity, combined with a deep connection to history means that these tales can often reflect the historical and social dynamics of the regions where they originated. Reading these stories can provide historical context and insights into the evolution of cultural practices.

Of course, like many folktales, Arabic stories often convey moral lessons and ethical principles. They address common human experiences and challenges, providing insights into virtues such as courage, kindness, and perseverance.

We should also never forget that Arabic storytelling has significantly influenced world literature. Many stories have been adapted and reimagined in various cultures, showcasing the universal appeal of these tales and their enduring impact on global storytelling traditions. Arabic folklore and fairy tales have been and remain a rich source of inspiration for writers, artists, and creators. The fantastical elements, unique characters, and imaginative plots can serve as a springboard for your own creative endeavours.

One of my favourite aspects of this tradition is the use of magical realism in storytelling: Arabic folklore often blends the ordinary with the extraordinary, creating worlds where mythical creatures, powerful jinn, and enchanted objects coexist with everyday life, adding a sense of wonder and imagination to the tales.

Above all, Arabic storytelling is filled with captivating stories that entertain and engage readers. Whether it's the adventures of legendary heroes or the magic of mythical creatures, these tales have an enduring appeal that transcends cultural boundaries. As with most storytelling traditions, these tales were originally told by firelight as a way of preserving histories and educating both adult and child. These tales form part of our shared heritage, witches, warts, fantastic beasts, and all. They can be dark and violent. They can be sweet and loving. They are we and we are they in so many ways. I've loved reading and re reading these stories. I hope you do too.

Clive

Bath,

January 2024

Aladdin And The Wonderful Lamp

This story has been adapted from Andrew Lang's version of the same tale that originally appeared in The Blue Fairy Book, published in 1899 by Longmans, Green and Co., London and New York. This tale is, of course, taken from the traditional collection often referred to as The Arabian Nights.

There once lived a poor tailor, who had a son called Aladdin, a careless, idle boy who would do nothing but play ball all day long in the streets with little idle boys like himself. This so grieved the father that he died, yet, in spite of his mother's tears and prayers, Aladdin did not mend his ways. One day, when he was playing in the streets as usual, a stranger asked him his age, and if he was not the son of Mustapha the tailor.

"I am, sir," replied Aladdin, "but he died a long while ago."

On this the stranger, who was a famous African magician, fell on his neck and kissed him, saying, "I am your uncle, and knew you from your likeness to my brother. Go to your mother and tell her I am coming."

Aladdin ran home and told his mother of his newly found uncle.

"Indeed, child," she said, "your father had a brother, but I always thought he was dead." However, she prepared supper, and bade

Aladdin seek his uncle, who came laden with wine and fruit. He presently fell down and kissed the place where Mustapha used to sit, bidding Aladdin's mother not to be surprised at not having seen him before, as he had been forty years out of the country. He then turned to Aladdin, and asked him his trade, at which the boy hung his head, while his mother burst into tears. On learning that Aladdin was idle and would learn no trade, he offered to take a shop for him and stock it with merchandise. Next day he bought Aladdin a fine suit of clothes and took him all over the city, showing him the sights, and brought him home at nightfall to his mother, who was overjoyed to see her son so fine.

The next day the magician led Aladdin into some beautiful gardens a long way outside the city gates. They sat down by a fountain and the magician pulled a cake from his girdle, which he divided between them. They then journeyed onward till they almost reached the mountains. Aladdin was so tired that he begged to go back, but the magician beguiled him with pleasant stories, and led him on in spite of himself.

At last, they came to two mountains divided by a narrow valley. "We will go no farther," said the false uncle. "I will show you something wonderful, only first gather up sticks while I kindle a fire."

When it was lit the magician threw on it a powder he had about him, at the same time saying some magical words. The earth trembled a little and opened in front of them, disclosing a square flat stone with a brass ring in the middle to raise it by. Aladdin tried to run away, but the magician caught him and gave him a blow that knocked him down.

"What have I done, uncle?" he said piteously, whereupon the magician said in a kindlier tone, "Fear nothing, but obey me.

Beneath this stone lies a treasure which is to be yours, and no one else may touch it, so you must do exactly as I tell you."

At the word treasure Aladdin forgot his fears, and grasped the ring as he was told, saying the names of his father and grandfather. The stone came up quite easily, and some steps appeared.

"Go down," said the magician, "at the foot of those steps you will find an open door leading into three large halls. Tuck up your gown and go through them without touching anything, or you will die instantly. These halls lead into a garden of fine fruit trees. Walk on until you come to a niche in a terrace where a lighted lamp stands. Pour out the oil it contains and bring it to me." He drew a ring from his finger and gave it to Aladdin, bidding him prosper.

Aladdin found everything as the magician had said, gathered some fruit off the trees, and having got the lamp, arrived at the mouth of the cave. The magician cried out in a great hurry, "Make haste and give me the lamp." This Aladdin refused to do until he was out of the cave. The magician flew into a terrible passion, and throwing some more powder on to the fire, he said something, and the stone rolled back into its place.

The magician left Persia for ever, which plainly showed that he was no uncle of Aladdin's, but a cunning magician, who had read in his magic books of a wonderful lamp, which would make him the most powerful man in the world. Though he alone knew where to find it, he could only receive it from the hand of another. He had picked out the foolish Aladdin for this purpose, intending to get the lamp and kill him afterward

For two days Aladdin remained in the dark, crying and lamenting. At last, he clasped his hands in prayer, and in so doing rubbed the ring, which the magician had forgotten to take from him.

Immediately an enormous and frightful genie rose out of the earth, saying, "What would you have me do? I am the Slave of the Ring and will obey you in all things."

Aladdin fearlessly replied, "Deliver me from this place!" whereupon the earth opened, and he found himself outside. As soon as his eyes could bear the light he went home but fainted on the threshold. When he came to himself, he told his mother what had passed, and showed her the lamp and the fruits he had gathered in the garden, which were, in reality, precious stones. He then asked for some food.

"Alas! child," she said, "I have nothing in the house, but I have spun a little cotton and will go and sell it."

Aladdin bade her keep her cotton, for he would sell the lamp instead. As it was very dirty she began to rub it, that it might fetch a higher price. Instantly a hideous genie appeared, and asked what she would have. She fainted away, but Aladdin, snatching the lamp, said boldly, "Fetch me something to eat!" The genie returned with a silver bowl, twelve silver plates containing rich meats, two silver cups, and two bottles of wine.

Aladdin's mother, when she came to herself, said, "Where has this splendid feast come from?"

"Don't ask, but eat," replied Aladdin.

So, they sat at breakfast till it was dinner time, and Aladdin told his mother about the lamp. She begged him to sell it and have nothing to do with devils.

"No," said Aladdin, "since chance has made us aware of its virtues, we will use it, and the ring likewise, which I shall always wear on my finger." When they had eaten all the genie had brought, Aladdin sold one of the silver plates, and so on until none were left. He then had recourse to the genie, who gave him another set of plates, and thus they lived for many years.

One day Aladdin heard a proclamation from the Sultan that everyone was to stay at home and close his shutters while the Princess, his daughter, went to and from the bath. Aladdin was seized by a desire to see her face, which was very difficult, as she always went veiled. He hid himself behind the door of the bath and peeped through a chink. The Princess lifted her veil as she went in and looked so beautiful that Aladdin fell in love with her at first sight. He went home so changed that his mother was frightened. He told her he loved the Princess so deeply that he could not live without her and meant to ask her in marriage of her father. His mother, on hearing this, burst out laughing, but Aladdin at last prevailed upon her to go before the Sultan and carry his request.

Aladdin's mother fetched a napkin and laid in it the magic fruits from the enchanted garden, which sparkled and shone like the most beautiful jewels. She took these with her to please the Sultan, and set out, trusting in the lamp. The Grand Vizier and the lords of council had just gone in as she entered the hall and went to stand in front of the Sultan. He, however, took no notice of her. She went every day for a week and stood in the same place.

When the council broke up on the sixth day the Sultan said to his Vizier, "I see a certain woman in the audience chamber every day carrying something in a napkin. Call her next time, that I may find out what she wants."

Next day, at a sign from the Vizier, she went up to the foot of the throne and remained kneeling till the Sultan said to her, "Rise, good woman, and tell me what you want." She hesitated, so the Sultan sent away all but the Vizier, and bade her speak frankly, promising to forgive her beforehand for anything she might say.

She then told him of her son's violent love for the Princess. "I begged him to forget her," she said, "but in vain, and he threatened to do some desperate deed if I refused to go and ask your Majesty for the hand of the Princess. Now I pray you to forgive not me alone, but my son Aladdin."

The Sultan asked her kindly what she had in the napkin, whereupon she unfolded the jewels and presented them. He was thunderstruck, and turning to the Vizier said, "What do you say? Ought I not to bestow the Princess on one who values her at such a price?"

The Vizier, who wanted her for his own son, begged the Sultan to withhold her for three months, in the course of which he hoped his son would contrive to make the Sultan a richer present. The Sultan granted this, and told Aladdin's mother that, though he consented to the marriage, she must not appear before him again for three months.

Aladdin waited patiently for nearly three months, but after two had elapsed his mother, going into the city to buy oil, found every one rejoicing, and asked what was going on.

"Do you not know," was the answer, "that the son of the Grand Vizier is to marry the Sultan's daughter tonight?"

Breathless, she ran and told Aladdin, who was overwhelmed at first, but presently he thought of the lamp. He rubbed it, and the genie appeared, saying, "What is your will?" Aladdin replied, "The Sultan, as you know, has broken his promise to me, and the Vizier's son is to have the Princess. My command is that tonight you bring here the bride and bridegroom."

"Master, I obey," said the genie.

Aladdin then went to his chamber, where, sure enough, at midnight the genie transported the bed containing the Vizier's son and the Princess.

"Take this new married man," Aladdin said, "and put him outside in the cold, and return at daybreak."

The genie took the Vizier's son out of bed, leaving Aladdin with the Princess. "Fear nothing," Aladdin said to her, "you are my wife, promised to me by your unjust father, and no harm shall come to you."

The Princess was too frightened to speak, and passed the most miserable night of her life, while Aladdin lay down beside her and slept soundly. At the appointed hour the genie fetched in the shivering bridegroom, laid him in his place, and transported the bed back to the palace.

Presently the Sultan came to wish his daughter good morning. The unhappy Vizier's son jumped up and hid himself, while the Princess would not say a word, and was very sorrowful. The Sultan sent her mother to her, who said, "How comes it, child, that you will not speak to your father? What has happened?"

The Princess sighed deeply, and at last told her mother how, during the night, the bed had been carried into some strange house, and what had passed there. Her mother did not believe her in the least but bade her rise and consider it an idle dream.

The following night exactly the same thing happened, and next morning, on the Princess's refusal to speak, the Sultan threatened to cut off her head. She then confessed all, bidding him to ask the Vizier's son if it were not so. The Sultan told the Vizier to ask his son, who admitted the truth, adding that, dearly as he loved the Princess, he would rather die than go through another such fearful night, and wished to be separated from her. His wish was granted, and there was an end to feasting and rejoicing.

When the three months were over, Aladdin sent his mother to remind the Sultan of his promise. She stood in the same place as before, and the Sultan, who had forgotten Aladdin, at once remembered him, and sent for her. On seeing her poverty the Sultan felt less inclined than ever to keep his word, and asked his Vizier's advice, who counselled him to set so high a value on the Princess that no man living could come up to it.

The Sultan then turned to Aladdin's mother, saying, "Good woman, a Sultan must remember his promises, and I will remember mine, but your son must first send me forty basins of gold brim full of jewels, carried by forty ragged and dirty slaves, led by as many fair ones, splendidly dressed. Tell him that I await his answer."

The mother of Aladdin bowed low and went home, thinking all was lost. She gave Aladdin the message, adding, "He may wait long enough for your answer!"

"Not so long, mother, as you think," her son replied. "I would do a great deal more than that for the Princess."

He summoned the genie, and in a few moments the eighty slaves arrived, and filled up the small house and garden. Aladdin made them set out to the palace, two and two, followed by his mother. They were so richly dressed, with such splendid jewels in their girdles, that everyone crowded to see them and the basins of gold they carried on their heads. They entered the palace, and, after kneeling before the Sultan, stood in a half circle round the throne with their arms crossed, while Aladdin's mother presented them to the Sultan.

The Sultan hesitated no longer, but said, "Good woman, return and tell your son that I wait for him with open arms."

She lost no time in telling Aladdin, bidding him make haste. But Aladdin first called the genie. "I want a scented bath," he said, "richly embroidered clothes, a horse surpassing the Sultan's, and twenty slaves to attend me. Besides this, six slaves, beautifully dressed, to wait on my mother, and lastly, ten thousand pieces of gold in ten purses."

No sooner said than done. Aladdin mounted his horse and passed through the streets, the slaves strewing gold as they went. Those who had played with him in his childhood no longer knew him, he had grown so handsome. When the Sultan saw him, he came down from his throne, embraced him, and led him into a hall where a feast was spread, intending to marry him to the Princess that very day.

But Aladdin refused, saying, "I must build a palace fit for her." He took his leave. Once home, he said to the genie, "Build me a palace of the finest marble, set with jasper, agate, and other precious stones. In the middle you shall build me a large hall with a dome, its four walls of massy gold and silver, each having six windows, whose lattices, all except one which is to be left unfinished, must be set with diamonds and rubies. There must be stables and horses and grooms and slaves, go and see about it!"

The palace was finished by the next day, and the genie carried him there and showed him all his orders faithfully carried out, even to the laying of a velvet carpet from Aladdin's palace to the Sultan's. Aladdin's mother then dressed herself carefully, and walked to the palace with her slaves, while he followed her on horseback. The Sultan sent musicians with trumpets and cymbals to meet them, so that the air resounded with music and cheers. Aladdin's mother was taken to the Princess, who saluted her and treated her with great honour.

At night the Princess said goodbye to her father, and set out on the carpet for Aladdin's palace, with his mother at her side, and followed by the hundred slaves. She was charmed at the sight of Aladdin, who ran to receive her.

"Princess," he said, "blame your beauty for my boldness if I have displeased you."

She told him that, having seen him, she willingly obeyed her father in this matter. After the wedding had taken place Aladdin led her into the hall, where a feast was spread, and she supped with him, after which they danced till midnight.

Next day Aladdin invited the Sultan to see the palace. On entering the hall with the four and twenty windows, with their rubies, diamonds, and emeralds, he cried, "It is a world's wonder! There is only one thing that surprises me. Was it by accident that one window was left unfinished?"

"No, sir, by design," returned Aladdin. "I wished your Majesty to have the glory of finishing this palace."

The Sultan was pleased and sent for the best jewellers in the city. He showed them the unfinished window and bade them fit it up like the others.

"Sir," replied their spokesman, "we cannot find jewels enough."

The Sultan had his own fetched, which they soon used, but to no purpose, for in a month's time the work was not half done. Aladdin, knowing that their task was vain, bade them undo their work and carry the jewels back, and the genie finished the window at his command. The Sultan was surprised to receive his jewels again, and visited Aladdin, who showed him the window finished. The Sultan embraced him, the envious Vizier meanwhile hinting that it was the work of enchantment.

Aladdin had won the hearts of the people by his gentle bearing. He was made captain of the Sultan's armies, and won several battles for him, but remained modest and courteous as before, and lived in peace and contentment for several years.

But far away in Africa the magician remembered Aladdin, and by his magic arts discovered that Aladdin, instead of perishing miserably in the cave, had escaped, and had married a princess, with whom he was living in great honour and wealth. He knew that the poor tailor's son could only have accomplished this by means of the lamp, and travelled night and day until he reached the capital of China, bent on Aladdin's ruin. As he passed through the town, he heard people talking everywhere about a marvellous palace.

"Forgive my ignorance," he asked, "what is this palace you speak of?"

"Have you not heard of Prince Aladdin's palace," was the reply, "the greatest wonder of the world? I will direct you if you have a mind to see it."

The magician thanked the man who spoke, and having seen the palace, knew that it had been raised by the Genie of the Lamp, and became half mad with rage. He determined to get hold of the lamp, and again plunge Aladdin into the deepest poverty.

Unluckily, Aladdin had gone hunting for eight days, which gave the magician plenty of time. He bought a dozen copper lamps, put them into a basket, and went to the palace, crying, "New lamps for old!" followed by a jeering crowd. The Princess, sitting in the hall of four and twenty windows, sent a slave to find out what the noise was about, and she came back laughing, so that the Princess scolded her.

"Madam," replied the slave, "who can help laughing to see an old fool offering to exchange fine new lamps for old ones?"

Another slave, hearing this, said, "There is an old one on the cornice there which he can have."

Now this was the magic lamp, which Aladdin had left there, as he could not take it out hunting with him. The Princess, not knowing its value, laughingly ordered the slave to take it and make the exchange. The slave went and said to the magician, "Give me a new lamp for this." He snatched it and bade the slave take her choice, amid the jeers of the crowd. His work was done and he cared little for his old task, and he left off crying his lamps, and went out of the city gates to a lonely place, where he remained till nightfall, when he pulled out the lamp and rubbed it. The genie appeared, and at the magician's command carried him, together with the palace and the Princess in it, to a lonely place in Africa.

Next morning the Sultan looked out of the window toward Aladdin's palace and rubbed his eyes, for it was gone. He sent for the Vizier and asked what had become of the palace. The Vizier looked out too and was lost in astonishment. He again put it down to enchantment, and this time the Sultan believed him, and sent thirty men on horseback to fetch Aladdin in chains. They met him riding home, bound him, and forced him to go with them on foot. The people, however, who loved him, followed, armed, to see that he came to no harm.

He was carried before the Sultan, who ordered the executioner to cut off his head. The executioner made Aladdin kneel down, bandaged his eyes, and raised his scimitar to strike. At that instant the Vizier, who saw that the crowd had forced their way into the courtyard and were scaling the walls to rescue Aladdin, called to the executioner to stay his hand. The people, indeed, looked so threatening that the Sultan gave way and ordered Aladdin to be unbound, and pardoned him in the sight of the crowd. Aladdin now begged to know what he had done.

"False wretch!" said the Sultan, "come here," and showed him from the window the place where his palace had stood. Aladdin was so amazed that he could not say a word. "Where is my palace and my daughter?" demanded the Sultan. "For the first I am not so deeply concerned, but my daughter I must have, and you must find her or lose your head."

Aladdin begged for forty days in which to find her, promising, if he failed, to return and suffer death at the Sultan's pleasure. His prayer was granted, and he went forth sadly from the Sultan's presence. For three days he wandered about like a madman, asking everyone what had become of his palace, but they only laughed and pitied him.

He came to the banks of a river, and knelt down to say his prayers before throwing himself in. In so doing he rubbed the magic ring he still wore. The genie he had seen in the cave appeared and asked his will. "Save my life, genie," said Aladdin, "bring my palace back."

"That is not in my power," said the genie, "I am only the Slave of the Ring, you must ask the genie of the lamp."

"Even so," said Aladdin, "but you can take me to the palace, and set me down under my dear wife's window."

He at once found himself in Africa, under the window of the Princess, and fell asleep out of sheer weariness. He was awakened by the singing of the birds, and his heart was lighter. He saw plainly that all his misfortunes were owing to the loss of the lamp, and vainly wondered who had robbed him of it.

That morning the Princess rose earlier than she had done since she had been carried into Africa by the magician, whose company she was forced to endure once a day. She, however, treated him so harshly that he dared not live there altogether. As she was dressing, one of her women looked out and saw Aladdin. The Princess ran and opened the window, and at the noise she made Aladdin looked up. She called to him to come to her, and great was the joy of these lovers at seeing each other again.

After he had kissed her Aladdin said, "I beg of you, Princess, in God's name, before we speak of anything else, for your own sake and mine, tell me what has become of an old lamp I left on the cornice in the hall of four and twenty windows, when I went hunting."

"Alas!" she said, "I am the innocent cause of our sorrows," and told him of the exchange of the lamp.

"Now I know," cried Aladdin, "that we have to thank the African magician for this! Where is the lamp?"

"He carries it about with him," said the Princess. "I know, for he pulled it out of his breast to show me. He wishes me to break my faith with you and marry him, saying that you were beheaded by my father's command. He is for ever speaking ill of you but I only reply by my tears. If I persist, I doubt not but he will use violence."

Aladdin comforted her and left her for a while. He changed clothes with the first person he met in the town, and having bought a certain powder, returned to the Princess, who let him in by a little side door.

"Put on your most beautiful dress," he said to her "and receive the magician with smiles, leading him to believe that you have forgotten me. Invite him to sup with you, and say you wish to taste the wine of his country. He will go for some and while he is gone I will tell you what to do."

She listened carefully to Aladdin and when he left she arrayed herself gaily for the first time since she left China. She put on a girdle and head dress of diamonds, and, seeing in a glass that she was more beautiful than ever, received the magician, saying, to his great amazement, "I have made up my mind that Aladdin is dead, and that all my tears will not bring him back to me, so I am resolved to mourn no more, and have therefore invited you to sup with me, but I am tired of the wines of China, and would fain taste those of Africa."

The magician flew to his cellar, and the Princess put the powder Aladdin had given her in her cup. When he returned she asked him to drink her health in the wine of Africa, handing him her cup in exchange for his, as a sign she was reconciled to him. Before drinking the magician made her a speech in praise of her beauty, but the Princess cut him short, saying, "Let us drink first, and you shall say what you will afterward."

She set her cup to her lips and kept it there, while the magician drained his to the dregs and fell back lifeless. The Princess then opened the door to Aladdin and flung her arms round his neck, but Aladdin pushed her away, bidding her leave him, as he had more to do. He then went to the dead magician, took the lamp out of his vest, and bade the genie carry the palace and all in it back to China. This was done, and the Princess in her chamber only felt two little shocks, and little thought she was at home again.

The Sultan, who was sitting in his closet, mourning for his lost daughter, happened to look up, and rubbed his eyes, for there stood the palace as before! He hastened there, and Aladdin received him in the hall of the four and twenty windows, with the Princess at his side. Aladdin told him what had happened, and showed him the dead body of the magician, that he might believe the tale. A ten days' feast was proclaimed, and it seemed as if Aladdin might now live the rest of his life in peace, but it was not to be.

The African magician had a younger brother, who was, if possible, more wicked, and more cunning than himself. He travelled to China to avenge his brother's death, and went to visit a pious woman called Fatima, thinking she might be of use to him. He entered her cell and clapped a dagger to her breast, telling her to rise and do his bidding on pain of death. He changed clothes with her, coloured his face like hers, put on her veil, and murdered her, that she might tell no tales. Then he went toward Aladdin's palace, and all the people, thinking he was the holy woman, gathered round him, kissing his hands, and begging his blessing.

When he got to the palace there was such a noise going on round him that the Princess bade her slave look out of the window and ask what the matter was. The slave said it was the holy woman, curing people of their ailments by her touch, whereupon the Princess, who had long desired to see Fatima, sent for her. On coming to the Princess the magician offered up a prayer for her health and prosperity. When he had done this, the Princess made him sit by her and begged him to stay with her always. The false Fatima, who wished for nothing better, consented, but kept his veil down for fear of discovery.

The Princess showed him the hall and asked him what he thought of it. "It is truly beautiful," said the false Fatima. "In my mind it wants but one thing."

"And what is that?" said the Princess.

"If only a roc's egg," replied he, "were hung up from the middle of this dome, it would be the wonder of the world."

After this the Princess could think of nothing but the roc's egg, and when Aladdin returned from hunting he found her in a very ill humour. He begged to know what was amiss, and she told him that all her pleasure in the hall was spoiled for the want of a roc's egg hanging from the dome.

"If that is all," replied Aladdin, "you shall soon be happy."

He left her and rubbed the lamp, and when the genie appeared commanded him to bring a roc's egg. The genie gave such a loud and terrible shriek that the hall shook. "Wretch!" he cried, "is it not enough that I have done everything for you, but you must command me to bring my master and hang him up in the midst of this dome? You and your wife and your palace deserve to be burnt to ashes, but I know that this request does not come from you, but from the brother of the African magician, whom you destroyed. He is now in your palace disguised as the holy woman, whom he murdered. He it was who put that wish into your wife's head. Take care of yourself, for he means to kill you." So saying, the genie disappeared.

Aladdin went back to the Princess, saying his head ached, and requesting that the holy Fatima should be fetched to lay her hands on it. But when the magician came near, Aladdin, seizing his dagger, pierced him to the heart.

"What have you done?" cried the Princess. "You have killed the holy woman!"

"Not so," replied Aladdin, "but a wicked magician," and told her of how she had been deceived.

After this Aladdin and his wife lived in peace. He succeeded the Sultan when he died, and reigned for many years, leaving behind him a long line of kings.

The Doom Of Al Zameri

*This story has been adapted from Henry Iliowizi's version of the same
tale that originally appeared in The Weird Orient, published in 1900 by
Henry T. Coates and Company, Philadelphia. This tale references
elements of Surah 20 of The Koran.*

Nothing is known in nature which, in awful impressiveness,
compares with the overpowering scenery forever associated with
God's revelation to man. That arm of the Indian Ocean called the
Red Sea bifurcates into the westerly gulf of Suez and the easterly
one of Akabah, and the triangular peninsula thus formed embraces
the region that bears the name of the sky consecrated Mount Sinai.
He who, from an overtopping height, once surveys those prodigies
of this globe's eternal framework, pile on pile, varied by solitary
peaks raising their heads above the clouds, amid a confusion of
innumerable gorges, wadis, and ravines, the red of the stupendous
mass interspersed with porphyry and greenstone, will, apart from
their spiritual reminiscences, bear the impression to the end of his
days that he has been in the very heart of creative omnipotence.
About the entire system there is such a ghostly air, such a terrific
frown, as is recalled by no other chain of crests and cliffs, however
bold or life deserted. If the bleaker rocks that encompass the basin
of the Dead Sea are more deterring, those of Horeb are of a thrilling

sublimity, and if this is true in broad daylight, night invests them with an inexpressible mystic awe, intensified by an inexplicable rumbling and roaring not unlike distant thunder. But all other feelings are merged in the one of terror when, as it sometimes happens, a heavy thunderstorm breaks over the wilderness of Sinai. Rendered impervious by a rarely disturbed aridity, the barren rocks retain little more water than would the glazed incline of a pyramid, so that the mountain torrents rush down with cyclonic impetuosity, uprooting trees and sweeping off settlements, with no trace left of what man and nature combine to produce.

It was in one of those spasmodic storms that, in the year 1185 after Mohammed's flight from Mecca, a muffled figure moved cautiously in the heart of a cloudburst which was accompanied by blinding flashes of lightning and such thunderbolts as shook the very bedrock of the mountainous desolation. The Bedouin's watch fires, nightly seen all along the gentler acclivities, vanished before the elemental fury, and though the plain of al Rahe opened before him, the lonely wanderer turned his face toward Jebel Musa, or Mount of Moses, betraying his anxiety to remain unrecognized. Wind and rain forced the man to seek shelter somewhere, but he seemed to prefer a dark hollow to the sure hospitality of the Arab's tent. From the heights the torrents came roaring like waterfalls, carrying along piled up masses of uprooted tamarisks, palm trees, struggling sheep and goats, and even boulders were swept down like pebbles.

While stopping for a moment, irresolute as to the direction he should take, the muffled figure discerned a human form stranger than his own, overwhelmed by the flood and on the point of being either engulfed or crushed to death by the wreck encumbered torrent. With a rush which endangered his life, the mysterious wanderer caught hold of the forlorn victim, tearing him out of the destructive tide, and landed him near a cave which he had not seen before.

"Touch me not!" cried the rescued creature in a voice that startled his preserver. Yet compared with the rest of his individuality, the voice was the least appalling of his features. There stood a bare headed being, bent with age, pale as a ghost, lean as starvation, wrinkled as a shrivelled hag, shaggy as a bear, his beard descending to his knees, and his hair to his waist. Death stared from his eyes, misery from his face, in all an image of hopelessness, tottering toward the grave. Barely strong enough to drag his limbs, the wretch waddled into the rayless hole, whining and groaning.

The weather's inclemency would have hardly induced the other to divide the cave with one whose aspect suggested the tenant of the graveyard, but the tramp of approaching horses left no time for reflection. Like a shadow the muffled figure disappeared just in time to escape the notice of two Mamluks on horses, who, perceiving the hole, drew in their reins with an oath, "Allah tear the devil! If it were not for my poor horse I would crawl into that black pit to get out of this infernal tempest. See this cataract! Why, this beats the Nile! And the hawk we are looking for may as well be leagues out of this wilderness as within it. If we do not hurry to Wadi Feiran, the fever will settle in my belly. I feel cold about the heart," said one of the horsemen.

"Shall we give up the thousand purses set on Ali Bey's head?" asked his fellow.

"Give up the chase of the devil! The slave Sultan is not within these black reaches, I say, and we are fools to follow our noses until the breath is out of our stomachs," answered the other impatiently.

A red zigzag flash tore the clouds, the crash threw the horses on their haunches. Had not the astounded Mamluks scampered off like the wind, the lightning would have revealed to them the object of their hunt, Egypt's celebrated Sheikh el Beled, a title tantamount to the power and dignity of Caliph. Such was Ali Bey who, at the close of a career of adventure and romance, was a fugitive in the wilds, with a price set by his enemies upon his head.

"The bloodhounds have lost the spoor of the game, and if my messengers reach Acre safely, my friend Daher will be out in force, but where will I hide till then?" thought Ali Bey and proceeded to close up the entrance to his retreat by a pile of rubbish near at hand, darkness favouring the operation.

"Unless there are snakes in this hole, I shall have an hour's rest," said Ali to himself, having completed the hiding wall. A moaning ululation in the dark reminded him of the other presence he had enclosed with himself, and his alarm was not lessened by the sudden glimmer of something which broke the gloom of the den. Coming as it did from the deep of the hollow, it could not be mistaken for a flare of lightning from without. Another glimmer left no doubt as to its source.

Ali Bey was not a man to quail before anything another man could face, but here was a phenomenon to stop the pulsing of the stoutest heart. A burning jewel, not in the palsied hand of a decrepit dotard, but in the hold of one in the prime of manhood, who resembled the other as closely as a heifer does its dam. Who was he? A son of the former old hag? Or had there occurred the miracle of instantaneous rejuvenescence? Or was it Satan bent on some diabolical performance?

"Man or demon, good or evil power, whoever you are, I demand of you in Allah's name that you unfold your mystery to me. Are you he whom I saved from the fury of the elements? He was nearer a hundred than thirty years, nearer death than life. You look like him but could be his grandchild as to age and vigour. Are you and he the same? Or are you an illusion, perhaps the spirit of this mountain? If you are a spirit, you know who I am. If you are human I charge you to speak to Ali Bey, the Sheikh el Beled of Egypt, who is waiting for assistance to defeat the conspiracies of his enemies," spoke Ali with the firmness of despair.

"Sheikh el Beled," answered the one spoken to in a tone as changed as his form, "there is less of spirit in me than in you, yet am I less human than man ever was, deathless yet mortal, tossed about on the ocean of time from age to age, century to century, cycle to cycle, millennium to millennium, denied the peace of soul, the comfort of hope, the blessing of prayer, the nepenthe of oblivion, yes, the rest of the grave. Tremble not at the sound of my name. I am Al Zameri, the accursed roamer of the times, doomed since the making of the golden calf to begin, rejuvenated after a lapse of every hundred years, anew my unblessed career, homeless, godless, hopeless, shunned, feared, and hated!"

"Al Zameri!" cried Ali, who had moved some steps backward in horror.

"That is my name, and credulity couples it with sin, greed, famine, war, inundations, hurricanes, and pestilence. While you are within the reach of my breath, warned by instinct, no man will do you harm," promised the wretched wanderer.

"Allah confound the devil! You would have perished in the flood if I had not rescued you, there must be a hidden purpose in the accident of our meeting. Born a slave, destiny has given me the power to defy and defeat the Caliph of Islam. My sword has made me sole ruler over the empire on the banks of the Nile. In open battle I fear no foe, but it is conspiracy and the assassin's dagger that I am fleeing, and your thwarting my pathway, or my thwarting you, means something to me, Al Zameri. I am in the hand of Allah, the most merciful. But speak, you man of immortal woe, how did you provoke the anger of your people's God? Why was the golden idol fashioned? Was it done by you? What has been your experience since? For few are the Prophet's words in his reference to your transgression in the Koran," resumed Ali, making the best of his unique acquaintance.

"Sheikh el Beled, your kindness, not your service, requires my acknowledgment. Your succour was wasted on a man whom perdition would not have. For three thousand years death shuns me as ruthlessly as I long to hug it. My tale is a nightmare of three millenniums, taking me back to ancient Egypt, where I, a Hebrew, was born into abject slavery. My hot blood resented the taskmaster's rod. In a moment of rage I struck back at one of my tormentors, blow for blow, and was with other rebels doomed to dig in one of Pharaoh's copper mines on the coast of Akabah in the valley of Semud. Here many of the Egyptian idols were fashioned, and here I learned the secret of the priests, who caused metallic forms to utter sound, to articulate oracular speech. Certain instruments were skilfully inserted into the interior of the idol, and the priest manipulated them to the great wonderment of the populace, who lay prostrate before their all-knowing, warning, or blessing gods. The fraud was guarded by the loss of the tongue that betrayed it.

"I was young and strong when the joyous tidings penetrated our penal colony, that a man of God had afflicted Egypt with plague after plague, insisting that the Israelites be freed from bondage, and we soon read Egypt's doom in the face of our taskmaster. We conspired, made a desperate break for liberty, and marked our track with the blood of those who offered resistance. Love for parents long missed impelled me to disdain danger. Disguised as an Egyptian, I was determined to steal into the land of the Pharaohs, when one night my progress was stopped by a manifestation in the desert, which filled me with consternation. A pillar of lurid flame, having its base on earth, advanced eastward with a rotatory motion, its upper end obeying a force among the stars. It was a glowing meteor, enormous in volume, endless in height, and terrible to behold, setting earth and heaven on fire, and bathing the desert in fearful glory. As I hurried to get out of the pillar's reach, lest I be consumed, I fell in with the vanguard of my liberated brethren in the rear of their fiery guide. What I saw and heard thrilled me with awe. A power greater than Osiris lowered Egypt to the dust, and that was the God of my people. My father was no more, I embraced my aged mother and one surviving sister, and we wept for joy.

"Before I had been an hour in the great camp, which extended over many miles, the cry ran from lip to lip, 'We are pursued! The Egyptians are at our heels!' Terror and confusion seized the enormous multitude, men, women, and children acting like maniacs, while a throng of lusty fellows, myself among them, pressed on to see what the Man of God was going to do. We found him in company of Aaron and Hur, his countenance beaming, as though it had concentrated the blaze of the flaming pillar to reflect it in a milder beam. He was Moses, the son of Amram. In his hand a staff, his grey beard and curly locks setting off a face of manly firmness, tempered by feminine grace and a visionary dreaminess, his eyes turned fixedly where the top of the fire pillar lost itself in azure. As if in compliance with his tacit prayer, the prodigious beam swerved from its forward course, wheeled backward to the right, and thus transferred its base from the front of the moving camp to its rear, interposing its volume between the pursuer and the pursued. It was the second watch of the night, we were within a short hour of the Yam Mitzrayim, the Egyptian Sea known as The Red Sea, and a dense fog left us in doubt as to the distance of the enemy behind us. The suspense was unbearable, and Moses was besieged by the rebellious and the craven, who rent the air with reproaches and appeals. He spoke a few words of encouragement, asking the people to faithfully await the salvation of the Lord, but his voice was drowned in the vociferation of the threatening crowd.

"At a hint from Aaron five thousand armed men of the tribe of Levi threw themselves between the great leader and the clamouring mob. It was a critical moment. The undaunted chief spread out his hands in prayer.

"The third watch of the night came with a freezing gale, it raised the fog and revealed a sea lashed by the fury of the growing tempest. It was dawn when the leader, inspired from On High, struck the flood with his staff. The waters rose high, broke, scattered in dust, rose again, tumbled, divided up, and froze, leaving a broad highway dry as the shore. With his brother the leader entered the depth followed by the people, till the whole multitude found themselves between the icy walls, emerging on the opposite shore happy and jubilant.

"Just now the blush of morning in the east was eclipsed by a wave of effulgence west of the Sea of Egypt, and as we turned our eyes there we were amazed to behold the burning pillar replaced by a sun crowned power that illumined the heavens with his dazzling panoply and his sword of many flames. That presence sealed the doom of the Egyptians. In their impetuous onward rush they plunged into the jaws of death. The miraculous road was not meant to give them passage, and no sooner were they in the heart of the dry abyss than, by a touch of the leader's staff, the frozen walls, melted by the sun crowned power, gave way to the devouring sea, burying Egypt's mighty army. The air shivered with the multitudinous shout of joy sent up by our myriads of grateful fugitives. Song, dance, and praise commemorated the great event, to be shortly followed by one greater than anything I know of in the annals of man.

"Ah, let me come to the cause of my doom! What happened between the crossing of the Red Sea and the Day of Revelation is on record, but eternity will not efface the picture burned into my memory of what I have, thousands of years ago, witnessed in this wilderness of Zin.

"After a short encampment hereabout, the leader, he the chief of chiefs, made it known that in three days the Majesty Divine would reveal Himself and His truth on the top of Sinai, the interval to be spent in purifying preparations.

"As though all the earthquakes and thunders of the ages were to spend their furious energy within the space of one daybreak, a convulsed earth and a bursting firmament roused a terrified people from their sleep, summoning them to gather at the foot of the fire belching, quaking, night shrouded mountain, there to receive the first commandments of the Torah, the Law of the world. They obeyed the summons but succumbed to the supernatural manifestations. Himself unseen, the voice of the leader was heard from the thick of the clouds, communing with Omnipotence, the blasts of mighty trumpets intermingling with the bellowing, rumbling, and growling of the roused elements. Suddenly a profound silence superseded the universal agitation. Clearly stood out the apex of the mountain, clear spread the horizon, and ear, heart and soul were entranced by the ineffable melody of utterance which came floating from the empyrean. Like the symphony of an angelic chorus, the Ten

Commandments vibrated throughout the ethereal spaces, reclaiming the people from their torpor, to be overawed by a wonder exceeding anything they had yet seen. With a background of azure, and the three summits of the Sinaitic range as base, there spread in the clear infinite blue the likeness of inexpressible Majesty in the transcendental shape of a sovereign, crowned with supernal glory, compassion and benign grace radiating from His dimly discernible features, in His hand an open scroll, covering half the firmament, and showing the Decalogue in sunny splendour, each letter proving but the reflex of a yet grander copy visibly set in stars far back in the deepest heavens.

"A season of tumultuous rejoicing followed the closing of that soul thrilling scene, and the emancipated slaves abandoned themselves to indulgences bordering on license. In the whirl of excitement nobody noticed the absence of the venerated prophet, who had not been seen nor heard from since the Day of Revelation, and his family and closest associates were as ignorant of his whereabouts as the rest of the people. But when a whole month had passed by without a token of the prophet's being or doing, the craven hearted mass took umbrage, fearing they had been deserted both by Moses and his God. Aaron was called upon to allay their apprehensions, but he proved unequal to the exigency. Pressed to supply them with a power to worship, and somebody to lead them, instead of bidding them to have patience and wait, in a moment of weakness he yielded, suggesting that all the golden ornaments of the women be delivered to him, that he might fashion for them a god. If the High priest hoped that the women would not sacrifice their jewellery, he was soon undeceived. And I was at hand to lure him into the most heinous of human transgressions.

"Herein centres the enormity of my guilt. Aaron could have never fulfilled his promise had not an evil spirit prompted me to offer him my service in moulding for him a golden calf after the pattern of Egypt's idolatry. Doubting my ability to materialize what I proposed, he gave his assent. I cast into the fire all that I and the hordes had donated, and my experience in metal work enabled me to produce a golden calf with the trick of articulating words.

"When the people saw the image and heard it declare itself their god, they went wild with delight, Aaron himself catching the infection. An altar was built, a feast proclaimed, sacrifices offered, and the masses delivered themselves up to orgies.

"The riot of debauch was broken up by the unexpected arrival of the prophet. With his countenance shining like the sun, he rushed down from the mountain, dropped and shattered the tablets, which bore the Commandments he had received from the hand of God, and reduced the idol to powder which he scattered to the winds. Aaron exonerated himself by pointing to the madness of the people, and to me as the real culprit. 'This Azazel has brought the great sin on the head of the people,' cried he, his eye fixed in fierce hatred on my detested self. What could I advance in extenuation of my devilish authorship?

"Severe punishment was meted out. Four thousand prominent offenders fell under the sword, but I was singled out for a special fate as a warning to coming ages. 'Al Zameri shall not die, Al Zameri shall henceforth wander like Cain, shunned, feared, cursed and hated, Al Zameri shall, at the lapse of a hundred years, revisit the scene of his crime, shall be restored to his present condition, and thus go on and on, until time shall wipe out the memory of his evil deed,' was the verdict I heard. The prophet spoke it under the spell of inspiration, and I was set free.

"And free I was, and free I am to roam forever like a mad beast, driven here by the fury to be transformed at the appointed hour into the young man that I was when malicious folly stamped me as the outcast of the human race.

"That same hour I conceived an irrepressible impulse to seek the vast, the void, the desert, the jungle, the swamp, the unlighted cavern, the place of graves, the ruin, evading the blessed haunts of man, abhorring sunshine and courting darkness. Daylight blinds me as it does the owl, the sight of gold confounds, its touch burns me. The ferocious beast flees at my approach, the serpent hisses, and writhes away. However teeming the region with animal life, however vocal with the song of bird, my passing turns it into a soundless, lifeless wild. I speed with the wind, sweep with the storm, welcome the lightning's flare, the thunder's growl, rage with the elements, curse with the fiends of black Abaddon. The tiger's den is my shelter, my pillow a coil of venomous reptiles. I throw myself into the jaws of the lion. If I swallow the essence of poison, it does not avail me. Death is in league with all creation against me. If I try to end my misery by falling into a chasm, I am lighter than air. Water will not drown me, fire will not burn me, steel will cut my flesh but spares my life, and my dread is life. My dread is time, endless, hopeless, hateful years, decades, cycles, millenniums! Such is the sky ruled destiny of Al Zameri!"

"Horrible is your fate! Yours is hell on earth, O, son of guilt, who did ingraft on the race an evil growth, the worship of gold! Ah, the glittering fetish! What crimes are not traceable to his glossy fascinations! But the potency of prayer, the tear of remorse dear to Allah the most merciful, the King of the Day of Judgment, are they denied you?" inquired Ali Bey.

"Prayer, prayer, man's inward heaven, the unction of life, the solace of the soul, prayer, the heart feeding stream, with God as its fountainhead and influx, swelled by springs unrevealed and currents vainly searched," exclaimed Al Zameri, striking the palms of his hands together with a clap of pain. "Prayer would just as readily commingle with my being as Eden's blessed rivers with the flames of hell. What heaven and earth reveal of the wonderful and holy is deterring to me, whom neither the sublime nor the beautiful inspires, filled as I am with doubt as to whether there be mercy ample enough to cover my guilt.

"Yes, once, but once, long before the Orient felt the Roman's iron grip, my lips, prompted by the whisper of a cherub, stammered prayer, and with that inspiration died my feeble hope, leaving a seething caldron in a heart of flint. Ah, from my gloom of hell I had a glimpse of paradise. You have heard of Balbec's ancient glories, of which her magnificent ruins tell, I saw her in her palmy days, a city of palaces for merchant princes to dwell in, the rival of Tyre, Tadmor and Damascus. Perched on the side of the Anti Libanus, high above the fertile plain of Sahlat Ba'albec, and encircled by groves and gardens watered by the valley's never-failing spring of Ra'as el Ayn, Balbec gloried in rearing great monuments, while the temples dedicated to her gods stood among the marvels of the world. Whatever was precious, useful, or ornamental, was to be had in the bazaars of Balbec. Caravans carried invaluable treasures through her gates, and the royalties she levied enabled her to display a princely munificence in her domestic affairs. With Syria's fluctuating fortunes, Balbec realized every change, but her deadliest enemy was the earthquake's fearful visitation. Often did I wish to see creation sink in chaos, and myself engulfed in the universal wreckage, but my attempt to find death in one of Balbec's catastrophes, instead of bringing deliverance, brought heaven within my touch, with redoubled anguish as the sequel. Satan has his sport with Al Zameri.

"My memory is aglow as I recall the day of lurid skies, an atmosphere saturated with oppressive vapours, an ominous fluttering of birds, and a spasmodic rumbling, as of explosions underground. Too familiar with the symptoms to misunderstand the nature of the impending disturbance, I was thankful to be near Balbec, in whose ruins I hoped to be buried. Quick as my limbs could carry me, I hurried to the doomed city, and entered it through one of her gates, which gave me a full view of her famous Great Temple. Terror distracted the multitude, who rushed about, tumbling one against the other, and bellowing like frightened cattle. Repeated shocks opened gaping crevices in the ground, swallowing houses and closing over man and brute. Down came monumental shafts of skilful workmanship, buildings of massive masonry were either lying in heaps, the graves of their inmates, or stood cracked, ready to tumble at the next upheaval. Death was lurking everywhere. Little affected by the wrecks around me, my only thought was to corner death where escape was wellnigh impossible, and I rushed up the grand flight of steps, which took me to the eastern portico of the stupendous edifice, landing me in a large, hexagonal space. It had the dimensions of a court, which it was not, but a vestibule with one main entrance and two side doors to the great court, a peristyle circumscribed by columns of artistic chiselling, back of which were numerous recesses adorned by statues of gods. With no one to question my intrusion into the sacred place, I stood undetermined and purposeless, when a subterraneous force shook the rock-built foundation of the entablature, which descended with a crash, wrecking the fine statuary by the weight of the fragments. A scream of horror drew me irresistibly in the direction of the voice that uttered it, where, behind a pedestal, I saw a damsel stretched on the floor writhing in convulsions. Bending over the form and raising it from the ground, I held in my arms a being too perfect to be mortal, too substantial to be divine. She was unhurt, except for fright, and, bearing her to the open quadrangle of the peristyle, I seated myself on the floor, allowing her head and shoulders to rest on my lap. 'Are you the goddess to whom this temple is dedicated?' breathed I. In answer a pair of eyes opened wide, to my indescribable confusion, eyes that would tame the tiger and charm the hydra, but they soon closed again.

"Sheikh, I have seen Sisygambis, Persia's imperial mistress, the dame of Darius, her cheek shaming the jewelled tiara meant to grace majesty. On the tide of the Cydnus, on a galley, carved, gilded, and inlaid with ivory, gliding to the rhythmic stroke of polished oars, under sails of silk, I saw Cleopatra reclining on the deck, in the shade of a star-spangled canopy, arrayed as Venus, in the midst of voluptuous music, with her women dressed as nymphs, and little boys as Cupids, she moved me no more than did a score of others famed for beauty in their time. But I was stirred and stricken by the matchless damsel chance had thrown in my way, and I sat there intoxicated by a quaff from some heavenly spring thitherto unknown to me. 'If you were mine for eternity, then what would it matter to me whether the heavens favour me or curse?' I muttered half audibly.

"Once more her opened eyelids laid bare the fountains of bliss, and once more I asked, 'Are you that one whom the denizens of Balbec worship?'

"Like one waking from a vision she raised her head, raised herself, rose to her height a majestic figure, and, looking down on me with an expression of awe, she answered my question with a question. Was I one of the gods to whose worship her father had consecrated her? 'I am the priestess of chaste Istar. Only a god could save me as you did,' cried the maiden, sinking prostrate before me.

"A momentary rocking of the entire structure left but few of the remaining columns erect. The others brought down the Corinthian capitals and the heavy entablature with a tremendous fall, and the great court was one mass of debris scattered in every direction.

"The eastern portico being barred by a confused pile of broken columns, the only escape left open was the western end, and here I carried the fainting priestess, issuing with my burden from the wreck, and finding myself before another building still more beautiful and not yet greatly injured. This was Balbec's Temple of the Sun, a blossom of architecture and sculpture, profusely ornamented by figures of gods and heroes, and finished with a great lavishness of skill and art.

"It was the end of the day, and anxious to shun observation I laboured up the stately stairway to seek a refuge in the safer place, not on my own account but for the sake of the precious creature in my charge. Through a lofty portal I reached two staircases to my right and left, each one leading to the upper story, which was the Temple proper. Here I stopped to take breath, the burden having proved too much for me, and here again I had to look into those open eyes that beamed unutterable things for me. 'Save me, save me, and I will praise and worship you, god of the sun,' whispered the deluded creature.

"'Be undeceived, fair ministress, I am no god but a man of flesh and blood and untold woes, woes unknown to any mortal but myself,' said I.

"'You are not a god, but a man of untold woes? You are unlike any mortal in look, and who sent you here to save me, all others having deserted this place, priest and priestess fleeing for life? Surely you are more than mortal, thus to face death undeterred?'

"'Let not a guilt encumbered fugitive practice deception on you, ministress of Istar. You are right, alas! I am not mortal, but cursed to wander and suffer, because of a great sin committed thousands of years ago,' cried I, and briefly enlightened her as to my nature and my doom.

Tender compassion radiated from her immaculate countenance as, seizing my hand with a hold that thrilled my frame with ravishing delight, she spoke these words, 'O, let me alleviate your suffering by sharing your misery, poor, erring man, who did offend Zicara and his progeny! Yes, I will pray on your behalf! Hear me, all powerful Zicara, and you, Ea, the holder of life and knowledge, the ruler of the abyss, the king of the rivers and gardens, the mate of Bahu, who begot Bal Merodach, hear me and restrain the seven evil spirits from besetting Al Zameri, but send the good ones to placate his conscience, that he have rest and peace, after an atonement long and awful! Yes, my life for his, Zicara, if propitiation cannot otherwise be had since he has imperilled his life for mine!'

"Even while these fervid words dropped from the sweet lips of the kneeling supplicant, the roving mania seized me deliriously. I turned my face toward the nearest exit, but felt my garment caught by the hands that had been folded in prayer. 'Flee not before I kiss the hands which brought me succour,' cried the maiden passionately. Burning kisses covered my hands, a tingling woe permeated the core of my being, I kissed the head, the cheek, the mouth of the one in the wide world, who had offered to share my fate, had offered her life for mine. But adamantine chains could not check my madness to fly, I broke away from her embrace, whose lamentations cut into my heart.

"A pack of hell hounds yelping at my heels would have added little to the mad pace that carried me to the dreary haunts of the mountains, the wailing of the girl, and her image, following me as new fuel to feed the fire of despair. Broken by overwhelming wretchedness, I fell where a steep rock barred my way, and then, after a chain of tearless cycles, I wept, yes, and prayed for mercy, to be delivered as it may please Him, whom I displeased!

"With sleep came a figure clad in supernatural brightness. 'Matatron the messenger of grace, who spreads man's prayers before the Throne, speaks to you, Al Zameri! Between your prayer and His Mercy stands a world of evil, fostered by the fetish of your making. You have seduced the people chosen to redeem mankind. When the race shall deem the chase of gold a thing as base as rapine, as vile as lust, then will the fever of your soul abate. Till then live on, the symbol of insatiate greed, a living Sodom, weltering in the fetid pool of spiritual stagnancy!'

And Al Zameri was silent, burying his wretched face in his hands.

"Truly, gold in itself is not an evil, it is the root of the world's evil, the leprosy of the heart, incurable as the lung's consumption that reddens the cheek while it drains the life, and your guilt in reference to it is as dark as your punishment is great," spoke Ali. "I am that country's lord where I have been a slave. Courage has done much for me, but gold the most, yes, and the worst to make woman foul, and man her villain. Here Mammon is the king of kings. Ali Bey is a fugitive from assassins bought for gold, and Islam's Caliph depends for sovereign ease and safety less on valour and loyalty than on the bribe. You have raised gold to be an idol, on whose altars man's heart, his honour and his peace, and woman's virtue, are too often sacrificed. Therefore, run your course, Al Zameri, fulfil great Allah's decree, that man take heed lest in His just anger He drown this world in a boiling flood of liquid gold!"

A few stones removed from the entrance of the cave enabled the cursed roamer to slip out like a phantom, and with him passed the storm, leaving a chill around the heart of the Bey.

"Allah Akbar! This meeting forebodes Ali's downfall, I fear. It is my evil star that caused the wretch to stand in my way," said Ali Bey to himself. Subsequent developments proved his presentiment prophetic, in an ambush placed for his destruction, the celebrated Sheikh met his death.

Fortune And The Woodcutter

This story has been adapted from Andrew Lang's version of the same tale that originally appeared in The Brown Fairy Book, published in 1904 by Longmans, Green and Co., London and New York. This tale is based on an original taken from Traditions Populaires de l'Asie Mineure by Jean Nicolaides & Émile Carnoy, published by Maisonneuve in 1889.

Many centuries ago a wood cutter and his wife and children lived in a large forest. He was very poor, having only his axe to depend upon, and two mules to carry the wood he cut to the neighbouring town, but he worked hard, and was always out of bed by five o'clock, summer and winter.

This went on for twenty years, and though his sons were now grown up, and went with their father to the forest, everything seemed to go against them, and they remained as poor as ever. In the end the wood cutter lost heart, and said to himself, "What is the good of working like this if I'm never any richer at the end? I shall go to the forest no more! And perhaps, if I take to my bed, and do not run after Fortune, one day she may come to me."

So the next morning he did not get up, and when six o'clock struck, his wife, who had been cleaning the house, went to see what the matter was.

"Are you ill?" she asked, surprised at not finding him dressed. "The cock has crowed ever so often. It is high time for you to get up."

"Why should I get up?" asked the man, without moving.

"Why, to go to the forest, of course."

"Yes, and when I have toiled all day I hardly earn enough to give us one meal."

"But what can we do, my poor husband?" said she. "It is just a trick of Fortune's, and she'll never smile upon us."

"Well, I have had my fill of Fortune's tricks," he cried. "If she wants me she can find me here. But I have done with the wood for ever."

"My dear husband, grief has driven you mad! Do you think Fortune will come to anybody who does not go after her? Dress yourself, and saddle the mules, and begin your work. Do you know that there is not a morsel of bread in the house?"

"I don't care if there isn't, and I am not going to the forest. It is no use your talking, nothing will make me change my mind."

His agitated wife begged and implored in vain, but her husband persisted in staying in bed, and at last, in despair, she left him and went back to her work.

An hour or two later a man from the nearest village knocked at her door, and when she opened it, he said to her, "Good morning, mother. I have got a job to do, and I want to know if your husband will lend me your mules, as I see he is not using them, and maybe he can lend me a hand himself?"

"He is upstairs, you had better ask him," answered the woman. And the man went up and repeated his request.

"I am sorry, neighbour, but I have sworn not to leave my bed, and nothing will make me break my vow."

"Well, then, will you lend me your two mules? I will pay you something for them."

"Certainly, neighbour. Take them and welcome."

So the man left the house, and leading the mules from the stable, placed two sacks on their back, and drove them to a field where he had found a hidden treasure. He filled the sacks with the money, though he knew perfectly well that it belonged to the sultan, and was driving them quietly home again, when he saw two soldiers coming along the road. Now the man was aware that if he was caught he would be condemned to death, so he fled back into the forest. The mules, left to themselves, took the path that led to their master's stable.

The wood cutter's wife was looking out of the window when the mules drew up before the door, so heavily laden that they almost sank under their burdens. She lost no time in calling her husband, who was still lying in bed.

"Quick! Quick! Get up as fast as you can. Our two mules have returned with sacks on their backs, so heavily laden with something or other that the poor beasts can hardly stand up."

"Wife, I have told you a dozen times already that I am not going to get up. Why can't you leave me in peace?"

As she found she could get no help from her husband the woman took a large knife and cut the cords which bound the sacks on to the animals' backs. The sacks fell at once to the ground, and out poured a rain of gold pieces, till the little courtyard shone like the sun.

"A treasure!" gasped the woman, as soon as she could speak from surprise. "A treasure!" And she ran off to tell her husband.

"Get up! get up!" she cried. "You were quite right not to go to the forest, and to await Fortune in your bed, for she has come at last! Our mules have returned home laden with all the gold in the world, and it is now lying in the court. No one in the whole country can be as rich as we are!"

In an instant the wood cutter was on his feet, and running to the courtyard, where he paused dazzled by the glitter of the coins which lay around him.

"You see, my dear wife, that I was right," he said at last. "Fortune is so capricious, you can never count on her. Run after her, and she is sure to fly from you, stay still, and she is sure to come."

Jaafer Ben Yehya And Abdulmelik Ben Salih The Abbasid

This story is adapted from Tales From The Arabic, by John Payne, privately published in 1901. This story is based on the Breslau and Calcutta editions of The Book of the Thousand Nights and One Night originally produced between 1814 and 1818. This tale derives from the Breslau text.

It's said that Jaafer ben Yehya the Barmecide once decided to have a private gathering with his close friends. He sent for his favourite companions, with whom he enjoyed spending time. Jaafer instructed his chamberlain to allow only one of his companions, Abdulmelik ben Salih, to join the gathering at a late hour because Abdulmelik was running errands. They all put on their colourful clothes, as was their tradition when they gathered to drink. They wore garments made of red, yellow, and green silk. As they sat down to drink, the cups circulated, and the lutes played.

Now, there was a man related to the Khalif, Haroun er Reshid, named Abdulmelik ben Salih ben Ali ben Abdallah ben el Abbas. He was known for his seriousness, piety, and decorum. The Khalif had repeatedly invited him to join in his revelries, offering him great wealth, but Abdulmelik always declined. One day, Abdulmelik arrived at Jaafer ben Yehya's door to discuss certain matters with him. The chamberlain, thinking he was the same Abdulmelik ben Salih that Jaafer had mentioned, allowed him to enter, believing that no one else should be admitted.

When Jaafer saw Abdulmelik, he was overcome with embarrassment. He realized that the chamberlain had been fooled by the similarity of the name. Abdulmelik, too, understood the situation and saw the embarrassment on Jaafer's face. So, he put on a cheerful demeanour and said, "Please, no harm done. Bring me some of those colourful clothes."

They brought him a dyed robe, which he put on. He then engaged in cheerful conversation and jokes with Jaafer and his friends. He asked for a glass of wine, saying, "Please be patient with us, as we are not accustomed to this."

He continued chatting and joking until Jaafer's tension disappeared, and he felt relieved. He turned to Abdulmelik and asked, "What brings you here?"

Abdulmelik replied, "I have three requests. First, I have a debt of a substantial sum of money that I would like to settle. Second, I want my son to be appointed as the governor of a province to raise his status. Third, I wish for you to arrange a marriage between him and the Khalif's daughter, who is his cousin and a suitable match."

Jaafer responded, "Your wishes are granted. As for the debt, the money will be delivered to your house immediately. Regarding the governorship, your son will become the governor of Egypt. And for the marriage, I'll arrange the wedding between him and the daughter of our esteemed Khalif, at the agreed-upon dowry. Go in peace, and may God be with you."

Abdulmelik returned to his home, where he found that the money had already been delivered. The next day, Jaafer met with the Khalif and informed him of the decisions. The Khalif approved and confirmed the appointment and the marriage. Jaafer then sent for the young man, who didn't leave the Khalif's palace until he received his appointment as the governor of Egypt. The necessary documents, along with the marriage contract, were prepared, and the wedding took place as planned.

Sheddad's Palace Of Irem

This story has been adapted from Henry Iliowizi's version of the same tale that originally appeared in The Weird Orient, published in 1900 by Henry T. Coates and Company, Philadelphia.

Sheddad and Sheddid, the sons of Ad and the grandsons of Uz, gained great renown in Hadramaut, where they were born in Ahkaf, a desert region encircled by desolation, as desolate as Hejaz, as barren as Tehamah, as scorching as Dahna 'the red', as eerie as the Gobi, and less explored than the Sahara. The ancient Hebrews referred to Hadramaut as Hazarmaveth, the 'court of death,' a name that is aptly justified by its dark rocks that sporadically rise above the shifting sand dunes, resembling colossal coffins in the gloomiest of graveyards. It was here that the Ad tribe thrived and achieved deeds that would forever be recounted in tales and songs.

While journeying through the Han Hai desert, Marco Polo reported seeing spectral apparitions and hearing them speak, calling people by their names, and startling the caravan drivers with strange noises like the galloping of horses, the beat of drums, and the blare of trumpets and other musical instruments. Some people consider these ghostly manifestations in the deserts as a facet of the world's spiritual mystery, and the ancient Arabs would never venture into a dark wilderness without uttering a prayerful expression of confidence, "I seek refuge with the guardian of this realm, that he may protect me from the foolish of his domain."

The Bedouins believe that long before the creation of Adam, countless Jinn or genies were formed from fire and lived in this world under successive rulers, all bearing the name Suliman. These ethereal beings, however, were not bound by mortal needs such as eating, drinking, and procreation. They were, however, susceptible to corruption and decay. When their malevolence angered Allah, he commanded Eblis to exile them to the harshest deserts, where they remained secluded but with a certain degree of freedom. They were allowed to exert their supernatural powers and follow their various inclinations, whether for good or ill. The fairy-like Peri, the colossal Div, and the ominous Tacwins or fates are mentioned in the Koran, leaving no room for doubt regarding their existence.

Now, the secret to Ad's prosperity, which allowed his people to thrive and multiply in the midst of desolation, lay in an army of Jinn at their disposal, granted to them by Ad's father, Uz, the son of Aram, who was in turn the son of Shem, one of Noah's descendants. With these otherworldly agents to carry out their will, Ad conceived the grand idea of constructing the most magnificent palace on Earth in the wilderness of Yemen. He shared this vision with his elder son, Sheddad. Sheddad's imagination soared, but the enormity of the endeavour made its realization seem uncertain, despite the available resources.

"Your plan, father, surpasses even the grandeur of the Tower of Babel. But with sufficient means, I would surround the grandest palace beneath the heavens with a garden reminiscent of Paradise," the eldest son of Ad proposed.

"The palace and the garden will be erected by unseen hands!" Ad exclaimed proudly, sketching his design in the sand.

The palace was to be built on a plateau as high as the tallest peak in Yemen, capable of accommodating their multiplied progeny, and its crowning feature was to be a hall of unparalleled splendour, housing a king's throne at its centre. This grand structure would be encircled by a garden resembling Eden, visible and accessible only at the king's command.

Ad's incredible vision was further embellished by his inventive son, who suggested a city of princely residences surrounding the palace, all enclosed by a wall with majestic entrances. Ad approved this addition, and the execution of the plan was not without an element of danger that the architects were unaware of, which ultimately led to the demise of its originator. Believing the time had come to commence the work, Ad ventured alone into the desolate region on a dark night, seeking to align himself with the powerful beings he had counted on to bring his dream to life. Whether it was the eerie desolation of the desert that unnerved him or an innate dread of the supernatural forces he was about to invoke, but the conjurer misspoke the incantation, resulting in a horrifying outcome. Instead of the benevolent spirits he expected to bow to him, a horde of menacing entities with wagging tails descended upon him like a storm, scowling and grinning with eyes filled with fury and malice. Unwittingly, Ad had disturbed the dreaded Tacwins, who would have torn him apart if not for the mystical seal he held in his hand - the same talisman that, in a later age, allowed Solomon to subdue Ashmodai and control myriad genies. Yet the terror of the moment overwhelmed the unfortunate sorcerer, and Ad was found lifeless, deeply mourned by his family and his namesake tribe.

Unfazed by his father's tragic end, Sheddad, now the acknowledged leader of his tribe and the possessor of the potent seal, confided in his brother Sheddid. He asserted that it was their filial duty to carry on what their father had initiated at all costs. Sheddid, however, was not the adventurous type, preferring the comfort of the tent to ventures fraught with peril. He implored his brother to desist from an endeavour that had already claimed a life, content with simply being a member of the tribe. Nevertheless, Sheddad, the sole master of the situation, burned with impatience to see his radiant vision materialize. He proceeded, undeterred by danger, to enact the plan as devised by his father and himself and was remarkably successful in establishing contact with the obedient Jinn under his command. He astonished them with an expanded version of the plan, which by now included even more elaborate features, and issued his commands with unwavering authority.

"You are required to build for me a city never to be equalled, still less to be excelled, by anything art or skill may attempt to produce, it is to be the home of a people a thousand times more numerous than the tribe of Ad, and its crowning marvel is to be my palace, of a splendour befitting a king of kings, and of an amplitude to afford room for a great court and an army. Grounded on a rocky foundation on a level with Yemen's highlands, the city's walls and dwellings shall be white as alabaster, but the palace shall be of onyx, trimmed with gold and set with gems. Twelve gorgeous halls shall be named after the signs of the zodiac, all opening upon one grander than them all, beneath a dome as lucent as the firmament, illuminated by a sun, a moon, and scintillating stars, moving at the king's will around his throne that shall blaze with what is most precious and brilliant in those jewels which rival the lustre of the constellations. Vaults for treasures, apartments for feasting, pavilions for ease, recesses for love, grottoes for coolness, cisterns for bathing, colonnades for pleasure, balconies for survey, and seats for delight, shall make my palace inimitable for all time. And city and palace shall be embedded in an Eden of foliage, blossom, and fruit, animated by birds of lustrous plume and sweetest song. Tax your skill to build more perfect than I know to ask for, but never less, and let your magic make the retreats inaccessible without the pleasure of the king." As he finished speaking, Sheddad was inwardly sorry that his inventive faculty lagged behind his vaulting ambition, and he feared that his dream would be less than he imagined.

"Master of the potent seal," replied the chief of the shining creatures, "your wish is our command. In eleven nights Sheddad shall stamp our work with his approval."

Elevated in his own estimation to the rank of a king of kings, and conscious of a power equal to that of a god, it required but a slight incentive for Sheddad's vanity to overleap itself, and infernal Eblis was at hand to furnish it. In the guise of an angel, the devil bewildered the architect of Irem by saluting him as a god. "Born of a woman, yours is the homage due to a prince of the skies, before whom spirits bow, exalted Sheddad!" spoke the Satanic deceiver with a profound salaam. Then the devil rose on his mighty wings to vanish in the void of the desert.

After this Sheddad would not have been astonished to hear the stars proclaim his majesty, but he was surprised when, having listened to his marvellous tale of the city the Jinn would build for him, Almena, his favourite wife, beheld an evil omen in the fact that, in his plan of sumptuous building, Sheddad had neglected to provide for the worship of the only true God.

"How could Sheddad forget him who created the heavens and the earth, the stars and the spirits, and whose just wrath wiped out the people in the time of our ancestor Noah? God's temple ought to rise high above your palace, or it will not stand, even according to the prophecy of Hud, your uncle, whose words were confirmed by signs from On High," expostulated Almena.

"Woman, your Sheddad is a god, and shall be worshipped because of his potency, and the favours he may bestow on those who shall please him. A heavenly power paid me homage before I entered this tent, and in eleven nights the tribe of Ad will see the wonder of the world. My palace shall be their temple, my throne their altar, you their goddess, and Sheddad their god!" cried the infatuated chief.

Almena was a frail daughter of Eve, and Sheddad's picture of their prospective divinity, sustained as it was by an angel's confirmation, converted her to share her husband's madness. The thoughts that occupied them during the day came in weird visions during the night, throngs kneeling in adoration before them, burning incense and wafting expiatory invocations, and kings hurrying from the ends of the earth to receive their crowns and sceptres from Sheddad's grace. On the tribe, it was deemed best that their chief's godship should burst as a revelation.

While the tribe of Ad were soundly asleep in their tents, a man and a woman slipped cautiously out of the encampment. They were mounted on two fast dromedaries and glided like spectres into the heart of the desert, buried in night and silence. Once more Eblis played his infernal trick on the deluded Sheddad, now in company of his bewitched Almena, by a renewed mock adoration offered as by a winged cherub. For it is hardly necessary to state that the infatuated couple were on their way to the abode of their future felicities. They had not been riding many hours before the level, blank face of the waste softened into undulations scantily covered with that vegetation which the camel alone is capable of digesting, its gastric capacities being almost equal to that of the ostrich, and the outlook indicated rising ground. A stretch had to be crossed punctuated by black rocks in ever increasing number, until the wilderness looked like a stony maze of dismal projections worn smooth by the grinding sands, ever moving with the gusts of hot air, and the East indicated daybreak when Sheddad and Almena ascended a height from which they could survey a vast horizon, bordered on the southeast by sea, but presenting otherwise the sterility of the Arabian Desert. A curious and perplexing paralysis of speech deprived them of the interchange of sentiments, and an uphill advance of a mile or so brought them before an arched portal of imposing stateliness, opening on a great city, half hidden from view by the sylvan and floral wealth of an Eden.

Husband and wife exchanged a look of amazement, strangely debarred from an audible articulation of feeling just when there was so much to be wondered at. There being nobody to hinder, no one to welcome them, Sheddad and Almena tied their brutes to the glittering handles of the brazen gates, and proceeded to take sovereign possession of what they considered their indisputable domain. The ascending avenue before them might have been called 'The Vista of Enchantment'. Sinuous in its course, its moss bedded windings were bordered by crystal rivulets which came down, broken by impediments, in bounding cascades, the water teeming with fish of tints recalling the changeful blushes of Aurora. Towering trees shaded, with their intertwining crowns of delicious leafage, a tropical exuberance of lesser growths weighed down with luscious fruit or glowing and sparkling with soft colours forming part of a delightful disorder of shrubs and vines, climbing, winding, crawling, hanging and blooming, but receding here and there to uncover the placid mirror of a lake limpid as beryl, or a spring of the coolest and purest liquid, all approachable by a hundred intercrossing pathways, lined and so softly carpeted that the unsandaled foot paced as on a silken rug of the finest texture. Here the bulbul's note was drowned in a concert of rival warblers, whose melodies were as sweet as their feathers were coruscant.

With ravenous greed Sheddad and Almena surrendered to the garden's temptations, swallowing great quantities of precious fruit, but feeding a hunger that seemed to grow with its glutting, nor did the cooling drink they greedily imbibed allay their parching thirst. But the whetted appetite rendered the sensuous enjoyment resistlessly fascinating, and the choice of the food being seemingly unlimited, husband and wife would have abandoned themselves altogether to physical indulgence, had not an overpowering sight burst on them, like a vision from a suddenly opened heaven.

They were on the point of ascending a terrace laid out with all the arts of magic, and wreathed with all the bounties of nature, when they reached the entrance to an enormous square, superbly enclosed by what appeared a score of palaces blended in one mass of variegated splendours, the one at the opposite end overtopping the others by a dome which blazed in the sun's radiance, as though set with carbuncles. Symmetrically proportionate to the size of the grand space ran a depression defined by a line of artistic shafts of alabaster, capped with globes of burnished gold studded with gems, and rising majestically above a grove of enamelled green, thick with odiferous bloom. In the heart of the depression was a basin filled with a rushing water as transparent as the sky and enlivened by star dotted swarms of the finny tribes. It was an azure stream in an Elysian garden, in the heart of a succession of edifices far beyond the limits of human resources and ingenuity. Except for the feathered musicians, and the zephyr which stirred the air and foliage, not a sound was heard, nor a creature seen. The overawing majesty of an architecture that dwarfed pantheons into monuments of man's vain endeavour to imitate the inimitable, and the gorgeousness which could not be thought of without remembering the limitations of earthly art and treasures however great, justified Sheddad's conceit that he was more than human, a consciousness now at last fully shared by Almena. Still unable to express their wonderment in words, they resorted to gestures and grimaces, as though the tale of Babel was to have a sort of counterpart in the story of Sheddad's palace of Irem. And their wonder rose in intensity as, entering the left wing of the palace by a sublime portico, the lofty vaulted spaces, communicating by exquisitely carved arches, imparted the illusion that the ceilings were as high as heaven and sparkled with real stars.

An implied welcome was extended to them in the first apartment by a banquet set in a begemmed service of golden vessels, dainties and beverages fit for gods. Hours busily spent at the sumptuous board neither appeased their hunger nor quench their thirst. Every morsel and every quaff sharpened the craving for more. When they succeeded in tearing themselves from the table's inexhaustible dishes, their progress through the palatial spaces consumed more time than they were aware of, the fascinations being as varied as they were marvellous. No matter how incomputable their new wealth might be, and no matter how lavish the ornamental art bestowed on each and every room might be, their main charm lay in the optic illusions, causing Sheddad and his companion to laugh with amusement and wonder, to scream with astonishment, or to shudder with horror.

Yielding to a woman's inquisitiveness, Almena was always a little in advance of her husband, always eager to be yet more surprised, and her eagerness was fully gratified. Once when a scream of laughter brought Sheddad to his wife's side, he found that what she had mistaken for clear water, rippled by a breeze, was indeed the solid floor of a long green archway, imparting the illusion of a stream flowing under cover of beautiful trees, Almena had prepared to cross it, with her sandals off, and her skirts raised, imagining the water to wave gently in a bed of golden sand. Here, again, she recoiled with terror from the glaring eyes of a crouching lion, ready to fly at her in a rage, there she stood paralyzed at the sight of the deadly rukta, rolled up in a coil on an imperial divan, with her fangs pointed, and her eyes glaring. In this manner the most formidable species of the animal kingdom faced them in threatening postures throughout the entire palace, often set in their natural conditions, always in a pose of aggressive ferocity.

Yet all this notwithstanding, Sheddad affected the lofty bearing of a god in his realm, and strode haughtily along the mysteriously echoing halls, the echoes of which before long mixed with strains of music sweet beyond expression. Drawn by the swelling harmonies, they descended a stately flight of stairs landing on a platform where, descending another flight, they beheld themselves at the extreme end of an enormous cavern bathed in a translucent haze of an unearthly luminousness. The muffled rumble of a distant waterfall blended enchantingly with waves of melody that floated incomprehensibly through the weird mazes of the honey combed hollow extending endlessly in cavernous, inaccessible spaces, passes and galleries.

Availing themselves of conveniently protruding stepping stones, the explorers ventured into the nethermost ranges, fairly brightened by the reflex of a stalactitical display, grotesque in shape, bulky in size, and indefinable in colour, every known hue blending into a magic play of ever-changing spectra and suggesting the idea that the palace above was the blossom of which the underground masses were the roots. Here they stood bewitched by the symphonies they could not account for, and by a scenery human genius may dream of, but never imitate.

While divided between the delights of the ear and the charm of the eye, Sheddad and Almena lost no sight of a crystal barrier behind which flowed a clear water alive with luminous fish, and through which they had a glimpse of things above, recognizing it to be the bed of the rushing stream that flowed in the court of the palace, fed by unexplorable cisterns, and discharging its volume into an unsounded abyss. As they advanced the wonders multiplied. Fluted pillars of snowy alabaster, draped and marvellously traced by invisible hands, towering shafts of white, red, amber, and blue, hanging balconies of gossamer lightness, trimmed with scarfs finer than the Indian shawl, canopies bristling with numberless crystals of every tint and shape, cataracts petrified in the act of precipitation, grottoes, fountains, streamlets, and cascades, with a myriad other exhibitions of magic art, filled subterraneous spaces of unmeasured magnitude.

Progressing through irregular archways and winding passages, Sheddad and Almena were lost in the labyrinth. Remembering, however, that the crystal basin ran along the grand court above, Sheddad followed its length and discovered a way to an ascent which took them to a broad stairway. This was the entrance from below to a colonnade of astonishing height and dimensions, covering the entire width of the court, and having, at both extremes, grand flights of steps, leading up to the wing of the palace crowned by the blazing dome.

If the son of Ad and his consort marvelled at what they had seen hitherto, they felt stupefied as ascending they stood before a golden arch wrought in imitation of the rainbow, revealing the wonders of the unsurpassed throne hall, rising high above the lofty throne. Four tigers erect on their haunches held up with their forepaws the seat of majesty, a gorgeous divan bedecked with priceless jewels, under a lofty canopy shaded by tapestries of matchless fabric and embroidery. To the right, suspended from the roof of the canopy, hung the sceptre, a mace incrusted with brilliants, to the left the crown, of dazzling splendour, above the throne sun, moon, and stars were scattered within the concave of the dome, while the twelve adjoining halls similarly represented the signs of the zodiac, thus completing a startling illusion of the heavens.

As though driven by an irresistible force, Sheddad, with the firm step of a king, advanced to take possession of his throne, Almena watching him with a throbbing heart. Nine steps had to be ascended before the seat could be reached. The aspirant to godship thought he felt the deadly breath of the tigers, whose distended claws and furious eyes threatened destruction, but he nerved himself and ascended the royal seat. Simultaneously with his touch upon the throne the crown descended on his head, the sceptre flew into his hand, while a mantle of radiance clothed his frame. Sheddad felt that he was a god, for his coronation was confirmed by the immediate action of sun, moon, and stars, which began to move in their respective orbits, shedding mellow light, and filling the spaces with sweet strains.

From his exalted seat Sheddad had for the first time an extended view of his dominion, and he realized that what he had seen thus far was but the heart of the whole, which seemed unbounded in extent and unapproachable in magnificence. It was manifest that palace and court formed the focus of a great city, spreading in many directions in avenues shaded by trees and cooled by delicious springs, placid lakes, playing fountains, and bubbling streamlets. Why should he lose a moment to reveal himself to his tribe as their god and lead them here triumphant in confirmation of his godship? Who on earth was mightier than he?

He rose. The sceptre slipped from his hand, the crown from his head, the mantle from his shoulders. Everything stood still. The song died. A dimness spread around him. The eyes of the tigers glared viciously. He stood by the side of his wife. They joined hands, hurried down and out into the open air to find that it was twilight and sultry. Surely the garden was less green, the flowers less fresh, the air less balmy, and the water less transparent than before. The song of the birds had changed into a melancholy chirrup, and their eyes glowed with threatening fierceness. From the water of the basin the fish pierced the royal pair with their fiery eyes, and the breeze moved lamenting through the corridors and trees. With a woman's instinct of impending danger, Almena led the way out of the court, but the garden was plunged in a mist, which made impossible a quick exit from the sylvan entanglements. While trying to strike the main avenue, they fell in with their dromedaries browsing contentedly in the thick of the most exquisite shrubbery, with neither saddle nor rope available for use. The brutes looked unaccountably shaggy, and hey turned to run at the approach of their master and did not stop until they had passed the gateway of which Sheddad was in quest. Here the saddles were found, shabby and mouldy, and were placed where they belonged, the camels having submitted to the goad, and the homeward journey began.

A deep sigh escaped Almena's breast as the distance widened between them and the enchanted city, and when she found words she began solemnly, "Sheddad, what is it we have seen and passed through? My blood runs cold when I think of the place, and do you mean to re-enter it as our permanent home?"

"You are a woman, or you would know that what Sheddad conjured out of naught, Sheddad will as master rule and own. Are not those spirits subject to my will?" was the imperious answer.

"You will bear patiently with your Almena, my lord, but are not the looming cities and splendid gardens often seen in the haze of the desert the dread of the lured Arab, who, mistaking them for fertile oases, rushes to destruction? Truly, the wiles of Eblis are numberless, and your great palace is destitute of the sacred place to prove it a work of the friendly Jinn. Your father's end should be your warning, O, light of my eyes!" cried the woman appealingly.

"Are you the wife of Sheddad, or of Sheddid? Let woman be timid, but no man be craven. The signet on my finger scorns infernal traps. You have seen me on the awful throne destined to be the worship of nations, and you are to share in the divine sovereignty of your Sheddad. But, O, Almena, why is your voice so unlike the one I have ever heard since the days of our youthful love? It sounds as though you are speaking to me from the hollow of a cave," spoke the son of Ad uneasily.

"You have taken this question from my lips, my lord, for your speech is so unfamiliar to my ear that, were I not near you, I should mistake it for an echo heard in the mountains of Yemen," confessed the daughter of the desert.

There was no time for another remark. The air swarmed with thousands of lurid Cupids, each one holding a tiny harp under his left arm. Flocking together, they interlocked in such a fashion as to form a stupendous arch, perfect in shape and burning like a crescent cut from the effulgent sun. On the top of the curve alighted one larger than his compeers, his outstretched arms pointing a glittering tiara in the direction of Sheddad, whose advance was greeted with voluptuous strains:

"Hail, our chief, your sceptre sway!

Rule Irem, Sheddad, we obey!

Your seal bade spirits be your thralls,

Hail, god of Irem's magic halls!"

With the dying of the choral apostrophe, the treacherous vision conjured by Eblis to dispel Almena's intuitive fear of something dreadful to come faded away. The sure-footed dromedaries picked their way among the bleak rocks and the sand ridges, with not a glimmer to break the darkness nor a syllable to spur them on. Sheddad and Almena continued silent under the overpowering spell of the sight, which soared before their mental vision long after it had vanished to the eye.

Daybreak found them near a solitary cliff known for the brackish water, oozing from one of its cracks, and the scanty browsing nearby fit for camels. Turning to his fresh water supply to appease his thirst, Sheddad found the water skin not only empty, but as dry as an old hide, while the figs he held in reserve were mouldy and hard as stone. Almena had the same experience. Unaccountable as appeared this discovery, it was less of a surprise than the cadaverous aspect of husband and wife, as they looked into each other's faces in full daylight. "You do not look like yourself, my lord, there is neither blood in your veins nor a beam of life in your eye," cried the startled mate of the aspiring god.

"And you've just described your own appearance, Almena. It's merely the withering of our mortal bodies as we're infused with immortal virtue," Sheddad assumed, feigning an air of supreme indifference, although his heart did not share this pretence. Almena's ashen countenance, once the embodiment of radiant beauty, stirred a deep, unspoken sorrow in the heart of her infatuated husband.

The consternation within the Ad tribe upon learning that a lifeless couple, riding on two robust dromedaries, were approaching their encampment can only be imagined. The news was brought by some passing Arabs who, upon spotting the approaching strangers, went out to investigate but quickly returned with a horrifying report, saying, "The dead are approaching!" Those who could run took off, leaving behind the frail elderly and helpless children to confront the apparitions. The spectral figures entered the encampment and took over the largest tent, the very one previously occupied by Sheddid, who had been among the first to disavow any involvement with the uninvited guests.

"If we've changed, so has this place, and everything around us, in just a few days. Our young camels have grown large and healthy, and who is this sleeping child?" Sheddad inquired, pointing towards a half-naked girl lying on a mat on the ground. "Could this be our Chaviva?"

"Our daughter!" the mother exclaimed in a hysterical tone, recognizing the two-year-old girl as the seven-year-old child they had left. "Either our eyes deceive us, or something is amiss," the woman added, deeply troubled.

"It's neither this nor that. We're not the same, and our vision isn't the same, but the world around us remains unchanged, only we perceive it as if magnified, much like higher beings might see it. How else could the powers above take notice of what transpires below?" Sheddad argued with self-congratulatory plausibility.

While Almena waited for their daughter to awaken, Sheddad decided to explore the surroundings in order to gather an audience to whom he could reveal his supposed divinity. Unluckily, the elderly and infirm members of the tribe were unable to hide from the searching gaze of the skeletal chief, who managed to find them and warned them about facing his wrath. "Inform the tribe and let Sheddid know that Sheddad and Almena have resided in the realm of the spirits as a god and goddess, and that I have come to take you to an Eden of everlasting bliss. All you need to do is say, 'Lead on, Sheddad.'"

"Have you not been living with the dead all this time?" inquired a trembling old woman.

"No, daughter of our noble tribe, during the five days we were away..."

"Five years!" interrupted a chorus of voices. "For five years, Sheddad and Almena have been missing and mourned as lost," the elderly woman added. Sheddad was utterly shocked. He had spent years, not just hours, in the enchanted palace, and every piece of evidence confirmed this astonishing fact. Nevertheless, despite his amazement, Sheddad's belief in his own divinity was so deeply ingrained that this new revelation was merely another indication of his supernatural destiny. To him, surviving for five years without regular food and rest was a compelling proof of his transformation, and the fact that many years had passed like mere hours affirmed the bliss of the world he had created.

The one member of the tribe who was most concerned and least thrilled by Sheddad's return from what he believed to be the real afterlife was Sheddad's own brother, Sheddid. He wished he could be a thousand miles away from this place, not out of jealousy regarding his brother's primogeniture but rather because he dreaded the thought of encountering him, not to mention his aversion to Sheddad's fantastical schemes. Nevertheless, facing the circumstances, Sheddid confronted his brother, questioning whether he was resolved to lead his people into a realm where they would return, like him, looking more dead than alive. "Your heart is under an evil influence, my brother. The children of Ad are content. Why tempt them with a snare laid by Eblis?"

Sheddad replied with a glowing description of the paradise that awaited those who followed him. "To ensure the truth of my words, this evening, a mist shall rise from the heart of Hadramaut, and with it shall appear the vision of the city and palace ensconced in gardens reminiscent of paradise. Those who prefer the marble dwelling, the pleasant stroll, the refreshing spring, the crystalline bath, the delightful fruit, the warm sunlight, the wondrous sights, and dominion over the world to the dark tent, meagre fare, and the arid wilderness are welcome to share in these blessings with me," he declared with a benevolent air befitting a god.

This offer was met with a jubilant shout from the fiery sons of the desert, and the promised mirage was eagerly anticipated. Later, within his tent, the mighty magician summoned the chief of the Jinn and instructed him to conjure up the image of the Palace of Irem. At sunset, all eyes turned towards the desert. As night fell, a radiant silver radiance enveloped the wilderness, transforming it into an ethereal canvas on which the city, palace, and gardens of Irem rose majestically, perfect in every aspect. Wild elation was soon replaced by a profound sense of awe before the man who had irrefutably proven his right to their reverent worship. "Lead us, divine Sheddad!" they cried, striking their tents and loading camels. The entire tribe was seized by a single passion: to possess and inhabit the grandest and most blissful of cities. Sheddid had no choice but to decide between remaining behind or joining the tribe, and he cast his lot with the multitude, setting aside his forebodings.

The march began with dancing and singing, with Sheddad and Almena leading the colourful caravan. However, soon the voices of beings other than humans began to disturb the eerie silence of the desolate desert. The name "Sheddad" could be heard, accompanied by heart-chilling laughter. As if incited by demons, the camels grew frenzied, tossing women and children from their backs and trampling them to death. Everyone yearned for the arrival of day to free them from this terror. Yet there was no break in the night, which felt as though it lasted three nights in one. When the light finally arrived, it came abruptly, nearly blinding the bewildered Arabs. And with it came a sound from above, a deafening noise akin to the roars of countless lions, intensifying, swelling, and echoing until it seemed as if heaven itself was in turmoil. The earth quaked, the desert glowed as if in a furnace, and the sands rose and twirled like a cyclone of ignited gases, exploding into sheets of fiery vitriol. Both humans and animals tried to bury their heads in the scorching sands, but the disaster was too cataclysmic for flesh to endure. In his agony, Sheddad felt the signet slip from his finger. Struck dumb and deaf, the son of Ad perished along with his entire entourage, consumed by the cyclonic flames, flesh and bone. Only those who, due to weakness or their love for young children, had stayed behind remained to rebuild the nearly obliterated Ad tribe.

Such was Sheddad's punishment for his delusions of godhood. His legend lives on in Arabian folklore. To this day, Allah preserves the city and palace as a testament to divine retribution. There are countless tales of wandering pilgrims and lost Bedouins who claim to have glimpsed Irem. Among them is Kalabah, who, after losing his way in the desert while searching for a missing camel, suddenly found himself standing at the gates of a dazzling city. He entered but was so overwhelmed by the eerie stillness within that he fled the premises in horror, taking with him a priceless gem as a keepsake. He showed this gem to Caliph Madwigah as proof of his incredible experience, as is duly recorded.

He Wins Who Waits

*This story has been adapted from Andrew Lang's version of the same tale
that originally appeared in The Olive Fairy Book, published in 1907 by
Longmans, Green and Co., London and New York. This tale is based on
an original taken from Contes Arméniens by Frédéric Macler, published
in 1905.*

Once upon a time there reigned a king who had an only daughter.
The girl had been spoiled by everybody from her birth, and besides
being beautiful, was clever and wilful, and when she grew old
enough to be married she refused to have anything to say to the
prince whom her father favoured, but declared she would choose a
husband for herself. By long experience the king knew that when she
had made up her mind, there was no use expecting her to change it,
so he inquired meekly what she wished him to do.

"Summon all the young men in the kingdom to appear before me a
month from today," answered the princess, "and the one to whom I
shall give this golden apple shall be my husband."

"But my dear –" began the king, in tones of dismay.

"The one to whom I shall give this golden apple shall be my
husband," repeated the princess, in a louder voice than before. And

the king understood the signal, and with a sigh proceeded to do her bidding.

The young men arrived - tall and short, dark, and fair, rich, and poor. They stood in rows in the great courtyard in front of the palace, and the princess, clad in robes of green, with a golden veil flowing behind her, passed before them all, holding the apple. Once or twice she stopped and hesitated, but in the end she always passed on, till she came to a youth near the end of the last row. There was nothing specially remarkable about him, the bystanders thought, nothing that was likely to take a girl's fancy. A hundred others were more handsome, and all wore finer clothes, but he met the princess's eyes frankly and with a smile, and she smiled too, and held out the apple.

"There is some mistake," cried the king, who had anxiously watched her progress, and hoped that none of the candidates would please her. "It is impossible that she can wish to marry the son of a poor widow, who has not a farthing in the world! Tell her that I will not hear of it, and that she must go through the rows again and fix upon someone else", and the princess went through the rows a second and a third time, and on each occasion she gave the apple to the widow's son.

"Well, marry him if you will," exclaimed the angry king, "but at least you shall not stay here." And the princess answered nothing, but threw up her head, and taking the widow's son by the hand, they left the castle.

That evening they were married, and after the ceremony went back to the house of the bridegroom's mother, which, in the eyes of the princess, did not look much bigger than a hen coop.

The old woman was not at all pleased when her son entered bringing his bride with him. "As if we were not poor enough before," grumbled she. "I dare say this is some fine lady who can do nothing to earn her living."

But the princess stroked the old woman's arm, and said softly, "Do not be vexed, dear mother, I am a famous spinner, and can sit at my wheel all day without breaking a thread."

And she kept her word, but in spite of the efforts of all three, they became poorer and poorer, and at the end of six months it was agreed that the husband should go to the neighbouring town to get work. Here he met a merchant who was about to start on a long journey with a train of camels laden with goods of all sorts and needed a man to help him. The widow's son begged that he would take him as a servant, and to this the merchant assented, giving him his whole year's salary beforehand. The young man returned home with the news, and next day bade farewell to his mother and his wife, who were very sad at parting from him.

"Do not forget me while you are absent," whispered the princess as she flung her arms round his neck, "and as you pass by the well which lies near the city gate, stop and greet the old man you will find sitting there. Kiss his hand, and then ask him what counsel he can give you for your journey."

Then the youth set out, and when he reached the well where the old man was sitting he asked the questions as his wife had bidden him.

"My son," replied the old man, "you have done well to come to me, and in return remember three things. First, remember that she whom the heart loves, is ever the most beautiful. Second, remember that patience is the first step on the road to happiness, and finally remember that he wins who waits."

The young man thanked him and went on his way. Early the next morning the caravan set out, and before sunset it had arrived at the first halting place, round some wells, where another company of merchants had already encamped. But no rain had fallen for a long while in that rocky country, and both men and beasts were parched with thirst. To be sure, there was another well about half a mile away, where there was always water, but to get it you had to be lowered deep down, and, besides, no one who had ever descended that well had been known to come back.

However, till they could store some water in their bags of goat skin, the caravans dared not go further into the desert, and on the night of the arrival of the widow's son and his master, the merchants had decided to offer a large reward to anyone who was brave enough to go down into the enchanted well and bring some up. Thus it happened that at sunrise the young man was aroused from his sleep by a herald making his round of the camp, proclaiming that every merchant present would give a thousand piastres to the man who would risk his life to bring water for themselves and their camels.

The youth hesitated for a little while when he heard the proclamation. The story of the well had spread far and wide, and long ago had reached his ears. The danger was great, he knew, but then, if he came back alive, he would be the possessor of eighty thousand piastres. He turned to the herald who was passing the tent and said out loud, "I will go."

"What madness!" cried his master, who happened to be standing near. "You are too young to throw away your life like that. Run after the herald and tell him you take back your offer." But the young man shook his head, and the merchant saw that it was useless to try and persuade him.

"Well, it is your own affair," he observed at last. "If you must go, you must. Only, if you ever return, I will give you a camel's load of goods and my best mule besides." And touching his turban in token of farewell, he entered the tent.

Hardly had he done so than a crowd of men were seen pouring out of the camp. "How can we thank you!" they exclaimed, pressing round the youth. "Our camels as well as ourselves are almost dead of thirst. See! Here is the rope we have brought to let you down."

"Come, then," answered the youth. And they all set out. On reaching the well, the rope was knotted securely under his arms, a big goat skin bottle was given him, and he was gently lowered to the bottom of the pit. Here a clear stream was bubbling over the rocks, and, stooping down, he was about to drink, when a huge Arab appeared before him, saying in a loud voice, "Come with me!"

The young man rose, never doubting that his last hour had come, but as he could do nothing, he followed the Arab into a brilliantly lighted hall, on the further side of the little river. There his guide sat down, and drawing towards him two boys, he said to the stranger, "I have a question to ask you. If you answer it right, your life shall be spared. If not, your head will be forfeit, as the head of many another has been before you. Tell me, which of my two children do I think the handsomer."

The question did not seem a hard one, for while the one boy was as beautiful a child as ever was seen, his brother was lain and ugly. But, just as the youth was going to speak, the old man's counsel flashed into the youth's mind, and he replied hastily, "The one whom we love best is always the most handsome."

"You have saved me!" cried the Arab, rising quickly from his seat, and pressing the young man in his arms. "Ah, if you could only guess what I have suffered from the stupidity of all the people to whom I have put that question, and I was condemned by a wicked genius to remain here until it was answered! But what brought you to this place, and how can I reward you for what you have done for me?"

"By helping me to draw enough water for my caravan of eighty merchants and their camels, who are dying for want of it," replied the youth.

"That is easily done," said the Arab. "Take these three apples, and when you have filled your skin, and are ready to be drawn up, lay one of them on the ground. Halfway to the earth, let fall another, and at the top, drop the third. If you follow my directions no harm will happen to you. And take, besides, these three pomegranates, green, red, and white. One day you will find a use for them!"

The young man did as he was told, and stepped out on the rocky waste, where the merchants were anxiously awaiting him. Oh, how thirsty they all were! But even after the camels had drunk, the skin seemed as full as ever.

Full of gratitude for their deliverance, the merchants pressed the money into his hands, while his own master bade him choose what goods he liked, and a mule to carry them.

So the widow's son was rich at last, and when the merchant had sold his merchandise, and returned home to his native city, his servant hired a man by whom he sent the money and the mule back to his wife.

"I will send the pomegranates also," he thought "for if I leave them in my turban they may someday fall out," and he drew them out of his turban. But the fruit had vanished, and in their places were three precious stones, green, white and red.

For a long time he remained with the merchant, who gradually trusted him with all his business, and gave him a large share of the money he made. When his master died, the young man wished to return home, but the widow begged him to stay and help her, and one day he awoke with a start, to remember that twenty years had passed since he had gone away.

"I want to see my wife," he said next morning to his mistress. "If at any time I can be of use to you, send a messenger to me, meanwhile, I have told Hassan what to do." And mounting a camel he set out.

Now, soon after he had taken service with the merchant a little boy had been born to him, and both the princess and the old woman toiled hard all day to get the baby food and clothing. When the money and the pomegranates arrived there was no need for them to work anymore, and the princess saw at once that they were not fruit at all, but precious stones of great value. The old woman, however, not being accustomed, like her daughter in law, to the sight of jewels, took them only for common fruit, and wished to give them to the child to eat. She was very angry when the princess hastily took them from her and hid them in her dress, while she went to the market and bought the three finest pomegranates she could find, which she handed the old woman for the little boy.

Then she bought beautiful new clothes for all of them, and when they were dressed they looked as fine as could be. Next, she took out one of the precious stones which her husband had sent her and placed it in a small silver box. This she wrapped up in a handkerchief embroidered in gold and filled the old woman's pockets with gold and silver pieces.

"Go, dear mother," she said, "to the palace, and present the jewel to the king, and if he asks you what he can give you in return, tell him that you want a paper, with his seal attached, proclaiming that no one is to meddle with anything you may choose to do. Before you leave the palace distribute the money amongst the servants."

The old woman took the box and started for the palace. No one there had ever seen a ruby of such beauty, and the most famous jeweller in the town was summoned to declare its value. But all he could say was, "If a boy threw a stone into the air with all his might, and you could pile up gold as high as the flight of the stone, it would not be sufficient to pay for this ruby."

At these words the king's face fell. Having once seen the ruby he could not bear to part with it, yet all the money in his treasury would not be enough to buy it. So for a little while he remained silent, wondering what offer he could make the old woman, and at last he said, "If I cannot give you the jewel's worth in money, is there anything you will take in exchange?"

"A paper signed by your hand, and sealed with your seal, proclaiming that I may do what I will, without let or hindrance," she answered promptly. And the king, delighted to have obtained what he coveted at so small a cost, gave her the paper without delay. Then the old woman took her leave and returned home.

The fame of this wonderful ruby soon spread far and wide, and envoys arrived at the little house to know if there were more stones to sell. Each king was so anxious to gain possession of the treasure that he bade his messenger outbid all the rest, and so the princess sold the two remaining stones for a sum of money so large that if the gold pieces had been spread out they would have reached from here to the moon. The first thing she did was to build a palace by the side of the cottage, and it was raised on pillars of gold, in which were set great diamonds, which blazed night and day. Of course the news of this palace was the first thing that reached the king her father, on his return from the wars, and he hurried to see it. In the doorway stood a young man of twenty, who was his grandson, though neither of them knew it, and so pleased was the king with the appearance of the youth, that he carried him back to his own palace, and made him commander of the whole army.

Not long after this, the widow's son returned to his native land. There, sure enough, was the tiny cottage where he had lived with his mother, but the gorgeous building beside it was quite new to him. What had become of his wife and his mother, and who could be dwelling in that other wonderful place. These were the first thoughts that flashed through his mind, but not wishing to betray himself by asking questions of passing strangers, he climbed up into a tree that stood opposite the palace and watched.

By and by a lady came out and began to gather some of the roses and jessamine that hung about the porch. The twenty years that had passed since he had last beheld her vanished in an instant, and he knew her to be his own wife, looking almost as young and beautiful as on the day of their parting. He was about to jump down from the tree and hasten to her side, when she was joined by a young man who placed his arm affectionately round her neck. At this sight the angry husband drew his bow, but before he could let fly the arrow, the counsel of the wise man came back to him and he said to himself, "Patience is the first step on the road to happiness." And he laid it down again.

At this moment the princess turned, and drawing her companion's head down to hers, kissed him on each cheek. A second time blind rage filled the heart of the watcher, and he snatched up his bow from the branch where it hung, when words, heard long since, seemed to sound in his ears, and he muttered, "He wins who waits." And the bow dropped to his side. Then, through the silent air came the sound of the youth's voice, "Mother, can you tell me nothing about my father? Does he still live, and will he never return to us?"

"Alas! my son, how can I answer you?" replied the lady. "Twenty years have passed since he left us to make his fortune, and, in that time, only once have I heard anything of him. But what has brought him to your mind just now?"

"Because last night I dreamed he was here," said the youth, "and then I remembered what I have so long forgotten, that I had a father, though even his history was strange to me. And now, tell me, please, all you can concerning him." And standing under the jessamine, the son learnt his father's history, and the man in the tree listened also.

"Oh," exclaimed the youth, when it was ended, while he twisted his hands in pain, "I am general in chief, you are the king's daughter, and we have the most splendid palace in the whole world, yet my father lives we know not where, and for all we can guess, may be poor and miserable. Tomorrow I will ask the king to give me soldiers, and I will seek him over the whole earth till I find him."

Then the man came down from the tree and clasped his wife and son in his arms. All that night they talked, and when the sun rose it still found them talking. But as soon as it was proper, he went up to the palace to pay his homage to the king, and to inform him of all that had happened and who they all really were. The king was overjoyed to think that his daughter, whom he had long since forgiven and sorely missed, was living at his gates, and was, besides, the mother of the youth who was so dear to him.

"It was written beforehand," cried the monarch. "You are my son in law before the world and shall be king after me." And the man bowed his head. He had waited, and he had won.

The Mystery Of The Damavant

This story has been adapted from Henry Iliowizi's version of the same tale that originally appeared in The Weird Orient, published in 1900 by Henry T. Coates and Company, Philadelphia.

As a somewhat distant offshoot of the Elburz the Damavant is a solitary pile, of imposing proportions, generally admitted to be Persia's most graceful mountain. Seen from a vantage point in Tehran, cloud crowned Damavant appears to be the real shoulder of sky bearing Atlas, losing its head in ether and its foot in a forest of the semi tropical varieties, dense to the degree of inaccessibility. The wild beast is here at home, the tiger, bear, wolf, panther, and wild boar, finding in these jungles an abundance of food, a safe retreat, and a cool spring to satisfy thirst. While the gentler slopes are covered by extensive, fruit bearing orchards, there are crests and hollows in the Elburz system which the eagle's eye alone has seen, and there are peaks which, but for the sinuous furrows cut by the wild torrents after heavy showers, no human foot could ever ascend. Spirits are believed to haunt the caves and impenetrable thickets of those mountains, a belief sustained by mocking echoes and multiple reverberations started by the least noise, and the Iranian folk look up to him with awe, who dares sojourn above the settled line of demarcation dividing the earthly from the unearthly. The history of religion, poetry and superstition is inextricably intertwined with the weird mystery which hangs over the unapproachable heights and deeps of mountains.

In the year 410 of the Hegira, two distinguished men, accompanied by four seasoned mountain climbers, were making their way up a challenging path through a bewildering gorge. This gorge, typically a dry riverbed, had turned into a raging torrent due to heavy rain. Their goal was to explore the seemingly impassable wonders of the south-eastern slope of Damavant.

The undertaking was arduous and filled with risks. What made it even more remarkable was that one of the two men showed clear signs of advanced age. Dressed as a dervish and with a shock of white hair, the elderly climber leaned on a sturdy staff for support. Occasionally, he needed the assistance of the strong arms of the vigilant attendants to overcome obstacles on the path.

The other man, much younger and stronger, exuded an air of nobility and authority. His attire and demeanour left no doubt about his position of power and command. As he forged ahead, he frequently glanced back at the frail figure following him. With a sympathetic smile, he assured the older man, "The return journey will be easier."

"You've spoken the truth; the journey here and existence itself, that's the challenge," replied the other, his aging and sorrowful face marked by deep wrinkles.

"Without Mahmud of Ghaznin on your mind, Firdusi, would you still feel this way?" asked the younger man in a gentle tone.

"Mahmud's court is a sea of evil that engulfed my island of happiness. Whom did I wrong to become a footsore fugitive, like the blood-stained son of Adam?" cried the old man with a shaky voice, pausing to catch his breath.

"Your pure spirit has vanquished the mundane, offering this world a taste of Eden. Your Shah Namah is the music of the heavens, and Eblis, who revels in discord and chaos, sought revenge by poisoning Mahmud's mind, oh Firdusi. Your own version does not portray Mahmud as your enemy, but rather his envious treasurer. It will end well, though. Nasir Lek's message will not leave Mahmud unmoved," assured the younger man, the Governor of Kohistan, a friend of the Sultan of Ghaznin, and an ardent admirer of Persia's renowned poet, Firdusi.

"May Allah bless your kindness. Yes, it will end well. It's good that things conclude here, for life in this world, filled with poverty, oppression, and the constant fear of the executioner's axe, would be a relentless hell. Ah, I've tasted the bitter cup to its last drop! But it cannot last much longer; my mortal frame is nearing its final decay. May Mahmud find misery in Firdusi's legacy!" cried the poet, raising his tearful eyes heavenward.

By this point, they had ascended to an altitude of over nine thousand feet above sea level. Tehran sprawled below them like a patchwork quilt covered with various shades. The sun was nearing the horizon, casting a golden glow that turned the landscape into a mesmerizing interplay of light and shadow beneath a sky suffused with rippling waves of translucent purple, crimson, silver, and gold. Facing eastward, the Muslims knelt and prostrated themselves in prayer. Once the prayers were completed, the escort was instructed to wait where they were, and the two men vanished into a labyrinth of crags, rocks, loose boulders, and heaps of stones, devoid of any plant life. Firdusi couldn't help but wonder how any living being could endure such a harsh and freezing environment. However, he kept his thoughts to himself.

As the chill grew in tandem with the desolation of the surroundings, they plunged into a dense fog, still ascending higher and higher, with the younger man assisting his elder companion. Finally, Nasir produced a horn, which he then blew. The sound reverberated with a haunting effect, followed by profound silence. There was no response. Another blast echoed through the mountains, sounding like muffled drums, and suddenly, there came a whistle-like note in reply.

"We are welcome here, Firdusi, and you will be duly rewarded," Nasir said.

The poet eyed Almazor sceptically. "Is he the enigmatic figure of Damavant?"

Nasir suggested, "You'll meet a man who could easily pass for the spirit of this mountain, and as for his mysterious abilities, you'll be the judge."

Firdusi inquired, "Am I allowed to ask him questions?"

"Ask nothing until his revelations unfold before you. You'll have little need for questions. While I've been amused by the tricks of jugglers, Almazor's abilities have taken me from one state of being to another. There he is. Say nothing. He understands my purpose and can read your thoughts," the Governor of Kohistan cautioned, his nerves on edge.

Firdusi strained to see the outline of a human figure and nearly stumbled into what could only be described as a cloaked, towering, and emaciated creature. It had a pallid complexion like the moon, with white hair as pure as newly fallen snow. The most striking feature was a single piercing eye, set deep in a sunken socket; the other eye was concealed, covered by skin like the rest of the face.

Almazor resembled more a prince of phantoms than a living being sustained by warm blood. His communication was through gestures, adding to the mystique of his enigmatic nature. He stood within a semi-circular enclosure before an opening too small for a person to enter without stooping.

Without a formal greeting or ceremony, Almazor turned and slithered into the gaping rock orifice, the others following him. Inside, it was brighter than expected, despite no obvious source of light. They watched in amazement as the emaciated hermit moved nimbly through steep and winding passageways, bridges, and tunnels, leading them up and down into the heart of the mountain. What became even more astonishing was the ease with which the men followed, almost as if carried by a force defying gravity.

The impression formed that the summit of Damavant couldn't be far away when their silent guide stopped in a well-lit, spacious area with an irregular cave-like structure, enhanced by a slanted passage resembling a polished silver funnel. At the upper end of this passage, the full moon's broad disk shone in all its glory. A stalagmite made of pure crystal sparkled like a reflector in the moonlight, providing seating for around twenty people. Next to it stood an unusually large chibouque with a green stem curving over the back of a shiny divan, and a box of sandalwood completed the equipment of the mystical laboratory.

When the sandalwood box was opened, a peculiar herb was revealed, cut and dried like tobacco but emitting a numbing fragrance. This herb was placed in the fire bowl of the chibouque, ignited, and filled the space with golden smoke and a drowsy atmosphere. Firdusi, almost involuntarily, sat down near the chibouque, facing the moon's radiant disk, and found himself with the pipe's mouthpiece between his lips.

As the smoke followed his breath, rising in swirls and rings above his head, he lost awareness of his surroundings. He experienced a sensation of bodily expansion, as though he were undergoing a transformation from a solid to an ethereal form. Simultaneously, the moon expanded dramatically, changing from a mottled globe to a land of dazzling peaks and dark chasms, drawing closer and closer, all while Firdusi felt himself being transported inexplicably from one world to another. He surrendered willingly to this experience, feeling weightless and spun lightly, and his next sensation was that of landing on a solid surface brilliantly illuminated.

In his wildest flights of imagination, the poet had never imagined the possibility of witnessing such a breath-taking sight as the lunar world unfolding before his eyes. The vantage point he stood on dwarfed the surrounding forest of sharp peaks and provided him with a view of countless deep craters that contrasted starkly with the brilliant lunar surface. If you could even call it that, given the endless expanse of spires, turrets, ridges, rocks, cliffs, and chasms, all twisted and contorted by immense forces into bewildering and otherworldly forms. It was a nightmarish realm of chaos and eternal silence, where death seemed to reign supreme.

The poet wondered, how had this desolation come to be? He speculated that it was once a sea of molten ores, tossed about and influenced by interstellar powers, and frozen into iron-hard rigidity as it passed through a frigid region. Now, it hung in perpetual darkness, a celestial mirror reflecting the unceasing light of the distant sun, away from our Earth.

With a heavy heart, Firdusi gazed upwards, trying to bear the unbearable brilliance. The darkness of the infinite space above was intensified by the enormity of the blazing sphere, convulsing with fiery oceans in tumultuous turmoil, shooting up, breaking, and bursting like violent waves colliding in a raging storm.

As he compared this aspect of the sun to its milder face as seen from Earth, the fiery orb began to visibly sink, and night rushed in from the opposite sky to swallow its last rays. It disappeared as if consumed by a cosmic beast, leaving no trace of its passage through the black expanse of the universe. Overwhelmed by this stupendous spectacle, Firdusi closed his eyes and fervently prayed, praising Allah the Most Merciful.

A more delightful sight soon graced the poet's eyes - a sphere rising above the dark horizon, larger than the moon as viewed from Earth, and just as captivating. It displayed a beautifully patterned disk with varying shades, zones, and colours, resembling those familiar to human eyes. The poet marvelled at the generosity of the Creator, reflecting on the beauty of this celestial body that now rose higher, radiating gently and leaving a profoundly moving impression.

Although it was impossible to distinguish individual features, Firdusi's poetic imagination attempted to identify the blue oceans, recognize the green zones, and trace the mountain ranges and vast deserts. As the world where humans played the roles of kings and slaves, saints and sinners, angels and demons, and experienced both joy and sorrow became more splendid with its ascent, the suffering bard, deeply empathizing with the struggles of humanity, allowed his tears to flow before he could find words to express his emotions.

"The Universe holds its secrets, Power Divine, but oh, I long for that peace found only in Your presence, that vision which unravels the great mysteries, and the life that knows no beginning, decay, or end! Who am I and why am I cast upon this shore of time, this island in the vast sea of space, to struggle alongside countless others like me, toiling and sighing, with death looming as the dark end of a disquieting nightmare? If humanity must perish like insignificant creatures, then the humble worm, ignorant of its misery, is blessed. Alas, the golden threads of hope lie in tatters here, and I wonder if my dreams of paradise are any less illusory. That radiant world has much to offer, sweetening a life embittered by the darkness within our human hearts. Why is humanity so closely related to the animal kingdom? Have I fallen from a higher spiritual state, sent here to atone and find redemption through that atonement? Or have I ascended from the lowly worm to my current state, progressing toward a higher, perhaps the highest, form of life, just as the Creator guides my path through the valley of sorrow and the shadow of death? Or perhaps the worm and I are mere specks in the vast expanse of time and space, summoned by a cruel fate to wriggle in agony and ultimately sink into eternal darkness? Divine Power, I implore you to banish this dark thought that threatens to extinguish the last flicker of hope, lest chaos consume all that is bright and rational in my small world."

As if in response to the poet's mood, the Earth itself began to undergo a remarkable transformation. Fiery and lurid hues rapidly spread across its luminous surface, engulfing it like a thickening shroud. It gave the impression of a red orb surrounded by a cloud of cinders, with the infinite blackness of space as its backdrop. However, the moon, though dimmed by the fading light of the Earth, did not remain completely obscured. Firdusi soon realized the reason for this as he turned his gaze to search for the source of the shimmer. What he witnessed was almost too much to contemplate without a shudder of reverence and awe. It was a glimpse of the vast starry heavens. For every star that was visible from the lunar surface, there now appeared a multitude of constellations, clusters of celestial bodies, with the closest ones surpassing the rainbow in size and outshining it in brilliance. The inky darkness of interstellar space served as a backdrop to highlight these radiant galaxies, creating the impression of an ethereal tree with a crown of sunlit stars stretching throughout the boundless expanse.

The vastness expanded even further, the depths grew deeper, and the wonders multiplied as countless hosts of stars emerged from the depths of infinity, wheeling and circling in celestial splendour, filling the boundless cosmos with soul-enrapturing melodies. Overwhelmed with joy, Firdusi's heart melted, and tears of rapture welled up in his eyes, mingled with a faint sense of sorrow arising from a lingering fear that this might all be a fleeting illusion. To his ears, the music of the spheres conveyed the inscrutable fate of humanity, their genuine tribulations, elusive hopes, unfulfilled dreams, and inevitable end. Yet, there was a comforting solace, an inherent peace in this heavenly spectacle.

Realizing the soothing balm of faith, the poet muttered with resignation, "Power Divine, as infinite as Your eternal glories, even I am a part of Your inscrutable plan, whatever it may be. In Your perfection, You have not created any being to remain forever imperfect, or to perish entirely after a glimmer of Your wisdom has once illuminated their minds."

Firdusi's lips quivered as he expressed this belief. His hand instinctively moved to his eyes, which were veiled by a dimness that blurred everything before him. The sensation of descending from another world filled his frail body with shudders of horror. When he opened his eyes, he found himself in the embrace of his friend, Nasir.

Despite his great creative imagination, it took some time for him to recollect his original circumstances, especially since the cave now appeared entirely different from before. There was no longer a beautiful vista or a moon to gaze upon. Instead, they found themselves in a dim passage, with no hermit to guide them. They had spent the entire night within the cave, and it was now broad daylight. Soon, Nasir's attendants responded to his horn's call, and they descended from the mountain in complete silence. They arrived at the palace gates simultaneously with a courier, who, dismounting from his horse, respectfully handed a package to the Governor of Kohistan. Nasir's face lit up with joy as he remarked, "This is Mahmud's response to my plea on your behalf, Firdusi, and I doubt the Sultan of Ghaznin could have been swayed by the devil this time."

Once they entered the Governor's residence, Nasir broke the seal of the message to discover its contents, and he read aloud, saying, "In the name of the one true, most merciful God! From Mahmud of Ghaznin to his friend Nasir Lek of Kohistan, on behalf of Abul Casim Mansur Firdusi. Peace and warm greetings. God alone is great. May truth and mercy prevail.

"As your heart has spoken, so has mine replied, moved by your just entreaty. Indeed, there is no finer poet than Firdusi, and the blame for his mistreatment rests with me for having listened to the slander of his enemies. The mischievous instigator of this slander, Hassan Meimendi, has met the executioner's axe. The all-knowing Allah never errs, but how can a ruler of nations avoid mistakes when misled by those whom he believes to be just, wise, and truthful?

"Once enlightened, Mahmud will not withhold the rewards and honours rightfully due to the one who has celebrated Iran's immortal heroes, inspiring future generations to follow in their footsteps. No matter how great, the departed were destined to remain forever lost, but through the magic of Firdusi's words, they are resurrected from the dust to be adorned in unfading glory. The national anthem of Persia has long awaited the arrival of Firdusi.

"As God is merciful, the author of the Shah Namah shall henceforth bear no grievance other than the memory of past wrongs. A greater load of gold than the one promised will be delivered at his request. If sympathetic regrets from his former friend and sovereign bring him comfort, Mahmud of Ghaznin hereby conveys his remorse for mistreating Abul Casim Mansur Firdusi. Firdusi is welcome at my court, welcomed as far as my rule extends."

Firdusi, dejected and silent, listened to the message from the king who had shattered his happiness. Only his tears revealed his deep heartache. His generous host understood the cause of his friend's sorrow. The author of Iran's great epic poems and Yusuf and Zuleikha had little to hope for in his remaining years, having experienced fear, poverty, and homelessness when he should have enjoyed a comfortable and prosperous life. He had outlived his only son and was separated from his only daughter. The vision of the stars he had seen in the Damavant cave intensified his melancholy. His earthly journey was coming to an end, and he wondered what lay beyond the grave.

Nasir noticed the change in his friend's demeanour and was concerned. "You must be in need of refreshment after the strenuous climb," he said with sympathy.

Firdusi replied with restrained emotion, "Please allow me to abstain from food for now, as eating might choke me, given the overwhelming emotions."

After satisfying his own hunger with a meal served by servants, Nasir asked Firdusi in a less reproachful and more anxious tone, "So, haven't the good news or the mysteries of the Damavant brought any relief to your gloom, Firdusi? Have they added to your spiritual wealth and ethereal dreams?"

Firdusi replied, moved deeply, "You are kind, and I should be happy with such a generous friend, but happiness has always eluded me. I stand on the precipice of my grave, with years wasted in undeserved disgrace and unrelenting misery. Ah, that vision revealed to me in the depths of the Damavant! If you know its nature, you can draw your own conclusions. Your hermit is more than you imagine."

Nasir explained, "Almazor is a well-guarded secret passed down from my father. My horn is the only way to call him, and he can't be found otherwise. Tehran knows as little about him as you did before I took you there. He is the mystery of the Damavant, more spirit than man, living in a way no one understands, impervious to hunger, thirst, or cold."

Firdusi contemplated, "A great secret and a precious heirloom indeed."

Nasir continued, "My grandfather blew the same horn I used last night and perhaps saw what you and I have seen."

Firdusi concluded, "Those sights are enough to challenge one's sanity."

Nasir added, "That herb only appears in a spring that defies nature, half liquid and half vapor, warm when everything else is frozen and cold when the sun blazes. It's invisible during the day but gives off a faint glow in the darkest of nights. My father told me that when this herb enters the human body, it makes the mind see whatever it can comprehend. Under its influence, I glimpsed paradise, a place and realm beyond description."

A fleeting smile crossed Firdusi's face as he looked into his friend's eyes. Then, in a deep, melodious, and expressive voice, he conjured terrifying and otherworldly visions, from desolate lunar landscapes to the celestial armies of stars. Nasir was moved to ecstasy, weeping, and kneeling before the revered poet, exclaiming, "And all this fails to bring you happiness, divine Firdusi!"

In Nasir's enthusiastic admiration, Firdusi perceived a reproach. He contemplated that perhaps blind faith was better than knowledge that led to doubt. He had tasted fame and favour but couldn't bear life's trials with the resignation expected by Islam. Rebelling against Allah's inscrutable decree was unworthy of a true believer. He believed that the universe's grandest symbol of divine omnipotence was the sun, just as Zarathustra had prostrated before it. He pondered how much more he should be in awe, having witnessed the grand procession of a billion suns with their countless planets and satellites.

Firdusi spoke thoughtfully, "Your words are not a reprimand, but they startle me with their implications. Even at my age, one's beliefs can be reconsidered, and new conclusions can be reached. How can we banish doubt, which creeps into the mind like a demon of madness? Let us work on the premise that life and death have harmonious relations. The connection between the smallest blade of grass and the mighty sun is as clear as that between a raindrop and the cloud and ocean. Both reveal the connection of the human soul to the universal spirit. When we recognize that the outer world is a manifestation of an intricate design, with God as the All in All throughout the Universe, then our souls transcend to the supernatural realm, inspiration turns into revelation, and the mind finds peace and the heart experiences happiness. Doubt yields to faith, and the raindrop, once lost in the darkest crevices of the rock, emerges as a crystal spring, flowing into the river, eager to unite with the vast ocean."

Whether Nasir comprehended his friend's philosophy or not, he was the last person to question the ideas of a man whose superior wisdom he never doubted. Muslim friendship is akin to Bedouin hospitality, and Nasir, who had welcomed the poet with all the honours, arranged to make his departure a grand event. Following a feast held in his honour, attended by the prominent figures of the province, the renowned poet, riding a fine dromedary, accompanied by another laden with valuable gifts, and escorted by a magnificent procession, set out hopefully from the gates of Tehran, accompanied by his loyal friend.

Firdusi's parting words of gratitude to his generous host were, "If Allah's mercy grants me the joys of paradise, I will pray that Nasir Lek shares them with me, unless your need surpasses mine, for I am less generous than you."

Upon reaching Tus, his birthplace, Firdusi discovered that the Sultan's promised gold had not arrived, which deeply troubled him. He feared that Mahmud's apologies might have been a trap set for his downfall. His anxiety was not alleviated when he overheard a child in the street reciting a verse from a sharp satire in which he mocked Mahmud as the illegitimate offspring of slaves. The verses insinuated that if Mahmud's ancestors had been of noble lineage, instead of deceiving him by offering silver instead of the gold prize promised for the Shah Namah, he would have adorned Firdusi's aged head with a golden crown.

Profound self-pity brought tears to the elderly man's eyes. His grievance echoed the lament of Iran, whispered by innocent voices into the ears of empathetic mothers. Once more, he relived the harrowing moments of his life, including the night when dawn was to witness him trampled under Mahmud's elephants because he had dared to protest the Sultan's deceit in sending him sixty thousand silver coins instead of the agreed-upon gold dinars. He recalled the time when, fleeing from Mahmud's wrath, he sought refuge in Mazenderan, where Kabous, the prince of Jorjan, dared not harbour him for fear of the relentless persecutor. The most agonizing memory was when El Kader Billah, the Caliph of Baghdad, who had initially been delighted by the fugitive's genius, asked him to leave when Mahmud of Ghaznin demanded his extradition. Overwhelmed with grief, the broken man returned to his daughter's home to pass away in her arms, resigned to the inscrutable decree of destiny.

Just as Firdusi's body was being carried out of Tus through one gate, the camels bearing the Sultan's gold entered the city through another. Firdusi's daughter declined to accept the treasure, but an elderly relative remembered his cherished desire to see his hometown improved with public works, especially a reliable and abundant water supply. In accordance with the poet's generous wish, the treasure was accepted and invested for the benefit of his grieving fellow townsmen. Over the ensuing centuries, their descendants have continued to commemorate the passing of Iran's immortal poet.

Story Of The King Who Would See Paradise

This story has been adapted from Andrew Lang's version of the same tale that originally appeared in The Orange Fairy Book, published in 1906 by Longmans, Green and Co., London and New York.

Once upon a time there was a king who, one day out hunting, came upon a fakeer in a lonely place in the mountains. The fakeer was seated on a little old bedstead reading the Koran, with his patched cloak thrown over his shoulders.

The king asked him what he was reading, and he said he was reading about Paradise and praying that he might be worthy to enter there. Then they began to talk, and, by and by, the king asked the fakeer if he could show him a glimpse of Paradise, for he found it very difficult to believe in what he could not see. The fakeer replied that he was asking a very difficult, and perhaps a very dangerous, thing, but that he would pray for him, and perhaps he might be able to do it, only he warned the king both against the dangers of his unbelief, and against the curiosity which prompted him to ask this thing. However, the king was not to be turned from his purpose, and he promised the fakeer always to provide him with food, if he, in return, would pray for him. To this the fakeer agreed, and so they parted.

Time went on, and the king always sent the old fakeer his food according to his promise, but, whenever he sent to ask him when he was going to show him Paradise, the fakeer always replied, "Not yet, not yet!"

After a year or two had passed by, the king heard one day that the fakeer was very ill - indeed, he was believed to be dying. Instantly he hurried off himself, and found that it was really true, and that the fakeer was even then breathing his last. There and then the king begged him to remember his promise, and to show him a glimpse of Paradise. The dying fakeer replied that if the king would come to his funeral, and, when the grave was filled in, and everyone else was gone away, he would come and lay his hand upon the grave, he would keep his word, and show him a glimpse of Paradise. At the same time he implored the king not to do this thing, but to be content to see Paradise when God called him there. Still the king's curiosity was so aroused that he would not give way.

Accordingly, after the fakeer was dead, and had been buried, he stayed behind when all the rest went away, and then, when he was quite alone, he stepped forward, and laid his hand upon the grave. Instantly the ground opened, and the astonished king, peeping in, saw a flight of rough steps, and, at the bottom of them, the fakeer sitting, just as he used to sit, on his rickety bedstead, reading the Koran.

At first the king was so surprised and frightened that he could only stare, but the fakeer beckoned to him to come down, so, mustering up his courage, he boldly stepped down into the grave.

The fakeer rose, and, making a sign to the king to follow, walked a few paces along a dark passage. Then he stopped, turned solemnly to his companion, and, with a movement of his hand, drew aside as it were a heavy curtain, and revealed - what? No one knows what was there shown to the king, nor did he ever tell anyone, but, when the fakeer at length dropped the curtain, and the king turned to leave the place, he had had his glimpse of Paradise! Trembling in every limb, he staggered back along the passage, and stumbled up the steps out of the tomb into the fresh air again.

The dawn was breaking. It seemed odd to the king that he had been so long in the grave. It appeared but a few minutes ago that he had descended, passed along a few steps to the place where he had peeped beyond the veil, and returned again after perhaps five minutes of that wonderful view. And what WAS it he had seen? He racked his brains to remember, but he could not call to mind a single thing. How curious everything looked too. Why, his own city, which by now he was entering, seemed changed and strange to him. The sun was already up when he turned into the palace gate and entered the public durbar hall. It was full, and a chamberlain came across and asked him why he sat unbidden in the king's presence.

"But I am the king!" he cried.

"What king?" said the chamberlain.

"The true king of this country," said he indignantly.

Then the chamberlain went away and spoke to the king who sat on the throne, and the old king heard words like 'mad,' 'age,' 'compassion.' Then the king on the throne called him to come forward, and, as he went, he caught sight of himself reflected in the polished steel shield of the bodyguard and started back in horror. He was old, decrepit, dirty, and ragged! His long white beard and locks were unkempt and straggled all over his chest and shoulders. Only one sign of royalty remained to him, and that was the signet ring upon his right hand. He dragged it off with shaking fingers and held it up to the king.

"Tell me who I am," he cried, "there is my signet, who once sat where you sit - even yesterday!"

The king looked at him compassionately and examined the signet with curiosity. Then he commanded, and they brought out dusty records and archives of the kingdom, and old coins of previous reigns, and compared them faithfully. At last the king turned to the old man, and said, "Old man, such a king as this whose signet you have, reigned seven hundred years ago, but he is said to have disappeared, none know where. Where did you get this ring?"

Then the old man smote his breast and cried out with a loud lamentation, for he understood that he, who was not content to wait patiently to see the Paradise of the faithful, had been judged already. And he turned and left the hall without a word, and went into the jungle, where he lived a life of prayer and meditation for twenty-five years, until at last, the Angel of Death came to him, and mercifully released him, purged and purified through his punishment.

The Gods In Exile

This story has been adapted from Henry Iliowizi's version of the same tale that originally appeared in The Weird Orient, published in 1900 by Henry T. Coates and Company, Philadelphia.

The year 1492 was a dark one for the sons of Shem. The fall of Granada and the expulsion of the Jews from Spain are events more generally commemorated than the equally dramatic episode which wound up with the tragic death of Bajazid, the dashing caliph of Damascus, surnamed Yildirim 'the thunderbolt'. At no time of the year is the Moslem world so deeply stirred as during the month Shawall, the fifteenth day of which marks the official opening of the great yearly pilgrimage to Mecca. The Haj is the name of the leading caravan which carries the Sultan's gift for Mohammed's shrine, that holds the black stone given by an angel to Abraham. No animal in creation has so many devout eyes concentrated on its unbeautiful outlines as the dromedary which conveys, under a canopy of green silk, the gorgeously embroidered covering for the walls of the Kabah. This Kiswa, as it is called, is made of black brocade, and its magnificent golden border spells divine utterance culled from the gems of the Koran. Exceeding it in costliness is a smaller curtain sent along for the Kabah's doors which swing in a frame of silver and gold.

Even in our days that train starts from Damascus with great ceremony, is accompanied by the municipal dignitaries led by the Pasha and escorted by a regiment in military pomp. No Moslem eye will miss the opportunity of witnessing the muhmil, or silken canopy, as it swings on the camel's back, shielding the sacred vesture of the most sacred of Islam's fanes, so that along the line of the procession the immense concourse of the faithful throng every available spot, from the terraced roof down to the gutters of the ill paved, sinuous lanes.

Such is the religious signal for hundreds of thousands to start for the centre of Moslem devotion from every quarter and corner as far as the crescent is revered, to fulfil the duty of adoring the object of the Prophet's worship. For he who has kissed that heavenly stone is not alone cleansed of all his sins but is thereafter distinguished by the surname of Hajj.

The departure of the Haj in the year of the discovery of the New World was one of unprecedented commotion. It was known that a great army was being concentrated and hurriedly drilled, and that Bajazid was on the point of taking the field himself, having gained signal triumphs in his repeated wars with Christian powers. That he appeared in his great mosque on the day of the Haj, and, surrounded by his bodyguard, followed the muhmil out of the city's confines, was interpreted as an ominous sign of impending danger. The Caliph's countenance was scrutinized with great anxiety by those who caught sight of it, and sombre deductions passed from lip to lip. As if to confirm the popular apprehensions, as Bajazid re-entered the city, a yelling saint, looking more like a satyr than a human being, emerged nobody knew from where, and, planting himself in the way of the white steed which carried the Commander of the faithful, cried, "Bajazid, Bajazid, the stars are against you. Woe! Woe!

Damascus! I see you and your sister cities swim in blood, your treasures plundered, your beauty rifled, your daughters outraged, with none to avenge you! Woe! Woe! Woe!"

A terrible frown darkened the brows of the hitherto invincible Caliph, but nobody dared lay a hand on the prophet of evil, who was allowed to lose himself in the next grove unmolested. The saint is only an instrument in the hand of Allah, and before the people had sufficiently recovered from their consternation to exchange a word about the fateful prophecy, a courier came tearing along the straightway of the city, another one was close behind, and another, their horses panting for breath. These events were followed by a sleepless night and feverish activity in the palace. Couriers were speeding to and fro, regiments were moving, batteries were mounted, and the greying dawn saw the Sultan at the head of a division marching out of his citadel never to return.

From the hand of fate Bajazid was to drink the dregs of the bitter cup. Like stubble before the fire, everything withered before the engulfing devastation of Timur's unconquerable host. Having swept nations and races before him, that celebrated Tartar conqueror made short work of Bajazid's mighty army. In the province of Angora host encountered host, the Caliph sustained a crushing defeat, his army was shattered, and the dreaded "thunderbolt" was himself among the prisoners in the hands of a merciless foe. With other cities, beautiful Damascus experienced the wrath of the Tartar's beastly nature. An indiscriminate slaughter of the population was followed by pillage, and whatever could not be plundered and taken off was delivered to the flames.

The Caliph's fate was sad in the extreme. Dragged along by the conqueror as a trophy in an iron palanquin, which looked more like a cage than aught else, death, more gracious than the savage Tartar, finally delivered Bajazid from a life of humiliation and torture.

The wizard who had foretold the downfall of the Caliph and the ruin of populous cities was never hereafter seen within the broad circuit of Damascus, a region exceeding in the exuberance of its semi tropic verdure and panoramic landscape the beauty of Granada's famous valley in its palmy days of Moorish rule. The fatalistic principle of Islam precludes spying into the inscrutable decrees of Allah, whose will is fate from which there is neither appeal nor escape. Why then waste a moment in identifying an oracle whose prophecies pass through him as water passes through a pipe? It is impious to search into the unsearchable.

There were two young men on the scene, however, whose antecedents account for that mad impetuosity with which they stormed onward in pursuit of the oracular saint as soon as it was possible for them to elude the eyes of the crowd. One was Damon Mianolis, a young Greek, who had inherited from his father an avidity for the occult science of astrology, the other was Selim Ebn Asa, a youthful Moslem, who had enabled Damon to witness in disguise the departure of the Haj. Damon's father was a physician, but had a secret laboratory, and had spent a fortune in attempts at fathoming the mysteries of alchemy and astrology. Damon had been early initiated into those mystic arcana, had learned to cast the horologue, but was woefully disappointed in the matter of extracting gold from other substances, and gave up the hope of ever discovering the elixir of life. The physician's death had put his son in possession of an extensive practice among his fellow Christians, and Selim's friendship was due to the Moslem's ambition to acquire a knowledge of French, which Damon spoke fluently.

The intimate relation of the two young men led to free discussions of the merits of their respective creeds, with the result that each one believed a little more in his friend's and a little less in his own scheme of salvation. The heavenly city built of gold and precious stones, with twelve gates and glittering streets, through which flows the river of life, bordered on its banks by the tree of life, which bears twelve sorts of fruits and leaves of healing virtue, was pointed to by Damon as the pattern of Mohammed's paradise of which Selim made much in his effort to convert his friend. Selim meant to astonish Damon by referring to those pavilions of pearls in which the houris dwell retired, each pearl sixty miles in dimension, but was met by the even more astonishing promise of St. John that 'the days shall come when there shall be vines which shall have each ten thousand branches, and every one of these branches shall have ten thousand lesser branches, and every one of these branches shall have ten thousand twigs, and every one of the twigs shall have ten thousand clusters of grapes, and every one of these clusters shall bear ten thousand grapes, and every one of these grapes being pressed shall yield two hundred and seventy five gallons of wine, and when a man shall take hold of one of those sacred branches, another one shall cry out "I am the better branch, take me and bless the Lord."

This left the youthful Moslem little to boast of in the concern of paradisial blessedness, and he was totally overwhelmed by a vivid picture of Dante's elaboration of hell. What impressed Selim, however, most profoundly was Damon's familiarity with the heavenly configurations, and his pretended ability to read future events. The fact is that the late Mianolis had shortly before his death predicted Bajazid's overthrow and captivity, and Selim had received a hint of the prediction. No sooner, therefore, had the saint's lamentation fallen on their ears than the young men exchanged a significant look, and the next instant both were on the track of the retreating soothsayer. In but a very few minutes Selim realized the impossibility of his overtaking the fleeing man, whose feet scarcely touched the turf, but not so Damon, who taxed his energies to their uttermost to keep the winged fugitive in sight. Not a living soul crossed them as they hurried onward, the saint leading through a maze of entangling thickets on pathways of his own, the other following almost out of breath, determined not to give up the chase.

In this way miles had been traversed before Damon noticed that they were at the foot of Anti Lebanon, and that Selim was not behind him. The ascent had to be made, or the game would have been lost in a moment. From an elevation of several hundred feet Damon's eye was fascinated by the superb view of Damascus, set in a garland of groves, bushes and gardens, distance enhancing the charm of the exquisite panorama. Along the banks of Abana, in the heart of a sea of verdure, rose a grand vision of terraced roofs, surmounted here and there by swelling domes, towering minarets, tipped with gilded crescents, glittering like burnished scythes from the thick foliage of blooming parks. An area of thirty miles in circuit spread like a dream, with a variance of grouping and shading, and a charm of blended tints such as are rarely vouchsafed to the eye even in regions of renowned picturesqueness.

Damon had never before seen Damascus in such a wreath of glory, but the few seconds the sight exacted of his attention frustrated his efforts to locate the wizard's retreat, who had disappeared as though dissolved in air. At the same time a feeling of exhaustion rendered a further ascent impossible, coupled with a somnolence which stole and gained upon the youth, until, succumbing to the spell, he lay stretched on the grass under a tree, lost in oblivion. Re appearing on the scene as suddenly as he had vanished, the haggard, half naked wizard waved his crooked staff over the sleeper's head, drew a circle around him, pointed southward, and vanished as before. On returning to consciousness Damon bit his tongue to assure himself that he was really awake, his hand dashed across his eyes, it was no vision. He felt deathly cold, although his touch left no doubt that he was robed in fur, his head, hands, and feet covered by the same material. It was night, and he in an air ship, under stars he had never seen before this, and sweeping with great speed through a world of mountains of ice and frozen seas, an icy desolation buried in dense fogs. Before him sat the controlling aeronaut, white as frost and silent as death, to his right sat a female in black, with eyes closed and the countenance of a corpse, to his left sat no one else but the saint as he had seen him in the street of Damascus, with no evidence of being in the least affected by the intense cold.

Damon suspecting that it was a dream within a dream, closed his eyes tightly to continue his slumber when he heard a voice addressing him thus, "Son of Mianolis the Wise, know that you are in the chariot of Auster, hurrying toward the great ice regions of the south with me, your sire's friend, and this dame, the Witch of Endor, on whose grave you had taken your rest this last day, thus disturbing her spirit that soars over the tomb of the body which held it when alive. Evil would have befallen you but for my interposition in your behalf, and I am indebted to your father for revelations in the stars and in the realms of nature, which give me foresight and power over spirits. What you shall see tonight was the awe of your ancestors and of those who gave rise to the mightiest progeny on earth, but hold your breath, lest the frost congeal your blood, and be not alarmed even if mountains quake and oceans burst," was the wizard's reassuring information.

Even before the last word had been spoken an enormous column of lurid flame and livid smoke shot up from the heart of an immense mountain, and in a continuous flow lost itself in the clouds, a deluge of fire ascending and descending with the tremendous crack and reverberation of thunder. "That southernmost volcano shall mark for generations to come the extreme limit of human penetration into the forbidding regions of ice, the other facing it to eastward burns no more but is likewise an insurmountable barrier set by nature against the intrusion of man into regions reserved for the dethroned gods. They shall in future years be respectively known and shunned as 'Mount Erebus' and 'Mount Terror'" volunteered the wizard as an explanation, but further mystifying the already confused aeronaut.

On the highest peak of Mount Terror the chariot alighted, and a puff of Auster's breath dissolved the mists around a group of crystal palaces, trimmed with gold, roofed with silver, clustering around an all outshining, sky towering edifice reaching up to an ethereal height, overarched by a blazing span of transcendental rainbowed glories, blending into golden haze below, and an indefinable silvery twilight above. "Asgard," were the first syllables uttered by the Witch of Endor.

Yes, it was Odin's celestial Court where, from his throne, he surveyed heaven and earth, and He was exalted high above all others. On his shoulders sat the ravens Hugin and Munin, who, in ancient times, daily traversed the world to report the happenings among the mortal race, and at his feet lay the two wolves Friki and Geri, whom Odin fed with the meat set before him, mead alone being sufficient for him who feeds all creatures.

Overpowering as was the presence of Odin on his throne, another spectacle forced itself on Damon's vision. In front of Valhalla's portal, an entrance as wide as the entire hall, a desperate struggle was raging between redoubtable combatants, who struck at each other with appalling fury. The broad arena was already strewed with numerous bodies cut to pieces. A relentless frenzy appeared to have seized those who were still engaged in the exterminating feud, while the gods looked on with complacence, as though the deathful affair was a mere tournament. When the battle was over there was but one hero left, and he bleeding from many wounds. Presently there came a blast from a horn in Valhalla, which sent a breath of animation through the bulky bodies of the slaughtered. Their wounds closed, their severed limbs knitted and healed, their eyes opened, their frames quivered, straightened, and pulsated with life. They rose, picked up their weapons, and straightway repaired to the festive hall where throngs of shining elves attended on them with food and drink. Damon knew then that these were the immortal heroes who, having fallen in battle, were permitted to dwell among the gods, partaking of the meat of Shrimnir, the ever-reviving boar, and of the mead of the she goat Heidrun. What looked like a fierce battle was simply an amusement.

The feast was rudely interrupted by a note of alarm sounded by Heimdall, the sleepless sentinel of Odin's Court. Heimdall's business is to make the round of the borders of heaven to prevent intruders from ascending by the way of Bifrost, that is the bridge built of the rainbow's light which links earth to Odin's ethereal Court. He is especially anxious to intercept the mischievous giants who are ever on the alert to annoy the powers of Asgard. As Heimdall's ears are so fine that he hears growing of the grass and of the wool on a sheep's back, it is no wonder that his warning of impending danger startled the gods. Thialfi, Thor's inseparable attendant and the swiftest messenger of Asgard, was forthwith despatched northward, from where, according to Heimdall's information, the storm was coming, while the gods and the heroes made ready for the emergency, whatever it might be. Invincible Thor, whose terrific hammer, Miölnir, splits mountains, and returns to the hand of the god when hurled against a foe, girded himself with his belt, which redoubles his terrors, and put on his iron gloves to render the shock of his mallet irresistible.

They soon beheld Thialfi returning all astounded, with tidings which made Thor's veins swell with rage. "A burning sun, O great Odin, accompanied by a host of gods, goddesses, and their dependents, carry with them here a city of supernal palaces, and will be upon us before your will can be heard in council," reported Thialfi.

Almost simultaneous with these words the first beam of a golden flood fell on the brilliant domes and towers of Asgard. Night fled to the darkest recesses of Antarctic gloom, the snow softened, the icebergs glittered like mountains of jewels, whale, dolphin and sealion gambolled with delight, but the black elves, who dread the sun, were turned by myriads into stones. Of vegetable life there was not as much as a blade of grass to be seen, not a withered leaf, nor a dry shrub to greet the radiant orb.

In his all-knowing wisdom Odin exclaimed, "It is the Olympian Thunderer who comes this way, if it means peace we shall open our hall to welcome him, should it mean war, it will be your task, Thor, to drive him there with ruin."

Quick as thought did Phoebus suspend his blazing chariot in mid heaven, eastward of Mount Erebus, which, crowned with light and glory, was instantaneously turned into an Olympus by the fiat of creative powers. Phoebus caused the earth to thaw, Pan called forth a garden of Hesperian richness, Ceres conjured up a crop of golden grain where glaciers had been slowly grinding their way for numberless cycles, the fire spitting Erebus smiled like May, garlanded by Flora, every god and goddess contributing his or her share to create an Elysium in the dreariest of ice buried deserts.

In less time than it takes to tell it, Jupiter established himself in a manner which left in Odin no doubt that the whilom sovereign of Olympus had come to stay. Thor burned for action, but Odin restrained his impetuous son, reminding him that if he had the rock blasting mallet to hurl, so had the Olympian chief something to send in return, which it might be wise to avoid if possible. First the most guileful schemer of Odin's Court was to be employed to ascertain the real purpose of the Thunderer's arrival, and this was the malicious Loki, one of the hostile giants, who had succeeded in securing a foothold in Asgard.

Loki's nature may be judged by his three offspring, they are the wolf Fenris, the Midgard serpent, and Hela, that is death. Fenris could not be allowed to roam at large, but to chain him was a problem the gods alone could solve. Every kind of chain having been tried in vain, the mountain spirits were required to fashion one that should not yield like cobweb to the teeth of the horrid monster. It was made of the beards of women, the noise of the cat's paw, the breath of fishes, the roots of stones, the spittle of birds, and the sensitiveness of bears, it was as pleasant to the touch as a silken cord and was named Glupnir. With this fetter on his neck Fenris was rendered harmless. His twin, the Midgard serpent, is so enormous that her length is thrown around the earth like a belt, she holding her tail in her mouth. Hela dwells in Elvidnir, a black hall in dark Niffleheim. She feeds on hunger, cuts her food with starvation, decks her bed with misery, employs slowness as her maid, delay as her servant, her threshold is precipice, her tapestries burning anguish. The father of this precious triplet was not a little pleased to be thus honoured with the important embassy to the sovereign of the Olympian dynasty, especially since the message was but little short of an ultimatum. Loki's mind was not of a frame to be surprised at anything or intimidated by any display of might, but the stream of blinding light he had to face, as he turned toward the point of his destination, caused his eyes to water, wholly unused as he was to a splendour which made Asgard's rainbow pale, as does the moon before the rising sun.

Whether it was for a purpose or by chance, Phoebus darted his rays with piercing penetration, focussing them on the visage of Odin's envoy, and his chariot, a master work of Hephæstus, forged of glittering metal, and set with resplendent gems, moved in an orbit with an ever-widening periphery. Winged Mercury met Loki halfway, bade him stop by a wave of his Caduceus, and required him to give an account of his mission. Satisfied with the answer, Mercury led the way to the gate of clouds guarded by the goddess Seasons, and Loki soon found himself in the radiant palace of Jupiter than which there could be nothing loftier and more glorious under the stars. Here the deities meet in council in the assembly hall of their chief, and here they indulge the divine feast of ambrosia and nectar served by the ineffably lovely goddess Hebe, while Apollo delights the immortals with the ravishing strains of his lyre, accompanied by the song of the nine Muses.

Ushered into the awful presence of the Olympian Thunderer, Loki beheld himself in the midst of a galaxy of deities, whose various attributes and aspects would have astonished him had they not been eclipsed by the overpowering grandeur of the son of Saturnus, who, enthroned in supernal majesty, with the Ægis, shining like the sun before him, and his thunder speeding eagle next to him, formed a striking contrast to Odin's dimmer environments.

At the sight of Loki, Apollo struck his lyre, the Muses joined their heavenly voices to swell the melody, and Hebe served to all the food and drink of the gods, including Odin's envoy in the divine conviviality. But ambrosia and nectar affected Loki's palate so differently from the meat of the boar Shrimnir and the mead of the she goat Heidrun that the first quaff of the new beverage made his facial muscles contract and distend in so ludicrous a fashion that the vast hall resounded with the laughter of the Olympians. Loki did not like the idea of being made the butt of ridicule, but, though stung to the quick, joined in the merriment at his expense, there being no hope for vengeance thus far. Required to state the purport of his message, he began thus, "It is Odin's wish that peace prevail betwixt his Court and you, O mighty Chief, and I am sent to remind you, that when Alfadur had doomed your rule and his in Midgard, a new order having risen with a new time, the compact was that you withdraw to the fields swept by Boreas, the Valkyrior kindling the north lights for your benefit, and he, undeterred by severer cold and longer night, should settle in this drearier end of earth, where Day returns but for a double month, allowing Night and Frost to rule supreme. What does your coming here with such consuming heat mean? Why do you come with such pomp as makes Odin's bleak retreat unbearable, unless he strive to hold by force what is his by treaty? In substance this is Odin's message. As guests he welcomes you and yours with all Valhalla has to entertain, and honours powers akin to him in weal and woe, who had tasted the bitters of dethronement and exile. But if your purpose be to fix a permanent abode within the bounds of Odin's hitherto undisputed empire, war will be the outcome, and war with Asgard means chaos and the end."

The Thunderer shook his locks, his eagle's eye flashed fire. Among the superior gods the face of Mars glowed like a meteor. Minerva assumed a menacing air, and the others gave evidence of a stern determination to go to the bitter end in whatever part they were able to sustain the right and dignity of their challenged head. But Jupiter, inclined toward conciliation if possible, dismissed Loki with earnest mien, promising his answer should reach Odin forthwith. And forthwith Mercury was at Loki's heels, and proceeded with him to Asgard, where Odin gave ear to Jupiter's reply thus conveyed.

"Great Odin, the cloud compelling power who wields the thunderbolt, but whose old sovereignty has been lamentably curtailed, deplores his condition and yours, True, when the empire over Midgard had to be abandoned in favour of Alfadur's anointed, the extremities of earth alone afforded refuge from the universal spread of those hateful inspirations which, like a deluge, submerged the better world, synagogue, church, or mosque supplanting those pantheons of art, poetry and beauty, which, in the golden age of dream and fable, song, dance and free love, made man as happy as an unbridled child. When the time had come for our stern trials, it is remembered that, to render our banishment bearable, you have benignly agreed to let the Olympian dynasty retreat northward of the habitable world, you and your being more seasoned to endure the severer rigors of this inclement zone. But where should we flee from the ever-swelling might of the cross and the crescent? Not satisfied with the conquest of blessed Midgard, their votaries dare penetrate the very extremes of the frigid north, and the cross may be seen where neither wolf nor vulture can breathe. Yea, the western hemisphere, hitherto unknown to the world, is being discovered, and before long will bristle with the spires of a myriad churches. This extreme alone seems forever barred against the intrusion of man, its terrors bringing death to him. Night, frost and sterility are here in league against mortal flesh. Necessity forced upon our father the resolution to seek once more a new home where, undisturbed by the detestable symbols of new creeds, we may continue with as much comfort as powers inalienable insure for us.

"Jupiter sends you peace, O, mighty Odin, not that he shrinks from war, or heeds threats, but because of his benign temper unless provoked when his wrath would prove too much even for the giants on whom Asgard has a watchful eye. For it is he who made Saturnus disgorge his progeny and holds him chained in the deeps of Erebus."

Mercury's bold language came near to costing him his head. Thor was restrained with difficulty by his father from sending his hammer against the brazen front of Jupiter's messenger, who was, however, allowed to depart unmolested. There was great commotion in Valhalla, and Odin sent his last word to the intruders requiring them to vacate the invaded heights forthwith, or Asgard would proceed to expel them by force. Thialfi imparted this warning to the Olympians and was dismissed with scorn. Heimdall's horn, Giallar, summoned all the Gods and heroes to battle, while Thor held his mallet in readiness to do fearful execution.

Odin's terrific frown was the signal given for the engagement, it isolated the hostile encampment, giving it the appearance of an illumined island in an ocean of dense night. The moments of suspense were being utilized on both sides to call in and muster all the reserves available. Nobody was happier than the mischievous Loki, who was charged to communicate by the roots of the Ygdrasil tree with the inhabitants of Jotunheim, it being the place where those prodigious giants live, the glove of one of whom Thor had once mistaken for a cavern wherein he spent a night and was disturbed in his sleep by the snoring of the colossus that shook him like an earthquake.

Should those Jotuns be slow in coming, Loki was to rouse Ymir from his rest, Ymir the terrific giant Frost, whose blood is the seas, whose body forms the earth, whose bones are the mountains, whose skull is the heavens, whose brains are the clouds and what they discharge in the shape of rain or snow, and whose eyebrows supplied the material for the making of Midgard, the habitable portion of the globe. Ymir sleeps under the Ygdrasil tree whose branches extend to every quarter of the universe, while its three roots connect Asgard with Niffleheim and Jotunheim. Ymir's disturbed slumbers make the earthquake and shudder, his awaking would bring about the end of things. Loki's malice had never been more gratified, he having thus far been an unwelcome presence among the gods of Asgard, who had even once gone to the trouble of slaying him for treason to Baldur, but Loki had another life to spare, and here he was bustling, busier than ever before.

Neither were they idle on Erebus. The response to Odin's threatening scowl was an intensified light and such a heat as began to dissolve whatever had remained frozen as stone since Time outspread his wings. Phoebus assumed the terrors of a bursting hell, so that whatever life there was in the sea buried itself deep under its surface. With a due appreciation of his dreadful adversaries, Jupiter arrayed himself in his most appalling panoply, and called on Tartarus to bring to light the pack of Titans prominent among whom were Cottus, Briareus and Gyes, each one having a hundred hands and fifty heads, well known as the subduers of Saturnus, who indulged the unpaternal habit of feasting on his own offspring. Useless to add, the other Olympians were prepared for the fray, but they waited for the aggressive deed to come from Asgard.

It came like a dart of lightning. Enraged by the consuming heat, Thor aimed a fatal blow at the sun's fiery steeds, hoping to shatter at one stroke the entire team. With its unfailing accuracy Miölnir struck the glowing chariot. Phoebus had a narrow escape, holding tightly the reins, the horses reared wildly, bleeding from many wounds, which closed, however, by virtue of their deathless substance. But as the mallet, by its nature, returned to Thor's grasp, the god roared like a hundred lions, for it was a red-hot mass of metal and could not be handled before another fling had passed it through a fathom's depth of a glacier's icy bed. By the time Thor was ready to renew his experiment he felt himself lifted off his feet and hurled headlong into an abyss at the back of Asgard. Such was the effect of a lightning bolt sent by Jupiter's hand, who had ascended the azurean height of his citadel where he caused an ominous thunder cloud to overshadow the Court of Odin. Though dazed by the blasting shock and the fall, Thor was on his feet, and from a cliff, which he quickly ascended, winged his hammer with unerring precision against the cloud enshrouded tower of Erebus. Miölnir was met halfway by another fulmination of the Olympian Thunderer, and the collision of the missiles reverberated like the crack of doom.

No less fierce was the engagement of the other powers on both sides, who, without deploying into battle array, strove with prodigious might, the one stunning or hurting the other. Malicious Loki, hugely amused to see the once invincible Thor wheel through the air and land ignominiously in a chasm, assumed the colossal proportions of the giant race to which he virtually belonged, making effective use of his enormous limbs. Having picked out Mars as his target, he aimed an iceberg at the Olympian war dog who was inflicting terrible punishment on the gods and heroes of Asgard, but Neptune was at hand with a tremendous billow of tepid water warmed by Phoebus. It struck the frozen mass, deflecting it from its fatal course, so that there was at once a great splash and a harmless crash.

The battle continued to rage along the line, the elements of fire, water, wind, and earth being wielded with whelming impetuosity. Between Thor and Jupiter the duel was incessant, with no turn in favour of Odin's most redoubtable combatant. In the general confusion Loki threw himself with a force on the enemy's flank, endeavouring thus to attack the gate which he had been permitted to enter as Odin's messenger. From his cloudy height the Olympian chief discerned the move of the perfidious strategist, brandished one of his forked lightning bolts, and Asgard beheld with amazement one of its mightiest hurled into oblivion.

Odin surveyed the situation, and recognized the hopelessness of the struggle, even if Ymir could be caused to budge and the giants of Jotunheim arrived in time. Where Thor failed who could succeed? And the dreaded Titans were likely to appear on the scene at any moment. Thialfi was, therefore, directed to recall Thor, and ask the Olympians to suspend hostilities, pending the consideration of a peaceful settlement. The brightening of the atmosphere around Asgard indicated Odin's change of mind. Jupiter agreed to a truce, and Phoebus relaxed the severity of his unbearable heat. Odin declared himself willing to withdraw his Court to the extreme south, provided the Olympians would not follow him there. Jupiter swore the irrevocable oath attested by the river Styx, that there shall be no further encroachments hereafter, come what may. And Mercury was instructed to convey peaceful greetings to Odin.

"Let our brother know that we properly appreciate his magnanimous offer to withdraw further south, that we reluctantly waged war against a kindred power dethroned by Him who is above all enthroned. No, not thus shall we part, mailed in threatening panoply, with grim war bristling and sullen. Festive joy, cordial intercourse and divine conviviality shall mark the season of our conciliation. Great Odin and his Court are to be honoured in this hall. Since man has ceased to pay us worshipful homage, our own felicity be our sole care."

In response to this effusion of friendship Odin signified his pleasure by ordering his black elves, to whose skilful workmanship Thor was indebted for his wonderful hammer, to throw an arched span of gold over the hollow which separated the mountains of Terror and Erebus. But the long nosed, dirty little artificers dared not face Phoebus, whose glare brought them death, wherefore the blazing chariot of the sun god made room for Aurora Australis, when the bridge rose like a vision, competing with the rainbow in multicoloured brilliancy. For once Vulcan confessed surprise at the exquisite mastery in metal work in which he had thought himself unrivalled, while Pluto was amazed at the lavishness of the precious material, which he knew to be limited in quantity. Once more did Heimdall sound his horn, this time to proclaim the opening of the grand feast in which all the gods, goddesses, heroes, and dependencies of Asgard were required to participate.

On their side the Olympians were neither to be eclipsed in splendour nor outdone in all that goes to make a feast of gods. Robed in supernal glory, each god and goddess, surrounded by their retinues, wore the symbols of their respective powers and attributes, but stood overawed by the transcendent magnificence of their chief, whom no mortal eye could behold without being consumed. From his throne above the clouds, surrounded by his family, who shone like stars, Jupiter beheld Odin issue from Valhalla, mounted on his eight-legged steed, Sleipnir, who could leap over mountains. He was followed by Frigga and Freya, his wife and daughter, the one as beautiful as Iris, the other, who stood for love, blushing like sweet Aurora, escorted by Thor and his inseparable attendant, Thialfi. Like a stream of radiant gold, a host of sunny elves, diminutive creatures flowed behind them, stirring the air with weird music. In their wake, leading another host of those unsightly elves clad in burnished brass, and blowing sonorous instruments of the same metal, came Frey in a chariot drawn by the boar Gullinbursti, along with Heimdall bestriding his horse, Gulltopp. The train's rear was taken up by a great number of inferior gods, heroes, and mountain giants, as well as their colossal frost companions.

Gratifying his mischievous nature, Cupid perched on the main entrance guarded by Seasons, and as this goddess opened it to admit Odin and his cortege, a shower of love's arrows descended on the unsuspicious powers of Asgard, who were received by Pluto and Neptune, and led into the assembly hall of Jupiter's palace. Here the Olympian dynasty were found standing, except Jupiter and Juno, who likewise rose, while Venus, wearing the Cestus which imparts ineffable grace to the wearer, welcomed the head of Asgard and escorted him to a lofty throne at the left hand of her father. A sweet fragrance was diffused among the star like assembly by a heavenly smile from Jupiter, who was at once captivated by the eyes of Freya, the goddess of love. Odin found it impossible to make a secret of his enchantment by Venus, while Thor had no eye for anyone but Hebe. Heimdall found in Juno the crown of sweetness, Thialfi bowed to Diana, and Frey paid his tender respects to Minerva. The other deities selected their partners in accordance with their natural bent of mind, or destined appointment in the divine economy.

Outside, the subordinate attendants grouped themselves harmoniously, so that no sooner were the strains of Apollo's lyre heard, accompanied by the enravishing song of the Muses, than the broad spaces between the dwellings of the gods teemed with the airy dancers. Elf, nymph, naiad, satyr, and dryad abandoned themselves to the spell of Apollo's music. This was only a faint reflex of what was happening in the star illumined hall of the Olympian Thunderer. Here the celestial food and beverage were being offered by Hebe, after the first grand march of the superior gods. Odin, who never tasted of Shrimnir's flesh, and indulged in but drink of the mead of the she goat Heidrun, now emptied a capacious goblet of nectar handed him by Hebe, at the same time that one was given to Thor. The head of Asgard's Court found it hard to swallow the strange liquid, so unlike mead, and, unable to retain it, ejected it in a manner to bring up the Olympian host and his entire house. As to Thor, the unspeakable drink and the mirth provoked by his ludicrous grimaces enraged him to such an extent that, but for the subduing charm of Hebe's look, he would have dashed his mallet against the very throne which filled gods with awe. Good nature prevailed, however, and as the refreshments passed around, the hilarity grew at the cost of Asgard.

Now Terpsichore struck her instrument, the graces joining to swell the strains which cause the gods to move in rhythmic measure. Looked at from the vantage ground occupied by Damon, the divine spectacle resembled a scattered constellation, the stars moving in pairs, then grouping in clusters, then spreading in lines, straight and curved, then forming in circles, then breaking up to renew and multiply the harmonious evolutions. There appeared nothing to intercept the minutest detail of the celestial scene, and Damon was intoxicated with felicity, ear and eye being equally ravished.

While the feast was at its height, Erebus shook with a convulsion which reminded Jupiter of the summons he had sent to Tartarus, and that the Titans had access to the upper world by way of the lava vomiting mountain. At the same instant Heimdall gave the alarm, his ear having recognized the tramp of the Jotuns for whom Odin had sent his son, Hermond the Nimble. Quick as were the gods in rushing to arms, and in manning every strategic and vulnerable point, they were not quick enough to prevent a collision between Briareus on one side and Skrymir on the other, each one sustained by his gigantic followers, who tore up glaciers and made icebergs fly as flakes of snow driven by a storm. As if by a tacit understanding, Thor and

Jupiter combined their terrific instruments of destruction, hurling them from opposite directions at the monstrous combatants, who heaped Pelion on Ossa in their furious efforts to crush each other. Briareus disappeared like a flash in the womb of Erebus, drawing his companions after him, the Jotuns took to their heels as fast as their gigantic limbs could carry them.

But there was no clearing of the atmosphere. The mountains trembled, the air grew oppressive and seemed saturated with fetid gases. A moment's ominous quiet was broken by another far reaching convulsion, followed by a crack which terrified the gods and threw Damon out of his seat deep down into a chasm. The womb of Erebus opened wide. A deluge of fire burst from the bowels of the earth, melting glaciers, and causing frozen seas to boil. Heaven glowed like a furnace, and Damon beheld with terror a stream of liquid metal pour down in a cataract from a height above his head. His attempt to flee from destruction proved his limbs to be of lead, he could not budge. He was going to be buried under fathoms of molten ore. Once more he tried to get to his feet, the glowing metal bursting on him from every side. In growing terror he grasped for something to assist him in his struggle for life, striking out right and left.

His numbness gave way, his limbs softened in their joints, and a vitalizing energy enabled him to raise his head. What did he see? A full rounded moon shedding a silver flood on a slumbering landscape, glorified by a weird maze of faraway dazzling white, varied by domes and spires of other hues. It was neither Asgard nor the heavenly city built by Hephæstus, for it was Damascus, oblivious of her impending doom. Damon was grateful to be here, conscious of the fact that the wizard he had followed had but sported with him. Yet what he had seen was worth the sacrifice. How much greater the

God of infinity, how much holier than they of Asgard and Olympus, He with whom a myriad galaxies count for naught as He sways the boundless Universe by the breath of His mouth!

The Wise Dey

This story is adapted from The Thousand And One Days by Julia Pardoe,
published in 1857 by William Lay, London.

After Chaaban, the Dey of Algiers, had passed away, the Turkish janissaries found themselves in need of a new Dey. Their aim was to select someone who was passive, feeble, and indifferent, someone who would let them have full control, whether it was just or not, and who wouldn't administer any punishments. As they roamed through the streets of Algiers, they came across Hadgi-Achmet, an elderly man peacefully seated at his doorstep, attentively repairing his old slippers. He seemed completely uninvolved in the noise, conversations, and chitchat happening around him. To the janissaries, he appeared to be the kind of apathetic man they were looking for – someone who wouldn't meddle in their affairs, allowing them to do as they pleased. In essence, they saw him as a mere figurehead for the position of Dey. So, they grabbed Hadgi-Achmet, forcibly pulled him away from his work, brought him to the divan, and made him the Dey against his will.

Forced into the position of Dey, Hadgi-Achmet didn't shy away from his new responsibilities. He diligently delved into the duties of his role, demonstrating the same dedication and enthusiasm he once had for the simple task of repairing his old slippers. He took on the task of safeguarding the nation's interests and upholding justice, dealing harshly with any wrongdoing that came to his attention. It was his peculiar habit to furrow his brows and flash his piercing eyes whenever confronted with anything dishonest or wicked. This unwavering commitment to justice and integrity didn't sit well with the Turkish janissaries and some members of the divan.

Four individuals in the council conspired to damage Hadgi-Achmet's public image. Since the Dey was directly involved in administering justice and meticulously examining even minor issues related to the people's well-being, these conspirators aimed to ridicule him. To accomplish this, they brought forth four apparently insignificant cases, thinking they weren't worth the consideration of a distinguished leader.

One of the council members addressed the Dey, saying, "My lord, we have a case that only you, the embodiment of justice, can judge. It involves a Tunisian merchant who recently set up shop in Bab-a-Zoun street, not far from the mosque. Initially, he conducted his business with some integrity, but over time, it became evident that he was nothing but a swindler. He cheated numerous customers in matters of weight, quality, and value of his goods. As you're well aware, the law prescribes that such wrongdoers should lose an ear. This man was apprehended, brought before the Cadi, and, given the glaring evidence of his deceit, the Cadi sentenced him to lose his left ear, reserving the right in case of future transgressions. However, when they removed his turban, it was discovered that his left ear was already missing. The Cadi, upon learning of this, ordered the removal of the right ear. To execute this order, they had to forcibly move the culprit's hand away from his right ear. And when they did, it was revealed that the Tunisian's right ear was missing as well. The Cadi then informed me, knowing your penchant for resolving weighty and significant matters, and I've come to present this case to your exceptional wisdom and illustrious justice."

Upon hearing these words, Hadgi-Achmet furrowed his brows, and his eyes blazed at the speaker and all those in the audience. He then turned to the man without ears and declared, "Since you've persistently been a rogue, and there's no hope of reform, I condemn you to spend your entire life without a turban or any head covering to hide the absence of your ears. Wise buyers will avoid you, for it's common knowledge that a merchant without ears is nothing more than a swindler."

The earless Tunisian left with a heavy heart. He was compelled to display his earless state to everyone at all times, a punishment far more severe than losing five hundred ears, had he possessed them.

With this judgment settled, another member of the council addressed the Dey, saying, "Hadgi-Achmet, our esteemed master, we have a dispute between two men that only your profound wisdom can resolve. One of these men is the father of a beautiful and promising boy. He had this son and two others. About ten years ago, his neighbour Ibrahim, who was childless, approached him and said, 'Chamyl, give me your youngest son. I will adopt him, and he will live in my house, inherit my wealth, and find happiness. If you agree, I'll give you my country house in Boudjaréah in exchange. You know it's blessed with a cooling north breeze during the hottest summer days.'

"Chamyl consented to give his son and accepted the house in Boudjaréah. Ormed, Chamyl's son, went to live with Ibrahim, who quickly developed a deep affection for the boy. In turn, Ormed, out of gratitude, grew very attached to him. Now, Chamyl has lost his other two sons and has become wealthy. He wishes to bring Ormed back, declaring, 'This child is now the sole hope of my family, the delight of my heart, and I want him to be my heir.'

"However, Ibrahim has lost almost half of his fortune but has not lost his love for his adopted son. In fact, his affection for the child, who possesses exceptional qualities of mind and a grateful, loving heart, continues to grow stronger by the day."

"To whom do you decide that Ormed shall belong? His adopted father or his biological father?" Hadgi-Achmet asked Chamyl.

Chamyl replied by enumerating his possessions: a house, a ship, several country houses, and merchandise.

Hadgi-Achmet questioned further, "Can you part with these possessions?"

Chamyl responded, "I can part with some of them."

"And the others," Hadgi-Achmet continued, "could you sell them if necessary and buy other things with the proceeds?"

"I could," Chamyl replied.

Hadgi-Achmet then inquired, "Could you transfer the affection you had for your deceased sons to other children?"

Chamyl sighed and replied, "No, that would be impossible."

"Affection cannot be transferred or exchanged," Hadgi-Achmet stated, "as it is an integral part of a person's heart and holds greater importance than material possessions, wouldn't you agree?"

"Yes, my lord," Chamyl answered.

"Thus," the Dey continued, "we can tell a person to sell or give away their belongings, but it would be absurd to instruct someone to stop loving the person they love. Therefore, Chamyl, I decree that you must leave with Ibrahim the child he loves and whom you willingly gave to him when you still had affection for your other two late sons. Your possessions, however, you may take with you wherever you wish because wealth is not the essence of the heart."

Chamyl protested, saying, "But I love my son, and I want him to be my heir."

Hadgi-Achmet responded, "You claim to love your son, but you showed no evidence of it while your other two children were alive. Furthermore, you exchanged your son for a house, which is no different than selling your child."

Chamyl defended himself, "I was poor."

The Dey retorted, "That's a weak excuse, as there are many poorer men than you who would never give up their children for any gain."

Chamyl insisted, "No, I didn't sell my son. He is still mine."

"No, your son is no longer yours," the Dey declared, "because you haven't shown yourself to be a father deserving of him. For a decade, your son has been under the care of the man to whom you traded him in exchange for a house. Ibrahim has proven himself worthy of the child's affection, and I order that he remain with him. But since you insist on having no one but your son as your heir, I further decree that all your property will pass to him after your death, which is only fair."

Ibrahim then spoke up, saying to the Dey, "My lord, Ormed and I have no need for Chamyl's wealth. What Allah has provided for us is sufficient for our needs. Allow Chamyl the right to choose an heir for himself, perhaps an orphan or a disadvantaged child, whom he may wish to adopt."

The Dey replied firmly, "No, the man who could calmly select one of his own children and trade him for a house can never genuinely care for an orphan or an unfortunate child. I see no reason to change the judgment I have delivered. Ormed will inherit the love of his adopted father and the wealth of his biological one."

Chamyl left, deeply angered by this verdict, which he found unjust but which the people of Algiers considered to be entirely fair.

The next member of the divan addressed Hadgi-Achmet with admiration, saying, "Your wisdom shines through every word you speak. Just listening to you is enough to understand and respect you. We are grateful for your endless patience and kindness. Now, look," he added, "there's a veiled woman, as the law dictates. She accuses her husband of letting her starve, but her husband claims she's lying and provides her with more than enough to eat. He even says she devours her food like a locust from the desert, yet she remains thin and weak, as you can see. The woman insists that her husband barely gives her enough to survive, and she seeks your compassion and justice."

Upon hearing this, Hadgi-Achmet furrowed his brows, and his eyes flashed with intensity as he looked at the man who had just spoken and those gathered for the audience. Then he asked, "Mahmoud, do you maintain that you provide sufficient nourishment for your wife?"

"Yes, my lord," Mahmoud replied.

"And you, woman," the Dey inquired, "do you still claim that your husband leaves you malnourished?"

"Yes, my lord," replied the frail woman, her voice barely audible, as she extended her translucent hands and thin arms in a pleading gesture toward her master and judge.

"Are you poor?" Hadgi-Achmet asked Mahmoud.

"No, my lord," Mahmoud answered, "I could support several wives if I wanted, but I prefer to have only this one in my house."

"Ah, you could support several wives," the Dey noted, "so why don't you give this one everything she desires, even if she were to eat as voraciously as a desert locust?"

"I never deny her anything," Mahmoud insisted.

The veiled woman sighed.

"Well," Hadgi-Achmet continued, "since you are both wealthy and generous, I will grant you the opportunity to defend yourself against such a disgraceful accusation of letting the woman you've married starve. To that end, I order that your wife shall reside in my palace, in the quarters designated for my women, and you will provide her with a stipend that enables her to buy any food she desires. If, after a year of peace and plenty, she still possesses that frail voice and excessive thinness that move my compassion, I will consider her afflicted with an incurable ailment and allow her to return and die in your home. But if, on the other hand, she regains her strength and voice, you will face execution. Not just for violating the law that commands husbands to provide for their wives but more so for lying before your lord and judge, who knows how to punish those who defy him."

Having delivered this verdict, Hadgi-Achmet fixed a menacing gaze on all the men present at the audience. Mahmoud departed, fully aware that he would face execution the following year, and an eerie silence enveloped the room for several minutes.

During this pause, Hadgi-Achmet inquired, "If there are any other matters requiring my judgment, let them be brought forth."

With considerably less self-assuredness and confidence than his colleagues had shown, a fourth member of the divan stepped forward. He addressed Hadgi-Achmet, saying, "My lord, we have a peculiar matter at hand, one that only you can adjudicate.

"These two men before you are twin brothers. They've always shared a deep bond and have never been apart. Recently, their father passed away. After mourning his loss, they agreed, 'Our father's house has been our sanctuary until now; let it continue to shelter us. We shall amicably divide whatever remains - arms, garments, or jewellery.

"But suddenly, an item emerged that defied division and for which no other compensation would suffice. It's a sacred amulet believed to grant wisdom to the one who wears it close to their heart beneath their tunic. Both brothers yearn for wisdom and desire to possess this invaluable heirloom left to them by their father."

Upon hearing these words, Hadgi-Achmet furrowed his brow, and once more, his eyes burned with intensity. He turned to one of the twins, Mozza, and asked, "Mozza, can you not consider giving the amulet to your brother, who desires it so greatly?"

Mozza replied, "No, my lord. I could accept my brother being wealthier than me, but not wiser."

Then, Hadgi-Achmet turned to the other brother, Farzan, and inquired, "Farzan, can you not yield the amulet to your brother, as he wishes?"

Farzan responded, "No, my lord. Wisdom not only bestows earthly possessions but also those belonging to heaven, and it's the latter that I desire above all else."

Hadgi-Achmet then instructed Mozza to wear the cherished amulet close to his heart beneath his tunic. Once this was done, he addressed the young man, saying, "I'm delighted to see that you value wisdom over wealth, for wisdom is of the utmost importance. However, can you not recognize that it is wise to be at peace with your brother, and that, for the sake of this peace, no sacrifice should be too great? To yield to your brother is the beginning and end of wisdom; the one who yields is always the best and the wisest. I am confident that you can now willingly offer this amulet to your brother for the sake of harmony."

Mozza replied, "I repeat, my lord, that I am willing to give up everything to my brother - slaves, diamonds, my house, my entire fortune. But I will never willingly part with this sacred amulet, for it is the only inheritance I desire."

Hadgi-Achmet responded, "Ah, you remain firm in your decision! Very well, then, give me your father's amulet."

Mozza reluctantly handed over the precious talisman to the Dey.

"Farzan," Hadgi-Achmet continued, "wear this amulet close to your heart, beneath your tunic."

Farzan followed the instruction, and as soon as he placed the amulet on his chest, he felt an overwhelming joy. He wanted to embrace his brother, but hesitated, and his eyes sparkled with delight.

"Ah!" exclaimed Hadgi-Achmet, addressing Farzan, "I can see that this amulet has a profound effect on you. It has opened your heart to wisdom, and you will renounce foolish conflicts, won't you? Will you yield to your brother the talisman he desires, which he may need more than you do?"

Farzan responded vehemently, "I would rather die than part with my father's amulet! I am capable of using my dagger against anyone who dares to try and take it from me, no matter who they are."

Hadgi-Achmet sighed and remarked, "Truly, it seems that this amulet falls short of granting all the wisdom you young men believe it possesses. In fact, it appears to sow discord between you, even though you've both worn it close to your hearts. You've held onto your enmity and unjust claims throughout this dispute. That's why I decree that this precious talisman, whose true power is uncertain, shall remain in my palace. In ten years, I will return it to the one of you who has provided the most indisputable proof of piety and virtue through their actions."

Upon hearing this judgment, the two brothers left the palace with heavy hearts. However, once they stepped outside, they quickly reconciled, acknowledging that the Dey's decision was just. From that point on, they lived happily and harmoniously, just as they had before the dispute.

In the meantime, after delivering these four judgments, Hadgi-Achmet furrowed his brow once more and turned to the members of the divan. He addressed them as follows, saying, "I have taken great pleasure in attending to even the smallest matters that concern the well-being and tranquillity of my subjects. I would not regret my time, even if it were spent on even more trivial affairs. Everything that relates to the welfare of those over whom Allah has made me their ruler seems important to me. I have no doubt that you appreciate my actions, and I know that you would rather demonstrate your zeal through deeds rather than words. Therefore, I'm entrusting you with a task that is of great significance to me because it concerns the most vulnerable members of my subjects – the most unfortunate among them. Before the start of Ramadan, I plan to distribute four sacks of rice among elderly men and widows who are in need. Unfortunately, the person who filled these sacks with rice made a mistake and mixed in some oats. I don't want these poor people to feel disrespected by receiving rice mixed with oats. So, I request that charitable hands sift the rice and remove the oats from it. I rely on you to carry out this task, and it will be waiting for you in one of the halls of my palace. At this moment, I can't be there to witness your dedication to obeying my orders and serving the people, but I will join you before your task is complete."

After these words, the Dey had his guards respectfully lead the members of the divan to a large hall where they found four sacks of rice and several baskets.

The members of the divan were convinced that this task was more about their reputations than the rice sacks. They began the unexpected work in silence, with the guards stationed at the hall's entrance where they sifted the rice for the benefit of the poor. Despite their quiet labour, they silently vowed to take revenge on Hadgi-Achmet if they ever had the opportunity.

Later in the day, Hadgi-Achmet joined them. He noticed that one of them was making slower progress than the others and said, "I won't accuse you of lacking zeal. Sometimes, people don't know what they truly want or what they're capable of. I'll help you with your task."

He earnestly began assisting the four members of the divan in sifting the rice for the poor.

Once the task was completed, the four sacks of rice were sealed. Hadgi-Achmet expressed his gratitude to his adversaries and had them escorted respectfully to the gates of his palace.

Alone and facing each other, the four men were filled with dismay and shame. They admitted, "We had intended to ridicule Hadgi-Achmet, but he ended up mocking us. From now on, let's refrain from critiquing his meticulous commitment to justice and instead focus on seeking revenge."

But they never found the opportunity. Hadgi-Achmet, who had begun his career by meticulously mending his old slippers, maintained a firm grip on power. While other Deys of that era often met violent ends by the hands of assassins or poison, Hadgi-Achmet peacefully passed away in his palace after living many long years.

The Bronze Ring

This story has been adapted from Andrew Lang's version of the same tale that originally appeared in The Blue Fairy Book, published in 1889 by Longmans, Green and Co., London and New York. This tale is based on an original taken from Traditions Populaires de l'Asie Mineure by Jean Nicolaides & Émile Carnoy, published by Maisonneuve in 1889.

Once upon a time in a certain country there lived a king whose palace was surrounded by a spacious garden. But, though the gardeners were many and the soil was good, this garden yielded neither flowers nor fruits, not even grass or shady trees. The King was in despair about it when a wise old man said to him, "Your gardeners do not understand their business, but what can you expect of men whose fathers were cobblers and carpenters? How should they have learned to cultivate your garden?"

"You are quite right," cried the King.

"Therefore," continued the old man, "you should send for a gardener whose father and grandfather have been gardeners before him, and very soon your garden will be full of green grass and gay flowers, and you will enjoy its delicious fruit."

So the King sent messengers to every town, village, and hamlet in his dominions, to look for a gardener whose forefathers had been gardeners also, and after forty days one was found.

"Come with us and be gardener to the King," they said to him.

"How can I go to the King," said the gardener, "a poor wretch like me?"

"That is of no consequence," they answered. "Here are new clothes for you and your family."

"But I owe money to several people."

"We will pay your debts," they said.

So the gardener allowed himself to be persuaded, and went away with the messengers, taking his wife and his son with him, and the King, delighted to have found a real gardener, entrusted him with the care of his garden. The man found no difficulty in making the royal garden produce flowers and fruit, and at the end of a year the park was not like the same place, and the King showered gifts upon his new servant.

The gardener, as you have heard already, had a son, who was a very handsome young man, with most agreeable manners, and every day he carried the best fruit of the garden to the King, and all the prettiest flowers to his daughter. Now this princess was wonderfully pretty and was just sixteen years old, and the King was beginning to think it was time that she should be married.

"My dear child," said he, "you are of an age to take a husband, therefore I am thinking of marrying you to the son of my prime minister.

"Father," replied the Princess, "I will never marry the son of the minister."

"Why not?" asked the King.

"Because I love the gardener's son," answered the Princess.

On hearing this the King was at first very angry, and then he wept and sighed, and declared that such a husband was not worthy of his daughter, but the young Princess was not to be turned from her resolution to marry the gardener's son.

Then the King consulted his ministers. "This is what you must do," they said. "To get rid of the gardener you must send both suitors to a very distant country, and the one who returns first shall marry your daughter."

The King followed this advice, and the minister's son was presented with a splendid horse and a purse full of gold pieces, while the gardener's son had only an old lame horse and a purse full of copper money, and everyone thought he would never come back from his journey.

The day before they started the Princess met her lover and said to him, "Be brave and remember always that I love you. Take this purse full of jewels and make the best use you can of them for love of me and come back quickly and demand my hand."

The two suitors left the town together, but the minister's son went off at a gallop on his good horse, and very soon was lost to sight behind the most distant hills. He travelled on for some days, and presently reached a fountain beside which an old woman all in rags sat upon a stone.

"Good day to you, young traveller," said she.

But the minister's son made no reply.

"Have pity upon me, traveller," she said again. "I am dying of hunger, as you see, and I have been here for three days and no one has given me anything."

"Let me alone, old witch," cried the young man, "I can do nothing for you," and so saying he went on his way.

That same evening the gardener's son rode up to the fountain upon his lame grey horse.

"Good day to you, young traveller," said the beggar woman.

"Good day, good woman," answered he.

"Young traveller, have pity upon me."

"Take my purse, good woman," said he, "and mount behind me, for your legs can't be very strong."

The old woman didn't wait to be asked twice, but mounted behind him, and in this style they reached the chief city of a powerful kingdom. The minister's son was lodged in a grand inn, while the gardener's son and the old woman dismounted at the inn for beggars.

The next day the gardener's son heard a great noise in the street, and the King's heralds passed, blowing all kinds of instruments, and crying, "The King, our master, is old and infirm. He will give a great reward to whoever will cure him and give him back the strength of his youth."

Then the old beggar woman said to her benefactor, "This is what you must do to obtain the reward which the King promises. Go out of the town by the south gate, and there you will find three little dogs of different colours, the first will be white, the second black, the third red. You must kill them and then burn them separately and gather up the ashes. Put the ashes of each dog into a bag of its own colour, then go before the door of the palace and cry out, 'A celebrated physician has come from Janina in Albania. He alone can cure the King and give him back the strength of his youth.' The King's physicians will say, 'This is an impostor, and not a learned man,' and they will make all sorts of difficulties, but you will overcome them all at last, and will present yourself before the sick King. You must then demand as much wood as three mules can carry, and a great cauldron, and must shut yourself up in a room with the Sultan, and when the cauldron boils you must throw him into it, and there leave him until his flesh is completely separated from his bones. Then arrange the bones in their proper places and throw over them the ashes out of the three bags. The King will come back to life and will be just as he was when he was twenty years old. For your reward you must demand the bronze ring which has the power to grant you everything you desire. Go, my son, and do not forget any of my instructions."

The young man followed the old beggar woman's directions. When he went out of the town he found the white, red, and black dogs, and killed and burnt them, gathering the ashes in three bags. Then he ran to the palace and cried, "A celebrated physician has just come from Janina in Albania. He alone can cure the King and give him back the strength of his youth."

The King's physicians at first laughed at the unknown wayfarer, but the Sultan ordered that the stranger should be admitted. They brought the cauldron and the loads of wood, and very soon the King was boiling away. Toward mid-day the gardener's son arranged the bones in their places, and he had hardly scattered the ashes over them before the old King revived, to find himself once more younger and heartier.

"How can I reward you, my benefactor?" he cried. "Will you take half my treasures?"

"No," said the gardener's son.

"My daughter's hand?"

"No."

"Take half my kingdom."

"No. Give me only the bronze ring which can instantly grant me anything I wish for."

"Alas!" said the King, "I set great store by that marvellous ring, nevertheless, you shall have it." And he gave it to him.

The gardener's son went back to say goodbye to the old beggar woman, and then he said to the bronze ring, "Prepare a splendid ship in which I may continue my journey. Let the hull be of fine gold, the masts of silver, the sails of brocade, let the crew consist of twelve young men of noble appearance, dressed like kings. St. Nicholas will be at the helm. As to the cargo, let it be diamonds, rubies, emeralds, and carbuncles."

And immediately a ship appeared upon the sea which resembled in every particular the description given by the gardener's son, and, stepping on board, he continued his journey. Presently he arrived at a great town and established himself in a wonderful palace. After several days he met his rival, the minister's son, who had spent all his money and was reduced to the disagreeable employment of a carrier of dust and rubbish. The gardener's son said to him, "What is your name, what is your family, and from what country do you come?"

"I am the son of the prime minister of a great nation, and yet see what a degrading occupation I am reduced to."

"Listen to me, though I don't know anything more about you, I am willing to help you. I will give you a ship to take you back to your own country upon one condition."

"Whatever it may be, I accept it willingly."

"Follow me to my palace."

The minister's son followed the rich stranger, whom he had not recognized. When they reached the palace the gardener's son made a sign to his slaves, who completely undressed the newcomer.

"Make this ring red hot," commanded the master, "and mark the man with it upon his back."

The slaves obeyed him.

"Now, young man," said the rich stranger, "I am going to give you a vessel which will take you back to your own country."

And, going out, he took the bronze ring and said, "Bronze ring, obey your master. Prepare me a ship of which the half rotten timbers shall be painted black, let the sails be in rags, and the sailors infirm and sickly. One shall have lost a leg, another an arm, the third shall be a hunchback, another lame or club footed or blind, and most of them shall be ugly and covered with scars. Go, and let my orders be executed."

The minister's son embarked in this old vessel, and thanks to favourable winds, at length reached his own country. In spite of the pitiable condition in which he returned they received him joyfully.

"I am the first to come back," said he to the King, now fulfil your promise and give me the princess in marriage.

So they at once began to prepare for the wedding festivities. As to the poor princess, she was sorrowful and angry enough about it.

The next morning, at daybreak, a wonderful ship with every sail set came to anchor before the town. The King happened at that moment to be at the palace window.

"What strange ship is this," he cried, "that has a golden hull, silver masts, and silken sails, and who are the young men like princes who man it? And do I not see St. Nicholas at the helm? Go at once and invite the captain of the ship to come to the palace."

His servants obeyed him, and very soon in came an enchantingly handsome young prince, dressed in rich silk, ornamented with pearls and diamonds.

"Young man," said the King, "you are welcome, whoever you may be. Do me the favour to be my guest as long as you remain in my capital."

"Many thanks, sire," replied the captain, "I accept your offer."

"My daughter is about to be married," said the King, "will you give her away?"

"I shall be charmed, sire."

Soon after came the Princess and her betrothed.

"Why, how is this?" cried the young captain, "would you marry this charming princess to such a man as that?"

"But he is my prime minister's son!"

"What does that matter? I cannot give your daughter away. The man she is betrothed to is one of my servants."

"Your servant?"

"Without doubt. I met him in a distant town reduced to carrying away dust and rubbish from the houses. I had pity on him and engaged him as one of my servants."

"It is impossible!" cried the King.

"Do you wish me to prove what I say? This young man returned in a vessel which I fitted out for him, an unseaworthy ship with a black battered hull, and the sailors were infirm and crippled."

"It is quite true," said the King.

"It is false," cried the minister's son. "I do not know this man!"

"Sire," said the young captain, "order your daughter's betrothed to be stripped, and see if the mark of my ring is not branded upon his back."

The King was about to give this order, when the minister's son, to save himself from such an indignity, admitted that the story was true.

"And now, sire," said the young captain, "do you not recognize me?"

"I recognize you," said the Princess, "you are the gardener's son whom I have always loved, and it is you I wish to marry."

"Young man, you shall be my son in law," cried the King. "The marriage festivities are already begun, so you shall marry my daughter this very day."

And so that very day the gardener's son married the beautiful Princess.

Several months passed. The young couple were as happy as the day was long, and the King was more and more pleased with himself for having secured such a son in law.

But, presently, the captain of the golden ship found it necessary to take a long voyage, and after embracing his wife tenderly he embarked.

Now in the outskirts of the capital there lived an old man, who had spent his life in studying black arts - alchemy, astrology, magic, and enchantment. This man found out that the gardener's son had only succeeded in marrying the Princess by the help of the genii who obeyed the bronze ring.

"I will have that ring," said he to himself. So he went down to the seashore and caught some little red fishes. Really, they were quite wonderfully pretty. Then he came back, and, passing before the Princess's window, he began to cry out, "Who wants some pretty little red fishes? "

The Princess heard him, and sent out one of her slaves, who said to the old peddler, "What will you take for your fish?"

"A bronze ring."

"A bronze ring, old simpleton! And where shall I find one?"

"Under the cushion in the Princess's room."

The slave went back to her mistress.

"The old madman will take neither gold nor silver," said she.

"What does he want then? "A bronze ring that is hidden under a cushion."

"Find the ring and give it to him," said the Princess.

And at last the slave found the bronze ring, which the captain of the golden ship had accidentally left behind and carried it to the man, who made off with it instantly.

Hardly had he reached his own house when, taking the ring, he said, "Bronze ring, obey your master. I desire that the golden ship shall turn to black wood, and the crew to hideous ogres, that St. Nicholas shall leave the helm and that the only cargo shall be black cats."

And the genii of the bronze ring obeyed him.

Finding himself upon the sea in this miserable condition, the young captain understood that someone must have stolen the bronze ring from him, and he lamented his misfortune loudly, but that did him no good.

"Alas!" he said to himself, "Whoever has taken my ring has probably taken my dear wife also. What good will it do me to go back to my own country?" And he sailed about from island to island, and from shore to shore, believing that wherever he went everybody was laughing at him, and very soon his poverty was so great that he and his crew and the poor black cats had nothing to eat but herbs and roots. After wandering about a long time he reached an island inhabited by mice. The captain landed upon the shore and began to explore the country. There were mice everywhere, and nothing but mice. Some of the black cats had followed him, and, not having been fed for several days, they were fearfully hungry, and made terrible havoc among the mice.

Then the queen of the mice held a council.

"These cats will eat every one of us," she said, "if the captain of the ship does not shut the ferocious animals up. Let us send a deputation to him of the bravest among us."

Several mice offered themselves for this mission and set out to find the young captain.

"Captain," said they, "go away quickly from our island, or we shall perish, every mouse of us."

"Willingly," replied the young captain, "upon one condition. That is that you shall first bring me back a bronze ring which some clever magician has stolen from me. If you do not do this I will land all my cats upon your island, and you shall be exterminated."

The mice withdrew in great dismay. "What is to be done?" said the Queen. "How can we find this bronze ring?" She held a new council, calling in mice from every quarter of the globe, but nobody knew where the bronze ring was.

Suddenly three mice arrived from a very distant country. One was blind, the second lame, and the third had her ears cropped. "Ho, ho, ho!" said the newcomers. "We come from a far distant country."

"Do you know where the bronze ring is which the genii obey?"

"Ho, ho, ho! We know. An old sorcerer has taken possession of it, and now he keeps it in his pocket by day and in his mouth by night."

"Go and take it from him and come back as soon as possible."

So the three mice made themselves a boat and set sail for the magician's country. When they reached the capital they landed and ran to the palace, leaving only the blind mouse on the shore to take care of the boat. Then they waited till it was night. The wicked old man lay down in bed and put the bronze ring into his mouth, and very soon he was asleep.

"Now, what shall we do?" said the two little animals to each other.

The mouse with the cropped ears found a lamp full of oil and a bottle full of pepper. So she dipped her tail first in the oil and then in the pepper and held it to the sorcerer's nose.

"Atisha! atisha!" sneezed the old man, but he did not wake, and the shock made the bronze ring jump out of his mouth. Quick as thought the lame mouse snatched up the precious talisman and carried it off to the boat.

Imagine the despair of the magician when he awoke and the bronze ring was nowhere to be found!

But by that time our three mice had set sail with their prize. A favouring breeze was carrying them toward the island where the queen of the mice was awaiting them. Naturally they began to talk about the bronze ring.

"Which of us deserves the most credit?" they cried all at once.

"I do," said the blind mouse, "for without my watchfulness our boat would have drifted away to the open sea."

"No, indeed," cried the mouse with the cropped ears, "the credit is mine. Did I not cause the ring to jump out of the man's mouth?"

"No, it is mine," cried the lame one, "for I ran off with the ring."

And from high words they soon came to blows, and alas, when the quarrel was fiercest the bronze ring fell into the sea.

"How are we to face our queen," said the three mice "when by our folly we have lost the talisman and condemned our people to be utterly exterminated? We cannot go back to our country, let us land on this desert island and there end our miserable lives." No sooner said than done. The boat reached the island, and the mice landed.

The blind mouse was speedily deserted by her two sisters, who went off to hunt flies, but as she wandered sadly along the shore she found a dead fish, and was eating it, when she felt something very hard. At her cries the other two mice ran up.

"It is the bronze ring! It is the talisman!" they cried joyfully, and, getting into their boat again, they soon reached the mouse island. It was time they did, for the captain was just going to land his cargo of cats, when a deputation of mice brought him the precious bronze ring.

"Bronze ring," commanded the young man, "obey your master. Let my ship appear as it was before."

Immediately the genii of the ring set to work, and the old black vessel became once more the wonderful golden ship with sails of brocade, the handsome sailors ran to the silver masts and the silken ropes, and very soon they set sail for the capital.

Ah, how merrily the sailors sang as they flew over the glassy sea!

At last the port was reached. The captain landed and ran to the palace, where he found the wicked old man asleep. The Princess clasped her husband in a long embrace. The magician tried to escape, but he was seized and bound with strong cords.

The next day the sorcerer, tied to the tail of a savage mule loaded with nuts, was broken into as many pieces as there were nuts upon the mule's back

Story Of The Rich Man Who Gave His Fair Daughter In Marriage To The Poor Old Man

This story is adapted from Tales From The Arabic, by John Payne, privately published in 1901. This story is based on the Breslau and Calcutta editions of The Book of the Thousand Nights and One Night originally produced between 1814 and 1818. This tale derives from the Breslau text.

There was once a wealthy merchant who had a beautiful daughter, as lovely as the full moon. When she turned fifteen, her father decided to find her a suitable husband. He consulted with an old man and invited him to his home. The merchant welcomed the old man with food and drinks and told him, "I wish to marry my daughter to you."

The old man hesitated because of his own modest means and replied, "I am not worthy of her, nor am I a suitable match for you." The merchant insisted, but the old man said, "I won't agree to this until you explain why you want me. If I find your reason acceptable, I will agree, otherwise, I won't."

The merchant began his story, "I come from China and, in my youth, I was wealthy and good-looking. I paid no attention to women but was more interested in men. Then, one night, I had a dream where a scale was set up, and it said, 'This is the share of a certain person.' I heard my name called, and I saw the most repulsive woman. I woke up terrified, vowing never to marry, fearing that I would end up with such an unpleasant wife. I travelled to this city, where I engaged in trade, made friends, and accumulated wealth. Eventually, I decided to marry, and one day I saw a beautiful house. I stood in front of it, and a lovely woman appeared in the window. I asked around and discovered that the house belonged to a notary in this city.

"I rushed to a man with whom I used to do business, and he helped me reach the notary's house. When I spoke to him, I asked for his daughter's hand in marriage. He claimed that his daughter wasn't suitable for me. I insisted, saying, 'My interest is in you, not your daughter.' But he continued to refuse. His friends argued that I was a suitable match, but he said his daughter was hideous and filled with flaws. I accepted his offer, even if his daughter was as he described. I agreed to marry her, and they asked for a dowry of four thousand dinars. I accepted.

"We arranged the marriage, and I hosted the wedding celebration. However, when I saw my bride on our wedding night, I found her hideous beyond imagination. I thought it was a joke played on me, and I expected to see the woman I had previously glimpsed in the window. However, she never appeared. I laughed it off, assuming her family had played a prank. But as the days went by, I realized she was the same person, and I was in despair. I fasted for three days, refusing to eat.

"My wife noticed my misery and asked me to tell her the whole story. I shared everything with her, and she promised to help me. She revealed that the woman I saw was her slave, and she belonged to me. She decided to offer me her slave and told her to obey me in everything. Afterward, she joined me, and I never touched the slave. Instead, I married her, and she bore me a beautiful daughter.

"My wife shared that many respectable people had sought her daughter's hand in marriage, but I refused them all because I had a dream that revealed she was destined for you. I would rather have you marry her during my lifetime than anyone else after my death."

The poor man agreed to marry the merchant's daughter, and they lived happily together.

The Clever Weaver

This story has been adapted from Andrew Lang's version of the same tale that originally appeared in The Olive Fairy Book, published in 1907 by Longmans, Green and Co., London and New York. This tale is based on an original taken from Contes Arméniens by Frédéric Macler, published in 1905.

Once upon a time the king of a far country was sitting on his throne, listening to the complaints of his people, and judging between them. That morning there had been fewer cases than usual to deal with, and the king was about to rise and go into his gardens, when a sudden stir was heard outside, and the lord high chamberlain entered, and inquired if his majesty would be graciously pleased to receive the ambassador of a powerful emperor who lived in the east and was greatly feared by the neighbouring sovereigns. The king, who stood as much in dread of him as the rest, gave orders that the envoy should be admitted at once, and that a banquet should be prepared in his honour. Then he settled himself again on his throne, wondering what the envoy had to say.

The envoy said nothing. He advanced to the throne where the king was awaiting him, and stooping down, traced on the floor with a rod which he held in his hand a black circle all round it. Then he sat down on a seat that was near and took no further notice of anyone.

The king and his courtiers were equally mystified and enraged at this strange behaviour, but the envoy sat as calm and still as an image, and it soon became plain that they would get no explanation from him. The ministers were hastily summoned to a council, but not one of them could throw any light upon the subject. This made the king angrier than ever, and he told them that unless before sunset they could find someone capable of solving the mystery he would hang them all.

The king was, as the ministers knew, a man of his word, and they quickly mapped out the city into districts, so that they might visit house by house, and question the occupants as to whether they could fathom the action of the ambassador. Most of them received no reply except a puzzled stare, but, luckily, one of them was more observant than the rest, and on entering an empty cottage where a swing was swinging of itself, he began to think it might be worthwhile for him to see the owner. Opening a door leading into another room, he found a second swing, swinging gently like the first, and from the window he beheld a patch of corn, and a willow which moved perpetually without any wind, in order to frighten away the sparrows. Feeling more and more curious, he descended the stairs and found himself in a large light workshop in which was seated a weaver at his loom. But all the weaver did was to guide his threads, for the machine that he had invented to set in motion the swings and the willow pole made the loom work.

When he saw the great wheel standing in the corner, and had guessed the use of it, the merchant heaved a sigh of relief. At any rate, if the weaver could not guess the riddle, he at least might put the minister on the right track. So without more ado he told the story of the circle, and ended by declaring that the person who could explain its meaning should be handsomely rewarded.

"Come with me at once," he said. "The sun is low in the heavens, and there is no time to lose."

The weaver stood thinking for a moment and then walked across to a window, outside of which was a hen coop with two knuckle bones lying beside it. These he picked up, and taking the hen from the coop, he tucked it under his arm.

"I am ready," he answered, turning to the minister.

In the hall the king still sat on his throne, and the envoy on his seat. Signing to the minister to remain where he was, the weaver advanced to the envoy, and placed the knuckle bones on the floor beside him. For answer, the envoy took a handful of millet seed out of his pocket and scattered it round, upon which the weaver set down the hen, who ate it up in a moment. At that the envoy rose without a word and took his departure.

As soon as he had left the hall, the king beckoned to the weaver.

"You alone seem to have guessed the riddle," said he, "and great shall be your reward. But tell me, I pray you, what it all means?"

"The meaning, O king," replied the weaver, "is this. The circle drawn by the envoy round your throne is the message of the emperor, and signifies, 'If I send an army and surround your capital, will you lay down your arms?' The knuckle bones which I placed before him told him, 'You are but children in comparison with us. Toys like these are the only playthings you are fit for.' The millet that he scattered was an emblem of the number of soldiers that his master can bring into the field, but by the hen which ate up the seed he understood that one of our men could destroy a host of theirs."

"I do not think," he added, "that the emperor will declare war."

"You have saved me and my honour," cried the king, "and wealth and glory shall be heaped upon you. Name your reward, and you shall have it even to the half of my kingdom."

"The small farm outside the city gates, as a marriage portion for my daughter, is all I ask," answered the weaver, and it was all he would accept. "Only, O king," were his parting words, "I would beg of you to remember that weavers also are of value to a state, and that they are sometimes cleverer even than ministers!"

The Croesus Of Yemen

This story has been adapted from Henry Iliowizi's version of the same tale that originally appeared in The Weird Orient, published in 1900 by Henry T. Coates and Company, Philadelphia.

Sanaa, the capital of Yemen, is one of the noblest cities of Arabia Felix, and is said to rival beautiful Damascus in many of her exquisite features. The Imam of Yemen who ruled in the beginning of this century could claim rank among the most whimsical princes who ever sat on a throne. He was a man of weak intellect, strong passion, boundless vanity, and a religious enthusiasm entirely foreign to his subjects, who are indifferent followers of Mohammed. That eccentric Commander of the Faithful conceived the singular fancy that he was animated by the soul of the last Prophet, and he suited his conduct to his conceit, there being no one to dispute his ludicrous presumption. He dressed in green, sermonized his people in the style of the Koran, read surahs of his own creation, raved of his nocturnal visits to heaven, descanted on visions and revelations vouchsafed to him, and scrupulously arranged his household in imitation of Mohammed's, not forgetting the seventeen wives of the founder of Islam, including an Ayesha, who was the power behind the Imam's throne, being the flower of his harem.

The most important person who stood next to the Imam in power, and above him in wisdom, was the great Kadi, or judge, Omar, who presided over the supreme court of Sanaa, and was in fact the walking code and cyclopia of Yemen. What he did not know only Allah and His Prophet could reveal. The wise Kadi had no doubt at all that the Imam was a spiritual duplicate of the true Prophet, and he received in recognition the proud title of the "Lion of God," reminiscent of Mohammed's most devoted champion who fought his battles and died sword in hand.

Omar plied his legal profession so well, had so many questions of justice and equity referred to him from every quarter of the land, that he rose to be the wealthiest Moslem of Sanaa, exceeded in his opulence by one man only, and that was the renowned Ben Abir, surnamed "The Croesus of Yemen." Ben Abir was no Moslem, but a Hebrew, and one who feared nothing so much as the remote likelihood of slighting his faith.

The Imam's ruling passion for prophetic honours was equalled by his unprophetic mania for building monumental structures with an extravagance which drained his treasure. Lacking the vast resources of the Caliph of Istanbul, the prince of Yemen nevertheless aspired to rival the head of the faithful in the monumental magnificence of his great capital, and immense sums were lavished on the embellishments of a city which was meant to dazzle even the strangers who had wondered at the imperial palaces of the mighty Sultan himself. The drawback was the limited revenues of the Imam's domains, and the shrewd Kadi, forestalling the danger of a royal recourse to his riches, was instrumental in causing his master to draw on Ben Abir for large sums, in return for titles and privileges which enabled the misused Israelite to indemnify himself in a measure for advances he never expected to see returned. Unlimited in the extent of his commercial enterprises and furnished with as many military escorts as he chose to ask for, Ben Abir's caravans carried loads of silk, cotton, hardware, weapons, and trinkets as far as Hadramaut, Hejaz and Nejd, fearless of the dangers of the Tehamah and the deathful simoons of the arid desert, and they returned to the seashore with tons of coffee, packs of gum, ostrich feathers, dyes, and pearls, which foreign vessels carried to distant lands. To all this Ben Abir added the breeding of the finest Arabian horses, such as are only found in Nejd, and it became a current saying that whatever the Croesus of Yemen touched turned into gold.

Now, it happened that, previous to the closing celebration of the Ramadhan Fast, Ben Abir presented his sovereign with one of his choicest Nejdi stallions, of spotless white and a most fiery temper, caparisoned in the most approved fashion. Delighted with the gift, the Imam showed his appreciation by mounting the spirited animal on the solemn occasion brought about by the sacrificial ceremony which marks the close of the Fast. As ill luck would have it, a distracted saint, who had just issued from his cave looking more like a chimpanzee than a human being, threw himself in the way of the stallion with a yell that frightened both horse and rider. Snorting and balking in recoil from the object of terror, the high-spirited creature reared and fell backward injuring the Kadi, who was behind, and landing the second edition of the Prophet on a rock, with a broken leg and a dislocated jaw as mementos of the inauspicious incident. Somebody had to be burdened with the blame, and the Kadi realized his opportunity. As soon as sufficiently recovered from his own hurts to sit in judgment, Omar declared Ben Abir guilty of high treason for having tempted the Imam to mount a mad horse, and condemned him to perish by decapitation, unless he should ransom his life for a fabulous sum, which was named, with the additional condition that it be paid in solid gold. Within twenty-four hours the gold was in the hands of the Imam's treasurer, and Ben Abir was a poor man.

When Ayesha, the flower of the royal harem, who was of Hebraic origin, heard of the Kadi's sentence, she appealed to her prophetic lord's conscience against the flagrant injustice. The Imam was moved to the extent of offering to return a small portion of the robbery, provided the Hebrew would enter the mosque. Ben Abir would not listen to the thought of such treason to the God of his fathers and had a brave wife to sustain him in his trial, with two children, one an ineffably charming maiden, to comfort him. Nor was he entirely destitute, his commercial credit remaining good.

In one of the mountain ranges of Yemen one Friday afternoon, as the sun began to approach the rim of the horizon, a small caravan made a halt. The dromedaries were freed from their burdens and allowed to browse, and a dark tent was stretched for the use of the master of the caravan. On a matting on the ground a rug was spread and a few pillows were put thereon for the ease of a middle-aged person who, dismounting from his horse, took possession of the transient resting place. As soon as he found himself within the tent he washed himself with water drawn from the nearest spring, changed his garments, brought forth a silver lamp, which he filled with oil, a silver flask full of wine, and a goblet of the same metal. With nightfall the lamp illumined the tent, and the inmate stood lost in prayer, with his face turned to the east. A blessing uttered over the wine was followed by a frugal meal, and the rest of the evening was spent in study of sacred lore. At the entrance to the tent, near a spear struck into the soil, stood a black sentry, while at a distance the camel drivers made themselves comfortable for the night. The lord of the caravan was Ben Abir, his sentinel was Ibraeem, a freed slave, who, having been treated kindly by his master in his happier days, would not desert him now that fortune declined to smile on him.

The night was very dark and would have been voiceless but for the sighs and moans of the dromedaries, who seemed audibly to commiserate one with another upon the hardships of life. About midnight the silence was unbroken, the discontented animals having buried their sense of trouble in dreamless sleep. At this hour Ben Abir was roused by his faithful attendant, who informed him of a great marvel that was to be seen before the tent. A heap of gold cropped up from the ground, each coin scintillating like a star.

"Rise, O, master! Allah sends you a treasure," cried the devoted slave.

"What is it you are raving of, O, Ibraeem! Are you dreaming?" said Ben Abir.

"Indeed I am wide awake, O, master! Step forth and trust to your own senses if you doubt mine, here is the hoard Allah would have you take," insisted Ibraeem.

As Ben Abir peered out of his tent to convince himself of Ibraeem's illusion, he saw with amazement a golden pile of coin, the pieces glowing like lupine eyes in the dark. This is a temptation of the evil one, thought the scrupulous Israelite, who would not have touched pelf on his Sabbath for the wealth of the Indies.

"Touch not a piece of this hoard, Oh, Ibraeem! If you fear Allah, and would not disobey Ben Abir. If the treasure is to be mine, it will remain where it is till after my Sabbath, if it be not mine, the breaking of my holy day will not save it for me. What is to be, will be. Go to sleep," closed the pious Yemenite, and retired to his couch, Ibraeem, after a little natural hesitation, doing likewise. What right, after all, had he to question the deep wisdom and deeper faith of his generous master?

But sleep would not return to Ben Abir. Through the coarse goat hair texture that made up the covering of his tent the glittering mass stared at him like so many living eyes, and he felt a chill run through the marrow of his bones. While he was at a loss to explain how the glare of the hoard penetrated the opaque material of his tent, a new wonder diverted his attention. An inclined plane, broad as a valley and smooth as glass, stretched down from the deep heavens with both ends lost, one among the starry configurations, the other in the unfathomed abysses of the nether world. The only irregularity in the sweep of the prodigious highway was a terrace which made a connecting link between the upper and the lower part of the plane. In the heart of the terrace shone the hoard which a while before had been seen before the tent.

Ben Abir doubted not that there was an evil design at the back of this marvellous display, but he felt safe in the consciousness of his firm loyalty. His feeling of safety, however, was somewhat shaken by a terrific detonation, like the eruption of a volcano. It was the signal for a numberless host to ascend towards the terrace, who, dividing and subdividing, started to march up in frowning armies to the sound of wailing notes, clarions and clashing cymbals mixing with a chaos of noise produced by all the instruments of music known. The vanguard was made up of a serried division of vicious ghouls whose march resembled more the dance of droll harlequins than the pace of warriors. At their heels came a vast herd of monstrous bipeds, with head, tail, and hoofs of the boar, making the air shudder with their hideous grunts, and piercing the sable of night with their grim eyes. Next followed a division of bipedal beasts, rolling fiery eyeballs, striking their sides with tails like those of lions, and rending the atmosphere with roars of fury. Back of these came bounding an enormous pack of bellowing hell hounds, each one a Cerberus, armed with the deadly teeth and claws of the tiger. Close behind tramped an appalling herd of deformities, hunch backed elephants, with raised trunks that were hissing serpents, and tusks which reached down to the ground tearing up fragments of rock and hurling them against the terrace with diabolic fury. The rear was taken up by a grisly multitude of animated skeletons, who yelled, grinned, laughed, and danced, drawing up and thrusting out their bony limbs with wriggling motion, and varying the infernal performance by a series of somersaults. Back of all burst a deluge of red fire which shot with raging impetuosity among the hellish monsters, who instead of being deterred appeared to derive strength from the consuming element. But fierce as was the rush against the terrace, beyond its outer limits the demons could not pass.

Meanwhile, on the upper extension of the celestial highway there was a quick mustering of radiant squadrons, and an array of embattled lines which extended beyond the remotest galaxies. The summons had gone forth to be ready for the infernal invader, and the denizens of the stars responded in unnumbered myriads. Signals flashed from height to height and save the warning note of a trumpet faintly heard now and then, the pregnant silence of the ethereal combatants contrasted strangely with the fiendish defiance of the howling goblins.

The moments of suspense were intensified by the swelling of the hoard to amazing dimensions, not that the coins multiplied, but they grew in size and in lustre, until each one resembled the solar disk. It was no more a pile, but a pyramid, of gold set in a frame of thickening darkness.

A peal of thunder from on high was the sign for the encounter. Like a sea of lightning, the radiant vanguard swept down the terrace with a mien so dreadful and weapons so deterring that the black divisions fled in horror before the blasting might that shook the deeps to the foundation.

With all his attention concentrated on the engagement, Ben Abir had not seen that a cherub stood before him one of those precious disks in his hand, until the apparition spoke. "So much is you, O, righteous Ben Abir! The rest will come," were the mystic words of the benign power.

Ben Abir could not accept the gift without stretching his arms to their full length and found it impossible to hold it the moment his hands closed round the edge of the fiery wheel. Finding the priceless treasure was slipping from his grasp he called for Ibraeem to help.

"What is it you would have me do for you, master?" asked the attendant when roused from his sound sleep.

"Have I called you, Ibraeem? Yes, I did call you, but it was all a dream, a dream as awful as the vision of Jacob in the wilderness. How far advanced is the night? Is there anything left of the golden hoard?" inquired Ben Abir.

"The camels are astir, and the east is grey, but the gold is all gone, master, all gone. Had we taken it, you would again be the Croesus of Yemen," said Ibraeem, regretfully. "We ought to have taken it, ought we not?"

"It is well that we kept our hands from it, it was a temptation held out by the evil one, Ibraeem, who lures man into error. What is to be will be. Let me be alone for a little space, I am somewhat perturbed," concluded Ben Abir, who wished to think over his unearthly vision.

With eyes closed, the Hebrew endeavoured to recall the dark and bright phantoms of the night, pondering what it all might mean. And that hoard, which his humble servant had witnessed and referred to, had been too tangible a reality to be transferred to the domain of the spectral.

The radiant flood gates of heaven's light oceans opened wide. The Orient was ablaze with the glories of an early sunrise, which had been initiated by waves of gilded crimson, and Arabia Felix rose from a transcendental dream to bathe in dew as brilliant as the pearls of Halool and Katar. The air vibrated with the joyous notes of the feathered freebooters, there were the finch, the lark, and the thrush to lead in the matin concert, and the beautifully crested hoopoe, on whom Solomon bestowed a golden crown for services rendered him in the desert and for messages carried between His Majesty and Belkeys, the Queen of Sheba. Sweet was the scent of the air, and the sparkling dew was as yet unabsorbed by the glowing heat of the rising day.

Ben Abir issued from his tent to feel that nature donned her festal robes in honour of the Sabbath blessed of his Lord. Was it not his soul that made him realize the holiness of God's creation? How different the world looked to him on weekdays. But think of whatever he might, before his mental gaze still soared his vision undispelled by the cheer of sunshine and life. His heart throbbed with prophetic apprehension. Who was wise enough to enlighten him?

However, the day was passed in worship and study, and at the sight of the first three stars in the firmament, the scrupulous Ben Abir bade his farewell to the Sabbath by the blessing uttered over a cup of wine, and lantern in hand, proceeded to search the spot whereupon the golden hoard had been seen on the previous night. One gold piece only he found on turning up the sand with the tip of his sandal, but it was enough to make his heart flutter, conscious that the coin in his hand was not of human make. Returning to his tent, the precious piece was deposited on a pillow with a trembling hand, when lo, the thing began to dilate and grow in brilliance, until it reached the size and shape of the golden disk he had in his vision received from an angel's hand. Ben Abir bit his thumb to assure himself that he was awake. Was it not another illusion? To the touch it was an ordinary coin, to the eye it had the form of a mighty targe of burnished gold.

"It is mine, and I shall keep it as the secret and talisman of my life, a gift of the Most High, blessed be He!" whispered the loyal Israelite, and the mysterious coin was carefully wrapped up and put away.

The early dawn of the first day of the week found Ben Abir's caravan winding its way amid a wilderness of tropic vegetation and scattered rocks, but the tide of fortune still turned against him. Torrents of rain impeded the march of his camels and damaged the goods he depended on for the success of his journey. While the dromedaries were in the act of crossing a bridge the span gave way and three of the poor brutes went down never to rise again, and to complete his ruin, fire broke out at the caravansary where he had hoped to find refuge from the weather's inclemencies, and he had good cause to be grateful even for escape from death in the flames that consumed the remnant of his merchandise, largely secured on credit. The Croesus of Yemen found himself on the brink of poverty, a ruined man with a crowd of creditors to lodge him in one of Sanaa's abominable prisons. He knew the Kadi who would speak the sentence, and he prepared to face the inevitable, trusting that something would happen to render his painful situation bearable.

There lived at this time another person in Sanaa who actually rejoiced at the disgrace and impoverishment of Ben Abir, and this contrary both to his own temper, and to the popular sympathies with a man who in his better days alleviated human misery to the best of his ability. That exception was Hayem Cordosa. The cause of the ill feeling in Cordosa's breast was an unhappy, one-sided romance, which had driven his son, Menahem, to desperation. Until a certain morning that youth had but one dream, and that was knowledge. It was the fateful moment when he chanced to meet in the street an exquisitely lovely boy mounted on a pony in charge of a slave. The child's silken locks were darker than the weathered face of his attendant, his complexion was like milk and blood, his lips reminded one of the red coral, his teeth of the purest pearl, while his eyes suggested the dreams of angels in realms of ineffable felicity. A few questions put to the slave brought the information that infinitely fairer than the child was his elder sister Estrelia. In the glow of his loyal admiration Ibraeem, who had the child in charge, portrayed to the interested youth a maiden who was more beautiful than the Peri of Yemen. So great was her beauty that her pellucid witchery shone through her veil, while her perfect form would have been envied by the graces of antiquity. Ibraeem did not think that he exaggerated matters by assuring Menahem that Estrelia's loveliness illumined the apartments of her privacy, and that her eyes would enchant the deadly rukta. If the youth had any doubt about it, the cherub like sweetness of her little brother dispelled the doubt.

Menahem was not a youth to be despised. His fidelity to principle was as great as his learning in sacred literature was deep. He felt justified in offering his heart to Ben Abir's daughter, but met with a rebuff, and became desperate. The erstwhile cheerful youth grew gloomy, courted seclusion, brooded on vengeance, and finally resorted to the extremity of deserting his faith, to the great sorrow of his scrupulously religious parents. It was a mad step, but there was method in the madness. The apostate put himself under the protection of Omar, and the learned Kadi presented him to his royal master as a convert to Islam, the Imam received him with favour, assured him of a seat in Paradise, and made him his cup bearer. Menahem was where he wished to be, but Cordosa hated the house of Ben Abir.

It was during the last trip of the fallen Croesus of Yemen that the convert took an opportunity to speak to the Imam of the maiden who had driven him mad, and he spoke of her as the "luminous Peri of Yemen, whose radiant beauty enlightens Ben Abir's home."

Under ordinary circumstances there was not a thing within the boundaries of his dominion the Imam would hesitate to lay hand on if he deemed its possession desirable. In this especial case the remembrance of a broken leg and dislocated jaw seemed to justify any step calculated to afford some recompense for those injuries which gave the aspirant to prophetic veneration a hideous aspect.

When consulted in the matter, the Kadi failed to see it in any other light "You are the blessed rebirth of the last prophet, the prince of this great land, and there is no power in the heavens to interfere with your right, O, commander of the faithful, when you see fit to save a soul from perdition. As to the increase in your harem beyond the number consecrated by the will of Mohammed, your servant will be grateful for any of your Houris, if you deign to transfer her to the humbler home of your devoted Kadi," was Omar's suggestion.

Had the secret remained among its originators and been carried out promptly, the fate of Estrelia would have been sealed, but the removal of one from the Imam's harem put Ayesha on her mettle. She suspected a new arrival, and, having fathomed the mind of Yemen's lord, she was alarmed at the prospect of being eclipsed by superior charms, thus forfeiting her hitherto undisputed rule, and she lost no time in apprising the right persons of Estrelia's imminent danger. Thus did it come to pass that when, led by the apostate, the minions of the prince descended on Ben Abir's unprotected home, they had to report that their nocturnal invasion had been a failure. The "luminous peri of Yemen" had been warned in time.

For a man already under the pressure of great trials to return from a ruinous trip and be greeted by the news of his child's disappearance, is an experience more readily imagined than described. The last visitation was too overwhelming even for the Job like resignation of Ben Abir. His only comfort was his wife's assurance that Estrelia was not in the seraglio of the Imam. She had been carried away by two men in disguise through a back door, barely escaping the grasp of the vandals who knocked for admission in the front. The mother was so panic stricken that she failed to remember the names of the persons who had come to the rescue of her child, and she had not heard from them since, but she felt sure that everything would turn out right.

In his brighter days Ben Abir would have invoked the power of his sovereign to effect the restitution of his daughter, but matters had changed, and circumstances dictated prudence on his part. Imam and Kadi were alike interested in his ruin. To search quietly, wait patiently, hope and pray, were the only ways and means compatible with his safety. Besides, there were impatient creditors to be appeased and starvation at the door. The princely home had to be disposed of, but this afforded small relief. Whatever he touched, success was his adversary.

"If I made it my business to bury the dead, not a death would for years occur in the city of Sanaa," remarked the disappointed man to his wife.

The last trinket had been sold to keep the wolf away from the door, and now hunger stared his wife and child in the face. The devoted Ibraeem did his utmost to relieve the want of his master's family, but his fidelity was more of a comfort than a support. With the pride of a man who would rather die than appeal for help, Ben Abir yet had finally to yield to the entreaties of a starving wife. There remained but one thing for him to do, a bitter pill for him to swallow, and he acted like a man. Twice a year it was Cordosa's business to lead a caravan to one of Yemen's ports to exchange Arabian products for merchandise imported for the markets of the peninsula. What he did not do on his own account he did on commission for others. The leading merchants of Sanaa charged him with the purchase of their wares, and their commissions were all entered in a book to be referred to in due time.

The resources of Ben Abir having been exhausted, he remembered the precious coin he had sewed up in the hem of his coarse mantle, and he resolved to ask Cordosa to invest it for him in whatever way he should deem profitable. Curbing his pride he sought an interview with his enemy, made a frank statement of his pinching indigence, and requested Cordosa to buy for the only piece of gold he had in the world anything that could be sold in Sanaa. Ben Abir's sad plight and frankness moved Cordosa's heart, who not alone promised to do his best in the matter of business but insisted on relieving the distress of the fallen man's family. The reconciliation was complete, and the generous commissioner set out on his journey, accompanied by the best wishes of Ben Abir, and those who expected his return with more than usual interest.

The six long lines of dromedaries of Cordosa's caravan, each file held together by a hair rope, were preceded by a snow-white donkey of the best breed in Hasa, good luck being insured by that philosophic animal who gave Balaam a lesson. To the left of the sagacious quadruped rode the regular guide, a Bedouin who felt at home in the trackless waste, to the right, astride of a fine steed, was the Karawan Bashi, the caravan commander, a gorgeous display of gaudy trimmings, trappings, jingling bells, and tassels, in which, however, he was greatly eclipsed by the leading ass. At the Bashi's left side dangled a sword of Damascus, sheathed in a scabbard, and his warlike temper was formidably impressed on all whom it concerned by a spear of unusual length. Behind these three leaders, varying in their capacity, on his horse came Cordosa, the master of the caravan. Between the guide and the Karawan Bashi there was a tacit understanding to while away the monotony of the trip by tales of adventure in the desert, which they told with startling vividness, each one managing to pose as the hero of some thrilling episode.

After the usual number of days, and the accidents incidental to a journey through inhospitable regions, Cordosa reached the point of his destination. Here the unexpected happened to the experienced commissioner. Following his memoranda, he left no detail of business unattended to, except the order of Ben Abir, which he had omitted to enter on his book. As the caravan was on the point of proceeding homeward, Cordosa remembered Ben Abir's request, and felt guilty. Full of self-reproach, he turned to the Karawan Bashi and required him to hurry to the bazaar and buy for the gold piece he gave him anything he thought profitable or useful. The order was carried out to the letter, to the great mortification of Cordosa. The Karawan Bashi happened to meet a sailor, who had a cage full of Angola cats for sale, and proposing to strike a bargain, offered the gold piece in exchange for the feline colony, was taken at his word, and thus possessed himself of the freaky livestock. The sailor's tale was brief. The animals had kept a large vessel free of mice, the ship had foundered, the seaman saved the cats. He had nothing to live on.

It was a straight story. The vendor had the gold and Cordosa the cats. The only thing to be done was to take the feline company along.

Again the unexpected happened to Cordosa. For many days everything went on without a hitch, when the Karawan Bashi and the guide informed him that the high land they were traversing was entirely unknown to them, and that they did not know how they had come into it. "What I see around me I have never before seen, and I have led a hundred caravans across the width and breadth of Yemen," asserted the most experienced guide, and the Bashi shook his head significantly.

"And have you perceived the singular fact, that though the country hereabout resembles the garden of Eden, we have this long day not seen a single sign of life," said Cordosa, not undisturbed in his mind.

"Allah Akbar! What sea is it there we are drawing nearer to?" asked the Bashi in alarm. "A big water in the mountain!"

"By the beard of the Prophet, how can a big water climb up a mountain?" ejaculated the astonished guide.

"What you see is no water, but a heavy fog, which looks like water," corrected Cordosa, much surprised however at the phenomenal denseness of the cloud.

"True, it is a fog, but I have never seen one that looked so much like a rolling tide threatening to engulf us. Everything that is alive seems to have fled before we entered this region," observed the guide, apprehensively.

And a strange fog it was, which rolled forward like a tidal wave, and before long buried the caravan in a cloud so dense that one could not see his own feet, and the men became alarmed lest they go down unwarned over the brink of some precipice. The camels were allowed to grope their way, the guide having given up the idea of guiding, and the long string of animals progressed slowly amid a flood of vapor with nothing to vary the nerve trying suspense for fully an hour. Everything and everybody was soaked by the moisture, the air did not stir, and the stillness was oppressive. At last there was a rift in the hitherto impenetrable mass, and when a breeze lifted the fog, Cordosa rubbed his eyes to assure himself of being awake.

"Do you see what I see?" asked he of the Karawan Bashi.

"And what do you see, O, man, who have traversed the Red Desert?" asked in turn the Bashi of the guide.

"I see, high up, a city of marble palaces with roofs of silver and balconies of gold, as glorious as Balbec and Chilminar," cried the guide, enthusiastically.

"That is what I see, we have been lured into the domain of the genii, and harm will betide us if we fail to evade their crafty wiles," answered the Bashi, nervously.

"If we do not flee the malicious Div will hurl us into one of those bottomless chasms which swarm with venomous serpents," warned the guide.

"We must try to retrace our course, or the bird of prey and the hyena will pick the flesh from our bones," said the Bashi, in a mood of dark prophecy.

"Is it not God who rules this world and the stars? How can you be sure that evil will befall us if we enter that place? We are men of faith and stout hearts, and I propose that we proceed toward that dazzling city, no matter who they be who inhabit it," was Cordosa's fearless proposition.

"You shall not find me craven if there is danger to face. The point of this spear has been buried in the body of the lion, and this heel has bruised the head of the rukta, and if there be the evil one, I will face him," exclaimed the Karawan Bashi.

"Neither is your guide of the stuff that shrinks before spectres, however monstrous. Let us meet those who have built that marvellous city," cried the guide heroically, and toward the city the caravan advanced.

It was that hour of the day when the lengthened shadows indicate the descent of the glowing orb, but the striking absence of bird or insect in a quarter where every inducement for their presence was to be seen in abundance gave the surroundings an air of desolation, and produced the sensation experienced by him who suddenly lights on a corpse. A broad avenue shaded by treble lines of orange trees in blossom, diffusing delicious odours, led up to a high portal giving admission to a vast enclosure walled by grey stones perfectly fitted by masterful hands, a fortress looking as new as though the masons had just given it the finishing touch. The wall was not high enough to hide the gorgeous edifices within, but the wayfarers pricked their ears in vain to catch a sound of life, the quiet being that of the graveyard.

"This is a dead city," observed the guide, in the hope of shaking the courage of Cordosa, "perhaps the desolate city was built by the son of Ad."

"They are not dead at night who are dead during the day," added the Karawan Bashi, with a similar object in view.

"God is strong enough to afford us protection against all evil powers. Here may be a mystery we are destined to solve. Knock at the gate for admission," ordered Cordosa peremptorily.

"Allah illaha il Allah!" cried the Bashi, seized with a fit of unflinching heroism. "I will knock at the gate with my scabbard, be the place under the rule of grim Monkir, the faithful need not be afraid of the creatures of Eblis."

The rap on the gate gave forth a hollow sound in response, yet the gateway opened with a jar, revealing a scene at which the intruders gazed with amazement. Sheddad's garden of Irem could hardly equal the vernal luxuriance which hid the foundations of the wonderful buildings. Scattered here and there, among delightful flower beds and thick clusters of the luscious vine, stood groups of fairies motionless, so handsome that their cheeks rivalled the rose in sweetness. They were all barefooted, their little feet resembling those of children. For headgear they wore crowns of golden hair, their garb was a transparent gauze, shining like moonlight, and bespangled with gold, and they were all armed with spears of that precious metal. Awful was their silence, their expression yet showing an intense anxiety to utter speech. The gate slammed to with its jarring note as soon as the last camel was within the precincts, and the Yemenites shuddered at the realization of their being locked in a dead city.

Overcome by the awe of the surroundings, Cordosa exclaimed, "Great Lord, protect us!" Hereupon the whole mountain experienced a tremor, shared by the life like fairies, who appeared to shiver at the mention of the Supreme.

It being sunset, Cordosa directed the Bashi and the guide to take the caravan to the nearest khan, and the next moment the travellers entered a caravansary, compared to which the Asaad Pasha of Damascus is but an insignificant hostelry. They found the gate ajar, and within there was plenty of provender, and a playing fountain to quench the thirst of man and brute. A sumptuous divan furnished with the costliest rugs of silk, and such seats as are only reserved for caliphs, tempted the Arabs to rest their weary limbs, while the odours of savory viands betrayed the neighbourhood of a culinary institution of the highest order. Following the scent they entered a prodigious banquet hall of imperial splendour. On low tables a royal feast was set in glittering crystal under covers of gold. On the right side of each service lay a golden rod not unlike the sceptre of a king. Scores of fairies stood around in the attitude of attendants eager to serve, but stiff and lifeless as mummies, dead beauty radiating from their faces of immaculate purity.

Hunger yielded to temptation, and the Bashi's example was followed by the others, except Cordosa who, lost in wonder, would not avail himself of the magnificent hospitality impliedly offered by beings who to all appearances were dead, or if not dead then strangely enchanted for some unaccountable purpose.

Neither had the others time to appease the cravings of their appetites, for no sooner was the first dish uncovered than a multitudinous rustling, tripping and squeaking caused the astonished guests to turn their eyes toward the door, when lo, and behold, thick swarms of silvery mice came rushing and tumbling one over the other, and, flying up the limbs of the horrified men, as squirrels are often seen to run up trees, they devoured in the twinkling of an eye whatever had been laid bare to their voracity. The sumptuous banquet was turned into a scene of horror and disgust, the more so since the pests seemed heedless of those who were present and callous to the blows which were dealt them with the golden rods that were apparently there for that purpose.

"Bring the cats here," commanded Cordosa. And as the cage was brought forth and opened the cats leapt forth like tigers wild for prey. But nimble as pussy is, the agility of her game left her without a chance to do mischief. Quick as the vermin had appeared, they much more quickly disappeared, as though the swarms had been nothing but flitting shadows.

Before it was possible to restore the animals to their cage, Cordosa and his subordinates were not only startled by the sudden animation of the fairies in the banquet hall, but a muffled roar, as of a victorious army without, made them feel instinctively that a great change had come over the dwellers of the magic city. It was a tumult that stirred the air far and wide, was echoed and re-echoed, until the hills were vocal with the ringing vibrations of countless voices. Before a question could be asked, in marched a legion of those admirable creatures, who but a little before had been seen in a state of inanimation. Arraying themselves in military form, they presented arms and made a profound salaam in evident honour of Cordosa, thus acknowledging his title to their respect. With that unfailing politeness, which is the exquisite quality of the refined Oriental, the Hebrew begged to be informed why he was made the object of this distinguished attention. "Because you have broken the spell which for many hundred years held the denizens of this city enthralled by enchantment," was the answer.

There was a genial affability in the demeanour of the child like representatives of the city's population, so that the fear of their being malicious genii vanished, and a confiding intercourse took the place of shrinking suspicion. The story they told of their origin and subsequent enchantment is one of romance, necromancy, and dire vengeance. It is briefly as follows:

Lilithiana, the Peri Queen of the mountains of Yemen, had, in ages gone by, been wooed by the then two mighty magicians of Africa, known as El Akbor and Metemhagi. El Akbor was dreaded as the master of all the rodent species, which he had often sent on expeditions of destruction to avenge wrongs or to satisfy malice. There was no escape from the instruments of his ire. Persons and property were bitten, torn, and destroyed according to his order. The only power he feared was Metemhagi, who ruled all the feline tribes, and could be appealed to against the plague his rival was in a position to inflict. Long and assiduous was the courtship of the two necromancers, and the love contest closed with Lilithiana's declared preference for Metemhagi.

The Peri Queen controlled the untold wealth hidden in the mountains of her domain, was mistress of all the genii within the bounds of her empire and concluded to build an enchanted city accessible to none but her progeny. A host of her aerial subjects received orders to carry out their Queen's behest, and the city of marble, silver and gold was the result of one hour's workmanship. Here the queenly Peri retired with her mortal adorer, and an impenetrable zone of cloud was thrown around the region that had the weird city as its centre.

Lilithiana was not long to enjoy her marital felicity. Her intimacy with a mortal deprived her of the power over Yemen's genii, and the angel, who centuries before had expelled her from Paradise for a slight trespass, descended to inform her that her sin would be visited on her guiltless offspring, her own punishment being exile and separation from her dear ones. Aware of the Peri's fall and disgrace, El Akbor assumed the deterring form of a monstrous rat and, embracing his opportunity, threw himself among the genii of Lilithiana's realm during a dance in the moonlight. The shock transformed them into a swarm of silvery mice, and the magician having thus gained power over them, uttered another incantation, causing the whilom airy beings to raven with an insatiate hunger. This gluttony made them the terror of Lilithiana's descendants, who were doomed hereafter to live only from sunset to sunrise, held by witchcraft the rest of the time in a death like trance.

Metemhagi's devotion to his fairest of consorts made it impossible for him to part with her whose tender passion for him had caused her fall and banishment, and his absence enabled the diabolical Akbor to accomplish his purpose. Informed of the outrage, Metemhagi hurried to the spot as fast as the fleetest tiger could carry him, but found that the spell was to last until, prompted by a higher power, the intrusion of man with that feline species of whom the rodents are in terror should break the magic thrall, and restore matters to their original condition. This having happened, the disenchantment of the enthralled inhabitants of the superb city was followed by that of the genii who had been changed to mice. Lilithiana's return to majesty came next. Widowed and humiliated, she had hovered for centuries on the borders of her beloved empire till Cordosa's arrival in her city changed the aspect of things, and she was the Peri Queen once more.

Hitherto the nocturnal revellers could not indulge their feast without beating off the pestilent vermin with one hand while eating with the other, it was the first time that the banquet was being enjoyed in daylight, and without the use of the erstwhile indispensable weapon. The viands served appeared as inexhaustible as the multitudes who entered the dining hall to pay their respects to Cordosa, regale themselves, and file off again. Nor was music wanting to enliven conviviality. The charming attendants ravished the souls of the throng with song so sweet that the strangers had difficulty to prevent their eyelids from closing, lulled into obliviousness by the dulcet melody. At last Cordosa alone remained awake, the rest had succumbed to the irresistible charm of the bewitching voices. The honours showered on Cordosa were worthy of a great deliverer. In a palanquin of the most precious metal, studded with brilliant jewels, seated on cushions softer than air, he was carried through the festively decked boulevards and paradisial gardens, among dazzling palaces and amid the joyous ovations of jubilant crowds.

And as soon as the sun had withdrawn his last mellow beam from the crests of the mountains, unearthly splendours burst over the magic city. The spectacle was one of ghostly awe and august magnificence. A splendid illumination shed a flood of light on towering edifices and their resplendent decorations. In a second, grand triumphal arches spanned every highway, woven of the Orient's most exuberant foliage, flowers and blossoms, each one strewed thickly with the delicate petals of all the roses in creation, and the delighted denizens were transfigured in the reflex of the weird effulgence. Expectation sat visible on every face, and the reason became manifest when the faint vibration of a dreamy music came floating on the balmy breeze from the lower end of the main boulevard. The disenchanted genii celebrated their deliverance, and prepared to welcome their Peri Queen, whose time had come to return from her banishment to rule, surrounded by those whose image kept her lover's memory green. The event was to be commemorated by a transcendent jubilee.

The Queen's cavalry opened the triumphal entry with a division of diminutive and luminous horsemen, armed with golden spears, mounted on tiny zebras not larger than kittens, and blowing trumpets not unlike the calyx of the white lily. In an instant their files flew up the first triumphal arch, with no more effort than a bird makes when he hops from one twig to another. From their lofty position they watched the advance of the Queen's artillery, a glittering train of golden cannon, mortars, and howitzers, on silver carriages, pulled by little white elephants whose drivers in lustrous uniform swelled the chorus by bugles which varied the harmony with great effect. An inclined span thrown by the vanguard to the top of an arch served as a road to an elevated platform, where the ordnance was put in position, loaded, and pointed in every direction of the compass. Beneath came the body of the great army, battalion on battalion, ascending and occupying in succession arch after arch, until the vernal displays bristled and blazed with the gorgeousness of the shining host. A translucent haze like a veil of atomized jewels floated in the atmosphere, reflecting the hues of the rainbow, and a thousand bands accompanied a chorus as numerous as the voices of the entire army and population.

Cordosa's tears flowed freely, the symphony proved too much for his heart. The pageant around him looked like a dream of blessed childhood. He had neither time to feel nor to think. The chorus sang the prelude to the entrance of the Peri Queen. Wrapped in a cloud as intensely bright, as though the moon's light had been concentrated within a radius of a few leagues, Lilithiana entered the gate of her own city. Jubilant hurrahs greeted her and reverberated a thousandfold throughout the hills. As the queenly train drew nearer, Cordosa discerned in the heart of the mass of light a gliding chariot drawn by twelve fiery steeds as white as the blaze around them. In reclining ease Lilithiana rested on pillows of gossamer apparently filled out with light. Her golden hair hung like a beam of mild sunshine, leaving a countenance free, which with its star like eyes left no hope for mortal beauty to equal it. Of lesser witchery yet unmatched by flesh however fair were her nine attending nymphs, who in another equipage rode behind their mistress, each one holding a bag full of precious coin. The glorious pageant closed with a division of brilliantly mounted guards on stags with golden hoofs and antlers.

What was the sensation of Cordosa on perceiving that the Peri Queen had her eyes riveted upon him. Before the spot he occupied her chariot stopped. Without alighting from her royal seat, Lilithiana spoke thus to the astonished man:

"Not so much to you, O, Cordosa, do we owe our restoration, and our children their disenchantment, as to the righteous Ben Abir whose faith and reverence frustrated the designs of the evil one. Temptation lured him in vain, and trials failed to weaken his trust in Eternal Justice. Yet have you done your share to deepen his misery. Why knows he not where his daughter hides? Are you not afraid of retribution? Lead his child to his heart. And behold, these nine bags of gold are destined for him. Take them there and deliver them untouched as his need for virtues rare among men. His cause is in higher hands, they who injured him will suffer."

The air was rent with cries of applause, and the triumphal chariot proceeded onward. Filing down from the arches, the army stood in marching order, and followed in grand parade. The discharge of artillery shook the air, the musicians played, and the pageant moved on and out of sight, except the column of moonlight, which faded slowly in the hazy distance. The palatial buildings burst out with radiance from within, and the happy crowds abandoned themselves to feasting and dancing.

Cordosa's first business now was to load the dromedaries with the treasure intended for Ben Abir. At the khan he found it almost impossible to awaken his men. When the Karawan Bashi finally opened his eyes, he looked stupid as an ox and talked as if he had lost his senses. The guide was similarly affected. The Arabs seemed deaf and dumb, and Cordosa felt alarmed at their state of torpitude. When all his efforts to raise them failed, he bethought himself of the fountain and grasped a vessel with the intention of throwing cold water on the dull company. But the fountain was gone. Cordosa turned toward the door of the superb Divan, where they had spent hours on the previous day, there was neither a hall nor a door to be seen, and a sudden dimness had made all things uncertain. Still more disturbed by the startling situation, Cordosa tried to grope his way into the room of whose nearness he was sure, but, instead of striking one of the cushioned seats, he struck his head against the bark of a tree. Awaiting once more some unexpected change he strained his eyes to discern some object, and failing in the effort, knelt down to ascertain the nature of the ground he was on. Cold sand, gravel, and wet grass apprised him of surroundings other than those he had supposed to be about him. While fear was gaining on him, a passing wind raised the fog, and his astonished eye was sweeping in vain in search for the enchanted or disenchanted city.

The sun was just throwing out his multicoloured couriers to inform continents of his coming. A further effort to awaken his men proved successful, and Cordosa's next care was to discover whether the cats were in their cage, and whether the gold bags made a part of what he doubted not was a dream's phantom. His consternation was great when he found the cage empty and counted nine bags full to overflowing of the precious metal. Calling on the Karawan Bashi and the guide, he thought it was time to proceed homeward. "We have dreamed long enough," said he for a purpose.

"Yes, master, there must be some tricksy Div hereabout, I have a jumble in my head. I could swear by Allah that we have been in a grand city and have witnessed queer things," said the Bashi, with a yawn.

"By the beard of the Prophet, Bashi, the demon has blown something of that sort into my own brain," asserted the guide. The others said nothing. The caravan pursued its way, and Cordosa had his eyes on the camels that bore the enormous treasure. Sanaa was reached in safety. None of the men noticed the disappearance of the cats.

Immediately after his arrival Cordosa dispatched two trusty persons to his country retreat, and they returned with a third in a disguise which rendered identification impossible. He then sent for Ben Abir and insisted on being informed as to how he had come into possession of the mysterious coin that he had given him to invest. Filled with unutterable wonder at what he heard, Cordosa emptied one bag of gold after the other, asking each time whether the pile he had refrained from touching on the specified Friday eve had been as large as the one before him. Not before the contents of the ninth bag had been added to the heap, did Ben Abir exclaim, "So large, and not larger."

"Then take all this, and be once more the Croesus of Yemen, O, righteous Ben Abir!" cried Cordosa, and supplemented his words by the tale of the phantom city. It was Ben Abir's turn to be overwhelmed by astonishment. "And now has your time come to be perfectly happy," added Cordosa, knowing the contrary to be the case.

"Alas, Ben Abir's happiness will never, never return! My daughter, my daughter!" lamented the disconsolate father.

"Even your daughter returns with your fortune," said Cordosa, and disappeared through the door, which led to his private apartments. Another minute and the lost Estrelia lay sobbing in her father's arms. Ben Abir was a happy man, but the other felt that he owed his friend an explanation, which was substantially as follows.

When the jealous Ayesha had learned of the Imam's intention to glorify his harem by the incomparable loveliness of Ben Abir's daughter, she lost no time in warning Cordosa of the maiden's danger. Knowing that his recreant son was at the bottom of the infamous scheme, he felt himself called upon to frustrate it. But once in possession of the girl, whose charms had lost him his son, Cordosa hoped against hope to effect a change in her feelings toward the desperate Menahem. The plan did not work. Estrelia detested the youth who had worshipped her but was told that her safety required her removal to a hiding place. Cordosa was maturing a new plan when the supernatural incidents of his last journey left him no choice. The Peri Queen must be obeyed, lest misfortune betide his house.

Cordosa asked Abir's forgiveness, pointing to the great anguish of heart the love affair had caused him. The Croesus of Yemen, recognizing the higher hand that fashioned his destiny, would not have his friend refer to it hereafter. "I would to God I could heal your wound, O, kind-hearted Cordosa. My gratitude and sympathy are yours, and if a part of this hoard will give you ease, be it yours also," replied Ben Abir.

But Cordosa would not entertain the thought of being rewarded for services he had rendered accidentally, while Lilithiana's warning not to touch the gold was fresh in his memory.

As the two much tried men were considering the best way of conveying the treasure quietly to the house of its owner, Ibraeem knocked at the door. When admitted, the man could scarcely speak for excitement. "The Imam is dead!" cried the liberated slave out of breath.

"The Imam dead! Who killed him?" asked Cordosa, sure that death had not come peacefully, else why that commotion?

"He killed both the Imam and the Kadi," supplemented Ibraeem, "He ran amuck."

"Who is he?" asked Ben Abir with pardonable impatience.

"Menahem Cordosa," breathed the slave, betraying a delicacy of feeling slaves are not credited with. Cordosa grew faint and was caught in the arms of Ben Abir.

"Menahem Cordosa an assassin!" mourned the stricken parent. "It is well that it ended as it did," added Cordosa, having recovered his composure. "Take your hoard, friend, and may your house prosper."

"Do you remember ever having seen this heap of coin?" asked Ben Abir, seeing Ibraeem's eyes fascinated by the shining pile.

"That is the gold we saw that Friday eve before your tent," replied Ibraeem.

"Yes, Ibraeem, and then I told you that what is to be will be. This all goes to our house, yours not less than mine, faithful Ibraeem, who shall live to the end of your days with the Croesus of Yemen," said the grateful Ben Abir.

The Death Of Abu Nowas And Of His Wife

This story has been adapted from Andrew Lang's version of the same tale that originally appeared in The Crimson Fairy Book, published in 1903 by Longmans, Green and Co., London and New York. This tale is based on an original taken from Tunische Mahrchen

Once upon a time there lived a man whose name was Abu Nowas, and he was a great favourite with the Sultan of the country, who had a palace in the same town where Abu Nowas dwelt.

One day Abu Nowas came weeping into the hall of the palace where the Sultan was sitting, and said to him, "Oh, mighty Sultan, my wife is dead."

"That is bad news," replied the Sultan, "I must get you another wife." And he bade his Grand Vizir send for the Sultana.

"This poor Abu Nowas has lost his wife," said he when she entered the hall.

"Oh, then we must get him another," answered the Sultana, "I have a girl that will suit him exactly," and she clapped her hands loudly. At this signal a maiden appeared and stood before her.

"I have got a husband for you," said the Sultana.

"Who is he?" asked the girl.

"Abu Nowas, the jester," replied the Sultana.

"I will take him," answered the maiden, and as Abu Nowas made no objection, it was all arranged. The Sultana had the most beautiful clothes made for the bride, and the Sultan gave the bridegroom his wedding suit, and a thousand gold pieces into the bargain, and soft carpets for the house.

So Abu Nowas took his wife home, and for some time they were very happy, and spent the money freely which the Sultan had given them, never thinking what they should do for more when that was gone. But come to an end it did, and they had to sell their fine things one by one, till at length nothing was left but a cloak apiece, and one blanket to cover them.

"We have run through our fortune," said Abu Nowas, "what are we to do now? I am afraid to go back to the Sultan, for he will command his servants to turn me from the door. But you shall return to your mistress, and throw yourself at her feet and weep, and perhaps she will help us."

"Oh, you had much better go," said the wife. "I shall not know what to say."

"Well, then, stay at home, if you like," answered Abu Nowas, "and I will ask to be admitted to the Sultan's presence, and will tell him, with sobs, that my wife is dead, and that I have no money for her burial. When he hears that perhaps he will give us something."

"Yes, that is a good plan," said the wife, and Abu Nowas set out.

The Sultan was sitting in the hall of justice when Abu Nowas entered, his eyes streaming with tears, for he had rubbed some pepper into them. They smarted dreadfully, and he could hardly see to walk straight, and everyone wondered what the matter with him was.

"Abu Nowas! What has happened?" cried the Sultan.

"Oh, noble Sultan, my wife is dead," wept he.

"We must all die," answered the Sultan, but this was not the reply for which Abu Nowas had hoped.

"True, O Sultan, but I have neither shroud to wrap her in, nor money to bury her with," went on Abu Nowas, in no wise abashed by the way the Sultan had received his news.

"Well, give him a hundred pieces of gold," said the Sultan, turning to the Grand Vizir. And when the money was counted out Abu Nowas bowed low, and left the hall, his tears still flowing, but with joy in his heart.

"Have you got anything?" cried his wife, who was waiting for him anxiously

"Yes, a hundred gold pieces," said he, throwing down the bag, "but that will not last us any time. Now you must go to the Sultana, clothed in sackcloth and robes of mourning, and tell her that your husband, Abu Nowas, is dead, and you have no money for his burial. When she hears that, she will be sure to ask you what has become of the money and the fine clothes she gave us on our marriage, and you will answer, 'before he died he sold everything.'"

The wife did as she was told, and wrapping herself in sackcloth went up to the Sultana's own palace, and as she was known to have been one of Subida's favourite attendants, she was taken without difficulty into the private apartments.

"What is the matter?" inquired the Sultana, at the sight of the dismal figure.

"My husband lies dead at home, and he has spent all our money, and sold everything, and I have nothing left to bury him with," sobbed the wife.

Then Subida took up a purse containing two hundred gold pieces and said, "Your husband served us long and faithfully. You must see that he has a fine funeral."

The wife took the money, and, kissing the feet of the Sultana, she joyfully hastened home. They spent some happy hours planning how they should spend it and thinking how clever they had been.

"When the Sultan goes this evening to Subida's palace," said Abu Nowas, "she will be sure to tell him that Abu Nowas is dead. 'Not Abu Nowas, it is his wife,' he will reply, and they will quarrel over it, and all the time we shall be sitting here enjoying ourselves. Oh, if they only knew, how angry they would be!"

As Abu Nowas had foreseen, the Sultan went, in the evening after his business was over, to pay his usual visit to the Sultana.

"Poor Abu Nowas is dead!" said Subida when he entered the room.

"It is not Abu Nowas, but his wife who is dead," answered the Sultan.

"No, really you are quite wrong. She came to tell me herself only a couple of hours ago," replied Subida, "and as he had spent all their money, I gave her something to bury him with."

"You must be dreaming," exclaimed the Sultan. "Soon after midday Abu Nowas came into the hall, his eyes streaming with tears, and when I asked him the reason he answered that his wife was dead, and they had sold everything they had, and he had nothing left, not so much as would buy her a shroud, far less for her burial."

For a long time they talked, and neither would listen to the other, till the Sultan sent for the door keeper and bade him go instantly to the house of Abu Nowas and see if it was the man or his wife who was dead. But Abu Nowas happened to be sitting with his wife behind the latticed window, which looked on the street, and he saw the man coming, and sprang up at once.

"There is the Sultan's door keeper! They have sent him here to find out the truth. Quick! Throw yourself on the bed and pretend that you are dead."

And in a moment the wife was stretched out stiffly, with a linen sheet spread across her, like a corpse. She was only just in time, for the sheet was hardly drawn across her when the door opened and the porter came in. "Has anything happened?" asked he.

"My poor wife is dead," replied Abu Nowas. "Look! She is laid out here." And the porter approached the bed, which was in a corner of the room, and saw the stiff form lying underneath.

"We must all die," said he, and went back to the Sultan.

"Well, have you found out which of them is dead?" asked the Sultan.

"Yes, noble Sultan, it is the wife," replied the porter.

"He only says that to please you," cried Subida in a rage, and calling to her chamberlain, she ordered him to go at once to the dwelling of Abu Nowas and see which of the two was dead. "And be sure you tell the truth about it," added she, "or it will be the worse for you."

As her chamberlain drew near the house, Abu Nowas caught sight of him. "There is the Sultana's chamberlain," he exclaimed in a fright. "Now it is my turn to die. Be quick and spread the sheet over me." And he laid himself on the bed, and held his breath when the chamberlain came in.

"What are you weeping for?" asked the man, finding the wife in tears.

"My husband is dead," answered she, pointing to the bed, and the chamberlain drew back the sheet and beheld Abu Nowas lying stiff and motionless. Then he gently replaced the sheet and returned to the palace.

"Well, have you found out this time?" asked the Sultan.

"My lord, it is the husband who is dead."

"But I tell you he was with me only a few hours ago," cried the Sultan angrily. "I must get to the bottom of this before I sleep! Let my golden coach be brought round at once."

The coach was before the door in another five minutes, and the Sultan and Sultana both got in. Abu Nowas had ceased being a dead man and was looking into the street when he saw the coach coming.

"Quick! Quick!" he called to his wife. "The Sultan will be here directly, and we must both be dead to receive him."

So they laid themselves down, and spread the sheet over them, and held their breath. At that instant the Sultan entered, followed by the Sultana and the chamberlain, and he went up to the bed and found the corpses stiff and motionless.

"I would give a thousand gold pieces to anyone who would tell me the truth about this," cried he, and at the words Abu Nowas sat up.

"Give them to me, then," said Abu Nowas, holding out his hand. "You cannot give them to anyone who needs them more."

"Oh, Abu Nowas, you impudent dog!" exclaimed the Sultan, bursting into a laugh, in which the Sultana joined. "I might have known it was one of your tricks!" But he sent Abu Nowas the gold he had promised and let us hope that it did not fly so fast as the last had done.

The Fate Of Arzemia

This story has been adapted from Henry Iliowizi's version of the same tale that originally appeared in The Weird Orient, published in 1900 by Henry T. Coates and Company, Philadelphia.

In the ninth year of his reign, Chosroes Nushirvan, a ruler known for conquering kingdoms, sat on his gem-encrusted throne in a grand hall at his celebrated palace in Ctesiphon, his capital city. The palace was so immense that, on this occasion, his entire division of fifty thousand elite soldiers, known as the "golden spears," was needed to form a perimeter around its grounds in the heart of the splendid city located on the banks of the Tigris. The scene was one of opulence, with dazzling jewels, exquisite art, extravagant magnificence, and immeasurable wealth.

The golden throne was placed upon a massive silk carpet, intricately embroidered to resemble a semi-tropical garden, with various plants, leaves, and blossoms beautifully rendered in a spectrum of gemstones, from emeralds to sparkling diamonds and sapphires. The vaulted hall itself mimicked the firmament, adorned with golden orbs that moved in harmony with the planets and zodiac signs through a system of machinery.

Chosroes was clad in splendid armour, his hand resting on a jewel-adorned sword of immense value. His crown was so heavy that it required a golden chain to keep it suspended above the head of the mighty ruler of Persia. Seated beside him, at a lower position on his right, was Zarathustrotema, the esteemed leader of all sun worshipers and the highest-ranking priest of priests. Before the throne, the court's chiefs and attendants stood, ready to bow in submission to the autocratic monarch.

The people in the hall glanced nervously at the ruler, noticing the signs of his troubled state. Chosroes' demeanour was marked by discord, whether it was anger, melancholy, or despair, it remained unclear. There was no warmth in his expression, which was surprising given that the day marked a time of joy and celebration. It had been seven days since the birth of his royal child, and today was designated for naming and blessing the new-born. However, the powerful King of Persia had been haunted for the past six days and nights by a vivid and unsettling dream that chilled his very soul. His vision was unlike Nebuchadnezzar's vision of a human figure made of various metals shattered by a rock. Chosroes dreamt of strolling in one of his splendid gardens, brimming with melodious birds and delicious fruits. As he contemplated the great victories he had achieved and the colossal wealth that filled his vaults, enabling him to rival the Great Mughul in courtly luxuries, his thoughts turned to Rome, his only formidable adversary. Rome appeared to be bending to his will, leaving him with might, grandeur, royal comfort, and love. What more could he attain except the dominion of the entire world?

"First Rome, then India!" he declared.

But suddenly, a disturbing sight disrupted his reverie. There, very near his splendid marble palace, stood a grim Tower of Silence. He had never seen such a structure so close to his palace before. Towers of Silence were typically situated in remote groves, preferably on hills frequented by carrion-eating vultures. They were the places where followers of the Zoroastrian faith exposed their dead, allowing the birds to strip the corpses of flesh, as their belief held that human remains should not pollute the sacred earth. The King was deeply troubled. How had this tower come to be here, and by whose command?

Chosroes gazed up at the top of the eerie tower, where a swarm of vultures circled, as if a corpse had been placed there. His horror intensified when he noticed that the flock was descending upon him. In his confusion, he plucked a twig from a tree, intending to fend off the ravenous birds. Astonishingly, the tree bled as he wounded it with the twig, and the ominous swarm vanished. The Tower of Silence seemed to disappear as well, leaving Chosroes with a sceptre of gold adorned with resplendent gemstones in his hand. His torment continued when he was struck by an insatiable hunger. When he reached for the nearest fruit to satisfy his craving, his touch turned it into a transparent jewel. Every attempt to quell his hunger yielded the same result. Thirst followed hunger, and when he sought a nearby spring to drink, he found the clear liquid had solidified into diamonds.

In desperation, he prayed, invoking Ahura Mazda, pleading for help and guidance. In the midst of his suffering, a malevolent laugh echoed in the night. It came from a monstrous figure lurking behind a tree, a winged dragon with the head of a man – a head from the royal family. Terrified, Chosroes attempted to flee, but the same flock of vultures returned, landing on him like fiends. They carried him high into the air, and then, instead of tormenting him, they delivered him to the grating atop the Tower of Silence. The agony of being torn apart awakened him from the nightmarish vision. He awoke, breathing heavily and trembling.

His first sight upon awakening was that of the court's master of ceremonies, who stood with folded arms and lowered head, ready to inform the king of a significant royal birth. That very night, Shirin, his most envied and favoured sultana among his thousands of wives, had given birth to a beautiful daughter. The eerie timing of the child's birth, so close to the distressing dream, could not be ignored. Instead of consulting the Magi, the high priests known for their interpretations of dreams and the casting of horoscopes, Chosroes had chosen to wait until the seventh day after the birth, a day dedicated to naming the child and having her horoscope calculated, as was the custom among the followers of Zarathustra. To ensure that no deception was practiced by the cunning Magi, the King had secretly summoned the heads of three separate fire temples, located far from one another, to provide reports. Zarathustrotema himself had received a similar summons. And so, the throne room of Chosroes Nushirvan was filled with an intense sense of apprehension, not only by the ruler of the empire but by all those left uninformed and powerless at the foot of his throne.

"Great leader of the light-worshiping people of Iran, enlightened by Ahura Mazda Himself, I have summoned you here today with a significant purpose, soon to be revealed. I have called forth the wisest dasturs from the fire temples of Ardashir and Kanjak, instructing them to appear before me today to cast the child's horoscope. This child, to be named Arzemia, was born to Shirin, the favoured sultana of Chosroes Nushirvan. It is my decree that the horoscope of the princess be cast this very hour by three of the wisest Magi, each of whom remains unaware of the others' work. Your presence, Zarathustrotema, is to add your wisdom to theirs, in case some hidden aspect remains unexamined," the king said with a nervous demeanour.

At that moment, a venerable priest entered the royal chamber. After paying his respects, the Magian unfurled a parchment adorned with hieroglyphics, sketched various lines on it with a rod, and, with his gaze fixed on the zodiac symbols moving across the hall's celestial dome, he began his pronouncement, saying, "The divine stars under whose influence your new-born child came into this world reveal to me a realm of light set against an impenetrable darkness. I see a destiny marked by strength and beauty, a life where rays of sunshine will be consumed by the shadows of the night. These celestial beings favour Arzemia, O king, with more than ordinary grace and royal renown. She will stand among the immortal queens, but her years will be few, just as Mazda forbids her to rule and construct, as did Semiramis, the marvels of Nineveh, Babylon, with its hanging gardens, and towers soaring into the heavens. With her, Iran's might and glory will be reborn, but lurking behind it all is a looming chaos, crimson lightning, armies drenched in blood, kingdoms in ruins, and thrones fallen. The stars foretell an era of triumph that gives way to one of crime, sorrow, tears, and ruin."

The next astrologer spoke with the intensity of a prophet of doom, his prophecy darker still. "The forces of Angro Maniyush are arrayed against the offspring of Chosroes Nushirvan. Born under the constellation of Cleopatra, the child named Arzemia shall surpass the Egyptian enchantress in the qualities that make a woman a ruler and a sorceress that kings cannot resist. A veil shrouds the rest. Let it remain concealed. Iran's destiny unfolds before me, alternating between splendour and thunderous clouds that rise from an eternal abyss."

Then, the third prophet of ill omens continued, "Arzemia's fate is intertwined with the Sasanian dynasty, like the reign of Tadmor's queen. She will rule a vast empire, clashing with one even mightier.

But her fate will not mirror Zenobia's. Tremors seize me as I witness Iran's tragic future, scripted in the book of fate by Ahura Mazda, following an era of unparalleled victories. In the distance, I hear the whispers of malevolent spirits, and my lips will not utter their dreadful secrets. Why summon the night while the sun shines high? Rome is not your most formidable foe, O Chosroes Nushirvan. Beware of the serpent within your own bosom."

The echo of "in your bosom" reverberated in the king's ears, and the throne room fell silent, with everyone deeply affected by the eerie prophecies. With an air of disquiet, Chosroes turned his gaze to Zarathustrotema, who displayed signs of anxiety.

"Why does one see what the others do not? Are the god stars not constant in their alignment? They prophesy a queenship like that of three others, yet so different. Why? Unveil the truth, dispel all doubt. If Persia's fall is destined from above, let the horoscope reveal it clearly, and provide me with the truth," demanded the autocrat.

"Since the time of Zarathustra, O King of Kings, when has Ahura Mazda granted mortals the purest light? The celestial stars foretell our destiny but do not offer unequivocal predictions, and mankind should be thankful for the uncertainty that allows hope to nurture its dreams. Horoscopes indicate qualities shared by three famous queens under the same zodiac signs, leaving much unanswered to cultivate bright possibilities. Gracious Mazda, in order not to overshadow the joy of the future, withholds the full knowledge of our fate. I beseech you not to let foreboding events cloud your bright horizon. March onward in triumph, while we, the guardians of the sacred fires, pray for your victories. If we must fall, let it be in grandeur. May your empire flourish with Arzemia, her wisdom guided by Zarathustra, and her ambition inspired by Babylon's immortal queen," concluded the high priest of Iran, making a heartfelt plea.

Chosroes, burdened by a sense of impending doom, sought refuge in unrestrained activity, attempting to silence his apprehensions. His tide of fortune, still swelling, helped diminish the weight of his foreboding that inauspicious stars were frowning upon him. His avarice seemed to grow with the continual flow of treasures brought by victorious generals fighting against the Roman Emperor Heraclius. One feared component of the Persian army was a few battalions of well-trained elephants. Each division had its own group of these colossal creatures, but the fifty thousand "golden spears" primarily relied on fifty massive war elephants, led by a white mammoth known as Mahmud. Mahmud had previously carried the Ethiopian King Abraba when he invaded Mecca, and he was given the rank of a general. He performed his duties with remarkable dignity and strategic intelligence. His elephant forces were trained to follow his lead, to project volumes of water and mud stored in their capacious reservoirs into the eyes of the enemy, to use their trunks effectively in combat, and to break through enemy ranks. Mahmud's actions paved the way for many victories, and no other officer in the Persian army was as esteemed as this intelligent creature. Mahmud lived in quarters as lavish as those of the other generals, and his robe was adorned with gold and precious stones.

With the powerful momentum of these elephants leading his massive army, Chosroes Nushirvan not only wrested control of Asia Minor from the Roman Empire but expanded his conquests to Libya, Egypt, and Carthage. His white palace's extensive vaults were filled with the riches of vanquished nations. He would exhibit only trivial trophies to the general populace and a dissatisfied nobility. Chosroes' domestic life, however, revealed a ruler who was an unjust father, a tyrant, a coward, and an arrogant braggart. He owed his power and prestige to the courage of his generals, but unknown to him, conspiracy was brewing where he least expected.

The turmoil and warfare did not disrupt the early years of Arzemia's childhood. Sheltered within the imperial harem, she matured into a captivating young woman. Possessing exceptional talents and an extraordinary thirst for knowledge rarely seen in Oriental courts, Arzemia flourished. Infatuated with his enchanting daughter, Chosroes spared no expense in providing her with the luxuries befitting a queen and assigned wise tutors to impart both secular and Zarathustrian wisdom. At the age of sixteen, Arzemia astounded the court by appearing at her father's side in the audience hall. Draped in a purple gown with a heart-shaped array of dazzling gems on her chest and a sparkling tiara atop her head, the princess enthroned before the court resembled a goddess rather than an unusually mature maiden. To the courtiers gathered at the foot of the throne, she appeared as a vision from a dream, with flawless beauty and a magnetic allure, her eyes casting irresistible arrows of charm.

It was a grand celebration, with the true cross taken from Jerusalem by a famous general presented before the throne. An envoy from Arabia, appearing unkempt, was granted an audience, though the primary purpose was to introduce Shirin's enchanting daughter to the court.

"Is it homage or tribute that you bring from my subjects in Arabia?" Chosroes inquired of the Bedouin envoy, who appeared dishevelled and unrefined.

In response, the Arab silently delivered a written message and displayed no awe in the face of the opulence surrounding him. Translated, the message read, "In the name of the most merciful

God! Mohammed, son of Abdallah and apostle of God, to Chosroes Nushirvan, king of Persia."

"Stop, fool! What do I hear? Does a wild desert slave dare to place his name ahead of mine in writing?" the autocrat exclaimed, seizing the message and tearing it to shreds. "Remove this man from my sight, and instruct my governor in Yemen that a madman resides in Medina who claims to be a prophet. If he cannot cure him, send me his head."

With this, the scene came to an end, but it had significant repercussions for Iran and, not to be overlooked, for Arzemia. From that point forward, her visions differed from those she had experienced in the seclusion of the harem. There had been eyes in the hall that radiated an irresistibly sympathetic glow, and the enchanting look had captivated her entire being. It was her first taste of love, a sentiment she couldn't quite grasp. Before this event, her active imagination, when not exploring the mysteries of Zarathustra, delighted in weaving tales of heroes and heroines who heralded her future greatness. Destined by the stars to wear a crown and inherit the empire of Iran, she imagined herself outshining even the legendary accomplishments of Semiramis. With the entire world at her feet, kings and emperors would bow to her rule. Why settle for being a mere mortal's companion when she could be a goddess, untouched like the revered Mithra who illuminated the heavens without a mate? The words of Cleopatra and Zenobia came to her mind as she mused, "Why be one man's companion when you can be the awe and adoration of the entire world?" Shirin overheard these thoughts, recognizing that it was time to introduce the blossoming maiden to the outside world. Arzemia's childhood had come to an end.

*

"You know, my lord, that our child's extraordinary beauty is surpassed only by her brilliant intellect. She has mastered the languages spoken by great nations and has acquired the wisdom taught by the Magi. But ever since, following your wishes, I cautiously hinted at her horoscope, I've noticed a change in her behaviour that deeply concerns me. Arzemia has been seeking solitude in our gardens, as if she were in communion with spirits, talking about the hollowness of love and dreaming of a destiny beyond the reach of ordinary mortals, destined by the stars. Ahura Mazda has given us this precious child to brighten our later years. Our daughter is like a musical instrument, meant to dispel discord and darkness, not to be silenced by neglect. May the restless devas leave her, as she wanders into realms that are too ethereal to be safe," prayed the cunning sultana, confident in her schemes.

"What would you have me do, Shirin? Should I marry her off to the man whom I, Chosroes, esteem the most?" inquired the father authoritatively, as early marriages were in line with Zarathustra's moral teachings.

"Not now, my lord. Let the child experience the court, and let the court experience her, before the subject of love is brought up," suggested the emboldened sultana.

"Sultana, it was my love that elevated you above the most beautiful in my harem, just as it raised your son above his brothers. Love's triumph was yours. Now, our daughter, blessed by the stars, shall receive even greater favour. She shall be adorned like Arustra and take her first place at my side," promised the autocratic father. And so, Shirin once again outshone her rivals in royal favour.

Brought into the public eye at her mother's initiative, Arzemia captivated the court with her extraordinary beauty and her regal bearing. Yet, this was where she found herself ensnared by love's unfailing arrow, shattering her previous imaginings like a tower struck by lightning. A new scene unfolded before her, more captivating than all others, and at the centre stood a man whose mere presence could explain love as passionate as Zenobia's and madness as profound as Cleopatra's. Though of average height, this figure bore a striking resemblance to the war god feared by the Olympians. He was not classically handsome, but he was imposing. With an olive complexion, an aquiline nose, deep black eyes that were both fierce and gentle, and a chin concealed beneath a beard as black as the raven, he was a man of commanding presence. His thick, arched eyebrows and a sensuous, curling lip added to his allure. He had shapely feet and even shapelier hands, and he was dressed as a Persian general. This was Shahrbaraz, to whom Chosroes owed much of his most significant victories. Covered in glory and loaded with royal favour, Shahrbaraz was flattered by courtiers, idolized by the army, and lionized by the people. The general wanted for nothing, but when Arzemia's eyes met his they made all other ambitions fade in comparison to his all-consuming passion to worship this divine woman.

That day marked the destiny of Arzemia, and it was not over without an incident that sent alarm through both the king and his court. The cause was a sealed document discovered in front of Chosroes Nushirvan's famous grand palace gate, warning the king of an imminent conspiracy to overthrow him and implicating the royal bodyguards in the nefarious plot. Immediate action was needed, and Chosroes, seized with fear, called upon his bravest general to temporarily oversee the safety of the capital and the palace. Shahrbaraz pledged his unwavering vigilance until the conspirators were brought to justice.

"Within the walls of Ctesiphon, there are twelve thousand elite troops, with an additional twenty-five thousand ready for action. Fear not, my sovereign, Shahrbaraz will not rest," assured the resourceful strategist with a concealed chuckle, arranging matters to his liking.

Unaware of the cause of the court's sudden alarm, the people observed the feverish military activity. Large groups of soldiers departed, while even larger ones occupied the city's fortifications. As night fell, the palace was heavily guarded from all directions, giving Ctesiphon the appearance of a besieged city, ready to repel an aggressive foe. What was to happen on this night?

Meanwhile, Arzemia, untouched by the chaos, surrendered to an overpowering passion that burned at the core of her fiery nature. Succumbing to the fever of her soul, she escaped her luxurious chambers to seek the soothing night breeze in a secluded garden, a private area within the royal park. The moon, barely visible in its crescent form, offered limited illumination in the darkness as she made her way to a concealed spot on a terrace. In the daytime, it provided an expansive view of the garden. Here, in an elegantly appointed alcove, the maiden assumed a prayerful posture and called upon the help of Ahura Mazda, the revealed power of Zarathustra.

"Eternal Ahura Mazda, the god of gods, the creator of light, who upholds the good and the true, the holy and the beautiful throughout all space. You bright spirits who seek to carry out His will, if the fire burning in my heart is indeed love kindled by heaven, let no barriers stand between me and the one for whom my heart burns. Let no barrier exist longer than it takes for two wind-driven flames to come together, uniting in celestial fire. Messengers of Ahura Mazda, carry my message to the one fate has destined to be my love, let walls bend, and guards turn a deaf ear so that the one who loves Arzemia can reach me without obstruction," implored the maiden.

A mysterious glimmer appeared on the lower balconies of the palace, flaring up and vanishing before reappearing, followed by complete silence. However, near the garden's rear gate, where the signal was expected and understood, there were movements. An intruder, well-informed about his destination, silently glided through the shadows toward Arzemia's retreat. The man who entered was clearly aware of the danger that lay in his presence at this hour, and it wasn't until he reached Arzemia's side that she realized the identity of the person who had come to her.

"Who are you, the most daring of men, who fearlessly invades the inviolable privacy of Chosroes Nushirvan's daughter?" exclaimed the maiden in anxious apprehension, fearing the fulfilment of her prayer.

"Forgive me! I am not the same person I was before your gaze struck me with madness to be your devotee, your slave, or to not be at all," he replied.

"Ahura Mazda! Is it really you, the man honoured by Iran, Shahrbaraz?" the maiden exclaimed.

"Your servant, your eternal slave," he reiterated.

"The auspicious stars brought you. But do not humble Arzemia while you humble yourself. The stars have linked our destinies, and I am yours, just as you are eternally mine," the maiden declared.

"My heaven," was the brief utterance of the great general who then raised her up like a child, enveloping her cheeks with ardent kisses.

"Your tears of joy would bring tears to the eyes of angels in paradise, my dear," Persia's renowned hero whispered.

"The nightingale! I've never heard the nightingale sing so melancholic, so sweet, so prophetic. It seems to sigh, weep, and convey to my heart things that words cannot express. Some unseen force moves it to stir our emotions," Arzemia breathed with deep emotion.

"You are like a sympathetic instrument of creation, attuned to spiritual harmonies that escape those with lesser insight. The bird's song means little to me, but in your voice, I hear a celestial melody that stirs the heavenly spheres," Shahrbaraz said softly.

"It's a privilege to receive admiration from the lips of love, but what am I compared to you, the pride of Iran, the one who defeated the Romans and captured their holy city? Who can claim a greater accomplishment? If your armies were you, could you not conquer the entire world?" Arzemia asked.

"I've conquered the realms of Earth and Heaven, my star of happiness. With you as mine, there's nothing more to wish for in all the worlds. Smiting the Romans and capturing their holy city was a lesser feat than coming close to you, a treasure more challenging to reach than the depths of the ocean in search of hidden riches," the general declared.

"Alas, you're right! Oh, gods! Your life, your precious life, should you be discovered here with me at this hour! My dearest, how did you manage to elude the guards, whose very heads would be at stake for allowing your presence where only the king holds sway? You must leave, my adored one, my beloved. Depart now, before the divine beings intervene. I hear friendly spirits urging your departure," Arzemia pleaded, suddenly aware of the peril her lover faced.

"Your prayer, child of light, that urged the walls to bend and the guards to be deaf, and love, which Orpheus pursued into the world of shadows, have smoothed my path here, undaunted by fate. Those who enter heaven defy death. Your presence makes me invulnerable to mortal harm. Ah, don't waste a moment, my cherub, dwelling on thoughts of death or danger," Shahrbaraz fervently exclaimed.

"May it never be, Ahura Mazda, that Iran's glory is tarnished by treachery! But let's not toy with the envious fates, as they may grow envious of Arzemia's happiness. I would not trade heaven for what we have here on Earth," the girl implored.

"From now on, let all your worries be mine, divine Arzemia. My 'golden spears' hold every fort and gate, and they follow only your will and mine. I could be king right now if I wished. To be near you, I had to use whatever means necessary. A scheme concocted by me, taken seriously by the king, gave me control of Ctesiphon and the court," the strategist explained.

"The god stars decree that I will become queen one day, with you as my king, my Ninus to your Semiramis, with Rome and Iran bowing before us. Ah, there's a light!" the girl exclaimed in alarm, noticing a glimmer in the palace.

"It's the signal for me to leave," Shahrbaraz said, and a moment later, the gate closed behind him, after exchanging a kiss that tasted of divine ecstasy.

Their secret relationship, between Iran's greatest general and its most beautiful princess, continued for some time until a series of revolutionary changes threw Ctesiphon into turmoil. Chosroes Nushirvan's court was a hotbed of intrigue, and the harem was filled with vices and corruption stemming from absolute rule. Among the many jealous women in the palace, Shirin, the Christian sultana, held the most sway. She had captivated the king to the point where she managed to disinherit and imprison Kavadh, the legitimate heir to the throne, in favour of her son Mardanshah. However, Kavadh later seized the reins of power and executed his father, leaving him to die of starvation in a treasure vault. He also executed seventeen brothers to ensure his rule. His violent actions were driven by his passionate love for Shirin, not revenge, though this love eventually turned to hatred when she refused him and ended her own life. Arzemia was the sole surviving child, and Shahrbaraz ensured her safety. After Kavadh's fall, Arzemia succeeded her father as queen.

During the turbulent period following Kavadh's reign, Shahrbaraz plotted to seize Iran's throne. With his fifty thousand golden spears and Arzemia's support, he entered Ctesiphon in triumph, having himself crowned in Chosroes' palace. Arzemia's many suitors organized a conspiracy against Shahrbaraz, led by Faruch Zad, the powerful satrap of Khorassan, who was deeply in love with the princess. Shahrbaraz was assassinated on the day of his wedding to Arzemia, and his body was mutilated and paraded through the streets of Ctesiphon on an ass. Arzemia was horrified and filled with sorrow and vengeance. Her chance for revenge came when she succeeded her father, and Faruch Zad, who had pursued her aggressively, met a gruesome end, executed under her orders.

As the looming threat of Islam's conquest grew, Arzemia faced defeat at the hands of their hordes, including the loss of Mahmud, the intelligent elephant, which foreboded further misfortune. Fearing for her empire's demise, Arzemia turned to the Magi for her horoscope, along with her father's dream, which revealed dark prophecies about her destiny. She accepted her fate with resignation, understanding that her birth had displeased the god stars, and even contemplated whether it would have been better if she had never been born.

As Arzemia uttered these words, a commotion in the royal courtyard signalled her armed guards to rush toward the palace entrance, where they encountered a desperate group of conspirators led by one of Faruch Zad's relatives. The confrontation was brief, and Arzemia was taken captive by the avenger of the late satrap. She endured extreme torture and was ultimately put to death in a dishonourable manner.

With her, perished one of the noblest and most virtuous queens of one of the mightiest empires, which would eventually succumb to the forces of Islam.

Story Of The Rich Man And his Wasteful Son

This story is adapted from Tales From The Arabic, by John Payne, privately published in 1901. This story is based on the Breslau and Calcutta editions of The Book of the Thousand Nights and One Night originally produced between 1814 and 1818. This tale derives from the Breslau text.

Once, there was a wise man who had three sons and many grandchildren. Over time, disagreements arose among them. The wise man decided to gather his sons and address the issue. He said, "You must support one another and avoid belittling each other. Remember that unity is strength. If you seek help from outsiders against each other, you will only bring destruction upon yourselves. I have some wealth, which I will hide in a specific location. It will serve as a safety net for you in times of need."

After this talk, the sons left their father. However, one of them secretly watched his father bury the treasure outside the city. The next morning, the son went to the hidden spot, dug up the treasure, and took it for himself. When the old man was nearing the end of his life, he called his sons and told them where he had hidden his wealth. After his death, the sons went to the location, uncovered the treasure, and divided it among themselves. What they didn't know was that the first son had stolen a portion earlier and added it to the rest.

Years later, the first son had a son of his own, a remarkable child who grew up to be the most distinguished person of his time. Worried about his son's future, the first son decided to share the secret of the hidden treasure. He advised his son, "In my youth, I wronged my own family regarding the inheritance. I see that you are in a good position now, but if you ever face hardship, open the hidden chamber and find the treasure."

When the old man passed away, the young man couldn't resist the temptation. He opened the chamber, only to discover it was empty, with a rope hanging down and a message advising him to hang himself if he ever faced poverty. Disheartened, the young man tried to hang himself, but the rope broke, causing a portion of the ceiling to collapse. Hidden within were immense riches. He realized his father had used this elaborate scheme to teach him a valuable lesson.

The young man restored his wealth and prosperity and rejoined his friends who had distanced themselves from him during his hard times. He told them a fabricated story about locusts devouring a stone instead of bread to prove a point. They were perplexed by his tale but left him, and his fortunes thrived.

The Enchanted Head

This story has been adapted from Andrew Lang's version of the same tale that originally appeared in The Brown Fairy Book, published in 1904 by Longmans, Green and Co., London and New York. This tale is based on an original taken from Traditions populaires de toutes les nations (Asie Mineure) by Jean Nicolaides & Émile Carnoy, published by Maisonneuve in 1889.

Once upon a time an old woman lived in a small cottage near the sea with her two daughters. They were very poor, and the girls seldom left the house, as they worked all day long making veils for the ladies to wear over their faces, and every morning, when the veils were finished, the other took them over the bridge and sold them in the city. Then she bought the food that they needed for the day and returned home to do her share of veil making.

One morning the old woman rose even earlier than usual and set off for the city with her wares. She was just crossing the bridge when, suddenly, she knocked up against a human head, which she had never seen there before. The woman started back in horror, but what was her surprise when the head spoke, exactly as if it had a body joined on to it.

"Take me with you, good mother!" it said imploringly, "take me with you back to your house."

At the sound of these words the poor woman nearly went mad with terror. Have that horrible thing always at home? Never! Never! And she turned and ran back as fast as she could, not knowing that the head was jumping, dancing, and rolling after her. But when she reached her own door it bounded in before her, and stopped in front of the fire, begging, and praying to be allowed to stay.

All that day there was no food in the house, for the veils had not been sold, and they had no money to buy anything with. So they all sat silent at their work, inwardly cursing the head which was the cause of their misfortunes.

When evening came, and there was no sign of supper, the head spoke, for the first time that day, "Good mother, does no one ever eat here? During all the hours I have spent in your house not a creature has touched anything."

"No," answered the old woman, "we are not eating anything."

"And why not, good mother?"

"Because we have no money to buy any food."

"Is it your custom never to eat?"

"No, for every morning I go into the city to sell my veils, and with the few shillings I get for them I buy all we want. Today I did not cross the bridge, so of course I had nothing for food."

"Then I am the cause of your having gone hungry all day?" asked the head.

"Yes, you are," answered the old woman.

"Well, then, I will give you money and plenty of it, if you will only do as I tell you. In an hour, as the clock strikes twelve, you must be on the bridge at the place where you met me. When you get there call out 'Ahmed,' three times, as loud as you can. Then a slave will appear, and you must say to him, 'The head, your master, desires you to open the trunk, and to give me the green purse which you will find in it.'"

"Very well, my lord," said the old woman, "I will set off at once for the bridge." And wrapping her veil round her she went out

Midnight was striking as she reached the spot where she had met the head so many hours before.

"Ahmed! Ahmed! Ahmed!" cried she, and immediately a huge slave, as tall as a giant, stood on the bridge before her.

"What do you want?" asked he.

"The head, your master, desires you to open the trunk, and to give me the green purse which you will find in it."

"I will be back in a moment, good mother," said he. And three minutes later he placed a purse full of sequins in the old woman's hand.

No one can imagine the joy of the whole family at the sight of all this wealth. The tiny, tumble-down cottage was rebuilt, the girls had new dresses, and their mother ceased selling veils. It was such a new thing for them to have money to spend, that they were not as careful as they might have been, and by and by there was not a single coin left in the purse. When this happened their hearts sank within them, and their faces fell.

"Have you spent your fortune?" asked the head from its corner, when it saw how sad they looked. "Well, then, go at midnight, good mother, to the bridge, and call out 'Mahomet!' three times, as loud as you can. A slave will appear in answer, and you must tell him to open the trunk, and to give you the red purse which he will find there."

The old woman did not need twice telling but set off at once for the bridge.

"Mahomet! Mahomet! Mahomet!" cried she, with all her might, and in an instant a slave, still larger than the last, stood before her.

"What do you want?" asked he.

"The head, your master, bids you open the trunk, and to give me the red purse which you will find in it."

"Very well, good mother, I will do so," answered the slave, and the moment after he had vanished, he reappeared with the purse in his hand.

This time the money seemed so endless that the old woman built herself a new house and filled it with the most beautiful things that were to be found in the shops. Her daughters were always wrapped in veils that looked as if they were woven out of sunbeams, and their dresses shone with precious stones. The neighbours wondered where all this sudden wealth had sprung from, but nobody knew about the head.

"Good mother," said the head, one day, "this morning you are to go to the city and ask the sultan to give me his daughter for my bride."

"Do what?" asked the old woman in amazement. "How can I tell the sultan that a head without a body wishes to become his son in law? They will think that I am mad, and I shall be hooted from the palace and stoned by the children."

"Do as I bid you," replied the head, "it is my will."

The old woman was afraid to say anything more, and, putting on her richest clothes, started for the palace. The sultan granted her an audience at once, and, in a trembling voice, she made her request.

"Are you mad, old woman?" said the sultan, staring at her.

"The wooer is powerful, O Sultan, and nothing is impossible to him."

"Is that true?"

"It is, O Sultan, I swear it," answered she.

"Then let him show his power by doing three things, and I will give him my daughter."

"Command, O gracious prince," said she.

"Do you see that hill in front of the palace?" asked the sultan.

"I see it," answered she.

"Well, in forty days the man who has sent you must make that hill vanish and plant a beautiful garden in its place. That is the first thing. Now go and tell him what I say."

So the old woman returned and told the head the sultan's first condition.

"It is well," he replied, and said no more about it.

For thirty-nine days the head remained in its favourite corner. The old woman thought that the task set before him was beyond his powers, and that no more would be heard about the sultan's daughter. But on the thirty-ninth evening after her visit to the palace, the head suddenly spoke.

"Good mother," he said, "you must go tonight to the bridge, and when you are there cry "Ali! Ali! Ali!" as loud as you can. A slave will appear before you, and you will tell him that he is to level the hill, and to make, in its place, the most beautiful garden that ever was seen."

"I will go at once," answered she.

It did not take her long to reach the bridge which led to the city, and she took up her position on the spot where she had first seen the head and called loudly "Ali! Ali! Ali." In an instant a slave appeared before her, of such a huge size that the old woman was half frightened, but his voice was mild and gentle as he said, "What is it that you want?"

"Your master bids you level the hill that stands in front of the sultan's palace and in its place to make the most beautiful garden in the world."

"Tell my master he shall be obeyed," replied Ali, "it shall be done this moment." And the old woman went home and gave Ali's message to the head.

Meanwhile the sultan was in his palace waiting till the fortieth day should dawn and wondering that not one spadeful of earth should have been dug out of the hill.

"If that old woman has been playing me a trick," thought he, "I will hang her! And I will put up some gallows tomorrow on the hill itself."

But when tomorrow came there was no hill, and when the sultan opened his eyes he could not imagine why the room was so much lighter than usual, and why the sweet smell of flowers filled the air.

"Can there be a fire?" he said to himself, "the sun never came in at this window before. I must get up and see." So he rose and looked out, and underneath him flowers from every part of the world were blooming, and creepers of every colour hung in chains from tree to tree.

Then he remembered. "Certainly that old woman's son is a clever magician!" cried he, "I never met anyone as clever as that. What shall I give him to do next? Let me think. Ah! I know." And he sent for the old woman, who by the orders of the head, was waiting below.

"Your son has carried out my wishes very nicely," he said. "The garden is larger and better than that of any other king. But when I walk across it I shall need some place to rest on the other side. In forty days he must build me a palace, in which every room shall be filled with different furniture from a different country, and each more magnificent than any room that ever was seen." And having said this he turned round and went away.

"Oh, he will never be able to do that," thought she, "it is much more difficult than the hill." And she walked home slowly, with her head bent.

"Well, what am I to do next?" asked the head cheerfully. And the old woman told her story

"Dear me! Is that all? Why it is child's play," answered the head, and troubled no more about the palace for thirty-nine days. Then he told the old woman to go to the bridge and call for Hassan.

"What do you want, old woman?" asked Hassan, when he appeared, for he was not as polite as the others had been.

"Your master commands you to build the most magnificent palace that ever was seen," replied she, "and you are to place it on the borders of the new garden."

"He shall be obeyed," answered Hassan. And when the sultan woke he saw, in the distance, a palace built of soft blue marble, resting on slender pillars of pure gold.

"That old woman's son is certainly all powerful," cried he, "what shall I bid him do now?" And after thinking some time he sent for the old woman, who was expecting the summons.

"The garden is wonderful, and the palace the finest in the world," said he, "so fine, that my servants would cut but a sorry figure in it. Let your son fill it with forty slaves whose beauty shall be unequalled, all exactly like each other, and of the same height."

This time the king thought he had invented something totally impossible, and was quite pleased with himself for his cleverness

Thirty-nine days passed, and at midnight on the night of the last the old woman was standing on the bridge.

"Bekir! Bekir! Bekir!" cried she. And a slave appeared and inquired what she wanted.

"The head, your master, bids you find forty slaves of unequalled beauty, and of the same height, and place them in the sultan's palace on the other side of the garden."

And when, on the morning of the fortieth day, the sultan went to the blue palace, and was received by the forty slaves, he nearly lost his wits from surprise.

"I will assuredly give my daughter to the old woman's son," thought he. "If I were to search all the world through I could never find a more powerful son in law."

And when the old woman entered his presence he informed her that he was ready to fulfil his promise, and she was to bid her son appear at the palace without delay.

This command did not at all please the old woman, though, of course, she made no objections to the sultan

"All has gone well so far," she grumbled, when she told her story to the head, "but what do you suppose the sultan will say, when he sees his daughter's husband?"

"Never mind what he says! Put me on a silver dish and carry me to the palace."

So it was done, though the old woman's heart beat heavily as she laid down the dish with the head upon it.

At the sight before him the king flew into a violent rage.

"I will never marry my daughter to such a monster," he cried. But the princess placed her head gently on his arm.

"You have given your word, my father, and you cannot break it," said she.

"But, my child, it is impossible for you to marry such a being," exclaimed the sultan.

"Yes, I will marry him. He has a beautiful head, and I love him already."

So the marriage was celebrated, and great feasts were held in the palace, though the people wept tears to think of the sad fate of their beloved princess. But when the merry making was done, and the young couple were alone, the head suddenly disappeared, or, rather, a body was added to it, and one of the handsomest young men that ever was seen stood before the princess.

"A wicked fairy enchanted me at my birth," he said, "and for the rest of the world I must always be a head only. But for you, and you only, I am a man like other men.

"And that is all I care about," said the princess.

The Student Of Timbuktu

This story has been adapted from Henry Iliowizi's version of the same tale that originally appeared in The Weird Orient, published in 1900 by Henry T. Coates and Company, Philadelphia.

At the end of the year 1578, the slave markets of Mauritania were overflowing with captives, and, for once, the price of a male slave was lower than that of a donkey. This surplus of human beings was the result of the thousands of prisoners who had survived the decisive battle near Al Kesar Kebir, on the banks of the Elmahassen. The battle was fought between the invading army of Dom Sebastian, the young and arrogant monarch of Lusitania, and the forces led by Muley Abd al Melek, the formidable Emir al Mumemin, the Commander of the true believers, and the ruler of the Moorish Empire. It's worth noting that this account of the battle and Dom Sebastian's fate is in line with historical records.

As the market value of Christian slaves declined, the cruelty of their Muslim captors increased. Fanaticism revelled in the daily spectacle of crusaders who refused to convert to Islam by reciting the Fatha, being condemned to live entombment. The cruel irony of history was evident when the Catholic Auto da fè had its counterpart in the dreadful fate of a king and his army, including his noble knights. They found themselves less than a hundred miles from their kingdom's coast, facing a choice between renouncing their faith or being buried alive for the Moor's satisfaction. These unfortunate souls were forced to prepare their own graves, which were usually cells in the city's wall. One Christian would seal up another, only to meet the same fate himself.

Dom Sebastian, the zealous king, suffered a particularly melancholic fate. He had been defeated and humiliated, and with fewer than half of his once-mighty knights and soldiers, he found himself at the mercy of an unrelenting enemy. He was wounded and in chains, languishing in the wretched dungeon of Mequinez, one of the Sultan's capitals, the others being Fez and Morocco. After the funeral of the unmissed Seedna, who had perished on the battlefield, his son and successor, the newly proclaimed Sultan, chose to mark his coronation by burying the Christian king alive, who had invaded his father's empire despite the late Shereef's warning of inevitable ruin.

The new Sultan's fervent desire for vengeance was fuelled by the mysterious disappearance of his father's priceless crown, which the late Muley Abd al Melek had worn during the battle but was now nowhere to be found. This crown was a precious heirloom dating back to the great Caliphate of Omar, acquired by his victorious general Saad along with the immense treasures of the Chosroes. The crown had been worn by Chosroes Nushirvan in the grand palace of Madayn, the capital of ancient Persia. Its value had been further enhanced by a rare jewel that Emperor Heraclius had gifted to Omar.

These cumulative motives led to one of the cruellest executions devised by human atrocity. The new Seedna also inflicted tortures on his loyal attendants, such as the Mul el Ma, who quenched His Majesty's thirst from a gazelle skin in camp, the Mul Attai, who prepared and served the royal tea, and the most important Mul M'dul, the keeper of the Shereef's red umbrella. The reasons for these punishments remained unresolved.

The inhabitants of Mequinez, who had long provided the majority of the Emperor's devoted servants, were filled with excitement, and the entire population turned out to witness the live burial of a Christian monarch. A procession emerged from the imperial mosque, consisting of notable figures, long-bearded Kadis dressed in white robes, white turbans, and red sandals, with prayer books hanging from their belts. There were talebs, the doctors of law, emins, the mosque ministers, adools, the public notaries, and a group of fukies, who were the guiding lights for the faithful youth.

At the city's gate, they joined another procession, equally grotesque and sombre, reminiscent of the macabre processions of the Inquisition. This group included jubilant children playing tom-toms and horns, accompanied by comical dances and grimaces, much to the amusement of the sympathetic crowd. A frightening figure representing Azrael, the angel of death, followed, and on a donkey sat the woeful representative of Christian royalty, bareheaded and dressed in a black jellab, holding a human skull in his right hand, depicting terror and anguish. This was Dom Sebastian, heading to his grave, with Monkir on his right and Nakir on his left, the demons who would interrogate him about his faith and beat him with clubs if he failed.

The rear of this group was occupied by Eblis, grotesquely dressed in red and armed with instruments of diabolical torture. A group of naked, filthy saints ran alongside, howling and spitting at Portugal's former king, condemning his soul to the deepest pit and praying that Allah would show no mercy to the Christian "dog." Upon passing the city gate, the procession moved along a winding road through well-tended gardens, surrounded by an outer wall, leading to a cell about six feet high but barely wide enough to enclose a human body. The cell was open in the main wall and was intended for Sebastian's suffocation and eternal rest. Too weak to dismount on his own, Sebastian was roughly handled by Monkir and Nakir, who lifted him and placed him inside the cell. They twisted him so that the fanatical onlookers could see his face. Three wooden bars held the victim against the lifeless wall.

All attention was now focused on the mosque, where the signal to seal the king's grave was about to be given by firing a cannon and raising a flag. The eerie ceremony was arranged so that the bricking up of the living tomb would coincide with the prayer time. As the cannon boomed and the flag unfurled, muezzins perched atop their minarets called out, "Allah Akbar, Allah Akbar, God is great, and Mohammed is his Prophet!"

The crowd bowed down in prostration, reciting the Fatha prayer toward Mecca, "Praise be to God, the Lord of all creatures, the most merciful, the King of the Day of Judgment! You we worship, and of You we beg assistance. Direct us in the right way, in the way of those to whom You have been gracious, not of those against whom you are incensed, nor of those who go astray."

After the echoes of the Sulhama prayer had dissipated, the faithful rose from their prayer positions, and the supreme Kadi of the land delivered a decree. He declared, "Listen, worshippers of the true God! The Christian there had plotted the downfall of our nation and the eradication of Islam, but Allah had different plans. Our late Seedna, may Allah grant him paradise's joys, perished in his armour, battling that infidel, who came as an enemy and acted as a traitor, violating the truce. Therefore, our Emir al Mumemin decreed that he should die in disgrace, like the other slaves who refused to recite the

Fatha. May Allah smite the enemies of our Seedna. There is no God but God, and Mohammed is his Prophet!"

Bricks and mortar slowly sealed the open side of the vertical tomb. An hour later, there was no cell in sight, only a plain wall hiding a king who was quickly suffocating, while the triumphant mob returned to the city.

Under Muley Zidan's rule, a decree bearing the Grand Vizier's signature was posted in every mosque across his domain. It promised high honours and the opportunity to marry any maiden within the empire, from the daughter of the first Sultana to any local damsel, to anyone who could restore the lost crown to the ruling dynasty. There would be no inquiries into how the finder came into possession of the imperial diadem.

As time passed, the disastrous crusade and its tragic aftermath became the stuff of legends and tales, turning the historical event into a realm of romance. To this day, the people of Lusitania anticipate the return of Dom Sebastian, believing that he dwells among the Moors, in a state of suspended animation like Barbarossa. In the tribes of Western Barbary, it is commonly believed that the great battle is fought over periodically, always during the new moon, with phantom armies clashing on the banks of the Elmahassen, culminating in the historical defeat of the crusaders.

The audacious invasion would sound like a myth from the time of the Argonauts if the outcome had been less devastating for the adventurers. For a young king in his twenties, with limited resources, to embark on a conquest far from his supply base, aiming for an empire larger than the combined kingdoms of Spain and Portugal, and one that Christendom had learned to fear, was a daring endeavour. The circumstances surrounding the last battle, the death of the Sultan, the loss of the crown, and the grim fate of the prisoners, all added an air of mystique and ghostliness to the event.

The legendary development of the battle near Al Kesar Kebir can be traced back to the experiences of a student from Timbuktu who arrived in Fez at the beginning of the sixteenth century. During this time, the Kairouin was renowned for being one of the world's greatest centres of learning, attracting students from diverse regions. The student from Timbuktu was an exception. He shunned luxury, avoided the pleasures of the harem, and spent his days among ancient books and manuscripts in the Kairouin's underground library. He paid for his purchases without waiting for change and was known for his unique appearance, with eyes that glowed like living topaz stones.

This student, named Omeyya, was a mystery. He had a romantic origin, having grown up as the adopted child of the renowned sibyl Kadijah, who was known as the "owl witch." She was rarely seen by the people of Timbuktu, and her services were only sought in extreme cases. She had an unusual method of healing, involving a drawing of a long-necked bird, which she believed to be a powerful remedy. Omeyya's enigmatic nature and unusual history made him a figure of curiosity and fear among the people.

In Kadijah's dim dwelling, Omeyya grew into consciousness, nurtured with motherly care. As he matured, he was initiated into the secrets of her dark arts. Then, one day, the owl witch surprised him with the offer of a revelation about his life.

"You don't know who you truly are, my son," she began, sensing her approaching end. "And it's time I shared the truth about your birth parents. Here, in this place, Naïma, the daughter of Moadh, the most feared man in Timbuktu, gave birth to you. Your father was Abu

Sofian, the son of Abu Thaleb, whom Moadh had killed in a family feud. As soon as he was old enough, Sofian yearned to avenge his father's death, and his sole focus was on seeking vengeance. From the rooftop of his mother's house, he could see Moadh's terraced residence, and there he daily directed his curses, determined to breach it at the first opportunity and end the life of the ruthless killer.

"His chance came when a fire broke out near Moadh's house. Armed and unnoticed, Sofian slipped into the Saalemlik (reception room). But his target eluded him there. So, he dashed for the Haremlik, intent on striking down Moadh in the protected privacy of his wives. However, his rush was halted when a tiny, jewelled, alabaster hand swept aside a silken curtain, revealing a stunning Houri, so enchanting that Sofian questioned if he was even awake. In her excitement, the girl said, 'Have you come to save me from the flames? They've gone to watch the fire, and my father commanded me to wait for his return. He's a formidable man to disobey.' Her voice melted Sofian's heart, and he couldn't believe his eyes.

"'Radiant one, disguise your beauty in men's clothing so I can rescue you, even if it means my life,' Sofian replied with remarkable composure. The young girl transformed herself into a stately youth.

"'I'm Naïma, and if you'll be the light of my eyes and the breath of my life, I'll be the dust under your feet,' said the transformed maiden.

"Amid the general chaos, they escaped unnoticed and reached the street. That same day, under Sofian's roof, Naïma became his wife. But their secret elopement wasn't safe for long, and the city was soon in an uproar over the news.

"Moadh called upon his kin to avenge the outrage, but Sofian was vigilant. Armed kinsmen guarded his house around the clock to prevent any surprise attacks, and Naïma was placed in my care in case of defeat. There was a siege and a battle, and during the hand-to-hand combat, Sofian mortally wounded Moadh. But in return, Sofian was fatally stabbed by one of the avengers. The young widow stayed under my protection, and this was when you were born. She had no one to turn to or seek help from, so sorrow, shame, and guilt kept her hidden from the sight of men. She wouldn't venture out during the day for fear of being recognized and harmed by her own kin, who despised her.

"She didn't stay with me for long. One unfortunate day, she left her safe haven to enjoy the morning sun and fell prey to marauding Bedouins who attacked and looted the city. My arts couldn't save her, Omeyya. Since then, the daughter of Moadh has changed hands many times, serving as a slave or mistress, as her masters pleased. This happened nineteen years ago, when you came under my care and became my comfort.

"In my youth, I was loved by a man of the black arts who passed on to me the secrets of Egypt's great mystery, the land of his birth. He was knowledgeable, but not enough to elude death, and now I too feel the approach of the inexorable reaper. Tomorrow, I'll be no more, and this hollow will be my grave. Bury me as a son would his mother. Under that stone, you'll find gold to sustain you throughout your life. But you'll leave here to seek a better life, greater wealth, higher status, and the joy of love, along with your mother, in the renowned city on the River of Pearls. You must follow the instructions you'll receive. This dark abyss, Omeyya, conceals Egypt's great mystery, which will become your responsibility. Take this rod from my hand and trace the crescent symbol in the air, from right to left, toward the eastern wall," the witch commanded.

Omeyya complied, and the silvery crescent appeared on the bare rock, with its horns slowly extending downward to form an oval door that led to a brilliantly lit arched space. In the heart of the revealed chamber, perched on an onyx block, stood a large heron, its plumage white from the neck down, the rest adorned with sky blue feathers inscribed with multi-coloured hieroglyphics and an abundance of rubies and amethysts. The hieroglyphics were scattered irregularly across the body of the mystical bird, densest around its wings and thickest on the breast and its gracefully elongated neck. The bird's eyes were topaz, its long bill glistened with black diamonds, and its tail, lapis lazuli in colour, spread like a peacock's and was adorned with star-like patterns set in pearls, emeralds, sapphires, beryls, chrysolites, carbuncles, sards, and various forms of jasper and ligure. Even its black legs were inscribed with kabbalistic lines in rare gems.

"By the genii of Amenti, the masters who created you in the beginning as the symbol and oracle of Osiris, O Phoenix! I adjure you to accept this youth in my place as your favoured one and to heed his call once he interprets the emblems that activate your mystery," the sibyl cried out loudly.

Omeyya's eyes widened in astonishment. The inanimate bird suddenly showed signs of life, fluffing its feathers to display a shimmering array of gems that sparkled like brilliant stars. A golden orange haze radiated from its feathers, turning into a carmine flame that engulfed the bird, leaving the place as it was, dull and lifeless.

"Remember me well, for my time has come! The rod you hold contains the key to the mystery you are to unravel in Fatma's great school, during a period of strict abstinence from physical pleasures. For thirty-seven months, you must only drink morning dew, bathe in the River of Pearls at new moon, and sleep within canvas walls. Your purity is essential, as it makes you deserving of the power unlocked by the revealed arcana," the sibyl said in her final words.

Her frail body fell lifeless to the ground.

Omeyya realized the rod contained something more. In the full light, he discovered an upper end that looked like a carved handle. With a twist, he removed it, revealing a hollow inside. From this cavity, he withdrew a rolled-up papyrus. Unrolling the document revealed a larger sheet than it seemed at first, displaying a lifelike image of the phoenix, with intricate hieroglyphics beautifully rendered. With this scroll in his possession and having paid his last respects to his foster mother, Omeyya departed from the gloomy abode of his childhood, fully determined to follow the sibyl's instructions with utmost diligence.

*

Now, we encounter Omeyya at the Kairouin of Fez, where he has completed his period of probation. On the eve of the new moon, he stood by the banks of Elmahassen, rod in hand, ready to test the occult knowledge he had gained through years of intense study.

The night was cloudy, and Omeyya strained his eyes to spot the slender crescent. "Spirit of Kadijah, assist me," he prayed, and he used his rod to draw an imaginary crescent in front of the real one, now visible through a thin cloud. Like a burst of searchlight, a radiant glow emerged from the crown of a cedar tree, converging on a nest where the shining phoenix perched.

"Bird of Osiris, revered in Heliopolis! If I am as worthy of your masters' favour as I have been successful in comprehending the mystic lore that beckons your presence, then reveal to me the encounter of those armies that fought their last battle in this valley years ago. Let me learn what became of Abd al Melek's crown," Omeyya beseeched, tracing the area with his rod.

In response, the bird let out a prolonged scream, and echoes resounded, mimicking the sound of cavalry, artillery, cheers, and horse neighs. A foreign army is shown, engaging in strategic manoeuvres. They exclaimed in joy as a royal procession led by a young king arrived with a compact force of mounted cavalrymen, all armed to the teeth. Upon assessing the area, the king ordered the construction of a pontoon bridge across the river. The majority of the army divided into two groups, with one fortifying the current position while the other quickly crossed the river to do the same. It was a scene of intense activity on that cloudy night.

During the swift preparations in this part of the valley, a Muslim army suddenly emerged from the shadows of the surrounding groves, gardens, and thickets along the river. They surged forward with remarkable speed, forming ominous battle lines. They even had a group of horsemen ford the stream, positioning themselves on both sides of the water. At the centre, protected by a formidable bodyguard, was the Commander of the true faithful. His grand pavilion stood at the foot of the hill where Omeyya watched, surrounded by smaller pavilions housing His Majesty's ministers. The leader of this Muslim host was the Shereef Abd al Melek, seated atop a white horse, and his crown signified his central authority.

At a gesture from Abd al Melek, the Court's Emin signalled the start of the battle with the cry, "La illaha il Allah!" But before the echoes could return the call, a daring group of Portuguese cavalry charged into the front lines of the Moors. Their fierce attack was accompanied by artillery fire that took a heavy toll on the Muslim forces.

"Praise Allah! Crush the enemies of the faithful!" roared the Sultan, and his army surged forward like a storm sweeping through a forest. Although outnumbered three to one, Dom Sebastian's forces not only held their ground but also pushed their entire infantry formation against the enemy's left flank with such force that it forced the enemy back toward the royal pavilion, sowing confusion and panic. Abd al Melek, who had been watching the action with intense concern, was driven into a fury. He smote anyone within reach with his scimitar, cursed his own men, and in a fit of rage, tore his crown from his head and flung it into the river.

The outcome became uncertain for a moment, but the Christian forces fell like grass under the scythe. Finally, a white flag was raised in Sebastian's sector, leading the Moors to ease off their attack. The desperate king himself charged their ranks with his remaining knights, but the furious Moors swiftly overcame this brave band of Christians, slaying them as traitors. The Emin proclaimed the victory from a mound constructed of Christian heads. From this unique platform, the Sulhama resounded through the valley, "Allah Akbar! Allah Akbar!" The entire army prostrated, with the exception of the Shereef, whose head hung low, chin touching his chest. When help arrived, it was too late. Abd al Melek had passed away, and the dark of night once again reigned, causing the phantom armies to vanish. Omeyya's heart was filled with hope and anticipation. What would the daylight reveal in the river's waters?

As the early dawn broke, Omeyya found himself in the same spot he had occupied during the eventful night. He murmured, "Bismillah! Arrahmani! Arrahimi!" giving thanks to the "all-merciful God" for his incredible success. In the mud at the river's bed, about four feet below the swirling waters, his eyes clearly identified the precious object. In an instant, Omeyya plunged into the water, emerging with the tiara of Abd al Melek. This achievement would have intoxicated a less experienced person, but Omeyya had undergone a trial that left him in full control of his emotions.

Although he had succeeded beyond his wildest dreams, Omeyya returned to Fez with a profound sense of melancholy. He had no one on Earth to share his golden prospects, tied to the treasure he now guarded, along with the boundless potential held by his magical rod. Despite his sobering experiences over the years, Omeyya's thoughts inevitably drifted to the great prize to which he was now entitled. He had a rightful claim to the Seedna's daughter. However, he needed to determine whether the empire's foremost maiden was worth pursuing, and also whether it was prudent to proceed without adequate precautions, given the Shereef's tendency to eliminate bothersome rivals.

Filled with golden daydreams, the young sorcerer made his way to the enclosed bazaar the following day. Here, the Fazzi gathered after the yearly arrival of the Akabah, the grand caravan from Timbuktu, to inspect the displayed human merchandise. It was a paradise for slave dealers. The square marketplace had only one gate and hosted numerous businesses within its confines. The primary trade involved the auction and private sale of slaves. Men, women, and children were stripped of their clothing and examined like livestock, with assessments made on their teeth, eyes, mouth, nostrils, chest, arms, and legs. The agility of slaves was tested through the liberal application of whips to make them jump high, and their strength by lifting heavy weights. Attractive women were subjected to more considerate treatment. Bids were placed, accepted, or declined. Most of the human commodities were of African descent and attired to accentuate their figures.

Among the few white individuals was a woman for whom the owner demanded an astronomical price. He disdainfully rejected a bid of twenty-five doubloons, the highest amount ever offered for a slave above the age of thirty. She wasn't openly displayed like the other slaves, but was concealed behind a canvas screen in a corner, where prospective buyers could privately examine her. The most recent person to inspect her had just emerged from behind the partition. He was a black-skinned Muslim with a silk caftan that indicated his lineage from the Prophet. His fine satin shawl wrapped gracefully around his frame, suggesting that he enjoyed a comfortable income with little work and few worries. He was also a student at the Kairouin, but his studies were focused on the mystery of women, and the bags of gold sand he had brought from Tafilet allowed him to indulge in this pursuit with great diligence.

"What is the age of this beauty?" inquired the descendant of Mohammed.

"This beauty hails from Jannat al Ferdaws, where they remain ever young and sweet, like the blossoms of the Tuba tree," responded the slave dealer enthusiastically.

"If she were a virgin, your comparison might hold, but she has been someone's beloved, and she must have witnessed at least thirty Ramazans," observed the holy connoisseur of the fair sex.

"She'll see thirty more years and still be more beautiful than a twenty-year-old. She's worth her weight in gold," declared the slave dealer.

"Can I buy her for a pound of gold sand?" asked the descendant of the Prophet.

"One hundred doubloons will make Naïma yours," the master of the slave proclaimed.

"Naïma!" a voice nearby echoed. "Is that your slave's name?" inquired Omeyya, who had been observing the transaction.

"That's her name, Cid, as sweet as she is," replied the cunning dealer.

"I'll pay the price if you can satisfy me about her place of birth, her lineage, and her background," Omeyya promised without hesitation.

"What you ask of me, I cannot do. We buy and exchange slaves as we do with other commodities, without concerning ourselves about where they come from or who they are. Why does it matter? I obtained Naïma in Tenduf, but she might have come there from Timbuktu via Tandeng, an oasis in the desert, rich in salt and nourished by fresh springs," the merchant explained.

"She is mine. Have the taleb prepare the legal transfer," Omeyya declared without even looking at the person he had purchased. This surprised the onlookers, and the man in the green caftan left in disgust. In a few minutes, the document was drawn up and signed, the price was paid, and Omeyya, trembling with emotion, led the slave away, whom he was convinced must be his mother.

Once in his tent, he had her remove her kaik, the face cover, and had her sit on a cushion. He knelt before her, gazed at her beautiful face, kissed her hands, and spoke, "Your first response to my first question should be straightforward and concise. If your father was Moadh of Timbuktu, your husband was Sofian, son of Abu Thaleb, from the same city, if your friend was the owl witch Kadijah, if a child named Omeyya was born to you in her cave, then speak the word so that I may praise Allah's great mercy."

"What spirit has told you the story of my sorrow, master?" the woman exclaimed in an emotional tone. "You must be a descendant of the all-knowing Prophet!"

"No! Isn't it enough that I am your child?" replied Omeyya, tears welling up, and there was a moment of poignant emotion that words couldn't express.

Once again, it was a new moon night. Naïma now lived in a luxurious home, attended to by slaves. She moved through rooms adorned with silk draperies and soft Moorish rugs. Her eyelids were adorned with kohl, her fingernails painted with henna. Her harem opened onto a courtyard scented by mandragora and orange blossoms, cooled by the splashing of fountains and enlivened by storks, sacred birds in Morocco. Mother and son had bared their souls to each other, both confident that their dreams were about to be realized.

*

Omeyya found himself alone once more in the silent night, under the stars veiled by clouds. He had been waiting since before the sun set, gazing at the picturesque view of Western Mecca, the groves, and gardens spread across the slopes of the valley through which the Wad el Jubar flowed. Omeyya stood on the hilltop crowned by Mulai Ismael's bastion, providing a perfect view of Fez, especially when the dark night had fallen over the city and the golden globe atop the renowned Mulai Edris Mosque faded from view. This was when he heard the nightingale at its best, and his soul was attuned to its amorous melody. When the crescent moon ascended in the heavenly tapestry, the time had come for the revelation of Egypt's mystery. At the right moment, Omeyya's rod infused the bird with power, raising it above the courtyard and palace. A white radiance enveloped the area, and at its heart, the heron appeared in mid-flight.

"Bird of Osiris, revered in Heliopolis! By the unseen masters who created you, I demand to witness the one destined to be my partner," Omeyya implored with trepidation.

Omeyya was startled when the phoenix seemed to vanish, as if affronted by his request. However, in its place, just like Iris emerging from the clouds, appeared a smiling Hebe, with Muley Zidan and his chief Sultana standing regally behind her.

"Hamdillah!" exclaimed Omeyya, falling to his knees to praise "Allah, the Most Merciful, the King of the Day of Judgment!"

When he rose, the stars and the silvery crescent adorned the sky, while the valley of the River of Pearls resounded with the trill of countless nightingales.

The following morning, the streets of Fez resounded with the cries of the Sultan's heralds, summoning the one who was entitled to the great prize to come forth and claim it. "Bring the crown and receive your reward!" was the proclamation heard in the streets and bazaars, although no one knew what it meant.

Omeyya suspected that something had occurred in the palace and felt that his victory was assured. As he later discovered, the same night, the Shereef, the Shereefa, and their daughter Rehamina had shared the same vision, a coincidence that could only be explained in one way. Abd al Melek's crown had been found. The Sultan's criers were dispatched to inform the fortunate discoverer of his prize. Thus, doubly reassured, Omeyya presented himself before the Emir al Mumemin, who was deeply impressed by the student's account.

"What you saw, my child, was not the phoenix of Osiris, but rather Allah's splendid rooster, which sings each morning to delight the ears of the true God, as all birds of its kind join in its melodious praise. Only by a miracle, with the help of the bird our Prophet beheld in the heavens, could Abd al Melek's crown be restored," the Seedna concluded devoutly.

In the presence of the grand Divan, Omeyya displayed the crown, and in the throne hall, his engagement to Rehamina was solemnly confirmed. In due course, a royal wedding was held, and thereafter, Muley Zidan found in Omeyya not only a worthy husband for his lovely daughter but also a trusted confidant and wise counsellor in his council.

The Tunisian Sage; Or, The Powder Of Longevity

This story is adapted from The Thousand And One Days by Julia Pardoe, published in 1857 by William Lay, London.

Selim-ben-Foubi had spent twenty years in the world of commerce when he unexpectedly inherited a fortune that greatly exceeded his needs and desires. He had lost all his children, and this newfound wealth brought him little joy. In fact, he found it rather burdensome to possess so much gold and precious items he would never use.

He contemplated his situation and said, "I'm fifty years old now, and even if I were to live to a hundred, I couldn't possibly spend half of what I own. I can only eat one meal at a time, wear one outfit, and sleep in one bed. So, if I can live in a comfortable house, eat my fill, and share a meal with a friend, that's all I truly need. I've decided to give away half of my wealth while I'm alive, so I can experience the happiness of creating joy for others."

With this generous plan in mind, Selim wanted to seek the advice of two of his friends. Leaving his country house in Boudjaréah, he headed to Aldgezaire. There, in the garden of the grand mosque, resided a wise and venerable mufti. He sat next to the mufti under the shade of blooming pomegranate trees and began the conversation.

"Mehtem, I've come to visit you because I want to pour out my heart and seek your wisdom. As you know, I've suddenly become very wealthy, and I have no son to inherit my riches. Is my wealth too much for a single man? Please, share your thoughts," Selim inquired.

"That which Allah bestows should never be regarded lightly," replied the sage.

"I don't look down on my wealth," Selim explained, "but I'm thinking about sharing it with others and keeping only what I need to live out the rest of my days."

"You don't know how long your days will be," Mehtem cautioned.

"Assuming I enjoy the longest life possible - say, a hundred years - do you think I'll live any longer?" Selim asked.

"Only Allah knows that," the sage replied.

"Let's imagine five hundred years then," Selim continued. "Surely, that covers all possibilities. So, during this extended time, wouldn't it be more satisfying for me to know that my riches are being put to good use, rather than hoarded away in some vault, where they might arouse envy among the poor or attract the greed of wrongdoers?"

"Perhaps," said the mufti.

"So, you think it's a good idea?" Selim inquired.

"It might be," the mufti replied, "but whether it will work in practice is uncertain. Many people have wise thoughts, but it's rare to see them put those thoughts into action."

"Please advise me," Selim requested. "I want to fulfil the law and do good. How should I distribute half of my substantial fortune?"

The mufti pondered deeply and then responded, "I advise you to take at least a year to contemplate your project. Time is like the sun that ripens a person's thoughts. Reflecting before taking action is rarely a cause for regret. Reflect, and then come consult with me."

Selim left the mosque and went to Bab-a-Zoun street, to visit his other friend, a Moorish merchant who worked hard to make a living. He began the conversation with a question, "We've been friends for ten years now, and that's why I come to ask you this. How do you think a wealthy and benevolent man should use his fortune to be of service?"

The Moorish merchant replied, "You're making quite an unusual inquiry. I can't imagine why a man with a desire to give would find it difficult. He can build a mosque, assist the elderly, support widows and orphans, enrich his friends, if he has any, for the wealthy usually have friends."

Selim continued, "But what if it were you? What would you do if you had something to give away?"

"I?" the merchant responded. "I can't imagine myself having anything to give away, considering that I can barely afford to pay the rent for my modest shop and stock it with a few sacks of rice and some coffee. If I had money, I'd certainly start by buying a house and merchandise. There's no point in asking a poor man like me, 'To whom would you give your money?' But I'll tell you, there's no shortage of good deeds to be done. Fortunate is the one who only has to decide."

"You're absolutely right," Selim told his friend. With that, he left and returned to his country house in Boudjaréah. On his way, he encountered his neighbour Achmet the Arab. Selim stopped to chat with him and posed a question, "You're a man of mature age, well-versed in life's matters. Tell me, do you think it's wise for a wealthy childless man to give away half of his fortune while he's still alive and reserve the other half to maintain a decent life in his remaining years?"

Achmet responded, "I can't say whether it's more pleasing to Allah to give or keep the wealth He has blessed you with. As for me, I don't have much to give, given my modest fortune and the numerous children I have. But if I were rich and had no heirs, I would bury my gold in a corner of my garden rather than give it to satisfy people, most of whom tend to be either wicked or ungrateful. This gold would eventually be found by someone whom Allah meant to enrich, and so I wouldn't be responsible for how it was used."

"Your idea isn't necessarily a bad one," Selim acknowledged. "I'll certainly ponder it."

While Selim and Achmet were conversing, a poorly dressed Tunisian man approached them. This man was none other than Hussein Muley, a physician from Tunis. He was already advanced in age, known for his knowledge, but not for his wealth. Selim kindly invited him to rest at his home, and Hussein accepted the offer. After exchanging greetings with Achmet, Selim led his guest into one of the cool and refreshing rooms in his delightful residence. Hussein Muley, weary from a two-hour walk in the scorching sun, reclined on a divan while being served with a generous supply of fruits and coffee.

After taking some time to rest and recover, Selim addressed him amicably, "I'm delighted to have you in my home, as you are a wise man with a great reputation in your field. You've travelled, read, and experienced life, so you must surely be capable of offering sound judgment on matters pertaining to this life. I would greatly appreciate your opinion on a project I'm considering. I've come into significant wealth through inheritance and have no children. I'm contemplating giving away a substantial portion of my wealth while I'm still alive. How do you think I should best use this wealth?"

Hussein Muley looked at Selim with astonishment. "You want to give away a substantial part of your wealth," he said. "This is truly remarkable. I've travelled, read, and experienced life, as you mentioned, but I've never heard of anyone giving away most of their fortune while still alive."

"Does that mean it would be a mistake?" Selim inquired.

"I'm not sure," the Tunisian replied, lost in deep thought, his gaze fixed on the tips of his worn-out slippers rather than taking in the view of the ever-changing sea and the azure sky in the distance.

"What are you pondering?" Selim asked after a while.

"I was contemplating... I was thinking that if human life were longer, it would benefit both those who study science and those fortunate enough to possess great wealth. It would also be advantageous for the poor, as they might hope to enjoy the fruits of their labour if they worked hard to become wealthy."

"Why dwell on a matter that all of humanity's reflections can't change?"

"I don't believe that the current length of human life follows the course of nature. Until now, physicians have often shortened it unintentionally. My goal is to rectify the unintentional harm they've caused and be remembered with gratitude by future generations."

"What do you mean?" Selim exclaimed. "You want to alter the natural order of things, the entire course of nature?"

"Nothing can convince me that our natural course is to die at sixty or eighty years when people once lived for hundreds of years. I am convinced that we were created to live much longer, and I dedicate all my days, nights, and studies to the pursuit of a discovery that will extend human existence. It will return things to the way they were when people married at a hundred years old and lived to see their grandchildren grow up and marry in their turn. I often wonder, why should our lives be shorter than those of oak trees in the forest, serpents, or even vultures?"

"If we lived as long as oak trees," Selim responded, "the cedars and palm trees would still outlive us."

"You jest, but your jesting is misplaced, for nothing is more serious than the idea that consumes me. Imagine for a moment, wouldn't you be delighted to witness countless sunrises and sunsets, to marvel at the wonders of the heavens and the fertility of the earth for ages to come?"

Selim pondered for a moment and replied, "It's true that people don't embrace death, but life may not be as desirable as you suggest."

"So, you're not interested in extending your time on this earth? For me, I long for it greatly. In addition to my days and nights, I devote all the knowledge I gather from my scholarly pursuits to achieving this great goal. I'm already on the path, but unfortunately, I lack gold. This gold you either despise or don't know how to employ - it could, in my hands, contribute to the happiness of future generations. With gold, you can acquire valuable books, study the stars, unearth treasures from the depths of the earth, extract metals, decompose substances, and, in short, unlock countless mysteries. Yes, gold, which has never granted its possessor an extra day, not even an extra hour, would enable me to make an extraordinary discovery. I wouldn't keep the secret to myself, and I would first share it with the person whose wealth had aided me in obtaining it."

"But if you were to discover a means to extend my life for centuries, I wouldn't be wealthy enough to give away half of my fortune."

"What!" exclaimed the Tunisian physician. "Isn't life more valuable than all the riches in the world? If someone were to tell you right now, 'You must give up all your possessions or face a lethal blow from a yataghan or a gunshot to your chest,' wouldn't you willingly relinquish your wealth to avoid such a fate?"

"You puzzle me, but I think in that situation, I would indeed sacrifice my property to save my life."

"Then you see that life is precious, even to the poor. So why not strive to prolong your own? Even if my profound knowledge fails to achieve this, you would still be affluent enough to enjoy a life of somewhat shorter duration."

Listening to the erudite physician, Selim gradually fell into deep contemplation. The Tunisian, rather than continuing his discourse, joined Selim in introspection. Consequently, the two men became absorbed in their individual thoughts while in each other's presence, with only Allah knowing the nature of their reflections.

After an extended period of silent contemplation, Selim addressed Hussein Muley, saying, "Before meeting you, my intention was to give away half of my fortune to make others happy during my lifetime. I believe that aiding you in your scholarly endeavours, which aim to extend human life, aligns perfectly with my original purpose. Therefore, Hussein Muley, I propose to provide you with the gold you need right away. Come with me."

The Tunisian, who appeared more astonished than overjoyed by these words, gravely stood up and followed Selim to another room in the house. Selim handed him a small casket filled with gold coins.

"Use this wisely," Selim advised, "and keep me informed of your progress."

"I will not fail to do so," replied Hussein Muley. Clutching the precious casket to his chest, he declared, "With this, I have the means to quench my thirst for knowledge, overcome any obstacles, and uncover the long-lost secret that could add centuries to human life, extending our days to those of our ancestors. Selim," he added, "your generosity is commendable. I need not express my gratitude because I am about to work for you as I would for myself. Nonetheless, I genuinely thank you with all my heart."

After uttering these words, the erudite physician departed with a solemn and contemplative demeanour.

Selim, too, remained deeply absorbed in his thoughts. Left alone, he contemplated the conundrum of long and short lives, pondering the incredible feats achieved by science. He found himself questioning whether he should confide in the sage mufti, whom he would soon meet again, regarding his assistance to Hussein Muley and his hope to witness an almost indefinite extension of human life. Ultimately, he decided not to disclose his involvement to anyone and opted to silently await the miraculous discovery of his new acquaintance, Hussein Muley, the physician from Tunis.

Several months passed without any sign of the physician, but when he finally returned to Boudjaréah, he appeared even more emaciated, haggard, and fragile than a man who had traversed the vast expanse of the Sahara Desert on foot. His feeble frame seemed barely able to support his trembling form.

"Tell me," Selim inquired, "what has happened to you? Are you unwell, or have you returned to me on the brink of starvation?"

"No, but I have travelled ceaselessly beneath the dim starlight and the scorching sun's rays, often forgetting to take necessary sustenance due to my deep immersion in my studies."

"And what's the outcome?"

"Unfortunately, I haven't achieved what I had hoped for. So far, all I've managed is to secure the ability to extend our lives by fifty years."

Having uttered these words, Hussein Muley sorrowfully placed his withered hands upon his chest and continued, "I realize that such a discovery would bring great joy to anyone else, but it falls short of satisfying me. An additional fifty years, is that all?"

"It's still something," Selim responded, "so will you enlighten me on what's required to gain those extra fifty years of life?"

"Shall I reveal it to you?" exclaimed the Tunisian. "I've come here specifically for that purpose and to provide you with this powder. You must take it every morning on an empty stomach for a period of one year, three months, one week, and one day without fail."

"I must jot down these instructions," said Selim.

He promptly took note of the guidelines and then inquired, "Don't you think you should be content with your discovery, begin to live well, and get some proper rest to enjoy the remaining years of your life?"

"I have no desire to rest from my efforts yet. What's the significance of adding fifty years to sixty or eighty, which will soon be over for me? No, no, I wish to live for at least two centuries, relishing the fruits of my labour, securing the prosperity of my children, and even my children's children. Do you think we'll initially share this magnificent secret, which has cost us so much, with everyone for free? It's this secret that will allow us to live in luxury until the end of our days. You can, for substantial sums of money, distribute the powder I will have created to whomever you choose, just as I will exchange it for gold. And when we eventually pass away, sated with life, we'll bequeath our secret to the generations that come after us."

"This plan sounds fair and well thought out to me. However, I have no intention of selling the powder. Can I give it away immediately to one or two individuals whom I highly regard?"

"No, let's not draw attention to our good fortune just yet. We should wait until my discovery is completely perfected."

"Agreed. But it saddens me to see you so pale, thin, and frail as you are."

"Oh, that's of little concern," said the Tunisian, striking his forehead with his hands. "Don't let my emaciated appearance trouble you. I'd rather have nothing but skin on my bones and keep my secret safe. I'll soon regain my health and my colour. No, my health doesn't worry me; I'm simply anxious because I lack the money needed to continue my studies."

"Do you require much?" Selim inquired.

"Ah, yes, quite a substantial sum," replied Hussein with a sigh. "If I fail to secure it, instead of living fifty years longer than the typical lifespan, I will either starve myself or drown myself in my house's well."

"Be careful not to take such extreme measures," Selim cautioned. "I can still give you something. Use that, and later on, follow my advice to sell your powder to a wealthy individual to fund your extensive research."

Hussein Muley appeared to be deeply lost in thought, with his forehead resting in his hands. He seemed as if he weren't listening to Selim, but it's quite possible he heard him very well.

"You're not listening to me," Selim continued. "Hussein! Hussein! I will provide you with another small case of gold, but after this one, I have nothing left to give you. There will only be enough for me during the time I hope to live, thanks to your powder. If you discover something even more extraordinary, you'll share it with me, at least for my own benefit, won't you?"

Hussein Muley suddenly seemed to snap out of his reverie and exclaimed, "Ah! I have finally found what I've been seeking! Yes, there's only one herb missing now. I will search for it, even if it's at the far end of the earth, and I will resolve the great problem that has preoccupied me for over thirty years. Selim! Selim! Entrust what you can still dedicate to the well-being of humanity into my care, and rest assured that you'll earn the admiration and gratitude of future generations."

"I desire neither one nor the other," Selim replied. "I simply want to do a little good, that's all. Will I succeed in my endeavour? I'll admit to you, Hussein Muley, that I've regretted more than once devoting my fortune to a discovery that could turn out to be more harmful than beneficial to the world. The world is already crowded enough, and what would happen if people lived for several centuries? Wouldn't they end up killing each other due to lack of space?"

"Do they not already kill each other by sea and by land?" said Hussein Muley with a peculiar smile. "Come," he continued, "don't trouble yourself with what might happen on Earth in the future. Make use of the opportunities that fate offers you and enjoy extended days in peace."

After sharing these words, he accepted the second case of gold offered by Selim, tucked it under his arm, and stated in a solemn tone, "I'm about to embark on a journey to Asia. There, near the Indies, lies a towering mountain, Mount Himalaya - do you know of it?"

"No," Selim replied.

"Neither do I, actually, but I'm heading there to find a specific plant on its summit, which will complete the discoveries I've already made."

"I thought nothing grew on those mountain peaks covered with perpetual snow and frost?"

"Indeed, nothing does except for the one I require. I'm going to find it and will show it to you upon my return."

"Very well," Selim said, and they parted ways.

Hussein Muley retreated with swift steps.

Meanwhile, Selim meticulously stored the powder, which he was supposed to take daily on an empty stomach for a year, three months, a week, and a day. Luckily, he found the taste of this substance not too unpleasant.

The Tunisian, along with his wife, children, and several chests, presumably containing his books and research materials, departed from Aldgezaire. However, Selim never saw him again. He patiently awaited his return for three, five, ten years. Since he believed that ten years should be sufficient to travel to Asia and scale the highest mountain there, he began to suspect that the yellow, gaunt, and scholarly Tunisian was either deceased or had taken advantage of his lack of knowledge and gullibility.

As these thoughts consumed his mind, an epidemic swept through Aldgezaire, and Selim fell victim to it. He decided to seek the counsel of the wise mufti, who was still alive, and in a moment of candour prompted by danger, he confided in him. Selim revealed how he had given two caskets filled with gold to Hussein Muley with the hope of extending human life for many centuries.

The wise mufti stroked his long, white beard and remarked, "Selim, Selim, you've been taken in by a fraudster to whom you imprudently entrusted your noble intentions. This just proves the truth of what I once said to you, 'Even with the best intentions, we can commit the most foolish actions.'"

Selim sighed and replied, "Ah! My misfortune is that I didn't follow the spontaneous impulse of my heart. I genuinely wanted to do good, but in seeking advice from various sources, I followed the worst guidance."

The mufti nodded in agreement, "Yes, you might have acted wisely by following your initial instinct. However, if, as I advised, you had taken more time to reflect on your benevolent plans, you certainly wouldn't have given your gold to a swindler who only mocked your gullibility."

Selim admitted his mistake. He understood that seeking the wisdom of the learned is of no use if you don't intend to heed it. He humbly prostrated himself before Allah, gradually regained his health, and generously distributed a substantial sum of money to the needy at the mosques. He no longer placed his trust in the notion of hundreds of years of life from Mount Himalaya or the elixir of longevity.

The Golden Headed Fish

This story has been adapted from Andrew Lang's version of the same tale that originally appeared in The Olive Fairy Book, published in 1907 by Longmans, Green and Co., London and New York. This tale is based on an original taken from Contes Arméniens by Frédéric Macler, published in 1905.

Once upon a time there lived in Egypt a king who lost his sight from a bad illness. Of course, he was very unhappy, and became more so as months passed, and all the best doctors in the land were unable to cure him. The poor man grew so thin from misery that everyone thought he was going to die, and the prince, his only son, thought so too.

Great was the rejoicing through Egypt when a traveller arrived in a boat down the river Nile, and after questioning the people as to the reason of their downcast looks, declared that he was court physician to the king of a far country, and would, if allowed, examine the eyes of the blind man. He was at once admitted into the royal presence, and after a few minutes of careful study announced that the case, though very serious, was not quite hopeless.

"Somewhere in the Great Sea," he said, "there exists a golden headed fish. If you can manage to catch this creature, bring it to me, and I will prepare an ointment from its blood which will restore your sight.

For a hundred days I will wait here, but if at the end of that time the fish should still be uncaught, I must return to my own master."

The next morning the young prince set forth in quest of the fish, taking with him a hundred men, each man carrying a net. Quite a little fleet of boats was awaiting them and in these they sailed to the middle of the Great Sea. For three months they laboured diligently from sunrise to sunset, but though they caught large multitudes of fishes, not one of them had a golden head.

"It is quite useless now," said the prince on the very last night. "Even if we find it this evening, the hundred days will be over in an hour, and long before we could reach the Egyptian capital the doctor will be on his way home. Still, I will go out again, and cast the net once more myself." And so he did, and at the very moment that the hundred days were up, he drew in the net with the golden headed fish entangled in its meshes.

"Success has come, but as happens often, it is too late," murmured the young man, who had studied in the schools of philosophy, "but, all the same, put the fish in that vessel full of water, and we will take it back to show my father that we have done what we could."

But when he drew near the fish it looked up at him with such piteous eyes that he could not make up his mind to condemn it to death. For he knew well that, though the doctors of his own country were ignorant of the secret of the ointment, they would do all in their power to extract something from the fish's blood. So, he picked up the prize of so much labour, and threw it back into the sea, and then began his journey back to the palace. When at last he reached it, he found the king in a high fever, caused by his disappointment, and he refused to believe the story told him by his son.

"Your head shall pay for it! Your head shall pay for it!" cried he, and bade the courtiers instantly summon the executioner to the palace.

But of course, somebody ran at once to the queen, and told her of the king's order, and she put common clothes on the prince, and filled his pockets with gold, and hurried him on board a ship which was sailing that night for a distant island.

"Your father will repent someday, and then he will be thankful to know you are alive," said she. "But one last counsel will I give you, and that is, take no man into your service who desires to be paid every month."

The young prince thought this advice rather odd. If the servant had to be paid anyhow, he did not understand what difference it could make whether it was by the year or by the month. However, he had many times proved that his mother was wiser than he, so he promised obedience.

After a voyage of several weeks, he arrived at the island of which his mother had spoken. It was full of hills and woods and flowers, and beautiful white houses stood everywhere in fragrant gardens.

"What a charming spot to live in," thought the prince. And he lost no time in buying one of the prettiest of the dwellings.

Then servants came pressing to offer their services, but as they all declared that they must have payment at the end of every month, the young man, who remembered his mother's words, declined to have anything to say to them. At length, one morning, an Arab appeared and begged that the prince would engage him.

"And what wages do you ask?" inquired the prince, when he had questioned the newcomer and found him suitable.

"I do not want money," answered the Arab, "at the end of a year you can see what my services are worth to you and can pay me in any way you like." And the young man was pleased and took the Arab for his servant.

Now, although no one would have guessed it from the look of the side of the island where the prince had landed, the other part was a complete desert, owing to the ravages of a horrible monster which came up from the sea, and devoured all the corn and cattle. The governor had sent bands of soldiers to lie in wait for the creature in order to kill it, but, somehow, no one ever happened to be awake at the moment that the ravages were committed. It was in vain that the sleepy soldiers were always punished severely - the same thing invariably occurred next time, and at last heralds were sent throughout the island to offer a great reward to the man who could slay the monster.

As soon as the Arab heard the news, he went straight to the governor's palace. "If my master can succeed in killing the monster, what reward will you give him?" asked he.

"My daughter and anything besides that he chooses," answered the governor. But the Arab shook his head.

"Give him your daughter and keep your wealth," said he, "but, henceforward, let her share in your gains, whatever they are."

"It is well," replied the governor, and ordered a deed to be prepared, which was signed by both of them.

That night the Arab stole down to the shore to watch, but, before he set out, he rubbed himself all over with some oil which made his skin smart so badly that there was no chance of his going to sleep as the soldiers had done. Then he hid himself behind a large rock and waited. By and by a swell seemed to rise on the water, and, a few minutes later, a hideous monster - part bird, part beast, and part serpent - stepped noiselessly on to the rocks. It walked stealthily up towards the fields, but the Arab was ready for it, and, as it passed, he plunged his dagger into the soft part behind the ear. The creature staggered and gave a loud cry, and then rolled over dead, with its feet in the sea.

The Arab watched for a little while, in order to make sure that there was no life left in his enemy, but as the huge body remained quite still, he quitted his hiding place, and cut off the ears of his foe. These he carried to his master, bidding him show them to the governor, and declare that he himself, and no other, had killed the monster.

"But it was you, and not I, who slew him," objected the prince.

"Never mind, do as I bid you. I have a reason for it," answered the Arab. And though the young man did not like taking credit for what he had never done, at length he gave in.

The governor was so delighted at the news that he begged the prince to take his daughter to wife that very day, but the prince refused, saying that all he desired was a ship which would carry him to see the world. Of course, this was granted him at once, and when he and his faithful Arab embarked they found, heaped up in the vessel, stores of diamonds and precious stones, which the grateful governor had secretly placed there.

So, they sailed, and they sailed, and they sailed, and at length they reached the shores of a great kingdom. Leaving the prince on board, the Arab went into the town to find out what sort of a place it was. After some hours he returned, saying that he heard that the king's daughter was the most beautiful princess in the world, and that the prince would do well to ask for her hand.

Nothing loth, the prince listened to this advice, and taking some of the finest necklaces in his hand, he mounted a splendid horse which the Arab had bought for him, and rode up to the palace, closely followed by his faithful attendant.

The strange king happened to be in a good humour, and they were readily admitted to his presence. Laying down his offerings on the steps of the throne, he prayed the king to grant him his daughter in marriage.

The monarch listened to him in silence, but answered, after a pause, "Young man, I will give you my daughter to wife, if that is your wish, but first I must tell you that she has already gone through the marriage ceremony with a hundred and ninety young men, and not one of them lived for twelve hours after. So, think, while there is yet time."

The prince did think and was so frightened that he very nearly went back to his ship without any more words. But just as he was about to withdraw his proposal the Arab whispered, "Fear nothing but take her."

"The luck must change some time," the prince said, at last, "and who would not risk his head for the hand of such a peerless princess?"

"As you will," replied the king. "Then I will give orders that the marriage shall be celebrated tonight."

And so, it was done, and after the ceremony the bride and bridegroom retired to their own apartments to sup by themselves, for such was the custom of the country. The moon shone bright, and the prince walked to the window to look out upon the river and upon the distant hills, when his gaze suddenly fell on a silken shroud neatly laid out on a couch, with his name embroidered in gold thread across the front, for this also was the pleasure of the king.

Horrified at the spectacle, he turned his head away, and this time his glance rested on a group of men, digging busily beneath the window. It was a strange hour for anyone to be at work, and what was the hole for? It was a curious shape, so long and narrow, almost like… Ah, yes, that was what it was! It was his grave that they were digging!

The shock of the discovery rendered him speechless, yet he stood fascinated and unable to move. At this moment a small black snake darted from the mouth of the princess, who was seated at the table, and wriggled quickly towards him. But the Arab was watching for something of the sort to happen, and seizing the serpent with some pincers that he held in one hand, he cut off its head with a sharp dagger.

The king could hardly believe his eyes when, early the next morning, his new son in law craved an audience of his Majesty.

"What, you?" he cried, as the young man entered.

"Yes, I. Why not?" asked the bridegroom, who thought it best to pretend not to know anything that had occurred. "You remember, I told you that the luck must turn at last, and so it has. But I came to ask whether you would be so kind as to bid the gardeners fill up a great hole right underneath my window, which spoils the view."

"Oh, certainly, yes, of course, it shall be done!" stammered the king. "Is there anything else?"

"No, nothing, thank you," replied the prince, as he bowed and withdrew.

Now, from the moment that the Arab cut off the snake's head, the spell, or whatever it was, seemed to have been taken off the princess, and she lived very happily with her husband. The days passed swiftly in hunting in the forests, or sailing on the broad river that flowed past the palace, and when night fell, she would sing to her harp, or the prince would tell her tales of his own country.

One evening a man in a strange garb, with a face burnt brown by the sun, arrived at court. He asked to see the bridegroom, and falling on his face announced that he was a messenger sent by the queen of Egypt, proclaiming him king in succession to his father, who was dead.

"Her Majesty begs you will set out without delay, and your bride also, as the affairs of the kingdom are somewhat in disorder," ended the messenger.

Then the young man hastened to seek an audience of his father-in-law, who was delighted to find that his daughter's husband was not merely the governor of a province, as he had supposed, but the king of a powerful country. He at once ordered a splendid ship to be made ready, and in a week's time rode down to the harbour, to bid farewell to the young couple.

In spite of her grief for the dead king, the queen was overjoyed to welcome her son home, and commanded the palace to be hung with splendid stuffs to do honour to the bride. The people expected great things from their new sovereign, for they had suffered much from the harsh rule of the old one, and crowds presented themselves every morning with petitions in their hands, which they hoped to persuade the king to grant. Truly, he had enough to keep him busy, but he was very happy for all that, till, one night, the Arab came to him, and begged permission to return to his own land.

Filled with dismay the young man said, "Leave me! Do you really wish to leave me?" Sadly, the Arab bowed his head.

"No, my master, never could I wish to leave you! But I have received a summons, and I dare not disobey it."

The king was silent, trying to choke down the grief he felt at the thought of losing his faithful servant.

"Well, I must not try to keep you," he faltered out at last. "That would be a poor return for all that you have done for me! Everything I have is yours, take what you will, for without you I should long ago have been dead!"

"And without you, I should long ago have been dead," answered the Arab, "for I am the Golden Headed Fish."

A Night By The Dead Sea

This story has been adapted from Henry Iliowizi's version of the same tale that originally appeared in The Weird Orient, published in 1900 by Henry T. Coates and Company, Philadelphia.

Othman Ibn Saad was for many years a name for which that of Eblis was substituted because of his dare devil exploits in highway robbery, which prompted the Ottoman Government to set a price on his head. The chief of Kerak was especially interested in Othman's capture, offering to double the reward, but no claimant appeared on the scene, while every week added new outrages to the long list of the brigand's incredible perpetrations. Again and again the enforcers of the law had been on the track of the dreaded Eblis only to discover too late, after a hot but fruitless chase, that the object of their hunt had posed the while as their informer, guide, or delightful boon companion, filling their ears with tales of the blood curdling atrocities of the robber.

Othman had the means of impersonating Greek, Turk, Jew, Armenian, any officer, dervish, saint, beggar, foreign gentleman, or woman, and even resorted to the guise of the devil, which is why he was sometimes called Eblis. It was the study of his life, and he plied his trade with surprising dexterity and hardihood. Tall, wiry, of tawny complexion, flashing eye, an iron grip, black hair, short beard, easy manner, and ostentatiously scrupulous in matters appertaining to the mosque, it never occurred to those who had met him in friendly intercourse, that his hands reeked with the blood of murder committed with the least possible compunction.

The authorities were perplexed by the conflicting descriptions provided by those fortunate enough to encounter the bandit and survive his murderous attacks. They were also baffled by the strange coincidence of him shedding blood at two distant locations at the same hour. This led many to believe that the terrifying highwayman might be a manifestation of the devil, holding court in a remote hideout on the shores of the Dead Sea - a suitable dwelling for Satan's dark schemes. This belief was reinforced by the fact that Othman's crimes consistently occurred on the darkest nights in the Jordan Valley. He showed no favouritism between Muslims and non-believers, treating all his victims with malicious cruelty.

However, the supposed embodiment of Eblis, in reality, enjoyed a comfortable home in the Plain of Engedi. This hamlet eked out a living from meagre vegetation in a desolate oasis, surrounded by the harshest of wilderness - burnt mountains, pestilential marshes, rugged cliffs, deep ravines, a rocky shore, and small valleys covered in salt deposits - all framing the most lifeless and dead sea on Earth. The region was bleak, miasmatical, and suffused with sulphur, inspiring Milton's descriptions of infernal suffering.

Othman's modest dwelling was maintained by a devoted wife and brightened by an affectionate son named Yezed, in his early twenties. Yezed learned from the muezzin at the small village mosque, the sole public structure in their settlement. Othman had set up his base here for his business but ventured as far as his swift horse could carry him during the darkest hours, using paths known only to him.

Othman's household was sustained by a small plot of crops and livestock, including a cow, a few sheep, and a couple of donkeys. There was little in the robber's life to provoke envy among his neighbours, except for his fiery horse, El Barak, named for the Prophet's lightning-fast steed. El Barak was gentle with Othman and Yezed but fiercely hostile to strangers, attacking them with ferocity. No one suspected that the horse had been trained to harm people.

Othman was a friendly neighbour who didn't meddle in others' affairs and was considered one of the village's least threatening inhabitants. He earned a small income by guiding those curious to explore the mysteries of the desolation surrounding the Dead Sea. This served as a plausible reason for his ownership of El Barak.

However, the time had come to reveal the family secret to Yezed. The son needed to be acquainted with his father's business, and his mettle had to be tested. Yezed was well-versed in the Koran and had a dreamy disposition filled with fantastical Islamic traditions. While Othman disapproved of his son's visionary nature, he saw promise in Yezed's love for horses and his desire to own a horse like El Barak. This wish was granted on Yezed's twenty-first birthday, and the people of Engedi began to suspect that Othman was wealthier than he appeared.

In a few weeks, Yezed rode his horse like an experienced equestrian, and his father asked him to accompany him to a location they planned to visit the following evening. A dervish had passed through the village and mentioned that a group of foreigners would be passing south of Engedi on their way to see Jebel Usdum, a massive ridge of rock salt that extended for miles, glistening like diamonds in the tropical sun and appearing eerie under the moonlight. Othman seized the opportunity, and as the sun set, two riders emerged from

Engedi, leaving the fertile land behind and advancing between the lifeless Dead Sea on one side and barren cliffs on the other.

The fading light cast an atmosphere of indescribable gloom over the desolate landscape, with a leaden haze forming over the sea, making it resemble a vast pool of stagnant oil. There was no sign of life except for the sound of their horses' hooves. Othman, who had been silent until then, suddenly halted his horse and exchanged a glance with Yezed. Yezed's imagination had been ignited by the sight of the setting sun, thinking of the eternal joys of Jannat al Naïm, the Prophet's Garden of Delight.

"Yezed, I'm thinking that you've reached your twenty-first year, and you seem as helpless as a child. You lack ambition, and there's no driving desire to motivate you towards a courageous act. If I were to pass away tonight, what would become of you and your mother?" Othman began, scrutinizing his inexperienced son.

Yezed replied contentedly, "I wished to own a horse, and my father made me happy. What more could I desire? If one is happy, there are no other wishes. Why talk of death tonight? There's no reason for it. But while you are alive, I am willing to work for mother and for you, although you should live for pleasure and prayer."

Othman, disappointed by his son's indifference to things that didn't interest him, exclaimed, "You know too little of this world. You have no desire to become rich and strong, and that's why you don't have other wishes. But I ask you, what joy is there in spending one's days in a desolate place like this?"

Yezed responded, "Yes, this region may look desolate, but it serves to remind the wicked of their fate and the righteous of their reward. What does it matter? Are we not happy even in this unfriendly valley? It's not about where we live but how we live. Isn't this the essence of Islam? The pleasures of the mortal world, what are they compared to the indescribable joys we're promised?"

Othman asked, "If Allah didn't want us to enjoy this world, why are there so many good things that the weak and the poor can't have?"

Yezed piously replied, "Let Allah, in His wisdom, answer that question. We must be content and resigned, no matter where we are or what our circumstances, to avoid forfeiting eternal bliss."

Othman remarked sarcastically, "You're aiming for the gates of Jannat al Naïm, aren't you?"

Yezed responded firmly, "God has revealed the truth to Mohammed, and he, in turn, shared it with his followers. We've learned from them, and just as the sun is bright, the moon is blessed, and the stars are the work of Allah, so is the Koran His word, the Prophet His messenger, Jannat al Naïm the paradise of the faithful, and Jehennam one of the seven divisions of hell where the wicked suffer for their sins."

He passionately continued, "Those who cross the bridge al Sirat, finer than a hair and sharper than a razor, will enter the abode of bliss after drinking from Mohammed's cistern. Jannat al Naïm lies beneath the throne of God, with golden earth, pearled stones, and golden trees. One tree, Tuba, reaches every true believer's dwelling, offering an endless variety of fruits. The Elect enjoy silken garments, magnificent horses, and the company of heavenly maidens called houris. Israfil, the universe's greatest musician, leads them in heavenly melodies. What, then, do all earthly joys amount to?"

Othman fixed his gaze on his enthusiastic son's face, concealing his own disbelief. How could he reveal the truth, which would shatter Yezed's illusions instantly? How would it affect him?

"Tell me, son, are you a coward?" asked Othman in a different tone. "By my word, you speak like a woman, yet you are the son of a man who defies Eblis."

Yezed retorted challengingly, "What I speak comes from what Mohammed and his imams have taught me, father. I may seem like a woman's child, but I'm not a woman, and I'm not a coward. Give me a task, no matter how dangerous, and I'll do it."

"That's my true son," Othman said, pleased with Yezed's display of manly spirit. "There's a task for you tonight, and it's not for the faint of heart to undertake. Son, this world is divided between masters and slaves, with a few giving orders and the majority following them. It's my wish that you become one of the masters. Will you follow my guidance?"

Yezed declared, "Whatever Othman Ibn Saad tells his son to do, I will do."

Othman asked, "Will you face danger without hesitation?"

"If the task aligns with the duty of a Muslim," Yezed replied.

"Is it wrong to eliminate those who hate us, those we hate, and those whom Mohammed hated?" Othman insinuated.

"No, a Muslim cannot love those whom the Prophet hated. Yes, it was his wish to convert infidels by the sword if necessary. Shedding blood is dreadful, except for those deserving to be cast into hell. I would stab such a person in the heart right now and feed their remains to the dogs," Yezed replied, with evident anger toward his detested target.

"And who are you speaking of?" asked the father, pleased with his righteous son's anger. "He must indeed be a wicked person for you to hate him."

"I'm talking about the one whose evil deeds match his sinister name, Eblis, the highway murderer of men and women, destined for Monkir's club and eternal damnation," declared Yezed, his eyes flashing, and his fists clenched.

In silent shock, the father gazed at his son. He, who had mercilessly taken many lives, now felt a chilling horror at the intense hatred he had stirred in his unsuspecting child. Othman turned El Barak's head toward the last glimmer of the western sky, gazing there for a moment as if lost in thought. Then, with a composed demeanour, he said in a low voice, "Yezed, that's the very man we are going to intercept tonight. A hefty bounty has been placed on his head, and my information assures us that we can waylay him if we act swiftly and skilfully. This is the task I mentioned earlier. Are you ready to join me in this daring endeavour?"

"I will follow wherever you lead and face death in the name of Allah. There is no cowardice in Othman's faithful son," replied the youth.

"You are a true lion's cub," Othman concluded and urged his horse to ascend a steep gorge. This path, which in the rainy season allowed a mountain torrent to flow, was now dry. The trail El Barak navigated was narrow, steep, and treacherous, with a sheer drop to one side and overhanging rocks to the other.

After about an hour's ride through deepening twilight, Othman veered into a narrow crevice in the mountain, dismounted, and signalled for Yezed to do the same. The youth obeyed silently and followed his nimble father, who began to scale an almost vertical wall with remarkable agility, disappearing into a narrow hole that a person of average size would have difficulty passing through. Once inside, Othman extended a rope for Yezed to grab onto. The interior of the rocky hideaway was pitch black when Yezed entered.

The light was soon restored, and Yezed was astonished to find himself in a spacious, high, and dry hollow with an irregular shape, sloping downward into a narrowing chasm that seemed to reach unfathomable depths. A gentle breeze emanated from the heart of the mountain, carrying an unsettling aura.

Other discoveries held Yezed's attention. A niche a few feet above their heads led to a treasure trove of various costumes, masks, uniforms, weapons, and ammunition, concealed under a tiger skin. There were watches, valuable jewellery, money, and other loot taken from victims. Othman whispered huskily, "If you ask whose all of this is, I'll tell you it's all yours."

A sudden puff of air from the black pit extinguished the light, followed by a moan, a deep sigh, and a low rumble. Othman held his breath, and Yezed's pulse raced nervously. What could he say? He had eerie feelings but no thoughts, for it all felt like a dream.

The light flickered back on. "It's all right," Othman reassured his son. Nothing else occurred to confirm his suspicion that something had stirred in the uncharted depths. "Anyone who tries to take the fruits of my life must be willing to risk everything. Now, to business, Yezed. Here is a suit and a mask for you, and this is your armour. My outfit is here. Don't be alarmed, the devil must outwit the devil. Hurry, every minute counts, and the game won't wait for us."

With this, Othman stunned his son by transforming himself into the most terrifying demon Yezed had ever imagined. The real Eblis couldn't appear more menacing than the desperado in his black mask with red eyes, red mouth, long hooked nose, pointed beard, pointed shoes, and tight leg coverings all in one piece. A coat with a cow's tail, black gloves that elongated his fingers, and a red spear with many points completed the ensemble.

"You're too slow, son, for an expedition that demands both speed and courage," the bandit declared, shoving Yezed into a strange outfit, adjusting his mask, and securing a belt with pistols around his waist. "Ready!" was the signal, and Othman burst out of the wall like a cannonball fired from a fortress embrasure. Yezed refused to be left behind and found it easier to descend than to ascend the steep wall.

Now Othman was the real Eblis, and his impetuousness seemed to electrify El Barak. Fear and pride drove Yezed to keep up with his father. It was one of those moonless nights, and the outlines of the bandit, resembling a devil on a fiery horse, filled his son with dread. They sped through the night and desolation, Othman leading and Yezed following closely, in an eerie silence.

After covering several miles, Othman's keen ear alerted him that their prey was close. He spotted the pillar of salt, a petrified figure resembling Lot's wife, and heard the approaching travellers, and their erstwhile target."

Your first chance, Yezed, to prove yourself a hero or a coward. Here we leave our horses. You will stand in the path of their mounts, and I will strike like thunder. If it becomes too much for me, stab and shoot. If I continue, fight. If I give up, run. I'll yell 'Eblis' when I attack them. Once we're done with them, our horses will take us home before the moon is up," whispered the bandit, brimming with excitement.

For the first time in his life, Yezed felt the fighting spirit of his father, who was eager for the deadly confrontation. If they succeeded in capturing or defeating the scourge of the Jordan plain, their names would be on everyone's lips, including the Caliph of Istanbul. A lantern carried by one of the travellers provided a clear view of their party, consisting of an armed escort and two civilians, escorting a foreigner on horseback and an armed servant. Othman descended on the group with a bone-chilling yell, dismounting one and assaulting the other with savage ferocity. However, it was a trap set by the Chief of Kerak to ensnare "Eblis." The Chief had spread rumours of an approaching traveling party in the area where they expected Othman's attack.

Three burly Arabs stood by their Chief, and Othman fought like a cornered animal, and his red spear kept them at bay. However, there was no way for him to escape. Shots were fired from a distance, and the group struggled.

"Finish them off," Othman shouted in desperation. In response, more shots struck the melee from a distance. Three of the five men fell, never to rise again. Othman was one of the three, lifeless from a bullet fired by his own son, Yezed. The realization of the tragedy and the peril of his situation forced Yezed to flee into the darkness of the night, with no one in pursuit. He had killed his own father.

Where could he flee? In his current attire, he couldn't risk returning home, even if he had better news to bring than the tragic death of his father by his own hand. To retrieve his normal clothing, he needed to retrace his steps to that dreadful crevice in the rock that he had thankfully left earlier in the night. He dreaded the thought of it, but he had no choice. The real problem was how to find his way back there.

Fortunately, Yezed had mistakenly mounted El Barak in his hasty escape, and the clever horse instinctively led him to the right location, stopping beneath the entrance of the cavern his deceased father had frequented, especially after successful robberies.

"Allah Akbar," sighed Yezed as he dismounted and prepared to enter the dark hollow. The rope was there, beckoning him to climb up. It felt like a horrible nightmare. So much had transpired in just a few hours. Could anything worse happen to him? Come what may, he had to enter that hollow. Yezed pulled himself up, entered the cave, lit a torch, discarded his disguise, put on his normal clothes, and then knelt down to weep bitterly. The riches and jewels – could they bring his father back to life? Then it dawned on Yezed. The riches and jewels, what a dreadful thought! It struck him like a revelation. Great Allah! His father was Eblis, the very embodiment of that terrifying figure – a murderer! How could he doubt it? Everything pointed to the reality of that fact.

"Allah Akbar. I am the most wretched of sons," the despairing youth murmured.

But wait! Yes, he heard a sigh, then another, followed by a groan, and then a howl, all rising from the unfathomable black abyss of the hollow, staring at him like the malevolent eye of a Cyclops. His blood ran cold. Once more, a gust of wind, like a breath from a monstrous mouth, left him in total darkness. However, more terrifying than the pitch-black obscurity was the faint glimmer of a ghostly light that crept up from the depths – a phosphorescent glow that barely illuminated the sepulchral gloom, just enough to make the shadows visible. Terror drove Yezed to the brink of insanity. At any moment, he feared that some apparition might emerge from that eerie opening. Grabbing a loaded gun nearby, Yezed emptied it into the opening. The immediate response was a massive explosion, shaking the mountain and sending Yezed flying through the air, amidst fragments of rock as large as pyramids. It was a wonder he wasn't crushed, but he miraculously landed on a mound of rubble, unharmed. New developments made the previous events pale in comparison.

By now, it took a great deal to astonish Yezed. However, his vantage point allowed him to witness a somewhat hazy panorama that was more beautiful than anything he could have ever hoped to see this side of paradise. Through the shifting mists of uncertain darkness, his eyes beheld a tropical paradise along the shores of a serene, crystal-clear lake. A blaze of countless lamps ignited the scene, revealing an abundance of lush, noble vegetation, adorned with fruit-bearing trees laden with blossoms and the golden apples of the Hesperides. The melodious song of the nightingale filled the air. Fragrant gardens were covered in vibrant vines, weighed down by clusters of grapes that produced the finest wine. Sparkling fountains played in the glow of the mystic illumination. An elevated arcade, with countless multi-coloured lights, gleamed like a curved horizon, covering an expansive stretch of emerald meadow. It was a sight that even put day to shame, inviting fish to frolic in the transparent waters. Beneath the arched canopy, there was enough space for armies to march or stand in formation.

In fact, the sounds of cymbals, fifes, and timbrels filled the air, and a massive crowd of strange people moved toward the central arcade, drawn to its brilliance. It was a horde of half-naked, debauched beings, where genders mingled indecently. At their forefront, a savage figure led the way, his hair long and matted, eyes bloodshot, face tattooed, lips stained, his features reminiscent of a gorilla. He clutched a massive club and carried a shield on his chest and bronze plates on his shins. Yezed instantly recognized him the moment he let out a beastly cry.

"Listen to Nimrod the Huntsman, children of Sodom! The mighty sons of Anak and the Rephaim, born of the heavens, have come to help us build that tower over there, defying Him who drowned our ancestors for living as we do and refusing to worship Him as servants. We shall build higher than His mountains and scorn His wrath. Yes, we will ascend above His clouds, mock His floods, and challenge His heaven. Who is He to be feared? He wields power over the winds and the thunderbolt, and mistreats beings like Himself. This is our common foe, our tyrant."

The dehumanized masses shouted, leaped, twisted their faces into grotesque expressions, and uttered blasphemous curses, followed by unspeakable debauchery. Beastly women competed for the favour of their male counterparts, offering them intoxicating drinks that they consumed in excess, rendering themselves intoxicated as well. Wild dancing and vulgar gestures preceded the indulgence of unspeakable vices, marking the beginning of a debauched celebration.

"The Anakim, the Rephaim, make way for the heroes!" Nimrod the Huntsman thundered. The Sodomites divided into two lines, creating a path to the triumphant arcade, ablaze with fire. Emerging from a shaded path, an army of hideous giants, exuding arrogance and bristling with an array of weapons, advanced in two separate columns toward the blazing arcade, where they would be welcomed and celebrated. They wore bronze plates on their chests, knees, and shins and donned animal hides, the leader wearing a lion's pelt. As they neared the immense arch, their chief instructed them to break formation and perform a series of manoeuvres to the raucous applause of the drunken crowd. Nimrod himself was there to greet the warriors.

"Great leader of the invincible sons of giants, who dared to challenge heaven and dethrone the being who revels in cruelty, we welcome you. We, the Sodomites, offer no welcome except to those whom we can mutilate or kill, so as to satisfy our sense of honour. O chief, in our midst, strangers receive stones to quench their hunger, mud to quench their thirst, and beds to sleep on that are adjusted to their size. If they are too long, we cut their limbs; if they are too short, we stretch them to fit our standards. Our law is force, our god is valour, our trade is plunder, and our pleasure is excess. We despise what He loves and love what He despises. We harm the innocent, show no respect for a woman's virtue, and torment those who oppose us, causing Him, our common enemy, to fume and fret. That is why we called on you to help us build that tower, to rise above His clouds. If He sends another deluge to drown us, we will defy Him as we always have, making His clouds break against the tower's peak. But for now, let this hour be dedicated to feasting, pleasure, drinking, dancing, and indulgence."

What Yezed experienced next was a cacophony of sheer terror. It was as if the lake had transformed into a seething cauldron of oil, surging violently towards the sky, and the fiery inferno quickly consumed the surrounding shores. The earth convulsed, driven by a powerful force from below, and then, in a violent rebound, the lakebed plummeted beneath its banks, creating a fiery chasm.

Blazing streams of the all-consuming fire shot out from countless cracks, crevices, and fissures, obliterating everything in their path. The lewd revellers were swallowed by the fiery torrents, leaving behind no trace of the once-illuminated Eden that had been a scene of unimaginable debauchery just moments before. It all dissolved into a shroud of black smoke, carrying with it the scent of death, much like the foul vapour that had hung over the ruins of Sodom and Gomorrah. Yezed alone managed to escape, and his trembling heart recognized the justice and mercy of Allah. Surrounding him there were only sulphurous fumes, pitch darkness, and the eerie silence of death.

Where was he? How would he ever descend from the towering pile where he'd been placed by some mysterious force? What would he find when daylight illuminated the aftermath? He wished it was all just a terrible nightmare, including the death of his father, who had been disguised as the devil. Yet the night felt endless, as if day would never return, and his situation was filled with horrific uncertainty and discomfort. To make things worse, Yezed saw the bleeding figure of his father in the attire of Eblis, just as he'd witnessed him rushing to his doom. "Your hands are clean, my son! But I am doomed to forever swim in a pool of blood, the life force of the hearts I pierced!" The wailing words reached Yezed through the passing breeze as the apparition faded from his sight, sending chills down his spine.

Yezed tried to speak, but his tongue was paralyzed. He attempted to communicate through gestures, but his arms and fingers wouldn't respond. Summoning all his strength, he threw himself in the direction where he'd seen Othman vanish, only to collide with a stone. How did that stone get there? There had been nothing there before. Yezed stood up, and to his surprise, there was no more smoke. He extended his arms sideways and encountered a wall. There had been no wall before.

"Allah, great Allah, is this the hollow where I changed my clothes?"

Indeed, it was. He decided to create some light, and there he found the secluded nook, the armoury, the strange wardrobe, and the treasure left behind by the deceased bandit. Then there was the dreaded black hole, concealing the horrors he had witnessed. Yezed shook with cold and dread. He sensed that it was the dead of night, and the reality of the nightmare was unbearable. Would he ever return to that accursed cave? Never! Never! Shivering and trembling, Yezed crawled out of the cave, lowered himself to the ground, found the loyal El Barak patiently waiting for him, embraced the faithful horse, and wept bitterly. The horse neighed gently, as if understanding the profound sorrow of his new master.

Seated in the saddle, Yezed allowed the intelligent horse to take the lead, and shortly before daybreak, he arrived at his mother's home. The place was filled with weeping and lamentation due to the loss of Othman. Yezed decided to confide in his trusted mentor, the muezzin. The holy man shuddered as he listened to Yezed's account but advised him to keep the story a secret. He feared that if the widow and orphan were implicated in the crimes of the guilty Othman, they might end up in prison. Nevertheless, the muezzin took careful note of the location of the intriguing cave. In time, he was able to lead the widow and her son away from the humble village of Engedi to a brighter and safer place.

The Steel Cane

This story has been adapted from Andrew Lang's version of the same tale that originally appeared in The Olive Fairy Book, published in 1907 by Longmans, Green and Co., London and New York. This tale is based on an original taken from Contes Arméniens by Frédéric Macler, published in 1905.

Once upon a time there lived an old woman who had a small cottage on the edge of the forest. Behind the cottage was a garden in which all sorts of vegetables grew, and, beyond that, a field with two or three cows in it, so her neighbours considered her quite rich, and envied her greatly.

As long as she was strong enough to work all day in her garden the old woman never felt lonely, but after a while she had a bad illness, which left her much weaker than before, and she began to think that now and then it would be nice to have someone to speak to. Just at this moment she heard of the death of a shepherd and his wife, who dwelt on the other side of the plain, leaving a little boy quite alone in the world.

"That will just suit me," she said, and sent a man over to bring the child, whom she intended to adopt for her own.

Now the boy, who was about twelve years old, ought to have considered himself very lucky, for his new mother was as kind to him as the old one. But unfortunately, he made friends with some bad rude companions whose tricks caused them to be a terror to everyone, and the poor old woman never ceased regretting her lost solitude. Things went on in this way for some years, till the boy became a man.

"Perhaps, if he were to be married, he might sober down," she thought to herself. And she inquired among the neighbours what girls there were of an age to choose from. At length one was found, good and industrious, as well as pretty, and as the young man raised no objections the wedding took place at once, and the bride and bridegroom went to live in the cottage with the old woman. But no change was to be seen in the husband's conduct. All day long he was out amusing himself in the company of his former friends, and if his wife dared to say anything to him on his return home, he beat her with his stick. And next year, when a baby was born to them, he beat it also.

At length the old woman's patience was worn out. She saw that it was quite useless to expect the lazy, idle creature to mend his ways, and one day she said to him, "Do you mean to go on like this for ever? Remember, you are no longer a boy, and it is time that you left off behaving like one. Come, shake off your bad habits, and work for your wife and child, and above all, stop beating them. If not, I will transform you into an ass, and heavy loads shall be piled on your back, and men shall ride you. Briars shall be your food, a goad shall prick you, and in your turn, you shall know how it feels to be beaten."

But if she expected her words to do any good, she soon found out her mistake, for the young man only grew angry and cried rudely, "Bah! Hold your tongue or I will whip you also."

"Will you?" she answered grimly, and, swift as lightning she picked up a steel cane that stood in the corner and laid it across his shoulders. In an instant his ears had grown long and his face longer, his arms had become legs, and his body was covered with close grey hair. Truly, he was an ass, and a very ugly one, too!

"Leave the house!" commanded the old woman. And, shambling awkwardly, he went.

As he was standing in the path outside, not knowing what to do, a man passed by. "Ho! My fine fellow, you are exactly what I was looking for! You don't seem to have a master, so come with me. I will find something for you to do." And taking him by the ear he led him from the cottage.

For seven years the ass led a hard life, just as the old woman had foretold. But instead of remembering that he had brought all his suffering on himself, and being sorry for his evil ways, he grew harder, and more bitter. At the end of the seven years his ass skin wore out, and he became a man again, and one day returned to the cottage.

His wife opened the door in answer to his knock, then, letting fall the latch, she ran inside, crying, "Grandmother! Grandmother! Your son has come back!"

"I thought he would," replied the old woman, going on with her spinning. "Well, we could have done very well without him. But as he is here, I suppose he must come in."

And come in he did. But as the old woman expected, he behaved still worse than before. For some weeks she allowed him to do what he liked, then at last she said, "So, experience has taught you nothing! After all, there are very few people who have sense to learn by it. But take care lest I change you into a wolf, to be a prey for dogs and men!"

"You talk too much. I shall break your head for you!" was all the answer she got.

Had the young man looked at her face he might have taken warning, but he was busy making a pipe, and took no notice. The next moment the steel cane had touched his shoulders, and a big grey wolf bounded through the door.

Oh, what a yapping among the dogs, and what a shouting among the neighbours as they gave chase.

For seven years he led the life of a hunted animal, often cold and nearly always hungry, and never daring to allow himself a sound sleep. At the end of that time his wolf skin wore out also, and again he appeared at the cottage door. But the second seven years had taught him no more than the first - his conduct was worse than before, and one day he beat his wife and son so brutally that they screamed to the old woman to come to their aid.

She did and brought the steel cane with her. In a second the ruffian had vanished, and a big black crow was flying about the room, crying "Gour! Gour!"

The window was open, and he darted through it, and seeking the companions who had ruined him, he managed to make them understand what had happened.

"We will avenge you," said they, and taking up a rope, set out to strangle the old woman.

But she was ready for them. One stroke of her cane and they were all changed into a troop of black crows, and this time their feathers are lasting still.

The History Of Ali Cogia

This story has been adapted from Katherine Pyle's version of the same tale that originally appeared in Tales of Folk and Fairies, published in 1929 by Little, Brown and Company, Boston.

In the city of Baghdad there once lived a merchant named Ali Cogia. This merchant was faithful and honest in all his dealings, but he had never made the holy pilgrimage to Mecca. He often felt troubled over this, for he knew he was neglecting a religious duty, but he was so occupied with his business affairs that it was difficult for him to leave home. Year after year he planned to make the pilgrimage, but always postponed it, hoping for some more convenient time.

One night the merchant had a dream so vivid that it was more like a vision than a dream. In this dream or vision an old man appeared before him and, regarding him with a severe and reproachful look, said, "Why have you not made the pilgrimage to Mecca?"

When Ali Cogia awoke, he felt greatly troubled. He feared this dream had been sent him as a reproach and a warning from heaven. He was still more troubled when the next night he dreamed the same dream, and when upon the third night the old man again appeared before him and asked the same question, he determined to delay no longer, but to set out upon the pilgrimage as soon as possible.

To this end he sold off all his goods except some that he decided to carry with him to Mecca and to dispose of there. He settled all his debts and rented his shop and his house to a friend, and as he had neither wife nor family, he was now free to set out at any time.

The sale of his goods had brought in quite a large sum of money, so that after he had set aside as much as was needed for the journey, he found he had still a thousand gold pieces left over.

These he determined to leave in some safe place until his return. He put the money in an olive jar and covered it over with olives and sealed it carefully. He then carried the jar to a friend named Abul Hassan, who was the owner of a large warehouse.

"Abul Hassan," said he, "I am about to make the journey to Mecca, as you perhaps know. I have here a jar of olives that I would like to leave in your warehouse until my return, if you will allow me to do so."

Abul Hassan was quite willing that his friend should do this and gave him the keys of the warehouse, bidding him place the jar wherever he wished. "I will gladly keep it until you return," said he, "and you may rest assured the jar will not be disturbed until such time as you shall come and claim it."

Ali Cogia thanked his friend and carried the jar into the warehouse, placing it in the farthest and darkest corner where it would not be in the way. Soon after he set out upon his journey to Mecca.

When Ali Cogia left Baghdad, he had no thought but that he would return in a year's time at latest. He made the journey safely, in company with a number of other pilgrims. Arrived in Mecca, he visited the celebrated temples and other objects of interest that were there. He performed all his religious duties faithfully, and after that he went to the bazaar and secured a place where he could display the goods he had brought with him.

One day a stranger came through the bazaar and stopped to admire the beauty of the things Ali had for sale.

"It is a pity," said the stranger, "that you should not go to Cairo. You could go there at no great expense, and I feel assured that you would receive a far better price for your goods there than here. I know, for I have lived in that city all my life, and I am familiar with the prices that are paid for such fine merchandise as yours." The stranger talked with Ali for some time and then passed on his way.

After he had gone the merchant meditated upon what had been said, and he finally determined to follow the stranger's advice and to take such goods as he had left for Cairo and place them on sale there. This he did and found that, as the stranger had promised, the prices he could get there were much higher than those paid in Mecca.

While Ali Cogia was in Cairo, he made the acquaintance of some people who were about to journey down into Egypt by caravan. They urged Ali to join them, and after some persuasion he consented to do so, as he had always wished to see that country. From Egypt Ali Cogia journeyed to Constantinople, and then on to other cities and countries. Time flew by so rapidly that when, finally, Ali stopped to reckon up how long it was since he had left Baghdad, he found that seven years had elapsed.

He now determined to return without delay to his own city. He found a camel that suited him and having bought it he packed upon it such goods as he had left and set out for Baghdad.

Now all the while that Ali Cogia had been travelling from place to place the jar containing the gold pieces had rested undisturbed and forgotten in Abul Hassan's warehouse. Abul and his wife sometimes talked of Ali and wondered when he would return and how he had fared upon his journey. They were surprised at his long absence and feared some misfortune might have come upon him. At one time there was a rumour that he was dead, but this rumour was afterward denied.

Now the very day that Ali Cogia set out upon his return journey Abul Hassan and his wife were seated at the table at their evening meal, and their talk turned upon the subject of olives.

"It is a long time since we have had any in the house," said the wife. "Indeed, I do not remember when I last tasted one, and yet it is my favourite fruit. I wish we had some now."

"Yes, we must get some," said Abul Hassan. "And by the way, that reminds me of the jar that Ali Cogia left with us. I wonder whether the olives in it are still good. They have been there for some years now."

"Yes, for seven years," replied his wife. "No doubt they are all spoiled by this time."

"That I will see," said Abul Hassan, rising and taking up a light. "If they are still good, we might as well have some, for I do not believe Ali Cogia will ever return to claim the jar."

His wife was horrified. "What are you thinking of?" cried she. "Ali Cogia entrusted this jar to you, and you gave your word that it would not be disturbed until he came again to claim it. We heard, indeed, that he was dead, but this rumour was afterward denied. What opinion would he have of you if he returned and found you had helped yourself to his olives?"

Abul Hassan, still holding the light in his hand, waited impatiently until his wife had finished speaking. Then he replied, "Ali Cogia will not return, of that I feel assured. And at any rate, if he should, I can easily replace the olives."

"You can replace the olives, no doubt," answered his wife, "but they would not be Ali Cogia's olives. This jar is a sacred trust and should not be disturbed by you under any consideration." But though she spoke strongly she could see by her husband's face that he had not changed his determination.

He now took up the dish and said, "If the olives are good, I will bring a dish full from the jar, but if they are spoiled, as I suppose they are, I will replace the cover and no one will be any the wiser."

His wife would have tried again to dissuade him, but without listening further he went at once to the warehouse. It did not take him long to find the jar. He took off the cover and found that, as he had suspected, the olives were spoiled. Wishing to see whether those beneath were in the same condition he tilted the jar and emptied some of them out into the dish. What was his surprise to see some gold pieces fall out with the olives. Abul Hassan could hardly believe his eyes. Hastily he plunged his hands down into the jar and soon found that except for the top layer of fruit the whole jar was full of gold pieces.

Abul Hassan's eyes sparkled with desire. He was naturally a very avaricious man, and the sight of the gold awakened all his greed. It had been there in his warehouse, all unknown to him, for seven years. He felt as though he had been tricked, for, thought he, "All this time I might have been using this money to advantage by trading with it and with no harm to anyone, for I could have replaced it at any time I heard Ali Cogia was about to return."

For a while he stood there lost in thought. Then he returned the gold to the jar, covered it over with olives as before, and replaced the cover, and taking up the empty dish and the light he returned to his wife.

"You were quite right," said he carelessly. "The olives were spoiled, so I did not bring any."

"You should not even have opened the jar," said his wife. "Heaven grant that no evil may come upon us for this."

To this remark Abul Hassan made no reply, and soon after he and his wife retired to rest. But the merchant could not sleep. All night he tossed and twisted, thinking of the gold, and planning how he could make it his own, and it was not until morning that he fell into a troubled sleep.

The next day he arose early and as soon as the bazaar opened, he went out and bought a quantity of olives. He brought them home and carried them into the warehouse secretly, and without his wife's knowing anything about it. Then he again opened Ali Cogia's jar, and having emptied it of its contents, he filled it with fresh olives and replaced the cover in such a way that no one, looking at it, would have known it had been disturbed. He then threw the spoiled olives away and hid the gold in a secret place known only to himself.

About a month after this Ali Cogia returned to Baghdad. As his own house was still rented, he took a room in a khan and at once hastened to Abul Hassan's house to get his jar.

Abul Hassan was confounded when he saw Ali Cogia enter his house, for he had managed to convince himself that Ali must be dead. This he had done to try to excuse himself in his own eyes for taking the gold. However, he hid his confusion as best he could, and made the returned traveller welcome, and asked him how he had fared in his journeyings.

Ali Cogia answered his inquiries politely, but he was uneasy and restless, and as soon as he could make the opportunity, he inquired about the olive jar he had left in the warehouse.

"The jar is there where you put it, I am sure," answered Abul Hassan, "though I myself have not seen it. I do not even know in what part of the warehouse you left it. But here are the keys, and as I am busy, I will ask you to get it for yourself."

Ali Cogia made haste to seek out the jar and was much relieved to find it exactly where he had left it and apparently untouched. He had trust in Abul Hassan's honour, but a thousand pieces of gold was such a large sum that he could not but feel some concern until he had it in his own hands again.

After thanking his fellow merchant for keeping the jar, more earnestly than seemed necessary, he carried it back to his room in the khan and having locked the door he opened it. He removed the two top layers of olives and was somewhat surprised not to see the gold. However, he thought he must have covered the money more carefully than he had supposed. He took out more olives, and then still more, but still there were no signs of the gold.

Filled with misgivings, Ali Cogia tilted the jar and emptied out the rest of the olives so hastily that they rolled all over the floor, but not a single piece of gold was there.

The merchant was dismayed. He could scarcely believe that Abul Hassan would rob him of his money, and yet there seemed no other explanation. He knew that the merchant kept his warehouse locked except when he was there himself, and that no one was allowed to visit it but those with whom he was well acquainted, and then only upon special business.

Deeply troubled he returned to the merchant's house, determined to demand an explanation and, if necessary, to force him by law to return the gold.

Abul Hassan seemed surprised to see Ali return so soon. "Did you forget something?" he asked. "Or do you wish to speak to me upon some business?"

"Do you not guess what I have come to speak to you about?" asked Ali.

"How should I guess? Unless it is to thank me again for keeping your jar for you."

"Abul Hassan, when I went away I left a thousand pieces of gold in the jar I placed in your warehouse. The gold is now gone. I suppose you saw some way in which you could use it both for your advantage and my own. If such is the case, please give me a receipt for the money, and I am willing to wait until you can return it to me, but I think you should have spoken of the matter when I was here before."

Abul Hassan showed the greatest surprise at this address. "I do not know what you are talking about," said he. "I know nothing about any gold. If there was any in the jar, which I very much doubt, it must be there still, for the jar has never been disturbed since you yourself placed it in my warehouse."

"The gold certainly was in the jar when I placed it there, and you must know it, for no one else could have taken it. No one goes into the warehouse without your permission, as you have often told me and then only for some express purpose."

Ali Cogia would have said more, but his fellow merchant interrupted him. "I repeat I know nothing of any gold," he cried angrily. "Go away and do not trouble me any further, or you will find yourself in difficulties. Do you not see how your loud talking has gathered a crowd about my house?"

And indeed, a number of people had gathered in front of Abul's house, drawn there by the sound of the dispute. They listened with curiosity to what the merchants were saying and presently became so interested that they began to discuss the matter among themselves, and to argue and dispute as to which of the merchants was in the right.

At last Ali Cogia, finding that Abul would confess nothing, said, "Very well. I see you are determined to keep the money if possible. But you shall find it is not as easy to rob me as you seem to think." Then, laying his hand upon Abul's shoulder, he added, "I summon you to appear with me before the Cadi, that he may decide the matter between us."

Now this is a summons no true Muslim can disobey. Abul was compelled to go before the Cadi with Ali, and a great crowd of people followed them, eager to know what decision would be given in the matter by the judge.

The Cadi listened attentively to all the two merchants had to say and after reflecting upon the matter he asked, "Abul Hassan, are you ready to swear that you know nothing of the gold Ali Cogia says he left with you, and that you did not disturb the jar?"

"I am," answered the merchant. "And indeed, I wish to swear to it," and this he did.

"And you, Ali Cogia, have you any witnesses to prove there was gold in the jar when you left it in Abul Hassan's warehouse?"

"Alas! No, no one knew of it but me."

"Then it is your word against his. Abul Hassan has sworn that he did not touch the jar, and unless you can bring witnesses to your truth, I cannot compel him to pay you a thousand pieces of gold that you may never have lost."

The case was dismissed. Abul Hassan returned to his home, satisfied and triumphant, but Ali Cogia returned to his lodging with hanging head and bitterness of heart. But though the Cadi had decided against him, Ali was not willing to let the matter rest there. He was determined to have justice done him, even though he were obliged to appeal to the Caliph himself.

At that time Haroun al Raschid was Commander of the Faithful. Every morning Haroun al Raschid went to the mosque to offer up prayers, accompanied by his Grand Vizier and Mesrour the Chief Eunuch. As he returned to the palace all who had complaints to make or petitions to offer stationed themselves along the way and gave their complaints and petitions in written form to Mesrour. Afterward these papers were presented to the Caliph that he might read them and decide upon their merits.

The day after the Cadi had dismissed the case of the two merchants, Ali Cogia set out early in the morning and placed himself beside the way where he knew the Caliph would pass.

In his hand he carried his complaint against Abul Hassan, written out in due form. He waited until Haroun al Raschid was returning from the mosque and then put the paper in the hand of Mesrour.

Later, when the Caliph was reading the papers, he was particularly interested in the one presented by Ali Cogia, "This is a curious case," said he to his Vizier, "and one which it will be difficult to decide. Order the two merchants to appear before me tomorrow, and I will hear what they have to say."

That evening the Caliph and his Vizier disguised themselves, and, attended only by Mesrour, they went out to wander about the streets of the city. It was the custom of the Caliph to do this, as in this way he learned much about his people, their needs and wants and ways of life, which would otherwise have been hidden from him.

For some time after they set out they heard and saw nothing of importance, but as they came near to a court that opened off one of the streets they heard the voices of a number of boys who were at play there in the moonlight.

The Caliph motioned to his Vizier to be silent, and together they stole to the opening of the court and looked in. The moon was so bright that they could clearly see the faces of the boys at play there. They had gathered about the tallest and most intelligent looking lad, who appeared to be their leader.

"Let us act out some play," the leader was saying. "I will be the Cadi, and you shall bring some case before me to be tried."

"Very well," cried another. "But what case shall we take?"

"Let us take the case of Ali Cogia and Abul Hassan. We all know about that, and if it had come before me, I should have decided it differently from the way the Cadi did."

All the boys agreed to this by clapping their hands.

The leader then appointed one boy to take the part of Ali Cogia and another to be Abul Hassan. Still others were chosen to be guards and merchants and so on.

The Caliph and his Vizier were much amused by this play, and they sat down upon a bench so conveniently placed that they could see all that went on without themselves being observed.

The pretend Cadi took his seat and commanded that Abul Hassan and Ali Cogia should be brought before him. "And let Ali Cogia bring with him the jar of olives in which he said he hid the gold," said he.

The lads who were taking the parts of Ali Cogia and Abul Hassan were now led forward by some of the other boys and were told by the pretend Cadi to state their cases. This they did clearly, for the case had been much talked about by their elders, and they were well acquainted with all the circumstances and had discussed them among themselves.

The pretend Cadi listened attentively to what they said, and then addressing the lad who took the part of Abul he asked, "Abul Hassan, are you willing to swear that you have not touched the jar nor opened it?"

The pretended merchant said he was.

The lad then asked, "Has Ali Cogia brought the jar of olives into court with him?"

"It is here," said the boys who were taking the parts of officers of the court.

The feigned Cadi ordered them to place the jar before him, which they pretended to do. He then went through the motions of lifting the lid and examining the olives and even of tasting one.

"These are very fine olives," said he. "Ali Cogia, when did you say you placed this jar in the warehouse?"

"It was when I left Baghdad, seven years ago," answered the pretended merchant.

"Abul Hassan, is that so?"

The boy who acted the part of Abul said that it was.

"Let the olive merchants be brought into court," commanded the pretend Cadi.

The boys who were taking the parts of olive merchants now came forward.

"Tell me," said the feigned Cadi, "how long is it possible to keep olives?"

"However great the care that is taken," they answered, "it is impossible to preserve them for more than three years. After that time they lose both colour and flavour and are fit for nothing but to be thrown out." The boys spoke with assurance, for their fathers were among the most expert olive dealers in the city, and they knew what they were talking about.

The pretend Cadi then bade them examine the olives in the jar and tell him how old they were. "As you see," said he, "they are of a fine colour, large, and of a delicious fresh taste."

The feigned merchants pretended to examine them carefully and then announced the olives were of that year's growth.

"But Ali Cogia says he left them with Abul Hassan seven years ago, and to this statement Abul Hassan agrees."

"It is impossible they should have been kept that long," answered the feigned merchants. "As we tell you, after three years olives are worth nothing, and at the end of seven years they would be utterly spoiled. These are fresh olives and of this year's growth."

The boy who took the part of Abul Hassan would have tried to explain and make excuses, but the pretend Cadi bade him be silent.

"You have sworn falsely," said he, "and also proved yourself a thief."

Then to the pretend guards he cried, "Take him away and let him be hung according to the law."

The feigned guards dragged away the boy who was acting Abul Hassan and then, the play being finished, all the boys clapped their hands and shouted their approval of the way the feigned Cadi had conducted the case.

Seeing that all was over the Caliph withdrew, beckoning to the Vizier and Mesrour to follow him. After they had gone a short distance, Haroun al Raschid turned to the Vizier and asked him what he thought of the play they had just witnessed.

"I think," said the Vizier, "that the pretend Cadi showed a wisdom and a judgment that the real Cadi would do well to imitate. I also think the boy is a lad of remarkable intelligence."

"It is my own thought," replied the Caliph. "Moreover, I have a further thought. You know this very case between Ali Cogia and Abul Hassan is to appear before me tomorrow, I have it in mind to send you to bring this boy to the palace, and I will then let him conduct this case in reality as he has today in play."

The Vizier applauded this plan, and he and his master returned to the palace, still talking of the boy.

The next day the Vizier went back to the court they had visited the evening before, and after looking about he found the lad who had taken the part of the Cadi sitting in a doorway. The Vizier approached him and spoke to him in a kind and friendly manner.

"My boy," said he, "I have come here by order of the Commander of the Faithful. Last evening, when you were acting your play, he overheard all that was said, and he wishes to see you at the palace today."

The boy was alarmed when he heard this, grew pale, and showed great uneasiness. "Have I done something wrong?" he asked. "If I have I did it unknowingly, and I hope I am not to be punished for something I did without intention."

"You have done no wrong," answered the Vizier, "and it is not to punish you that the Caliph has sent for you. Indeed, he is very much pleased with your conduct, and his sending for you in this manner is a great honour." He then told the lad what it was the Caliph wished him to do.

Instead of being put at ease by this the lad showed even greater discomfort. "This seems a strange thing for me to do," said he. "It will be hard to decide a case between two grown men when I am only a child. I am afraid I will not be able to please the Caliph, and that he will be angry with me."

"Conduct the case as wisely as you did last night when you were playing," answered the Vizier, "and the Caliph will not be displeased with you."

The boy then asked permission to go and tell his mother where he was going and for what purpose, and to this the Vizier consented.

When the lad's mother heard that he was to go to the palace to act as judge in a case of such importance she could hardly believe her ears. She was frightened lest the lad should in some way offend the Caliph by saying or doing something ill judged.

The lad tried to reassure her, though he himself was far from being at ease. "If the Caliph was pleased with the way I conducted the case last night I do not think he can be so very much displeased with me today," said he, "for I feel sure that only in this way can we discover the truth between the two merchants."

When the lad returned to the Vizier he looked very grave, and as they went along together on their way to the palace the Vizier tried in every way to put him more at ease and give him confidence.

Immediately upon their arrival at the palace they were shown into the room where the Caliph was sitting. Haroun al Raschid greeted the boy with no less kindness than the Vizier had shown and asked him if he understood the purpose for which he had been brought there.

The lad said he did.

"Then let the two merchants come in," said the Caliph.

Ali Cogia and Abul Hassan were at once brought in by the officers of the court. Ali Cogia brought with him the jar of olives, for so he had been commanded to do.

The Cadi who had judged between the two merchants had also been ordered to attend, and he entered and took the place assigned to him.

The Caliph then turned to the lad and bade him open the case by bidding the merchants tell their stories, and this, after a moment's pause, the lad did.

Ali Cogia told his story just as he had before, stating that he had left with Abul Hassan seven years before a thousand pieces of gold packed in a jar and covered over with olives.

"Is this the jar you left with Abul Hassan?" asked the boy, pointing to the jar Ali had brought into court.

Ali stated that it was.

"Abul Hassan, do you also say this is the jar Ali Cogia left with you?" asked the lad.

Abul answered that it was. He also asked to be allowed to take his oath that the jar had not been disturbed after it was left in his warehouse until Ali Cogia had returned and removed it.

"That is not necessary at present," answered the boy. "First let some expert olive merchants be brought in."

Several olive dealers, the most expert in the city, had been sent for, and they now came forward.

The lad asked these real merchants the same questions he had asked of the feigned merchants the night before. "How long," said he, "is it possible to keep olives good?"

And the merchants answered, as had the boys, "Not more than three years, for no matter how carefully they have been packed, after that time they lose both colour and flavour."

"Look in that jar," said the lad, "and tell us how long you think those olives have been kept there."

The merchants examined the olives with the greatest care, and then they all agreed that the olives were of that year's growth and quite fresh.

"And do you not think it possible they may have been kept a year or so?"

"No, it is not possible," answered the merchants. "We know, of a surety, as we have already said, that these olives are of this year's growth, and have only recently been packed in the jar."

When Ali Cogia heard this, he gave a cry of surprise, but Abul Hassan was silent, his face grew as pale as ashes, and his legs failed under him, for he knew that the merchants, in saying this, had pronounced sentence against him.

But the lad turned to the Caliph and begged that he might now be allowed to hand over the case to him. "When I pronounced sentence last night, it was but in play," said he. "But this is not play. A man's life is at stake, and I dare not pronounce sentence upon him."

To this request the Caliph agreed. "Abul Hassan, you have condemned yourself," he said. He then bade the guards take Abul Hassan away and execute him according to the law.

Before the wretched man was hanged, however, he confessed his guilt and told where he had hidden the thousand pieces of gold that belonged to Ali Cogia.

After Abul had been led away the Caliph caressed and praised the lad for conducting the case so wisely and with so much judgment.

"As for you," said he to the Cadi, "you have not shown the wisdom I demand from my judges. Learn from this child that such cases are not to be dismissed lightly, but to be inquired into with judgment and care. Otherwise it may go ill with you."

The Cadi retired, full of shame, but the Caliph ordered that a hundred pieces of gold should be given to the boy and that he should be sent home to his mother with honour.

The Story Of Caliph Stork

This story has been adapted from Andrew Lang's version of the same tale that originally appeared in The Green Fairy Book, published in 1892 by Longmans, Green and Co., London and New York.

I

Caliph Chasid, of Baghdad, was resting comfortably on his divan one fine afternoon. He was smoking a long pipe, and from time to time he sipped a little coffee which a slave handed to him, and after each sip he stroked his long beard with an air of enjoyment. In short, anyone could see that the Caliph was in an excellent humour. This was, in fact, the best time of day in which to approach him, for just now he was pretty sure to be both affable and in good spirits, and for this reason the Grand Vizier Mansor always chose this hour in which to pay his daily visit.

He arrived as usual this afternoon, but, contrary to his usual custom, with an anxious face. The Caliph withdrew his pipe for a moment from his lips and asked, "Why do you look so anxious, Grand Vizier?"

The Grand Vizier crossed his arms on his breast and bent low before his master as he answered, "Oh, my Lord! whether my countenance be anxious or not I know not, but down below, in the court of the palace, is a pedlar with such beautiful things that I cannot help feeling annoyed at having so little money to spare."

The Caliph, who had wished for some time past to give his Grand Vizier a present, ordered his slave to bring the pedlar before him at once. The slave soon returned, followed by the pedlar, a short stout man with a swarthy face, and dressed in very ragged clothes. He carried a box containing all manner of wares - strings of pearls, rings, richly mounted pistols, goblets, and combs. The Caliph and his Vizier inspected everything, and the Caliph chose some handsome pistols for himself and Mansor, and a jewelled comb for the Vizier's wife. Just as the pedlar was about to close his box, the Caliph noticed a small drawer, and asked if there was anything else in it for sale. The pedlar opened the drawer and showed them a box containing a black powder, and a scroll written in strange characters, which neither the Caliph nor the Mansor could read.

"I got these two articles from a merchant who had picked them up in the street at Mecca," said the pedlar. "I do not know what they may contain, but as they are of no use to me, you are welcome to have them for a trifle."

The Caliph, who liked to have old manuscripts in his library, even though he could not read them, purchased the scroll and the box, and dismissed the pedlar. Then, being anxious to know the contents of the scroll, he asked the Vizier if he did not know of anyone who might be able to decipher it.

"Most gracious Lord and master," replied the Vizier, "near the great Mosque lives a man called Selim the learned, who knows every language under the sun. Send for him, it may be that he will be able to interpret these mysterious characters."

The learned Selim was summoned immediately.

"Selim," said the Caliph, "I hear you are a scholar. Look well at this scroll and see whether you can read it. If you can, I will give you a robe of honour, but if you fail, I will order you to receive twelve strokes on your cheeks, and five and twenty on the soles of your feet, because you have been falsely called Selim the learned."

Selim prostrated himself and said, "Be it according to your will, oh master!" Then he gazed long at the scroll. Suddenly he exclaimed, "May I die, oh, my Lord, if this isn't Latin!"

"Well," said the Caliph, "if it is Latin, let us hear what it means."

So, Selim began to translate, "You who may find this, praise Allah for his mercy. Whoever shall snuff the powder in this box, and at the same time shall pronounce the word 'Mutabor' can transform himself into any creature he likes and will understand the language of all animals. When he wishes to resume the human form, he has only to bow three times towards the east, and to repeat the same word. Be careful, however, when wearing the shape of some beast or bird, not to laugh, or you will certainly forget the magic word and remain an animal for ever."

When Selim the learned had read this, the Caliph was delighted. He made the wise man swear not to tell the matter to anyone, gave him a splendid robe, and dismissed him.

Then he said to his Vizier, "That's what I call a good bargain, Mansor. I am longing for the moment when I can become some animal. Tomorrow morning I shall expect you early, we will go into the country, take some snuff from my box, and then hear what is being said in air, earth, and water."

II

Next morning Caliph Chasid had barely finished dressing, and breakfasting, when the Grand Vizier arrived, according to orders, to accompany him in his expedition. The Caliph stuck the snuff box in his girdle, and, having desired his servants to remain at home, started off with only the Grand Vizier in attendance. First, they walked through the palace gardens, but they looked in vain for some creature which could tempt them to try their magic power. At length the Vizier suggested going further on to a pond which lay beyond the town, and where he had often seen a variety of creatures, especially storks, whose grave, dignified appearance, and constant chatter had often attracted his attention.

The Caliph consented, and they went straight to the pond. As soon as they arrived, they remarked a stork strutting up and down with a stately air, hunting for frogs, and now and then muttering something to itself. At the same time they saw another stork far above in the sky flying towards the same spot.

"I would wager my beard, most gracious master," said the Grand Vizier, "that these two long legs will have a good chat together. How would it be if we turned ourselves into storks?"

"Well said," replied the Caliph, "but first let us remember carefully how we are to become men once more. True! Bow three times towards the east and say 'Mutabor!' and I shall be Caliph and you my Grand Vizier again. But for Heaven's sake don't laugh or we are lost!"

As the Caliph spoke he saw the second stork circling round his head and gradually flying towards the earth. Quickly he drew the box from his girdle, took a good pinch of the snuff, and offered one to Mansor, who also took one, and both cried together "Mutabor!"

Instantly their legs shrivelled up and grew thin and red, their smart yellow slippers turned to clumsy stork's feet, their arms to wings, their necks began to sprout from between their shoulders and grew a yard long, their beards disappeared, and their bodies were covered with feathers.

"You've got a fine long bill, Sir Vizier," cried the Caliph, after standing for some time lost in astonishment. "By the beard of the Prophet I never saw such a thing in all my life!"

"My very humble thanks," replied the Grand Vizier, as he bent his long neck, "but, if I may venture to say so, your Highness is even handsomer as a stork than as a Caliph. But come, if it so pleases you, let us go near our comrades there and find out whether we really do understand the language of storks."

Meantime the second stork had reached the ground. It first scraped its bill with its claw, stroked down its feathers, and then advanced towards the first stork. The two newly made storks lost no time in drawing near, and to their amazement overheard the following conversation:

"Good morning, Dame Longlegs. You are out early this morning!"

"Yes, indeed, dear Chatterbill. I am getting myself a morsel of breakfast. May I offer you a joint of lizard or a frog's thigh?"

"A thousand thanks, but I have really no appetite this morning. I am here for a very different purpose. I am to dance today before my father's guests, and I have come to the meadow for a little quiet practice."

Thereupon the young stork began to move about with the most wonderful steps. The Caliph and Mansor looked on in surprise for some time, but when at last she balanced herself in a picturesque attitude on one leg, and flapped her wings gracefully up and down, they could hold out no longer, a prolonged peal burst from each of their bills, and it was some time before they could recover their composure. The Caliph was the first to collect himself. "That was the best joke," said he, "I've ever seen. It's a pity the stupid creatures were scared away by our laughter, or no doubt they would have sung next!"

Suddenly, however, the Vizier remembered how strictly they had been warned not to laugh during their transformation. He at once communicated his fears to the Caliph, who exclaimed, "By Mecca and Medina! It would indeed prove but a poor joke if I had to remain a stork for the remainder of my days! Do just try and remember the stupid word, it has slipped my memory."

"We must bow three times eastwards and say 'Mu...mu...mu...'"

They turned to the east and fell to bowing till their bills touched the ground, but, oh horror - the magic word was quite forgotten, and however often the Caliph bowed and however touchingly his Vizier cried "Mu...mu..." they could not recall it, and the unhappy Chasid and Mansor remained storks as they were.

III

The two enchanted birds wandered sadly on through the meadows. In their misery they could not think what to do next. They could not rid themselves of their new forms, there was no use in returning to the town and saying who they were, for who would believe a stork who announced that he was a Caliph, and even if they did believe him, would the people of Baghdad consent to let a stork rule over them?

So, they lounged about for several days, supporting themselves on fruits, which, however, they found some difficulty in eating with their long bills. They did not much care to eat frogs or lizards. Their one comfort in their sad plight was the power of flying, and accordingly they often flew over the roofs of Baghdad to see what was going on there.

During the first few days they noticed signs of much disturbance and distress in the streets, but about the fourth day, as they sat on the roof of the palace, they perceived a splendid procession passing below them along the street. Drums and trumpets sounded, a man in a scarlet mantle, embroidered in gold, sat on a splendidly caparisoned horse surrounded by richly dressed slaves, half Baghdad crowded after him, and they all shouted, "Hail, Mirza, the Lord of Baghdad!"

The two storks on the palace roof looked at each other, and Caliph Chasid said, "Can you guess now, Grand Vizier, why I have been enchanted? This Mirza is the son of my deadly enemy, the mighty magician Kaschnur, who in an evil moment vowed vengeance on me. Still, I will not despair! Come with me, my faithful friend, we will go to the grave of the Prophet, and perhaps at that sacred spot the spell may be loosed."

They rose from the palace roof and spread their wings toward Medina. But flying was not quite an easy matter, for the two storks had had but little practice as yet.

"Oh, my Lord!" gasped the Vizier, after a couple of hours, "I can get on no longer, you really fly too quick for me. Besides, it is nearly evening, and we should do well to find some place in which to spend the night."

Chasid listened with favour to his servant's suggestion, and perceiving in the valley beneath them a ruin which seemed to promise shelter they flew towards it. The building in which they proposed to pass the night had apparently been formerly a castle.

Some handsome pillars still stood amongst the heaps of ruins, and several rooms, which yet remained in fair preservation, gave evidence of former splendour. Chasid and his companion wandered along the passages seeking a dry spot, when suddenly Mansor stood still.

"My Lord and master," he whispered, "if it were not absurd for a Grand Vizier, and still more for a stork, to be afraid of ghosts, I should feel quite nervous, for someone, or something close by me, has sighed and moaned quite audibly."

The Caliph stood still and distinctly heard a low weeping sound which seemed to proceed from a human being rather than from any animal. Full of curiosity he was about to rush towards the spot from where the sounds of woe came, when the Vizier caught him by the wing with his bill and implored him not to expose himself to fresh and unknown dangers. The Caliph, however, under whose stork's breast a brave heart beat, tore himself away with the loss of a few feathers, and hurried down a dark passage. He saw a door which stood ajar, and through which he distinctly heard sighs, mingled with sobs. He pushed open the door with his bill, but remained on the threshold, astonished at the sight which met his eyes. On the floor of the ruined chamber - which was but scantily lighted by a small, barred window - sat a large screech owl. Big tears rolled from its large round eyes, and in a hoarse voice it uttered its complaints through its crooked beak. As soon as it saw the Caliph and his Vizier - who had crept up meanwhile - it gave vent to a joyful cry. It gently wiped the tears from its eyes with its spotted brown wings, and to the great amazement of the two visitors, addressed them in good human Arabic.

"Welcome, you storks! You are a good sign of my deliverance, for it was foretold me that a piece of good fortune should befall me through a stork."

When the Caliph had recovered from his surprise, he drew up his feet into a graceful position, bent his long neck, and said, "Oh, screech owl! From your words I am led to believe that we see in you a companion in misfortune. But alas, your hope that you may attain your deliverance through us is but a vain one. You will know our helplessness when you have heard our story."

The screech owl begged him to relate it, and the Caliph accordingly told him what we already know.

IV

When the Caliph had ended, the owl thanked him and said, "You hear my story, and own that I am no less unfortunate than yourselves. My father is the King of the Indies. I, his only daughter, am named Lusa. That magician Kaschnur, who enchanted you, has been the cause of my misfortunes too. He came one day to my father and demanded my hand for his son Mirza. My father - who is rather hasty - ordered him to be thrown downstairs. The wretch not long after managed to approach me under another form, and one day, when I was in the garden, and asked for some refreshment, he brought me - in the disguise of a slave - a draught which changed me at once to this horrid shape. While I was fainting with terror he transported me here and cried to me with his awful voice, 'There shall you remain, lonely and hideous, despised even by the brutes, till the end of your days, or till some one of his own free will asks you to be his wife. Thus do I avenge myself on you and your proud father.'

"Since then many months have passed away. Sad and lonely do I live like any hermit within these walls, avoided by the world and a terror even to animals, the beauties of nature are hidden from me, for I am blind by day, and it is only when the moon sheds her pale light on this spot that the veil falls from my eyes and I can see." The owl paused, and once more wiped her eyes with her wing, for the recital of her woes had drawn fresh tears from her.

The Caliph fell into deep thought on hearing this story from the Princess. "If I am not much mistaken," said he, "there is some mysterious connection between our misfortunes, but how to find the key to the riddle is the question."

The owl answered, "Oh, my Lord! I too feel sure of this, for in my earliest youth a wise woman foretold that a stork would bring me some great happiness, and I think I could tell you how we might save ourselves."

The Caliph was much surprised and asked her what she meant.

"The Magician who has made us both miserable," said she, "comes once a month to these ruins. Not far from this room is a large hall where he is in the habit of feasting with his companions. I have often watched them. They tell each other all about their evil deeds, and possibly the magic word which you have forgotten may be mentioned."

"Oh, dearest Princess!" exclaimed the Caliph, "say, when does he come, and where is the hall?"

The owl paused a moment and then said, "Do not think me unkind, but I can only grant your request on one condition."

"Speak, speak!" cried Chasid, "Command, I will gladly do whatever you wish!"

"Well," replied the owl, "you see I should like to be free too, but this can only be if one of you will offer me his hand in marriage."

The storks seemed rather taken aback by this suggestion, and the Caliph beckoned to his Vizier to retire and consult with him.

When they were outside the door the Caliph said, "Grand Vizier, this is a tiresome business. However, you can take her."

"Indeed!" said the Vizier, "So that when I go home my wife may scratch my eyes out! Besides, I am an old man, and your Highness is still young and unmarried, and a far more suitable match for a young and lovely Princess."

"That's just where it is," sighed the Caliph, whose wings drooped in a dejected manner, "how do you know she is young and lovely? I call it buying a pig in a poke."

They argued on for some time, but at length, when the Caliph saw plainly that his Vizier would rather remain a stork to the end of his days than marry the owl, he determined to fulfil the condition himself. The owl was delighted. She owned that they could not have arrived at a better time, as most probably the magicians would meet that very night.

She then proceeded to lead the two storks to the chamber. They passed through a long dark passage till at length a bright ray of light shone before them through the chinks of a half-ruined wall. When they reached it the owl advised them to keep very quiet. Through the gap near which they stood they could with ease survey the whole of the large hall. It was adorned with splendid carved pillars, a number of coloured lamps replaced the light of day. In the middle of the hall stood a round table covered with a variety of dishes, and about the table was a divan on which eight men were seated. In one of these bad men the two recognised the pedlar who had sold the magic powder. The man next him begged him to relate all his latest doings, and amongst them he told the story of the Caliph and his Vizier.

"And what kind of word did you give them?" asked another old sorcerer.

"A very difficult Latin word, which is 'Mutabor.'"

V

As soon as the storks heard this they were nearly beside themselves with joy. They ran at such a pace to the door of the ruined castle that the owl could scarcely keep up with them. When they reached it the Caliph turned to the owl and said with much feeling, "Deliverer of my friend and myself, as a proof of my eternal gratitude, accept me as your husband."

Then he turned towards the east. Three times the storks bowed their long necks to the sun, which was just rising over the mountains. "Mutabor!" they both cried, and in an instant they were once more transformed. In the rapture of their newly given lives master and servant fell laughing and weeping into each other's arms. Who shall describe their surprise when they at last turned round and beheld standing before them a beautiful lady exquisitely dressed!

With a smile she held out her hand to the Caliph, and asked, "Do you not recognise your screech owl?"

It was she! The Caliph was so enchanted by her grace and beauty, that he declared being turned into a stork had been the best piece of luck which had ever befallen him. The three set out at once for Baghdad. Fortunately, the Caliph found not only the box with the magic powder, but also his purse in his girdle, and he was, therefore, able to buy in the nearest village all they required for their journey, and so at last they reached the gates of Baghdad.

Here the Caliph's arrival created the greatest sensation. He had been quite given up for dead, and the people were greatly rejoiced to see their beloved ruler again.

Their rage with the usurper Mirza, however, was great in proportion. They marched in force to the palace and took the old magician and his son prisoners. The Caliph sent the magician to the room where the Princess had lived as an owl and there had him hanged. As the son, however, knew nothing of his father's acts, the Caliph gave him his choice between death and a pinch of the magic snuff. When he chose the latter, the Grand Vizier handed him the box. One good pinch, and the magic word transformed him to a stork. The Caliph ordered him to be confined in an iron cage and placed in the palace gardens.

Caliph Chasid lived long and happily with his wife the Princess. His merriest time was when the Grand Vizier visited him in the afternoon, and when the Caliph was in particularly high spirits he would condescend to mimic the Vizier's appearance when he was a stork. He would strut gravely, and with well stiffened legs, up and down the room, chattering, and showing how he had vainly bowed to the east and cried "Mu...Mu..." The Caliphess and her children were always much entertained by this performance, but when the Caliph went on nodding and bowing and calling "Mu...mu..." too long, the Vizier would threaten laughingly to tell the Caliphess the subject of the discussion carried on one night outside the door of Princess Screech Owl.

The Story Of Zoulvisia

This story has been adapted from Andrew Lang's version of the same tale that originally appeared in The Olive Fairy Book, published in 1907 by Longmans, Green and Co., London and New York. This tale is based on an original taken from Contes Arméniens by Frédéric Macler, published in 1905.

Now there was once a powerful king who ruled over a country on the other side of the desert, and, when dying, gave the usual counsel to his seven sons. Hardly, however, was he dead than the eldest, who succeeded to the throne, announced his intention of hunting in the enchanted mountain. In vain the old men shook their heads and tried to persuade him to give up his mad scheme. All was useless, he went but did not return, and in due time the throne was filled by his next brother.

And so it happened to the other five, but when the youngest became king, and he also proclaimed a hunt in the mountain, a loud lament was raised in the city.

"Who will reign over us when you are dead? For dead you surely will be," they cried. "Stay with us, and we will make you happy." And for a while he listened to their prayers, and the land grew rich and prosperous under his rule. But in a few years the restless fit again took possession of him, and this time he would hear nothing. Hunt in that forest he would, and calling his friends and attendants round him, he set out one morning across the desert.

They were riding through a rocky valley, when a deer sprang up in front of them and bounded away. The king instantly gave chase, followed by his attendants, but the animal ran so swiftly that they never could get up to it, and at length it vanished in the depths of the forest.

Then the young man drew rein for the first time and looked about him. He had left his companions far behind, and, glancing back, he beheld them entering some tents, dotted here and there amongst the trees. For himself, the fresh coolness of the woods was more attractive to him than any food, however delicious, and for hours he strolled about as his fancy led him.

By and by, however, it began to grow dark, and he thought that the moment had arrived for them to start for the palace. So, leaving the forest with a sigh, he made his way down to the tents, but what was his horror to find his men lying about, some dead, some dying. These were past speech, but speech was needless. It was as clear as day that the wine they had drunk contained deadly poison.

"I am too late to help you, my poor friends," he said, gazing at them sadly, "but at least I can avenge you! Those that have set the snare will certainly return to see to its working. I will hide myself somewhere and discover who they are!"

Near the spot where he stood he noticed a large walnut tree, and into this he climbed. Night soon fell, and nothing broke the stillness of the place, but with the earliest glimpse of dawn a noise of galloping hoofs was heard.

Pushing the branches aside the young man beheld a youth approaching, mounted on a white horse. On reaching the tents the cavalier dismounted, and closely inspected the dead bodies that lay about them. Then, one by one, he dragged them to a ravine close by and threw them into a lake at the bottom. While he was doing this, the servants who had followed him led away the horses of the ill-fated men, and the courtiers were ordered to let loose the deer, which was used as a decoy, and to see that the tables in the tents were covered as before with food and wine.

Having made these arrangements he strolled slowly through the forest, but great was his surprise to come upon a beautiful horse hidden in the depths of a thicket.

"There was a horse for every dead man," he said to himself. "Then whose is this?"

"Mine!" answered a voice from a walnut tree close by. "Who are you that lure men into your power and then poison them? But you shall do so no longer. Return to your house, wherever it may be, and we will fight before it!"

The cavalier remained speechless with anger at these words, but then with a great effort he replied, "I accept your challenge. Mount and follow me. I am Zoulvisia."

And springing on his horse, he was out of sight so quickly that the king had only time to notice that light seemed to flow from him and his steed, and that the hair under his helmet was like liquid gold. Clearly, the cavalier was a woman. But who could she be? Was she queen of all the queens? Or was she chief of a band of robbers? She was neither, only a beautiful maiden.

Wrapped in these reflections, he remained standing beneath the walnut tree, long after horse and rider had vanished from sight. Then he awoke with a start, to remember that he must find the way to the house of his enemy, though where it was he had no notion. However, he took the path down which the rider had come, and walked along it for many hours till he came to three huts side by side, in each of which lived an old fairy and her sons.

The poor king was by this time so tired and hungry that he could hardly speak, but when he had drunk some milk, and rested a little, he was able to reply to the questions they eagerly put to him.

"I am going to seek Zoulvisia," said he, "she has slain my brothers and many of my subjects, and I mean to avenge them."

He had only spoken to the inhabitants of one house, but from all three came an answering murmur. "What a pity we did not know! Twice this day has she passed our door, and we might have kept her prisoner."

But though their words were brave their hearts were not, for the mere thought of Zoulvisia made them tremble.

"Forget Zoulvisia, and stay with us," they all said, holding out their hands, "you shall be our big brother, and we will be your little brothers." But the king would not.

Drawing from his pocket a pair of scissors, a razor, and a mirror, he gave one to each of the old fairies, saying, "Though I may not give up my vengeance I accept your friendship, and therefore leave you these three tokens. If blood should appear on the face of either know that my life is in danger, and, in memory of our sworn brotherhood, come to my aid."

"We will come," they answered. And the king mounted his horse and set out along the road they showed him.

By the light of the moon he presently perceived a splendid palace, but, though he rode twice round it, he could find no door. He was considering what he should do next, when he heard the sound of loud snoring, which seemed to come from his feet. Looking down, he beheld an old man lying at the bottom of a deep pit, just outside the walls, with a lantern by his side.

"Perhaps he may be able to give me some counsel," thought the king, and, with some difficulty, he scrambled into the pit and laid his hand on the shoulder of the sleeper.

"Are you a bird or a snake that you can enter here?" asked the old man, awakening with a start. But the king answered that he was a mere mortal, and that he sought Zoulvisia.

"Zoulvisia? The world's curse?" replied he, gnashing his teeth. "Out of all the thousands she has slain I am the only one who has escaped, though why she spared me only to condemn me to this living death I cannot guess."

"Help me if you can," said the king. And he told the old man his story, to which he listened intently.

"Take heed then to my counsel," answered the old man. "Know that every day at sunrise Zoulvisia dresses herself in her jacket of pearls and mounts the steps of her crystal watch tower. From there she can see all over her lands and behold the entrance of either man or demon. If so much as one is detected she utters such fearful cries that those who hear her die of fright. But hide yourself in a cave that lies near the foot of the tower and plant a forked stick in front of it, then, when she has uttered her third cry, go forth boldly, and look up at the tower. And go without fear, for you will have broken her power."

Word for word the king did as the old man had bidden him, and when he stepped forth from the cave, their eyes met.

"You have conquered me," said Zoulvisia, "and are worthy to be my husband, for you are the first man who has not died at the sound of my voice!" And letting down her golden hair, she drew up the king to the summit of the tower as with a rope. Then she led him into the hall of audience and presented him to her household.

"Ask of me what you will, and I will grant it to you," whispered Zoulvisia with a smile, as they sat together on a mossy bank by the stream. And the king prayed her to set free the old man to whom he owed his life, and to send him back to his own country.

"I have finished with hunting, and with riding about my lands,' said Zoulvisia, the day that they were married. "The care of providing for us all belongs henceforth to you." And turning to her attendants, she bade them bring the horse of fire before her.

"This is your master, O my steed of flame," cried she, "and you will serve him as you have served me." And kissing him between his eyes, she placed the bridle in the hand of her husband.

The horse looked for a moment at the young man, and then bent his head, while the king patted his neck and smoothed his tail, till they felt themselves old friends. After this he mounted to do Zoulvisia's bidding, but before he started she gave him a case of pearls containing one of her hairs, which he tucked into the breast of his coat.

He rode along for some time, without seeing any game to bring home for dinner. Suddenly a fine stag started up almost under his feet, and he at once gave chase. On they sped, but the stag twisted and turned so that the king had no chance of a shot till they reached a broad river, when the animal jumped in and swam across. The king fitted his cross bow with a bolt, and took aim, but though he succeeded in wounding the stag, it contrived to gain the opposite bank, and in his excitement he never observed that the case of pearls had fallen into the water.

The stream, though deep, was likewise rapid, and the box was swirled along miles, and miles, and miles, till it was washed up in quite another country. Here it was picked up by one of the water carriers belonging to the palace, who showed it to the king. The workmanship of the case was so curious, and the pearls so rare, that the king could not make up his mind to part with it, but he gave the man a good price, and sent him away. Then, summoning his chamberlain, he bade him find out its history in three days, or lose his head.

But the answer to the riddle, which puzzled all the magicians and wise men, was given by an old woman, who came up to the palace and told the chamberlain that, for two handfuls of gold, she would reveal the mystery. Of course the chamberlain gladly gave her what she asked, and in return she informed him that the case and the hair belonged to Zoulvisia.

"Bring her here, old crone, and you shall have gold enough to stand up in," said the chamberlain. And the old woman answered that she would try what she could do.

She went back to her hut in the middle of the forest, and standing in the doorway, whistled softly. Soon the dead leaves on the ground began to move and to rustle, and from underneath them there came a long train of serpents. They wriggled to the feet of the witch, who stooped down and patted their heads, and gave each one some milk in a red earthen basin. When they had all finished, she whistled again, and bade two or three coil themselves round her arms and neck, while she turned one into a cane and another into a whip. Then she took a stick, and on the riverbank changed it into a raft, and seating herself comfortably, she pushed off into the centre of the stream.

All that day she floated, and all the next night, and towards sunset the following evening she found herself close to Zoulvisia's garden, just at the moment that the king, on the horse of flame, was returning from hunting.

"Who are you?" he asked in surprise, for old women travelling on rafts were not common in that country. "Who are you, and why have you come here?"

"I am a poor pilgrim, my son," answered she, "and having missed the caravan, I have wandered foodless for many days through the desert, till at length I reached the river. There I found this tiny raft, and to it I committed myself, not knowing if I should live or die. But since you have found me, give me, I pray you, bread to eat, and let me lie this night by the dog who guards your door!"

This piteous tale touched the heart of the young man, and he promised that he would bring her food, and that she should pass the night in his palace.

"But mount behind me, good woman," cried he, "for you have walked far, and it is still a long way to the palace." And as he spoke he bent down to help her, but the horse swerved on one side.

And so it happened twice and thrice, and the old witch guessed the reason, though the king did not.

"I fear to fall off," said she, "but as your kind heart pities my sorrows, ride slowly, and lame as I am, I think I can manage to keep up."

At the door he bade the witch to rest herself, and he would fetch her all she needed. But Zoulvisia his wife grew pale when she heard whom he had brought and begged him to feed the old woman and send her away, as she would cause mischief to befall them.

The king laughed at her fears, and answered lightly, "Why, one would think she was a witch to hear you talk! And even if she were, what harm could she do to us?" And calling to the maidens he bade them carry her food, and to let her sleep in their chamber.

Now the old woman was very cunning, and kept the maidens awake half the night with all kinds of strange stories. Indeed, the next morning, while they were dressing their mistress, one of them suddenly broke into a laugh, in which the others joined her.

"What is the matter with you?" asked Zoulvisia. And the maid answered that she was thinking of a droll adventure told them the evening before by the newcomer.

"And, oh, madam!" cried the girl, "it may be that she is a witch, as they say, but I am sure she never would work a spell to harm a fly! And as for her tales, they would pass many a dull hour for you, when my lord was absent!"

So, in an evil hour, Zoulvisia consented that the crone should be brought to her, and from that moment the two were hardly ever apart.

One day the witch began to talk about the young king, and to declare that in all the lands she had visited she had seen none like him.

"It was so clever of him to guess your secret so as to win your heart," said she. "And of course he told you his, in return?"

"No, I don't think he has got any," returned Zoulvisia.

"Not got any secrets?" cried the old woman scornfully. "That is nonsense! Every man has a secret, which he always tells the woman he loves. And if he has not told it to you, it is that he does not love you!"

These words troubled Zoulvisia mightily, though she would not confess it to the witch. But the next time she found herself alone with her husband, she began to coax him to tell her in what lay the secret of his strength. For a long while he put her off with caresses, but when she would be no longer denied, he answered, "It is my sabre that gives me strength, and day and night it lies by my side. But now that I have told you, swear upon this ring, that I will give you in exchange for yours, that you will reveal it to nobody." And Zoulvisia swore, and instantly hastened to betray the great news to the old woman.

Four nights later, when all the world was asleep, the witch softly crept into the king's chamber and took the sabre from his side as he lay sleeping. Then, opening her lattice, she flew on to the terrace and dropped the sword into the river.

The next morning everyone was surprised because the king did not, as usual, rise early and go off to hunt. The attendants listened at the keyhole and heard the sound of heavy breathing, but none dared enter, till Zoulvisia pushed past. And what a sight met their gaze! There lay the king almost dead, with foam on his mouth, and eyes that were already closed. They wept, and they cried to him, but no answer came.

Suddenly a shriek broke from those who stood hindmost, and in strode the witch, with serpents round her neck and arms and hair. At a sign from her they flung themselves with a hiss upon the maidens, whose flesh was pierced with their poisonous fangs. Then turning to Zoulvisia, she said, "I give you your choice - will you come with me, or shall the serpents slay you also?" And as the terrified girl stared at her, unable to utter one word, she seized her by the arm and led her to the place where the raft was hidden among the rushes. When they were both on board she took the oars, and they floated down the stream till they had reached the neighbouring country, where Zoulvisia was sold for a sack of gold to the king.

Now, since the young man had entered the three huts on his way through the forest, not a morning had passed without the sons of the three fairies examining the scissors, the razor, and the mirror, which the young king had left them. Hitherto the surfaces of all three things had been bright and undimmed, but on this particular morning, when they took them out as usual, drops of blood stood on the razor and the scissors, while the little mirror was clouded over.

"Something terrible must have happened to our little brother," they whispered to each other, with awestruck faces, "we must hasten to his rescue before it be too late." And putting on their magic slippers they started for the palace.

The servants greeted them eagerly, ready to pour forth all they knew, but that was not much, only that the sabre had vanished, none knew where. The newcomers passed the whole of the day in searching for it, but it could not be found, and when night closed in, they were very tired and hungry. But how were they to get food? The king had not hunted that day, and there was nothing for them to eat. The little men were in despair, when a ray of the moon suddenly lit up the river beneath the walls.

"How stupid! Of course there are fish to catch," cried they, and running down to the bank they soon succeeded in landing some fine fish, which they cooked on the spot. Then they felt better and began to look about them.

Further out, in the middle of the stream, there was a strange splashing, and by and by the body of a huge fish appeared, turning and twisting as if in pain. The eyes of all the brothers were fixed on the spot, when the fish leapt in the air, and a bright gleam flashed through the night. "The sabre!" they shouted, and plunged into the stream, and with a sharp tug, pulled out the sword, while the fish lay on the water, exhausted by its struggles. Swimming back with the sabre to land, they carefully dried it in their coats, and then carried it to the palace and placed it on the king's pillow. In an instant colour came back to the waxen face, and the hollow cheeks filled out.

The king sat up, and opening his eyes he said, "Where is Zoulvisia?"

"That is what we do not know," answered the little men, "but now that you are saved you will soon find out." And they told him what had happened since Zoulvisia had betrayed his secret to the witch.

"Let me go to my horse," was all he said. But when he entered the stable he could have wept at the sight of his favourite steed, which was nearly in as sad a plight as his master had been. Languidly he turned his head as the door swung back on its hinges, but when he beheld the king he rose up, and rubbed his head against him.

"Oh, my poor horse! How much cleverer were you than I! If I had acted like you I should never have lost Zoulvisia, but we will seek her together, you and I."

For a long while the king and his horse followed the course of the stream, but nowhere could he learn anything of Zoulvisia. At length, one evening, they both stopped to rest by a cottage not far from a great city, and as the king was lying outstretched on the grass, lazily watching his horse cropping the short turf, an old woman came out with a wooden bowl of fresh milk, which she offered him.

He drank it eagerly, for he was very thirsty, and then laying down the bowl, began to talk to the woman, who was delighted to have someone to listen to her conversation.

"You are in luck to have passed this way just now," said she, "for in five days the king holds his wedding banquet. Ah, but the bride is unwilling, for all her blue eyes and her golden hair! And she keeps by her side a cup of poison and declares that she will swallow it rather than become his wife. Yet he is a handsome man too, and a proper husband for her - more than she could have looked for, having come from no one knows where, and bought from a witch"

The king started. Had he found her after all? His heart beat violently, as if it would choke him, but he gasped out, "Is her name Zoulvisia?"

"Ay, so she says, though the old witch… But what ails you?" she broke off, as the young man sprang to his feet and seized her wrists.

"Listen to me," he said. "Can you keep a secret?"

"Ay," answered the old woman again, "if I am paid for it."

"Oh, you shall be paid, never fear - as much as your heart can desire! Here is a handful of gold, and you shall have as much again if you will do my bidding." The old crone nodded her head.

"Then go and buy a dress such as ladies wear at court, and manage to get admitted into the palace, and into the presence of Zoulvisia. When there, show her this ring, and after that she will tell you what to do."

So the old woman set off, and clothed herself in a garment of yellow silk, and wrapped a veil closely round her head. In this dress she walked boldly up the palace steps behind some merchants whom the king had sent for to bring presents for Zoulvisia.

At first the bride would have nothing to say to any of them, but on perceiving the ring, she suddenly grew as meek as a lamb. And thanking the merchants for their trouble, she sent them away, and remained alone with her visitor.

"Grandmother," asked Zoulvisia, as soon as the door was safely shut, "where is the owner of this ring?"

"In my cottage," answered the old woman, "waiting for orders from you."

"Tell him to remain there for three days, and now go to the king of this country, and say that you have succeeded in bringing me to reason. Then he will let me alone and will cease to watch me. On the third day from this I shall be wandering about the garden near the river, and there your guest will find me. The rest concerns myself only."

The morning of the third day dawned, and with the first rays of the sun a bustle began in the palace, for that evening the king was to marry Zoulvisia. Tents were being erected of fine scarlet cloth, decked with wreaths of sweet-smelling white flowers, and in them the banquet was spread. When all was ready a procession was formed to fetch the bride, who had been wandering in the palace gardens since daylight, and crowds lined the way to see her pass. A glimpse of her dress of golden gauze might be caught, as she passed from one flowery thicket to another. Then suddenly the multitude swayed, and shrank back, as a thunderbolt seemed to flash out of the sky to the place where Zoulvisia was standing, but it was no thunderbolt, only the horse of fire! And when the people looked again, it was bounding away with two persons on its back.

Zoulvisia and her husband both learnt how to keep happiness when they had got it, and that is a lesson that many men and woman never learn at all. And besides, it is a lesson which nobody can teach, and that every boy and girl must learn for themselves.

Historical Notes

This section contains some brief biographical notes about the original collectors and their books featured in this collection. These notes have been adapted from those primarily on Wikipedia along with other supporting sources and notes.

Katharine Pyle

Katharine Pyle (1863–1938) was an American artist, poet, and children's writer.

Born in Wilmington, Delaware, the youngest offspring of William Pyle and his wife Margaret, she was the sister of author and artist Howard Pyle. She was educated at the Women's Industrial School and the Drexel Institute, then studied at the Philadelphia School of Design for Women and the New York Art Students' League. She lived in Wilmington her whole life, except four years in New York during the 1890s.

Her art was exhibited at the World's Columbian Exposition in 1893. She found work as an illustrator no later than 1895, but her first major success occurred in 1898 with *The Counterpane Fairy*. Over the course of her career she wrote over 30 books and illustrated the works of others. Her works appeared in the Ladies' Home Journal and Harper's Bazaar. The Delaware Art Museum now has a substantial collection of her manuscripts.

Henry Iliowizi

Henry Iliowizi was born in Choinick, which is near Minsk in Russia on the 2nd of January 1850, the son of Elijah and Dinah Iliowizi. Henry was born into a strongly Hasidic community and was initially educated at a local heder and then at the yeshiva of Vietka. Aged fourteen, Henry was sent to Jassy in Romania as a means of avoiding military conscription in Russia.

Once established outside of Russia Henry then moved to Frankfort am Main in 1865, travelling from there to Berlin, Breslau, London, and Paris. From 1877 until 1880, Henry taught at the Alliance School in Tetouan in Morocco.

Henry studied and became a Rabbi during this period, following which he moved again to the United States of America, working for a short period with a congregation in Harrisonburg, Virginia, before settling in Minneapolis, where he was Rabbi of the Congregation of Sha'aré Tob.

In 1881 Henry married Mathilde Flesch, and they continued to live in Minneapolis until 1888. The couple had no children. In 1888 Henry became Rabbi of the Congregations Adath Jeshurun in Philadelphia. Henry remained in post until 1900, and it was only after this period that Henry committed his time to literature.

In 1910 Henry and Mathilde moved to England. Henry died aged 61 in 1911. Mathilde died later in Munich aged 59.

Henry Iliowizi's writings include *Sol,* an epic poem (1883), *Herod,* a tragedy (1884), *Joseph,* a drama (1885), *Through Morocco to Minnesota* (1888), *Six Lectures on Religion* (1889), *Jewish Dreams and Realities* (1890), *The Quest of Columbus* (1892), *Saul* and *A Patriarch's Blessing,* tragedies (1894), *In the Pale, Stories and Legends of Russian Jews* (1897), *The Weird Orient* (1901). Henry also published various articles in *The Jewish Messenger* and *The Jewish Exponent*

In a brief statement published in Book News (Philadelphia), in July 1897, Iliowizi wrote "The purpose of my writing In the Pale was to familiarize the English-speaking public with the legendary, romantic, and spiritual aspects of life in Russian Jewry, also to convey an idea of the folklore current among the oppressed millions of Jews in the Czar's domains. Another work in preparation is intended to complete the picture of reality and dreamlife in those regions of semi barbarism and intolerance."

Iliowizi's second collection of stories is pertinent to this small collection, *The Weird Orient, Nine Mystic Tales*, were gathered from Arabic and Persian sources while Iliowizi was teaching in Morocco. The first story, *The Doom of Al Zameri*, tells of the ancient Wandering Jew. In another, *The Gods in Exile*, a character has a vision of the gods of Asgard encountering the Olympians. In *The Mystery of the Damnavant*, Firdusi ascends Persia's most graceful mountain and has a mystical vision caused by the smoke of a mysterious herb. The tales are redolent in some ways of *The Arabian Nights*, but with added spiritual dimensions.

Andrew Lang

Andrew Lang FBA was a Scottish poet, novelist, literary critic, and contributor to the field of anthropology. He is best known as a collector of folk and fairy tales. The Andrew Lang lectures at the University of St Andrews are named after him.

Lang was born on 31st March 1844 in Selkirk. He was the eldest of the eight children born to John Lang, the town clerk, and his wife Jane Plenderleath Sellar, who was the daughter of Patrick Sellar, factor to the first duke of Sutherland. On 17th April 1875, he married

Leonora Blanche Alleyne, youngest daughter of C. T. Alleyne of Clifton and Barbados. She was (or should have been) variously credited as author, collaborator, or translator of Lang's Colour / Rainbow Fairy Books, which he edited.

He was educated at Selkirk Grammar School, Loretto School, and the Edinburgh Academy, as well as the University of St Andrews and Balliol College, Oxford, where he took a first class in the final classical schools in 1868, becoming a fellow and subsequently honorary fellow of Merton College. He soon made a reputation as one of the most able and versatile writers of the day as a journalist, poet, critic, and historian. In 1906, he was elected FBA.

He died of angina pectoris on 20th July 1912 at the Tor na Coille Hotel in Banchory, survived by his wife. He was buried in the cathedral precincts at St Andrews, where a monument can be visited in the southeast corner of the 19th century section.

Lang is now chiefly known for his publications on folklore, mythology, and religion. The earliest of his publications is *Custom and Myth* (1884). In *Myth, Ritual and Religion* (1887) he explained the "irrational" elements of mythology as survivals from more primitive forms. Lang's *Making of Religion* was heavily influenced by the 18th century idea of the "noble savage", in it, he maintained the existence of high spiritual ideas among so called "savage" races, drawing parallels with the contemporary interest in occult phenomena in England.

His *Blue Fairy Book* (1889) was a beautifully produced and illustrated edition of fairy tales that has become a classic. This was followed by many other collections of fairy tales, collectively known as *Andrew Lang's Fairy Books*. In the preface of the *Lilac Fairy*

Book he credits his wife with translating and transcribing most of the stories in the collections.

Lang was one of the founders of "psychical research" and his other writings on anthropology include *The Book of Dreams and Ghosts* (1897), *Magic and Religion* (1901) and *The Secret of the Totem* (1905). He served as President of the Society for Psychical Research in 1911.

He collaborated with S. H. Butcher in a prose translation (1879) of Homer's *Odyssey*, and with E. Myers and Walter Leaf in a prose version (1883) of the *Iliad*, both still noted for their archaic but attractive style.

Lang's writings on Scottish history are characterised by a scholarly care for detail, a piquant literary style, and a gift for disentangling complicated questions. *The Mystery of Mary Stuart* (1901) was a consideration of the fresh light thrown on Mary, Queen of Scots, by the Lennox manuscripts in the University Library, Cambridge, approving of her and criticising her accusers.

Lang was active as a journalist in various ways, ranging from sparkling "leaders" for the Daily News to miscellaneous articles for the Morning Post, and for many years he was literary editor of Longman's Magazine.

Émile Henri Carnoy

Émile Henri Carnoy was born on May 12, 1861, in Varloé-Baillon and died in 1930. He was a biographer and a collector of folk tales and lores.

Known as Henry, he contributed to various periodicals. From 1875, Henri Carnoy wrote for the *Journal d'Amiens*. By 1877, he was contributing to the *Mélusine* magazine about his legendary tales

Tales from the Hakawati: Tales from the Arabic Tradition

from Picardy. He followed this in 1879 with *Contes Populoères Picards* in the Romania magazine. Henry's particular interest in folk tales from Picardy culminated with his 1881 book, *Oral literature of Picardy.*

A more detailed list of works includes:

- *International Collection of Tradition*; directors: MM. Émile Blémont & Henry Carnoy. v. I-XIV, Paris, Tradition, 1889-1896
- *French Tales*, Paris, E. Leroux, 1885
- *Traditionalist Studies*, Paris, J. Maissonneuve, 1890
- *Folklore of Constantinople*, by Jean Nicolaïdes & Henry Carnoy, Paris, E. Lechevalier, 1894
- *The Tradition*; A general review of tales, legends, songs, uses, traditions & popular arts, folklore, traditionism, history of religions, literature. Year 1-21 1887-1907, Paris, Aux Bureaux de La Tradition, 1887-1907
- *Traditional Algeria*: legends, tales, songs, music, morals, customs, festivals, beliefs, superstitions, etc. ; contributions to Arab folklore, Paris, Maisonneuve & Leclerc, 1884
- *Doctor Cornelius*; travels and misadventures of a scholar among the Sioux, Geneva, Atar 1910
- *Animal Tales* in the Fox Novels, Paris, J. Maisonneuve, 1889
- *The Legends of France*, Paris, A. Quantin 1885
- *Islam, the Koran, Dogma, Religious Prescriptions*, Paris, Bureaux de La Tradition, 1896
- *Oral Literature of Picardy*, Paris, Maisonneuve, 1883
- *Saget (Abbé Louis)*, Paris, [S.n.], 1910
- *Popular Traditions of Asia Minor*, Comp. & tr. Jean Nicolaïdes, Paris, Maisonneuve & C. Leclere, 1889

Frédéric Macler

Frédéric Macler was born in 1869 and died in 1938. He was a French linguist, orientalist and translator.

A native of Mandeure, Macler learned Armenian, Assyrian, and Hebrew from Auguste Carriere. In 1911, he succeeded Antoine Meillet, taking a chair in Armenian at the Institut National des Langues et Civilisations Orientales, which he held until 1937. In 1919, he co-founded the Society for Armenian Studies. In 1920, he founded the *Revue des Études Arméniennes*, which he directed until 1933, with Antoine Meillet.

His works include a French translation of the Arabic *Vision of Daniel*.

Julia Pardoe

Julia Pardoe (December 4, 1804 – November 26, 1862) was a versatile English writer known for her talents in poetry, novel writing, history, and travel literature. Her best-known piece, *The City of the Sultan and Domestic Manners of the Turks*, published in 1837, portrayed the Ottoman Turkish upper class with empathy and a humane perspective.

Pardoe hailed from Beverley, Yorkshire, where she was born, the second daughter of Major Thomas Pardoe, who was rumoured to have Spanish ancestry, and his wife Elizabeth. She had a family background with military connections. Her father, as the family lore goes, had participated in the Peninsular campaigns during the Napoleonic Wars and fought at the Battle of Waterloo before retiring from the military service. Julia Pardoe's baptism took place in Beverley on December 4, 1804. Her literary inclination emerged early in her life, and she anonymously published her debut work,

The Nun: a Poetical Romance, and Two Others, in 1824 during her late teenage years.

Like many individuals in the early 19th century, she relocated to a southern region to escape the threat of tuberculosis. During her time there, she discovered the inspiration for her first book. In 1835, she embarked on a journey to Turkey alongside her father, a trip that served as the muse for some of her most renowned writings.

Pardoe resided in London until 1842 when overwork compelled her to return and live with her parents. They first settled at Perry Street and later moved to Northfleet, Kent. Her contributions to literature earned Julia Pardoe a civil-list pension in January 1860.

Julia Pardoe's life was marked by health challenges, including insomnia and chronic liver disease. She passed away on November 26, 1862, at Upper Montagu Street in London. She remained unmarried throughout her life. While her death certificate indicated her age as 56 at the time of her demise, records from her baptism suggested she was actually 58 years old. She was laid to rest in Kensal Green Cemetery in London.

Julia Pardoe was a versatile and gifted writer, known for her diverse body of work that spanned across various genres and often took on an international perspective. Many of her works were initially serialized in British and American periodicals.

Her literary endeavours expanded from her early poetry into the realm of novels. Her debut novel, published anonymously in 1829, was *Lord Morcar of Hereward*. Over the years, she authored several other novels, including *Speculation* (1834), *The Mardens and the Daventrys* (1835), *The Romance of the Harem* (1839), and *Hungarian Castle* (1842).

After returning to Kent, Pardoe continued to contribute to publications like *Fraser's Magazine* and the *Illuminated Magazine*. She also penned additional novels such as *The Confessions of a Pretty Woman* (1846), *The Rival Beauties* (1848), *Flies in Amber* (1850), *Reginald Lyle* (1854), *The Jealous Wife* (1855), *Lady Arabella* (1856), *A Life-Struggle* (1859), and *The Rich Relation* (1862).

Pardoe embarked on extensive travels that inspired her to write travel books and cultural studies. Her first travel book, *Traits and Traditions of Portugal*, was published in 1833. During her stay in Constantinople in 1835, she witnessed the devastating effects of a plague epidemic. These experiences led her to publish *The City of the Sultan and Domestic Manners of the Turks* in 1837, which presented a more empathetic portrayal of the Ottoman Turkish upper class. The book became immensely popular and was republished in multiple editions. In 1838, she published *The Beauties of the Bosphorus* and *The River and the Desert*, the latter being a collection of personal letters to a friend. In 1840, she released *The City of Magyar*, a comprehensive study of Hungarian economic and political life.

Pardoe's historical writings on the French courts of the 16th and 17th centuries have endured over time. Her notable historical works include *Louis the Fourteenth and the Court of France in the Seventeenth Century* (1847), *The Court and Reign of Francis the First, King of France* (1849), and *The Life of Marie de Medicis, Queen of France, Consort of Henri IV, and Regent of the Kingdom Under Louis XIII* (1852).

In addition to her own writing, Pardoe translated Guido Sorelli's *La Peste (The Plague)* in 1834. She also edited Anita George's *Memoirs of the Queens of Spain*, which was published in 1850. In 1857, she wrote the introduction to *The Thousand and One Days: A Companion to the Arabian Nights*.

Pardoe was remembered by her contemporaries as a warm-hearted, animated, and highly talented individual. Princess Augusta of Cambridge took an interest in her work and requested that Pardoe dedicate her work *Traits and Traditions of Portugal* to her, which significantly contributed to its rapid success. Poet Elizabeth Barrett Browning praised her work *City of Magyar* for its vivid word-painting. Pardoe is credited with leaving a positive impression of Hungary in England. Her work on Francis the First was commended for its comprehensive coverage of his public and private life. However, her study of Marie de' Medici was criticized for being diffuse and unfocused.

In her later years, the quality of Pardoe's work was noted to vary. *The Eclectic Magazine of Foreign Literature, Science, and Art* in 1857 praised her Hungarian travelogue for its deep research, accuracy, and being one of the best books of travel available to the public. They also highlighted the value of her book *The Hungarian Castle*, which delved into Hungarian folklore.

In *Novels and Novelists*, J. Cordy Jeaffreson praised Pardoe's intellectual development, crediting her delicate health in her early years for providing her with the quiet solitude needed for study and meditation. He regarded her life and literary career as exemplary due to her industry, perseverance, and unwavering dedication.

John Payne

John Payne was born on 23rd August 1842, and he died on 11th February 1916. He was an English poet and translator.

He initially pursued a legal career and associated with Dante Gabriel Rossetti. Later he became involved with limited edition publishing and the Villon Society.

He is now best known for his translations of Boccaccio's *Decameron, The Arabian Nights* and the *Diwan Hafez.*

After completing his translation of Omar Khayyam, Payne returned to the rendition of Hafiz that was eventually published in 3 volumes. in 1901. Payne argues that Hafiz takes the "whole sweep of human experience and irradiates all things with his sun-gold and his wisdom".

Payne once said that Hafez, Dante and Shakespeare were the three greatest poets of the world.

Payne's works include (but are not limited to):

The Masque of Shadows and other poems (1870), Intaglios; sonnets (1871), Songs of Life and Death. (1872), Lautrec: A Poem (1878), The Poems of François Villon.(1878), New Poems (1880), The Book of the Thousand Nights and One Night (1882–4) translation in nine volumes, and Tales from the Arabic (1884)

About The Editor

Born in 1962 into a household that lived and breathed sports, the editor's dad was a seasoned senior amateur and lower league professional footballer. Not just that, he managed his own businesses in cahoots with Clive's mum, who was no slouch either – she was a skilled and award-winning dancer.

After snagging a degree in History from Leeds University, our storyteller took a rather serendipitous stroll into the burgeoning world of information technology in the late '80s. Like father, like son, they say. Alongside a flourishing tech career, Clive dabbled in various writing and acting pursuits, from freelancing as a journalist and book reviewer (with a coveted by-line in The Sunday People) to gracing stages in village halls and even professional theatres all across the south of the UK for a good decade.

In a nod to the family's sporting legacy, Clive - long after hanging up his own boots - delved into the world of live TV broadcasts. Armed with a wealth of rugby knowledge, he became one of the go-to 'statos' for the BBC, ITV, TVNZ, and EuroSport, covering everything from Heineken Cups to Six Nations, World Sevens, and World Cups in the late '90s.

For a deeper dive into this fascinating journey, head over to clivegilson.com, where there's a whole trove of tales waiting to be uncovered!